THE FIRST EVO: UPRISING

Kipjo K. Ewers

THIS IS A EVO UNIVERSE BOOK

PUBLISHED BY EVO UNIVERSE, L.L.C.

www.evouniverse.com

ASIN: B09KNGJN7K
ISBN-13 : 979-8479388873

EVO: Uprising

ASIN: B09KNGJN7K

Printed in the U.S.A. by EVOUniverse

Email: info@evouniverse.com

On-Line Chat: go to our website, www.evouniverse.com.

For Jackie…

OTHER WORKS

THE FIRST: (THE FIRST SERIES BOOK 1)

GENESIS: (THE FIRST SERIES BOOK 3)

EYE OF RA

FRED & MARY

"HELP! I'M A SUPERHERO!": BOOK ONE

THE ELF AND THE LARP: BOOK ONE

WAR OF MORTAL GODS: BOOK ONE

FORWARD

I would personally like to thank the fans of my work and new readers for purchasing book number two of "THE FIRST…EVO: UPRISING," the next Chapter of the EVOUniverse. We finally made it!

I plowed into book two because of people like you who loved what you read and asked for more. For that, I thank you sincerely. I write dialogue as if I am watching a movie; I do this because I want to draw you, the reader, into the story blowing up your imagination, making you feel like you were actually there. Let us face it, in real life, people do not always talk properly. Some talk with slang and broken English, and sometimes we pause and hesitate in the middle of a conversation, which is why I use "...".

As I stated, you will find some broken English, street slang, Patwah (Jamaican slang), and Creole slang in some conversations. This is to keep the realism of this fantastical novel.

Now that you have a brief glimpse into the thought process used to write this next chapter in the EVO mythology, cozy up in a chair, sit comfy in your seat on the train, airplane, boat, or car. I hope and pray that you enjoy "THE FIRST…EVO: UPRISING."

CHAPTER 1

Friday, 10:45 p.m. East Flatbush, New York:

Eddie Brown knew what he was doing that night.

Two weeks ago, he bought a Beretta 92 from Sammy Fisher, the neighborhood crackhead, for fifty bucks. Sammy had lifted the gun from a house he had broken into and was anxious to unload it to pay for his habit. Eddie, a tenth-grade dropout with few prospects, wanted to increase his investment. He surveyed Chang's grocery and liquor store for three days to confirm the surveillance cameras' location, the type of traffic that went in and out, and the best time to rob it when there would be the most cash flow. He figured 10:45 p.m. Friday was perfect because most people getting off of work would head straight home to hear the lottery numbers announced on the news. There would be a gap between when the store would be empty.

Dressed in black jeans, a hoodie, combat boots, leather gloves, a ski mask, and shades to cover his eyes, Eddie drew a deep breath. He remembered he had to be in and out in less than two minutes, making sure his head was down with his back facing the cameras. Eddie could not get greedy, taking only what was in the register. He would walk out with eight hundred to a thousand dollars if all went well.

He marched right up to seventy-one-year-old Annie Chang, who was in the middle of watching "Real Time with Bill Maher."

"Put all of your shit from the register in a brown paper bag now, bitch!" Eddie screamed. "Do it, or I'll blow your fucking brains all over the Newports! Now!"

Annie Chang was born to Mr. and Mrs. Chang in Brooklyn during World War II; her father named her after the comic strip Annie he loved. At twenty-one, she married her childhood love with her parents' approval. At thirty, she and her husband took over her father's family grocery business from then until now while raising and sending three children to college. All three graduated and obtained professions outside the family business while nurturing their families.

After forty-four years of marriage, her husband went home to join their parents. Despite her children's behest, she continued to run her father's store, waiting for her time to go home and join her husband and family.

"I know you understand English, bitch!" Eddie roared. Money in a brown paper bag, now! Don't make me kill your old, wrinkled ass!"

A now desperate Eddie cocked the hammer to the Beretta to show he was serious; he clutched the gun tighter so she would not see him shaking. This was now big time for him. He did not want to go to jail, especially after spending a weekend in county lockup for a nickel bag of weed. He was still on probation for the misdemeanor. Working as a stock boy at the local dollar store was not getting him anywhere but bargain basement gear, fourth-rate women, and no respect. He couldn't even afford to keep his prepaid phone on. He just wanted the money to get a couple of nice things. He was well over his two minutes as Annie Chang leaned forward, turning up the volume so she could hear "New Rules."

"Goddammit, you fucking slant-eyed bitch!" Eddie yelled.

Finally, losing his patience, he went to pistol-whip Annie into taking him seriously when his heart stopped to see her turn to him with eyes ablaze. She lowered her glasses, firing two intense beams of light from her eyes, first burning a hole through his wrist, severing all his ligaments. Eddie's useless hand dropped his gun as he emitted a blood-curdling scream. Annie followed up using her eyebeams to blow a hole through his left kneecap. Smoke spewed from both Eddie's wounds as he fell forward with a sickening thud on the tile floor. Little blood spilled from the cauterized wound as he bawled and screamed on the floor. As the stench of charred flesh filled the air, Annie sighed, picked up her iPhone, and dialed 9-1-1.

"Hello? Dis Chang's Grocery and Liquor store at 875 East Flatbush. Ya betta get down hea. One a dees little beatches try ta roll up on me, an I had ta smoke dat ass again. Come get dis piece a sheet off my floor…"

Annie hung up her phone, placing it back down on the counter. She turned the volume up higher on her television.

"Punk beatch made me miss "New Rules," Annie muttered.

~~~~~~~~~~~~~~~~~~~~~~~~~~~~~~~~~~

Fox Five Saturday Evening News…

"Rounding up our number five spot," began news anchor Christina Park, "another robbery thwarted at Chang's Grocery and Liquor store in East Flatbush, Brooklyn. The suspect, identified as Edward Brown, was wounded when he attempted to rob Mrs. Annie Chang, the store owner, at gunpoint. Mrs. Chang, a registered superhuman, wounded Brown with her abilities, which was caught on tape. This would mark the third time Mrs. Chang singlehandedly prevented a robbery in her store. Mrs. Chang was not charged with physically injuring Edward Brown. In related news, an intense downtown battle erupted between known New York superhero Captain Omega and the super-powered Brooklyn gang, the Notorious Bastards. Captain Omega reportedly stormed one of their drug facilities, causing an all-out battle that raged from Bedford-Stuyvesant down to Central Park.

Several people were injured in the incident—six killed, including one of the Notorious Bastards at the hands of Captain Omega. The remaining members are on the run, while property damage is estimated at a hundred thousand. Captain Omega was not charged with the murder of the gang member and has issued a statement vowing to bring the remaining members to justice and continue his "true" war on drugs… now Audrey Puente for the weather."

~~~~~~~~~~~~~~~~~~~~~~~~~~~~~~~~~~

2014, 12:45 a.m. United States Pentagon, Washington DC:

United States Secretary of Defense Robert Graves walked the halls heading to his meeting, followed closely by his Executive Assistant, Michael Mendes. He adjusted his silver-rimmed glasses, amplifying his hazel eyes as he walked purposefully.

"Everyone is there, I presume," Graves addressed Mendes without looking his way.

"Yes, sir," Mendes confirmed, "Dr. Alexander is all set to present his findings."

"Good," Graves said with a nod, "I want to get this show on the road the second I get inside."

The two arrived at the fortified checkpoint protected by armed security personnel. They scanned their I.Ds and subjected themselves to a retinal scan before passing through the checkpoint and heading to the conference room housing the Private US Armed Forces session.

Entering the conference room, Graves, followed by Mendes, took the time to greet and acknowledge each Joint Chiefs of Staff member. He finished by greeting and briefly talking to the presenter before taking his place at the head of the long, deep brown, oval wooden table. Mendes took his place in a seat to his right.

"Call to order this U.S. Armed Forces Session," Graves began. "Dr. Egan Alexander, our current lead geneticists and expert on the EVO virus and EVOs, will begin with the current findings."

Dr. Alexander, a slender man in his mid-thirties with a Drew Carey appearance, rose to begin his presentation.

"Gentlemen, based on findings as we already expected, the EVO population is indeed increasing. No longer through the spread of infection but through natural procreation. The virus has mutated and ingrained itself within the human DNA coding… becoming an actual gene."

Rumbles and mutters came from those present as Dr. Alexander referred to his onscreen presentation of a standard human DNA strand on one side and an extremely abnormal DNA strand on the other.

"As you can see, the normal DNA strand on the left possesses a double helix. The set of chromosomes in a cell makes up its genome; the human genome has approximately three billion base pairs of DNA arranged into forty-six chromosomes," Dr. Egan Alexander said while pointing. "The EVO DNA possesses a quadruple-helix. Its genome ranges in the trillion base pairs of DNA arranged into one-hundred-eighty-four chromosomes… the majority of which we are still currently unable to identify."

After allowing this to sink in around the room, he clicked to the next section of his presentation.

"Spread of virus infection, which was caused by the Source colliding with a nuclear warhead in the upper stratosphere of the planet, now dubbed the "Big Bang 2 Incident" resulted in the virus being spread to the four corners of the planet."

Dr. Alexander clicked again, moving to the next slide.

"It contaminated our water and food supply worldwide and became an airborne pathogen. Extreme cases of infection resulted in either death or superhuman abilities. This has now decreased from one to zero percent; the last official death recorded by the virus was two years ago.

The current population of EVOs can be estimated at point three percent worldwide; however, this only concerns the infected. Currently, an estimated point one percent of four-hundred-ninety thousand children born annually over the past six years possess the EVO gene. Our studies over these EVO pregnancies revealed that EVO children are born to two parents with abilities, one parent having abilities in both males and females, and neither parent possessing powers, confirming another hypothesis. It is safe to say that every man, woman, and child living on this planet is infected with the virus."

The unsettled rumbling came from the room again as Dr. Alexander moved to the next part of his presentation.

"Children born with the EVO gene are no longer defined as infected. They are True EVOs and with good reason. Except for certain types, all True EVOs' muscle and bone density are three times greater than that of normal human beings; they also heal faster."

"How much faster?" Admiral James A. Murdock, Sr. U.S.N. Chief of NORAD, asked.

"Minor wounds heal almost instantly," Dr. Alexander replied. "Greater wounds, we speculate, may take a couple of minutes to an hour, maybe less, depending on the severity. Due to the subjects' age, we cannot test the maximum limits of their healing capability. The blood samples we took determined them to be exceptionally greater than regular humans."

"Can you please review the types again?" General James N. Steiner of the USMC asked.

"Through studies, we can categorize EVOs by types based on their abilities," Dr. Alexander answered. "Prometheans are EVOs with superhuman intelligence and mental abilities such as telekinesis, mind reading, and telepathy.

Mercurians are EVOs with great superhuman speed, reflexes, strength, durability, and regenerative healing. Moleculars or Elementals are EVOs capable of alternating their genetic properties. We identify these types as mutations because they do not fall within the power set of the Source. Next are Apollos, EVOs capable of harnessing, manipulating, and unleashing certain energy types such as solar, electrical, nuclear, hydro, and even sound. Finally, we have Titans EVOs possessing tremendous superhuman strength, endurance, durability, and regenerative healing. These are the basic classes of EVOs thus far; we expect to find new classes as True EVOs begin to mature."

"Aside from physical traits, what other differences are there between True EVOs and the infected?" General Thomas Welsh, Chairman of the Joint of Staff, asked.

"Our comparison tests have revealed that currently, True EVOs at the age of three and four years old are ten percent equivalent ability-wise to most adult infected EVOs. Unlike the infected whose powers and abilities increase by honing or training," Dr. Alexander replied, "True EVOs' powers grow and develop with age. It is estimated that there is no limit to a True EVO's power levels. We won't know until one reaches full maturity, but it is speculated that some of them could very well rival or surpass the Source."

A significant degree of uneasy rumbling and muttering came into the room as Dr. Alexander adjusted his glasses, concluding his presentation.

"We estimate that at the current rate of birth, over the next twenty years, the purebred population will grow to 14,700… maybe even more."

The mutters and rumblings became words.

"Over fourteen thousand EVOs… with powers equal to the Source."

A great uneasiness filled the room as images of a possible dark and bleak future were imagined—a future where regular humans were knocked several notches down on the evolutionary ladder.

"Isn't there a way to detect a child with abilities before birth?" General Norton B. Matthews of the USAF asked.

"Currently no," Dr. Alexander answered, "other than the obvious physical traits that can be seen within eight to nine months, such as increased muscle and bone density, some powers and abilities do not manifest until the child reaches one to two years."

"What about treatment… a cure?" General James N. Steiner of the USMC asked.

"To put it bluntly, there is no cure," Dr. Alexander returned. "At its current evolutionary state, the gene is immune to any form of treatment administered to it. It is, for all intents and purposes, incurable."

One could cut the uneasiness throughout the room with a knife as Secretary of Defense Robert Graves took control of the meeting once again following the end of the doctor's presentation.

"Gentlemen, due to the actions of one of our own, Pandora's box has been opened and unleashed onto the world, and there's no way we can close the lid. The latest in biological weapons are superhumans. Our allies and enemies are paying a fortune to enlist EVOs as super soldiers.

It is like the N.F.L. draft out there. In the past, the White House has refrained from allowing the recruitment of EVOs into the United States Military. Under the current Administration, that order has been rescinded. We can no longer afford to fall behind as a superpower, especially on this level."

"What about the current superhero activity going on in the country?" General Norton B. Matthews (USAF) asked. "It's still reported that the majority of EVOs reside in the United States."

"Reside, yes," Graves answered. "Acting under, and on behalf of this government, no, and that is what needs to change. The White House is not happy at all with what's going on in the streets of this country. Many of these costume-wearing individuals have caused more harm than good both on the human and property damage level costing this country billions of dollars. A bill is currently being drafted to regulate superhuman activity. Vigilantism will no longer be tolerated in any state by powered or non-powered individuals."

There was a clear divide in the room as some agreed with his statement, while others were not thrilled that superhumans became a part of the United States Military's staple. Graves's face read that he didn't care what either side thought.

"Before that bill is introduced, it is imperative that an EVO division under the United States military is in place. Ready to aid in enforcing the laws of this land and defending both its borders and abroad if necessary," Graves ordered. "To make this perfectly clear, this new division will provide service and have authorization within all five branches of the United States military. This is not open for debate. Our Commander-in-Chief expects results within six months; my office and staff will be heading the review and recruiting process for this new division."

"Well, if you're taking the reins on this Graves," General Thomas Welsh scoffed, "what's there for us to do?"

"Prepare your branches to happily receive and give them aid by any means necessary." Graves answered with a smile. "Let's get it done, gentlemen."

~~~~~~~~~~~~~~~~~~~~~~~~~~~~~~~~

After the meeting, the Secretary of Defense walked the Pentagon's hallways, followed by Dr. Egan Alexander and his Executive Assistant, Michael Mendes.

"How do you think that went, Mendes?" Graves nonchalantly
~~~~~~~~~~~~~~~~~~~~~~~~~~~~~~~~

asked.

"I think it went as well as expected, sir," Mendes answered.

"Considering we didn't have to use an ounce of lube, I think they took it very well," Graves replied with a smirk.

Mendes sneered, comprehending the Secretary of Defense's comment.

"What is the E.T.A. on viable candidates, Dr. Alexander?"

"Screening takes place tomorrow," the doctor answered. "We should have a list of candidates in the next three weeks."

"Make it two, please," Graves requested. "The sooner we can get this three-ring circus underway, the better."

CHAPTER 2

Nadiya Romanenko was sixteen years old. Two months away from her birthday, her world would end. Two years ago, she dreamt of becoming a veterinarian. In her hometown of Poltava, she brought home small, injured animals and cared for them. Her mother passed away due to illness when she was six years old. For some time, it would be just her and her father, who loved her dearly. Every day, he walked her to school and picked her up afterward. On Fridays, he brought home honey cake for them to share after dinner. She was his Маленький ягня, which stood for "little lamb" in Ukrainian.

This simple life lasted four years until her father remarried the local butcher's wife. The childless woman, who was a widow two years before him, was unable to conceive by either her former husband or her father. Behind her father's back, she had nothing but contempt for Nadiya. Thinking only of her father's happiness after being so long without her mother, Nadiya held her peace despite full knowledge of the woman's hatred for her.

She would not know that after three years of enduring, fate would take away her father when he intervened in a knife fight at a local bar.

No more honey cakes came after that night.

In their stead were verbal abuse and vicious beatings. No longer was Nadiya allowed to attend school. Instead, her stepmother rented her out as cheap labor cleaning houses and businesses from dawn to late evening to keep a roof over her head and food in her belly. For a while, Nadiya skimmed money from the pay she received in hopes of saving enough to run away until her stepmother found out and almost beat her to death.

Four nights after the savage beating, men ripped a screaming Nadiya from her bed. The last glimpse of the inside of her home was of her stepmother taking a sizable stack of cash from the man who would be her new owner.

Yuri Bondarchuk was a well-known dealer of narcotics and white slave prostitution. A sadist with the local police in his back pocket, he purposely sought out virgins to hold auctions and sell them to the highest bidder. Age did not matter to him as long as he could get away with it. The Ukrainian government's laid-back position on the situation allowed him to get away with a lot.

Yuri dashed away Nadiya's dreams of becoming a veterinarian for grooming to become a sex slave. He forced her to take heroin between her toes to make her dependent and made her watch a girl two years older than her being beaten to death with a lead pipe by Yuri himself to instill fear. Her virginity would go to the highest bidder, not her boyfriend or husband. Afterward, she would be raped repeatedly, every day for the remainder of her life, or until she died from a drug overdose, disease, or at the hands of Yuri.

Nadiya sat curled up on her bed in the middle of her cell-like room, wearing a worn-out cheap schoolgirl outfit two sizes smaller than anything she had ever worn. She wept for a father who would never come. The cheers and howls outside meant the auction was over. The man coming to take her would be in her room soon. She tried to pull herself together, remembering Yuri's warning enforced by the other girls if she did not perform as expected.

She wished Yuri had doped her up before casting her into hell, but he wanted the client to have the entire virgin experience. To feel and see the agonizing pain and tears as he ruined her with each thrust. She quickly wiped her eyes and sat up on the bed at the sound of heavy footsteps getting closer. On her first night in the house, Yuri told her to pray to her heart's content because there was no God. No one was coming for a little whore.

She continued to pray, begging God to save her from this horrific fate. She never stopped until her first John walked through the door. She did not know what revolted her more—that he could be her grandfather or still had his wedding ring on. He stumbled over in his construction work clothes, the stench of booze raining down as he towered over her. It got worse as he cupped his filthy, callus-ridden hand around her face, forcing her to her feet.

"Pretty face…" he grinned. "I paid good money to break you into a whore tonight, and I intend to enjoy every cent."

Nadiya closed her eyes, screaming one final prayer in her thoughts.

"Please! Someone…anyone! Help me!"

She heard the sound of him unbuckling his belt, unzipping his fly, and letting his pants fall to the floor.

What followed was a thunderous quake all around her, followed by a massive explosion that viciously rattled everything. Smoke filled her small room as the old man, knocked on his rear with his pants around his ankles, cried out in fear. She crawled over to the door, where she heard more yelling and screaming. Yuri's voice, filled with obscenities, was the loudest. Nadiya found the courage to enter the hallway, thick with smoke. Most of the girls stayed in their rooms, only poking their heads out along with their Johns. She moved toward the chaos; to her, it was far better than spending another second in that room.

Nadiya got as far as the end of the hallway, looking into the bar where the front entrance was no more. As the evening moonlight cast into the room, she could not see Yuri's face because his back was turned to her, but she could sense fear and rage coming from him. All of it was directed toward the woman standing in the obliterated entranceway. She was tall with dark caramel skin; Nadiya had only seen a person with her complexion once before. She wore a simple, thin red leather jacket and long black tights. Her long, dark woolen mane and red cherry-toed bare feet captivated Nadiya, while her piercing, deep, glowing blue eyes told her that Yuri, the Devil, was a liar.

There was a God, and angels walked the earth.

"You have no right, bitch! This is not your country!" Yuri howled.

The woman answered him back in fluent Ukrainian.

"No, asshole, but it's my world."

"You fucking monkey," Yuri sniggered. "I come ready for you."

Nadiya knew who Yuri was referring to. Her heartbeat sped up at the sound of the footsteps. She clutched the corner of the wall, praying they would not notice her. Kostyantyn and Anastasiya, the two superhumans Yuri employed four months ago, now she knew why. She witnessed the almost seven-foot wall of pure muscle with piercing gray eyes, known as Kostyantyn, crush both the forearms of a customer while suspending him in midair for busting up the face of one of the girls because she puked out his semen instead of swallowing it.

Yuri had him punished because he refused to pay extra for the damages to his merchandise. The girl's punishment was to service every man in the building that night. He promised to bash her skull with a sledgehammer if a single drop spilled from her mouth.

Nadiya didn't know Anastasiya's abilities. All she knew was that the platinum blonde's eyes had a similar glow to the woman who stood before them, except hers was a piercing white. Lights flickered when she walked by. They popped when she was angered. Also, men made sure to avoid her at all times, while Yuri showed her the utmost respect. She looked at the girls in the stable with disgust and unbridled hatred, as if they were weak and deserving of their fate. The woman standing before them showed neither fear nor concern. Instead, she just pointed to Kostyantyn.

"You, I can see," she addressed Kostyantyn before wagging her finger at Anastasiya. "You, I find to be disgusting."

"Don't think you can lecture me bitch," Anastasiya mocked. "This is the land of wolves and sheep. I could give a fuck about the "would be eaten" just because they have a twat like me."

"Then I won't have any regrets about what happens next," the woman with the black lion-like mane responded.

With no more words between the two, Anastasiya kicked off her open-toes and planted her bare feet firmly on the ground. In an instant, the room's temperature increased significantly as parts of Nadiya's frayed blonde hair stood up on end.

It was then that she bore witness to Anastasiya's truly terrifying power. Pure, raw electricity poured from her slender, toned frame. It violently snapped and crackled, slithering about her. The white surge lashed out, either popping some of the remaining light bulbs in the vicinity or cutting through the wooden floorboards with the strength of a high-powered arc welder. The display of power made Yuri duck behind the bar for cover. Anastasiya raised her hands and allowed the current to surge between them, showing her control. Nadiya now knew why Anastasiya only wore skintight rubber outfits, the only material capable of withstanding the massive heat she generated.

She cowered as she watched Anastasiya lift almost three feet off the ground. The electricity flowing from the tips of her toes scorched the floor underneath her. It was like watching a furious demigod awaken. The only two people unfazed by her terrifying show of power were Kostyantyn and the woman, who just sighed and rolled her eyes.

"If you're done showboating, I got someplace to be."

"Roll your eyes to this, bitch," Anastasiya snarled.

She unleashed a violent bolt of electricity from the palm of her right hand, hitting the woman in the middle of her chest and making an ear-splitting sound. Nadiya crouched low, barely able to stay near the room, which became a severe hot zone. It was amazing; it did not go up in blazes from the extreme heat generated. The woman buckled slightly from the bolt of human-generated lightning.

To Nadiya's surprise and Anastasiya's fearful shock, the electrical blast that could turn a woodblock into a cinder appeared slightly uncomfortable for the woman. In fact, the charge meant to hurt her seemed to feed her as her eyes glowed brighter.

A savage grin formed on the woman's face as she coyly asked.

"So, what else you got?"

"Kos... Kostyantyn!"

Anastasiya nervously screamed his name for help as she continued to pour on the heat that did nothing but sear the woman's leather jacket.

"Yeah, Kostyantyn, let's see what you got," the woman taunted.

Kostyantyn growled, rushing the woman with blinding speed, breaking floorboards and shaking the building's structure. He hauled off with a right cross to the side of the woman's face, emitting a mini shockwave violently rocking the building. Nadiya fell on her rear while a staggered Anastasiya broke off her electrical attack. The building's seismic quaking did not stop as Kostyantyn rained down building toppling blows on the woman. But as destructive as his blows appeared, they neither staggered the woman nor forced her backward.

Out of nowhere, the onslaught was over with one earth-shattering blow. Neither Nadiya nor Anastasiya could see when she landed the punch, but it was clearly a body blow. Kostyantyn came almost two feet off the floor before dropping to his knees. He clutched his gut as he hacked up a massive amount of blood. His entire body trembled as he groaned.

The woman placed a hand on his back.

"Breathe… breathe… slowly. Your body will regenerate… just breathe slowly. Now, do you want another?"

Kostyantyn shook his head, yielding to her.

"Then stay there and don't move," she ordered him. "As for you…"

She locked onto a terrified Anastasiya.

"Get away from me, you fucking monster!"

Anastasiya blew out the roof of the building with another massive lightning bolt. She planned to break for it amidst the falling burning rubble and smoke. The superior superhuman thwarted her attempt to flee, snatching her out of mid-takeoff.

"Please! Please!" Anastasiya pleaded.

The woman she had ridiculed a couple of minutes before the fight held her by the neck, displaying her propulsion and shaking the building's structure. Nadiya covered her head, believing all the unnatural power would bring the brothel down on top of everyone. The energy she generated was far more potent than Anastasiya's, yet controlled. Some heat was behind it, but not enough to set the floors on fire. It pounded the wood and vibrated everything, bringing down almost every bottle behind the bar's shelf. Yuri screamed as a couple clocked him while coming down.

The woman tightened her grip on Anastasiya's throat, stopping her annoying pleas for leniency.

"The big bad wolf is begging for mercy now? Well, I'm not in a forgiving mood today."

Anastasiya let out a blood-curdling scream as she lit up like a Christmas tree. Nadiya coiled back, shielding her eyes as bolts of electricity shot everywhere, scorching walls and blowing out the remaining lights in the bar. At first, it appeared as if she was electrocuting Anastasiya, which made no sense to her.

Nadiya did not need to be a rocket scientist to know that Anastasiya was immune to electrocution's fatality. Looking closer, she realized the woman was drawing energy from out of Anastasiya. Her eyes flickered, reverting to normal, while the woman's eyes became an intense burning blue.

Anastasiya, drained of almost all of her power, went limp. The woman lowered herself back to the floor, releasing her where she collapsed into a heap.

"What… what did you do… to me?" Anastasiya asked while wheezing.

"Think that would be obvious," the woman informed her. "I drained you of your power. Electricity is one of the power sources that feeds me, and allows me to do that. I could have taken it all, in which case you would be a lifeless, burnt-out husk right now. For now, I just took enough so that you'd be incapable of conjuring up a spark. Unless you find a massive generator, it's going to take you a while to get back to full power. How does it feel to be just a sheep?"

Anastasiya mustered enough strength to roll to her side and slowly curl into a ball.

"Yeah, Van Dam, you ain't," the woman dismissively said.

She returned back over to Kostyantyn, who remained kneeling on the floor.

He stopped gasping and puking up blood, apparently healed from the earth-cracking gut check he received. As instructed by the goddess who brought him to his knees, the big man moved not an inch. She now stood over him, contemplating his fate.

"On your feet," she ordered.

Kostyantyn slowly rose, clutching his gut and towering over her. It was clear he still felt the effects of the thunderous blow.

"Do you have a sister?" she plainly asked.

Kostyantyn shook his head no.

"Do you have a mother?"

Kostyantyn nodded yes.

The next thing to follow was a vicious slap across the face that sounded like a thunderclap. Kostyantyn's eyes widened with rage as his nostrils flared. His chest expanded rapidly as if preparing for round two. However, he did not budge an inch as the woman stuck a finger in his face before scolding him.

"Shame on you! How dare you use the gift you were given for this. Using it to hurt and subjugate others, squandering it to line the pockets of that animal cowering behind the bar. I should knock that stupid looking head clean off your shoulders. Guess why I haven't done it yet?"

He did not answer her as he continued to stare her down; she did not wait for him to ask as she stepped closer.

"Because my parents taught me to never look down at a man unless you're picking him up."

Her words proved more hard hitting than her fists as Kostyantyn hunched his shoulders and bowed his head. Nadiya was dumbfounded to witness a man, who was once Yuri's savage right hand of fear and intimidation, swat away tears of shame and regret from his eyes.

"Raise your head."

Kostyantyn obeyed, staring into her blazing blue eyes again.

"I'm going to give you a chance to straighten out your life," she said, pointing at him again. "You get only one chance to clean up your act. If I ever catch you in a place like this or doing anything remotely similar to something like this, I mean running drugs, guns, a hitman for the Mafia, anything illegal. You will know me as your mother on that day. I will take you out of this world, and no amount of begging or pleading will stop me. Do we understand each other?"

"Yes," Kostyantyn nodded.

Nadiya was floored again, as this was the first time she had heard the big man speak.

"Get out of here."

An instructed Kostyantyn left through the brothel's obliterated entrance, not giving a thought to his former employer whimpering behind the bar. Nadiya's nervous smile grew as she hid near the doorway leading to the bedrooms. The woman sauntered to the bar, touching the beer-stained wood top and slowly tapping her fingernails across it.

"If you make me rip this bar apart to get to you, I will bludgeon you to death with it," she warned him.

The pimp, rapist, sadist, and murderer of women fearfully rose to his feet with cuts on his hands and face from broken glass. He reeked of booze that splashed on him during the demigod battle in his bar. He timidly raised his hands, searching for mercy.

"Please… please, let us negotiate."

She leaned forward, sneering at him.

"The 'F'n monkey doesn't negotiate."

The woman purposely put a fraction of her weight down on the bar, causing the middle to crack and splinter as she caved it in. It appeared like the whole bar would rip from its foundation, folding in two. Yuri fell back against the shelves that held the liquor. Two more bottles came down on top of him. He stooped down, nursing his bruised skull.

"I said, stand up!"

The powerful voice made even Nadiya weak in the knees with fear. Yuri timorously rose to his feet, whimpering like a child fitting to get a lashing. Then, Nadiya felt like a deer in headlights as the woman looked in her direction. She wore kind softness upon her face as she stared at her, something Nadiya had not seen since her father. It kept her rooted in place, even though her heart attempted to beat itself out of her chest. Her fear was natural after witnessing the terrible power of the woman who gestured to Nadiya, extending her hand as if coaxing a fawn in her native tongue.

"Hi, it's okay. You don't need to fear me. Come."

A fraction of her wanted to run, thinking she was trading one monster for a more terrifying one. Nadiya slowly crept forward, believing that before she was salvation sent by God.

"That's it. It's okay; you're safe now. He can't hurt you anymore. What is your name, child?"

"Na… Nadiya… my name is Nadiya," she said slowly.

"Nadiya," the woman said, her face lighting up.

It was a sincere smile that put Nadiya more at ease.

"Lovely name, how old are you?" she asked.

She glanced over at Yuri, who looked at her, sending a sliver of intimidation her way to keep her mouth shut. Unfortunately for him, the woman caught it. The next thing Nadiya felt was a whirlwind, making her scream.

With one hand, Yuri screamed louder as the woman grabbed the bar and snapped a vast portion of it off, tossing it near the smashed open entrance. It hit the ground, returning to reality of how heavy it was. She stomped to Yuri, shaking the floor, and let her fist fly. It went past his skull, blowing out the wall, bringing in the open air on the other side. From the look of Yuri, as he cringed, it appeared as if he soiled himself.

"Ya mad?! Yah ah try fe intimidate dee pickney right in fronta me?! Ya wan me murdah you?!" the woman howled.

Nadiya could barely make out the weird, broken English she spoke. However, she did not need to understand it to tell that she was beyond livid and through with Yuri.

"No! No! I swear! Please! Please!" Yuri screamed with trembling legs.

"Bow your head!" she roared in Ukrainian.

He quickly complied.

"And keep it bowed unless you want me to rip it from your shoulders," she growled.

She took a minute to let her kindness return before addressing Nadiya again.

"How old are you, child?"

"Sixteen," Nadiya shyly answered. "I will be seventeen in two months."

"Sixteen… years old."

The rage came back as the woman turned around to Yuri.

"Please! Please! I did not know she was that young!" he pleaded.

Yuri's body shook violently, expecting a vicious pummeling.

"He's lying!" Nadiya broke down hysterically with tears. "He bought me from my stepmother! He gave me drugs! He sold my virginity to the highest bidder! A dirty old man in the back was about to rape me!"

"She's..."

Before the word "lying" came from his lips, the woman grabbed him by his bottom jaw, standing him up on the tips of his toes. Yuri let out a muffled scream as it felt like she was going to crush or rip his jawbone out.

"Shut your lying tongue before I tear it out," she ordered him. "How many girls are in the back, honey?"

"Twenty, no, twenty-five," Nadiya returned nervously, "Twenty-five, I am sure of it."

"Let's make sure," the woman said.

She walked to the entrance leading to the bedrooms while dragging a squealing Yuri by his jaw.

Her voice boomed with a flawless Ukrainian dialect for all to hear.

"Alright, everyone in the back! Listen up! Nadiya will be walking to the back, going from room to room! When she opens the door, each girl will walk out fully clothed, and the John in the room will have all of his clothing removed down to his underwear, ready to hand to her! He will also give Nadiya his wallet if he has one and all his money!

He will then remain in the room until called! If you give Nadiya or the girl in the room a hard time, I will come back there and kill you! If you attack the girl in the room or try to attack Nadiya, I will come back there, and I will kill you!

If you attempt to run, I will hunt you down and kill you in the most painful way possible! Basically, the only way you are walking out of here alive is if you do as you are told! If you understand what I am saying, all Johns bang on the walls three times!"

On command like trained monkeys, three loud bangs came from the back.

"Nadiya, when you go to the back and get the first girl, ask her to help gather the next set of clothes, and so on, and so forth."

Nadiya nodded and slowly walked to the back, her stomach knotted as she opened the first door. As commanded, the John, on his knees, stark naked, held out his clothes and wallet, ready for her to take. It was hard to tell if he was trembling because it was cold or if he was racked with fear. The girl in the room was Kateryna, two years older than her. Kateryna sat on the bed with her head down, afraid to move.

"Kateryna, come, it is time to go. You do not have to be afraid anymore."

Kateryna coiled backward as she moved toward her, shaking like a leaf. She had been there a year longer than Nadiya and had to see and endure more horrors than her.

"Who is out there, Nadiya?" Kateryna asked, not looking up. "Who is she?"

"Our freedom," Nadiya said with a smile, "She is our freedom. Come! You have to come."

With those words, Kateryna slowly got to her feet and followed Nadiya, going from room to room, collecting the girls inside and the clothing from the Johns. Nadiya was off by two girls; there were twenty-seven, including her. Except for her and Kateryna, who held her hand tightly, everyone else huddled into a group like penguins trying to keep warm. All the Johns's clothes sat on the floor while the wallets and money were on a table that survived the battle.

The woman wore the softness of a mother as she held Yuri's jaw, forcing him down to his knees. She looked at each of the girls in the room. Some were clearly younger than Nadiya, others older with worn-out, hallowed eyes. Some had the shakes, going through withdrawals from not getting their regular fix used to keep them compliant. All of them, except for Nadiya, had fear written on their faces. They looked down at the floor, unsure if they were trading one master for another.

"Big man you are," the woman rumbled, "subjugating innocent women and children to fill your pockets. I wonder if I was to ask them all what I should do with you. What do you think they would say?"

Yuri swallowed hard, looking up at the group of women and children he tormented, terrorized, and forced to do his will, enduring rape, torture, and humiliation just to make him wealthy. Some found the courage to lift their eyes and look at him. All those eyes that met his gaze had hatred and rage.

"The reason why I am not going to ask them is that I already know what the answer would be, and I won't allow your filthy blood to be on their hands. However, that doesn't let you off the hook. You're my bitch now. You can come in!"

To everyone's surprise, a woman wearing a black biker helmet covering her identity in a complete skintight leather bike outfit with matching boots and gloves strolled through the massive hole that used to be the entrance to the bar/brothel. She stood next to the superwoman, looking down at Yuri. The superwoman reached into Yuri's back pocket, pulling out his wallet to look at his I.D. as he squealed again.

"Yuri Bondarchuk," she announced, "you have been found guilty of kidnapping, slavery, rape, molestation, and sexual assault of women and minors, distribution of narcotics to unwilling parties as well as minors, and murder. Your sentence, which is to be carried out immediately, is a life sentence to live just as you have treated others… as a whore in my stable."

She pulled Yuri up to his feet, yoking him up by his jawbone to extend his neck. As he gagged, the woman in the bike helmet pulled out what appeared to be a pink collar with a small pink box attached to it. She strapped it around Yuri's neck and locked it with a unique key. She stepped back as the superwoman switched from holding his jaw to grabbing him by his new collar, forcing him to his knees like a dog.

"Your new name is Bitch Number Four," she informed him. "The woman standing before you in black is your official handler. You don't need to know her name. Her job, which she is being paid handsomely to do, is to track you. And I will have you know she was willing to do this gig for free. The collar around your neck is both waterproof, tamper-proof, and unbreakable. In fact, the only way you can get it off is to lop your ugly ass head from your shoulders."

She pulled him up to his feet so that she could look him in the eyes.

"Your new job is to do what I say," she barked. "That entails doing the exact opposite of what you've been doing. As of now, you are out of the drug business. You take this rat hole you own and turn it into a proper boarding home. You will then go out and find women and children suffering the way you have made these women and children suffer.

You will take them in, clothe them properly, feed them, and ensure they get a proper education and the work skills they need to survive. You will protect them. You will be a true father to the weak and defenseless in your country. While doing that, you will lobby to change laws to protect women and children. You have six months to do this."

"How…" Yuri gagged, "how am I to do this?"

"Not my problem, bitch," she snarled, yoking him up. "You're a ho now, and whatever a ho's got to do to get the job done, he better get it done. If you try to run, I will find you and kill you. If you attempt to find out who your handler is, and she will know if you try, I will find you and kill you slowly and painfully. And if you haven't done what I just ordered, you to do in the next six months…"

Out of nowhere, she grabbed his right hand and squeezed it. He wailed as she crushed it. Nadiya and the girls slightly cringed as they heard the sound of breaking bones—much like pretzels snapping.

"I just broke eight bones in your hand," she explained to him, "next time, I will be back to re-break it along with your wrist. Next time it will be the hand, the wrist, and the forearm… and so on… and so on."

She finally released him. He collapsed, sobbing hysterically, clutching his broken right hand.

A sarcastic look of shock fell on the woman's face.

"Oh dear, are those tears I see? Are you scared? Do you feel humiliated? Am I treating you like an animal?"

She stooped down, giving him a look that would scare the Devil himself.

"Good, now you know how they felt. And that is how I break a bitch."

Yuri crumbled into a heap, bawling hysterically, still grasping his destroyed hand. The woman drew a deep breath and turned to the masses huddling close, bracing themselves.

"My name is Sophia Dennison," she softly announced in their native language, "and I will not hurt you. I am here to make sure no one will ever hurt you again."

Cries and sobs erupted within the flock of women. Nadiya quickly grabbed Kateryna around her waist, keeping her from collapsing, as she clutched her chest, weeping uncontrollably.

"Today, you have two choices," Sophia explained, "you can go with my friend here. She has a place where she can care and provide for you until you can get back on your feet. If you are addicted to drugs, she can get you clean. If you need counseling, we can get you the help that you need to get through this. If you have family that you know is looking for you, we can, and will, get you back to them. She can also provide you with the means to begin a new life anywhere in Europe that you want to go, with either school or a job waiting for you. We can do this for you."

"What is our other choice?" one of the older women of the group nervously asked.

"You can come and live with me," Sophia said with a smile. "I have a place where there is warm tropical weather, blue sea water all around, and pearl white sands."

"For how long?" Nadiya lifted her hand, asking.

"For as long as you like," Sophia said. "You can each decide for yourselves what you want to do."

Sophia once again turned her attention to the brothel's back with rooms filled with stark naked Johns waiting to hear their fate.

"All Johns in the back, listen up! You have all been found guilty of rape and soliciting sex from unwilling women and minors! All of your money is forfeited along with whatever this flea-ridden mutt has, which will be divided and given to the women and children you subjugated and terrorized! Your clothes will be burnt to ash! Now with two knocks, how many of you are going to go home and tell your wives, girlfriends, and families what you did here today?"

A couple of knocks rang out, which made Sophia sneer in disgust.

"Stop! Stop!" Sophia yelled back. "You lying sons of bitches, stop! You all know damn well if you make it out of here alive; you will not tell anyone what happened here. And that doesn't sit well with me. I like my rapists to be seen and known. Fortunately for all of you back there, we have a way of making that happen."

"How will you do this?" Kateryna nervously asked

"Anyone see Inglorious Bastards?" Sophia innocently asked.

The women looked around at one another, unfamiliar with the cult classic Quentin Tarantino movie.

"Well, my friend, here, has her own twist that she loves to do, minus the Apache knife."

Without a word, the woman pulled out what appeared to be a black telescopic baton from her right jacket pocket, snapping it open to a whole foot-long length. She pulled a large metal letter "R" from her left pocket, screwing it on tight to the baton's top. Sophia heated the large metal letter "R," turning it bright red with a concentrated blue atomic eyebeam blast as she held it out.

The women's eyes widened as they fully understood the fate of the

Johns in the back, who treated them less than animals.

"Anyone who doesn't have the stomach for roasted flesh," Sophia suggested, "can wait outside."

That night, the only screams and cries that could be heard were from cowardly evil men.

Not one woman or child left to wait outside.

CHAPTER 3

Two weeks later, within a secure and disclosed facility underneath the Pentagon, Secretary Graves sat at the head of an enormous conference room table. He sifted through his secured computer tablet, viewing digital files of superhuman candidates prepared by Mendes and Doctor Alexander. Both men patiently sat, flanking him on opposite sides of the conference room table as he viewed their report.

"So," Graves asked with a dull smile, "what do we have to offer the American public out of this pool of genetic misfits?"

Dr. Egan Alexander scrolled through his tablet before beginning.

"Based on both standard and newly implemented tests for EVO recruits, we found five possible candidates."

Robert Graves grabbed his coffee and took a sip.

"One of them, Captain Omega?"

"No," Dr. Alexander responded.

"He never applied," Executive Assistant Mendes clarified.

Graves gave a dry snort with a sigh, rolling his eyes.

"Why am I not surprised? America's number one' hero.' America's number one failure, I should do well to remind him of that someday."

Mendes and Dr. Alexander gave each other concerning eye contact, bearing witness to the Secretary of Defense's subtle rant.

Graves returned from his thoughts.

"So, who did we acquire? God help us if it's any of those idiots from Chicago."

"Abraham Rogers," Dr. Alexander announced.

Graves cocked an eyebrow.

"Who?"

Mendes tapped on his tablet, bringing Roger's file to the theater-sized conference room flat screen.

"Sergeant Abraham Rogers. Widower… age forty-eight…"

"Ancient," Graves groaned with furrowed eyebrows.

"Former United States Marine receiving the Medal of Honor for the Iran-Iraq War; a silver star for the Invasion of Panama," added Mendes, "served during Desert Storm. He received the Purple Heart after injury by an I.E.D. with full honors. Almost ninety percent of his eyesight was gone in his left eye."

Graves took another sip from his coffee.

"Ancient and crippled."

"Eyesight **was** gone," Dr. Alexander said, stepping in. "It was restored when he was infected by the EVO virus. He is currently a class five Titan, possessing tremendous superhuman strength, lifting in the fifty-ton range. It is nowhere near Captain Omega's level, but still impressive. He also has almost high-level superhuman durability, endurance, stamina, and regenerative healing.

"Combine that with his former military background, you have…" Mendes added, attempting to close.

"The perfect soldier," Graves finished his sentence. "I retract my cynicism, gentlemen. Good pick; who else do we have?"

Mendes selected the following file.

"Oliver Brandon, age twenty-two, born in Milwaukee, Wisconsin. A class nine Apollo EVO"

"What can he do?" Graves dryly inquired.

"Mr. Brandon possesses the ability to store, channel, and manipulate electricity on an immense scale," Dr. Alexander informed him.

"How large?" Graves inquisitively asked.

The doctor viewed his notes again before answering.

"We didn't get an accurate reading, but if I had to guess, he has the potential to drain all of the energy out of half the Northern Hemisphere. He can take the same energy and engulf a portion or all of his entire body in a plasma form of pure electricity.

He can achieve flight and move at one-hundred-eighty-six thousand miles per second. His electrical output produces heat greater than any electrical arc ever created, allowing him to burn through some of the hardest metals on this planet. Very few Apollo types in the electrical class possess various abilities."

Secretary Graves watched with disturbing fascination as Brandon, wearing a unique protective black bodysuit, stood in a controlled testing room. Without uttering a word, he transformed into a being of pure electricity. Extending his right arm, he unleashed a blinding electrically charged beam at a brick wall forty feet away, obliterating it on impact.

"I think I like this one," Graves said with a nod. "Another good pick. I must say I am impressed so far."

Dr. Alexander adjusted his glasses before selecting two more files on his tablet to project on the flat screen.

"Rosann and Adrian Esposito, both twenty-three… paternal twins from Staten Island, New York."

Secretary Graves's brows knitted as he leaned forward.

"Brother and sister EVOs?"

"An extreme rarity," Dr. Alexander explained, "but plausible considering they are twins who share some of the same traits, both are classified as mutants and sub-categorized as Elemental EVOs. Rosann Esposito is an organic Elemental. As her adrenaline levels rise, microscopic hollow barbs protrude from her fingertips, allowing her to collect DNA samples from carbon-based lifeforms. Once it enters her bloodstream, her body morphs, taking on the person's physical traits or animal she touches. The original form returns once her adrenaline levels normalize. The sample does not have to be alive for her to change. With animal DNA, she transforms, becoming a half-human, half-animal hybrid form. Strength, speed, endurance, and agility vary depending on the animal. The transformations seem extremely painful but are easier as long as she remains within classes such as mammals, reptiles, and certain amphibians.

The last recorded organic Elemental that attempted to assimilate bird DNA died due to incompatibility; the same fatal results also appear to happen with all aquatic DNA. Also, she can only assume one form at a time. The barbs in her fingertips retract and remain so once in a transformed state."

Graves carefully scanned her file with interest.

"What about humans?"

"The transformations seem much easier," Dr. Alexander said. "Slight changes occur, turning Ms. Esposito into the subject's monozygotic or identical twin, although sex does not change when she comes into contact with male subjects. Height, weight, eye and skin color, and hair all change to match any subject Ms. Esposito touches. What makes her extremely interesting is when she comes in contact with another EVO. She is capable of mimicking their abilities, not on an extremely high level as the subject she encounters, but enough to be quite formidable."

A faint smile grew on Graves's face.

"That's very useful; what of her brother?"

"An inorganic Elemental, the barbs in his fingers, are apparently stronger than his sister's. When he touches noncarbon-based materials such as wood, stone, or metal, his entire body, including internal organs, transforms into the same properties. His transformations appear to be painless. Strength, durability, and endurance also increase based on whatever he touches. His sister can duplicate his abilities when she touches him; however, he cannot do the same when it comes to her. It is also unclear why they react differently to carbon and noncarbon-based materials."

"Always thought twins were weird," Graves said with a huff. "Even my brother's set. Who's the final member of our list?"

Dr. Alexander projected the final candidate on the screen.

"Last, we have Erica Champion, originally from San Francisco, California… age sixteen and a Promethean class eight EVO."

Graves narrowed his eyes.

"Wait, what age again?"

"Age sixteen," Dr. Alexander reiterated. "A child prodigy diagnosed with autism until the EVO virus infected her, curing her of her autism while granting her intelligence on a superhuman level with access to eighty percent of her mental capability. Her abilities include reading minds, telepathy, psychokinesis, extrasensory perception, and low-level telekinesis."

"No recruiting of children," Graves emitted with passive sternness. "They're a pain when it comes to taking orders and a P.R. nightmare waiting to happen."

"Actually, Ms. Champion is already on the payroll, sir," Mendes informed Graves. "She's also known as Lady Tech."

Graves leaned back in his seat for the first time, stunned by Mende's news.

"**She's** Lady Tech?"

"The top anti-cyber terrorist in the agency responsible for re-firewalling all of the United States government's security systems." Mendes clarified with a nod. "Harvard graduate at the age of eleven with a master's in biology, biomechanics, biophysics, bionics, robotics, Aerodynamics, quantum physics, nuclear physics, atomic physics, astrophysics, cybernetics, computer science, and criminal law. She is also the top expert on EVOs. She volunteered to become a part of this group."

"Her knowledge and intelligence would give this group an extreme advantage like none other, in addition to her technological advances," Dr. Alexander interjected.

"Technological advances?" Secretary Graves asked with a spark in his eye.

"Ms. Champion holds several patents on fully functional combat ready applications that she is willing to share should she be picked for this group," Dr. Alexander informed him.

Graves narrowed his eyes while leaning back further in his seat as he tapped his chin. He sprang forward in his chair, reversing his decision.

"She's in; we'll just keep her out of combat situations; focus her strictly on R&D. So this is the 'best' this country has to offer?"

"Those willing to take the offer," Mendes said.

"God damn Bush," Graves muttered, "he's made it that even superhumans don't want to be all that they can be. This bunch will have to do for now."

"How do we proceed?" Mendes asked.

"Set up a base of operations for them," Graves instructed, "Pick an old facility we no longer use. I don't want them interacting with our regular kids."

"As for training?" Mendes asked, taking notes on his tablet.

"Considering we've never trained EVOs for combat before."

"Well, we've got that covered right here."

Graves pulled up Abraham Rogers's profile again on his tablet.

"The good Sergeant also has experience as a drill sergeant. I don't think he'll have any problem whipping this crew into a lean, mean fighting team."

Mendes and Dr. Alexander's eyes briefly met again with concern before looking back at the Secretary of Defense as he switched to Lady Tech's profile.

"And I'm sure the brainchild can provide the educational data needed to make them the best.

That's how you balance the budget, gentlemen. Get Rogers onboarded and up to date first, along with 'Lady Tech' before you drag the rest of them in. I want the base and them assembled within three weeks for orientation and training, and I want them combat-ready in six months. Make it happen."

CHAPTER 4

Alison Jefferies would be a statistic by tonight. She was already a statistic, being one of the 633,782 people across America who were homeless. She lost her job in the recession of 2008, along with her health benefits. Her unemployment wasn't enough to cover her condominium mortgage despite selling her car and other possessions, leading to foreclosure and losing her home altogether. With no family in New York, she bounced from friend to friend's house, sleeping on their couch. They all gave her the same story as if reciting from a textbook. She could only stay for a week or two; after that, she had to have a job to get back on her feet or find another place to stay. With no job prospects and wearing out all the welcomes of people she thought were her friends, she spent her first night with what little possessions she had left on a bench in Central Park.

Almost five blocks from where she used to work, she remembered the day she sat on one of the same park benches eating lunch, only to get up in disgust as a vagrant sat down next to her. That night, she contemplated suicide; being a Catholic, all be it, not a steadfast one, prevented her from taking her life. Within four years, she endured four muggings, two of them happening within a shelter, two physical assaults, and one sexual, also within a shelter. The hardened life on the streets put an additional twenty years on the thirty-two-year-old's face and body in less than seven years.

Four days ago, Alison found herself caught in the middle of a freezing March downpour. Fear of the shelters kept her from seeking warmth and cover. She now sat huddled in the corner of a building on Park Avenue, dazed with a sickening cough and a heavy wheezing in her chest, all clear signs of full-blown pneumonia.

Her eyes watered, and snot ran from her nose as she cried out for help, but the difficulty of her breathing kept her voice small among the noise of the concrete jungle. She was now among the ignored. People walked by, not even giving her a second glance as if she was a part of the trash on the street, while those who did acknowledge her tossed whatever spare change they had into her plastic cup. Clearly, it was not the assistance she was looking for. Each attempt to breathe became more painful. Alison would not last another cold night. The police or cleaning crew would walk by tomorrow and give her corpse a sharp kick, ordering her to move. She doubted she would even get a proper burial. She slowly closed her eyes, accepted her fate, and dreamed of better days. She dreamed of finding true love and children, things no longer in her future.

Teetering between the land of the dead and the living made Alison oblivious to the world coming to a halt. Everyone else around her was forced to lift their heads as they witnessed an angel descend from the heavens.

An angel donned in a skintight blue and black two-piece running outfit. Debris kicked up as vehicles, both big and small, shook from the powerful force of propulsion, keeping her airborne as Sophia hovered closer and closer to the streets of Manhattan. She canceled out the power two feet off, landing on her cherry-toed bare feet.

At the sight of cameras and other video recording devices aimed at her, her eyes blazed, disrupting them with an electromagnetic pulse. The masses became invisible again as she walked with purpose to the only person Sophia felt warranted her attention. Now towering over a semi-conscious Alison, she knelt down, gently touching her cheek.

"Hey… honey, are you with me?" Sophia asked.

The warmth of Sophia's touch made Alison slowly open her eyes.

Immediately, she believed she had passed on, beholding a woman whose glowing eyes were a bright, warm blue. However, she could still feel cold, her throat soreness from coughing, and breathing difficulty. She should not feel pain if she passed on.

"You've come to take me… to the light?" Alison asked as tears fell from her eyes.

"No, dear," Sophia smiled.

"You're not an angel?" Alison inquired.

"I'm a doctor," Sophia responded, "And from what I can tell, you have a severe case of pneumonia… can you tell me how long you've been like this?"

"I… I don't know," Alison got out between violent coughs, "Am I… am I… going to die?"

"Not on my watch," Sophia reassured Alison, stroking her hair. "Can you tell me your name?"

"Alison…" she answered.

Alison could not remember the last time someone spent more than a minute with her. She knew she smelled putrid, with snot and bile running from her nose and mouth, and yet this woman was stroking her thin, greasy black hair and dirt-ridden cheeks as if they had been friends for ages.

"Alison… would you like to come home with me," Sophia asked, extending an invitation, "so I can take care of you?"

"Till I get better?" Alison asked, nodding in and out of consciousness.

"No… for as long as you'd like."

Alison was conscious enough to hear the words "as long as you'd like." She burst into tears, hunching forward as a violent cough rang through her again, allowing her only to nod. Sophia scooped her up in her arms without hesitation, cradling her like a newborn. Images of her late father holding her whenever she fell asleep in the back of his station wagon came to mind. She rested her weary head against Sophia's bosom, feeling the warmth and a mighty heart.

Sophia walked back to the center of the street, ignoring the flabbergasted masses.

She whispered into Alison's ear, "Hold on tight… the take-off is a little bit rough."

Sophia coiled her powerful legs, causing the ground to shake underneath her before leaping into the air, leaving a small crater where she stood. The powerful energies that gave Sophia flight erupted from her feet's soles, allowing her to ascend above the skyscrapers into the heavens above Manhattan. She would go slow, adjusting to the precious cargo in her arms. Alison Jefferies looked down and saw that she was no longer one of the ignored. She was not a statistic. Those who looked up would remember her and this day.

CHAPTER 5

0800 hours—Marine Corps Mountain Warfare School located in Bridgeport, California—a small base amid a vast national forest, founded during the Korean War to prepare Marines for mountain warfare. Later, it was mothballed during the Vietnam War when the Corps determined it was no longer needed. A CH-46 Sea Knight helicopter disrupted the land's tranquil peace as it descended on the once-active base. Waiting for it to land was a party of ten standing next to a jet-black twin-engine Sikorsky private helicopter.

With arms folded behind his back, Secretary of Defense Robert Graves stared at the descending helicopter. He was flanked by Dr. Alexander and Executive Assistant Mendes while his Department of Defense agents remained vigilant to ensure that the perimeter was secure. Sitting on the Sikorsky folding steps was a teenager in her own world with bright sea-blue dyed hair similar to a Japanese Anime character. Her hi-tech glasses, skintight bodysuit, and boots separated her from everyone else in the group as she fiddled around on what appeared to be an exact glass version of a computer tablet.

The Sea Knight powered down after a ten-point landing; the exit door opened as the folding steps lowered, allowing the occupant inside to exit. Stepping out with a military duffle bag in his grip, dressed in a standard issued Marine service uniform with the rank of Sergeant on his right breast, was a man who looked like he was not born but forged out of raw iron by God Himself. His face showed his age, while his facial scars, especially the one across his left eye, revealed how he weathered a brutal world. Physically, he looked as if he could bring down Everest. If the Marine Corps were the known pitbulls of the United States Military, Sergeant Abraham Arthur Rogers was one of the fathers that sired generations.

Rogers stepped down from the helicopter, marching with purpose over to the party waiting for him. He halted within a respectful distance from the Secretary of Defense, snapping a crisp salute as he reported for duty again.

"Sergeant Rogers, great to finally meet you, soldier." Graves greeted him, "Welcome to Project Regulators. You already know Executive Assistant Mendes. This is Dr. Egan Alexander, lead geneticist and expert on the EVO virus and EVOs."

"Sir, a pleasure to be here," Rogers answered gruffly. "Are all the new recruits present?"

"Negative. Three of them will be here tomorrow at 1100 hours; we thought it best to get your orientation squared away before bringing them in," Graves returned, getting down to business as well. "We're looking for a six-month turnaround on this Sergeant. We need a superhuman fighting force our nation can both respect and be proud of. In the meantime, allow me to introduce you to one of your new teammates who is currently here."

Graves rolled his eyes as he attempted to introduce Rogers to the blue-haired young woman more interested in playing Candy Crush on her tablet than Rogers's introduction.

"Dr. Erica Champion, also a lead geneticist and expert on the EVO virus and EVOs. Also, she is the lead tech specialist and strategist of this facility with a background in many other fields…"

"That would make Einstein himself look like a retard," Dr. Champion blurted out while focusing on her game. "I also prefer to be called Lady Tech, gramps, if you don't mind."

Both Graves and Rogers had mirrored expressions of contempt for today's youth's lack of respect. Lady Tech turned her gaze long enough from her game to catch it and responded with an apologetic smile laced with sarcasm.

"I'm sorry, I forgot what the PC terminology is for geriatrics these days."

Lady Tech switched off the game with a slide of her hand and sprung to her feet, strolling over to the group standing before Rogers.

"Sergeant Abraham Arthur Rogers, forty-eight years old," Erica began to recite. "Born in Manhattan, New York. Former Marine receiving the Medal of Honor for the Iran-Iraq War from 1987 to 1988, a Silver Star for the Invasion of Panama, and a Purple Heart for injury from a landmine during Operation Desert Storm ended your military career.

In addition, a former professional wrestler for Battlefield Wrestling Alliance, holding four World Championship titles, on top of being the company's third Triple Crown Champion and second Grand Slam Champion. You also don't like the fact that you have a kid on your team."

"You got all of that from reading my mind?" Rogers steely asked.

"Heck no," Lady Tech grinned, "I follow the Xavier code of ethics. The first part, I got through your files; the second part, you can just Google. Not to mention, my little brother is a huge fan of yours. My parents took us to the Memorial Coliseum to see you fight $ee Money to retain the BWI Undisputed Platinum and American Championship belts in that Prison Rules match. One of the best matches of your career, and then at the Garden when you defeated Scott "The Crippler" Bentley at 'Legacy Three' to win your first World Heavyweight Championship."

With a slide of her hand and a couple of taps, her tablet projected a holographic YouTube video feed of Rogers wearing his wrestling attire, a Desert Storm-colored wrestling leotard topped off with matching knee/elbow pads and black boots. Patriot tattoos adorned his left breast, right shoulder, right forearm, and left shoulder. He set up a three-point stance in a ring corner before hollering, "Charge!" Rogers bolted, slamming a dazed opponent with a vicious shoulder tackle, driving him into the ring's mat. He then pulled the same opponent to his feet, slapping on a front facelock while throwing the challenger's arm over his neck. Abe saluted the fans before hoisting him into the air as if going for a vertical suplex.

Instead, he moved his arm from around his neck, letting him fall back down to Earth. He timed it, plowing him into the mat with a side slam, completing his Search and Destroy finisher. Rogers hooked him up, getting the three-count. Kid Rock's "Warrior" blared as Rogers sprung to his feet, marching over to a turnbuckle and leaping on the second ropes. He saluted the cheering fans celebrating one of his latest victories. With another hand swipe, she cut off the feed.

"The rest about not liking me," Erica said with a shrug. "I got from your facial features."

There was a calm silence as Rogers leaned forward, looking her in the eyes, removing the cockiness she had; Erica flinched a little while holding her ground.

Rogers leaned in closer, giving her a look over, and then lunged forward to whisper into her ear.

"First off, I don't hate kids," Rogers said sternly, "I hate disrespect and disobedience, things that children such as yourself are full of these days. You want to prove me wrong; you tighten up right now and do, as I say when I say… no discussion. You disobey or challenge me; I won't give a damn if you built the entire world. I will throw you out on your ass faster than you can calculate the speed at which I do it… do you understand me?"

Erica swallowed as she struggled to meet Rogers's intimidating gaze, which felt like it was putting a ton of weight on her.

"Yes…" Lady Tech began to utter.

"Sir. Yes, Sir." Rogers calmly snapped at her.

"Sir! Yes, Sir!!" Erica quickly barked out, snapping to attention.

Rogers stood tall again, looking down at her. Graves smiled, approving that he had chosen the perfect candidate for this new operation.

"Well, expert," Abe said, motioning to her, "show me what I'm working with."

"Gentlemen," Lady Tech coughed, getting her groove back, "welcome to the Ranch. Ninety percent of the facility is operational. The completion of the other ten percent will be by the end of this week. With my modifications and upgrades, this is the most fortified base of operations on the planet."

All four men looked around at the abandoned base, which had not been touched.

Graves raised an eyebrow as he turned to her.

"What modifications?"

Erica smacked her forehead while laughing.

"Oh, right! I forgot; this is the ten percent, this way, please."

Minus the Secretary's security detail, Rogers, Graves, Dr. Alexander, and Mendes followed Lady Tech, taking the lead to one of the old hangers used to maintain helicopters. As they neared the massive doors, a giant black orb twice the size of a basketball emitted an array of green and red beams that scanned each individual present.

"Please stand still for scanning," a female voice echoed from hidden audio speakers within the hanger, "recognize, Dr. Erica Champion, EVO Class 8 Promethean, and Creator. Recognize, Robert Edward Graves, human, United States Secretary of Defense. Recognize Dr. Egan Nathanial Alexander, human, a specialist in human genetics and biology. Recognize, Michael Eduardo Mendes, human, Executive Assistant to Secretary of Defense. Recognize, Abraham Arthur Rogers, EVO Class 5 Titan; reinstated United States Marines Sergeant under the Regulators project. Bio-scan is completed and stored in memory for future records. Welcome to the Ranch."

The massive hangar doors slid open, revealing an empty room. Graves's face scowled as he glared at Mendes, unimpressed with what he had seen. Lady Tech strolled into the hangar before the four men.

"Step lively, gentlemen!" Lady Tech requested in her best British voice. "Step lively; these doors close fast."

Rogers stepped through without hesitation, followed by Graves, Mendes, and Dr. Alexander in unison. The doors closed behind them, locking shut, leaving them in darkness for a split second before bright interior lights brought sight back into the room.

"Brace yourselves, boys, the initial disengage is kind of jolting,"

Erica warned.

Aside from Abe and Dr. Alexander, Graves, and Mendes didn't notice that the floor of the hanger that was originally concrete was entirely metal. Yellow and red siren lights flipped up from each corner of the ground. Half of the flooring, which ran the high school football field's length, disengaged underneath them, descending on a sliding slant into a massive complex. As the lift brought them down, the Secretary of Defense looked in amazement at the underground facility but more so at the assortment of two-armed, quadruped-legged droids. Some clung to steel rafters like spiders drilling, welding, and installing structures and electronic components. The underground complex was three-quarters the size and length of a supercarrier.

"They're called Doozers, multi-application droids created to build, run, maintain, and defend this facility if need be. The entire facility runs underneath the camp, and a little beyond," Lady Tech explained. "Topside will be reconstructed to give the illusion of a regular military base, while the real operations will take place down here. 360-degree surveillance on both ground and air. The entire complex is fortified from top to bottom with a new metal alloy that I created called dark metal."

"Dark metal?" Graves asked.

"Tungsten mixed with titanium, carbon nanofibers, and a dash of a woman's best friend. Very difficult to mix and blend, but once you get it right, it's virtually indestructible. This place can take more punishment than the President's safe room."

The floor rested at the bottom of the underground base, locking into place with the ground floor.

"Welcome home, Miss," the same female voice emitted from the facility's speaker system.

"Thank you, Maxine," Erica acknowledged. "She's the central computer that runs everything within the facility with the most advanced AI system created to date. Maxine runs the Doozers, security, and defenses and can link to worldwide surveillance and satellite systems in every country.

There's really nothing she can't do. Currently, she is compiling research on every EVO on the planet and categorizing them by type, power level, threat level, and location. If they're affiliated with a government or terrorist organization, if they're just civilians, whether they're current superheroes or criminals."

"What does Maxine stand for?" Graves asked.

"Uh, nothing," Erica said with a shrug, "I just thought it was a cute name for an AI."

Rogers and Graves turned their attention to four human-size Doozers. Two worked on a sizeable aircraft-type vehicle, smaller than a cargo jet with a space shuttle look. The other two assembled a heavily armored vehicle that appeared to cross between a tank and a Humvee.

"That's the Tornado," Lady Tech pointed out, "our mission air transport. It has V/STOL capabilities like a Harrier and can outmatch the speed of an SR-71. It even has suborbital capabilities, which have not been tested yet. It also includes an advanced targeting system for tracking up to twenty multiple targets and can fire anything from armor-piercing, heat-seeking, and heat plasma-based rounds."

"We have someone to fly this?" Graves questioned her.

"Yep, me."

"Come again?" Mendes inquired, stepping into the conversation.

"When I got my driver's license, I also went for my pilot's license," Lady Tech huffed. "It was pretty easy. Tornado has signature recognition protocols, recognizing only me as its pilot. So only I can fly it. In the worst-case scenario, if I cannot fly, Maxine is capable of remoting in and piloting it.

Next is the Warthog, an all-terrain transport with aquatic capability. Heavily armored with dark metal and outfitted with various guns and cannons, some possessing anti-aircraft armament. No conventional combat vehicle on land, sea, and air can beat it."

"Fascinating toys, Ms. Champion," Graves dryly sighed, "but I didn't hand you over a two-point-five-billion-dollar budget to bring to life things that you see in a blockbuster movie."

"My apologies," Erica returned with a sardonic tone, "I should have shown you the flashing Regulator signal first, but I'm still deciding between the middle finger and the forearm salute."

"Young lady."

Graves's tone had steel coursing through it, which Lady Tech turned to match her own.

"You gave me a two-point-five-billion-dollar budget to put together a superhuman unit capable of handling threats both domestic and abroad, Mr. Secretary. Every piece of equipment that I have fabricated here is essential to doing just that. So excuse me if I take offense to you thinking I'm not taking my job seriously just because I'm below the drinking age. Especially since this place will be charged with housing some of the most dangerous superhumans on the planet."

"What do you mean by "housing"?" Rogers sternly asked.

An awkward silence lasted for half a minute before Lady Tech burst out with a chuckle, shaking her head.

"Holy shit, he never told you."

"Watch your mouth," Rogers warned her, "Tell me what?"

Graves sighed while switching to a delicate tone.

"Rogers, there were slight changes made to your role and that of your new team after your signing on."

The bass in Abe's voice became more forceful.

"What changes?"

It made the conversation all the more uncomfortable for everyone except for Lady Tech, who stepped in.

"Sir, you weren't just recruited for this new unit to be a soldier again; you were also recruited to be a cop and a prison warden. Maxine, project an entire layout of the facility, please."

Her tablet lit up again as the camera projected a holographic schematic of the entire base, revealing a lower level underneath them.

"I call it Purgatory," Erica sighed. "A fortified prison facility constructed to incarcerate EVOs."

"Why is there a prison located on this base?" Rogers demanded.

"Because no regular human wants to be a CO in a prison where the inmates can either tear you apart with their bare hands or turn you to ashes with a snap of a finger." Lady Tech bluntly answered. "Why do you think we were given this big ole space in the middle of nowhere? Superhumans may be the norm of society now, Sergeant Rogers, but we still make regular folk a tad bit nervous. We're good enough to protect them, but just not good enough to be in the same room as them. Ain't that right, Mr. Secretary?"

A chainsaw could cut the awkwardness and tension that had developed; Dr. Alexander, a man of science, stood in an uncomfortable spot between the Secretary of Defense with loyal Mendes at his side and the superhumans.

"I can smell bull manure a mile away, Secretary Graves," Erica sneered. "I don't need my nose rubbed in it. I think I speak the same for the Sergeant even though I just met him."

Rogers changed his stance, standing next to her.

"What the kid said, sir."

Graves's face said it all. With formality thrown out the window, he shifted into a more authoritative stance to project the point of who was really in charge.

"Let's get an understanding here, shall we? This unit was only authorized because POTUS could no longer ignore the threat growing at our doorsteps. China, Russia, the UK, North and South Korea, and Israel and

Iran either have or are assembling superhuman units of their own.

It is an entirely new Cold War, and we do not intend to lose it. However, do not make the mistake of believing that you are irreplaceable. If I have to, I will take away all of your toys and find someone more suitable to run this operation for the right price."

"I'd love to see you try," Erica scoffed at him.

Graves raised a finger to warn Erica that she was testing his patience when Rogers stepped in.

"Last I checked, sir, there was me, the kid, and only three other recruits for this job," Abe dryly stated. "So unless you intend to throw a couple billion more of the tax payer's money into this, I believe your claim is slightly over-exaggerated."

Graves focused on the Sergeant, whose visual intimidation had his beat ten-fold. Graves, nonetheless, did not back down from him.

"We're not going to have a problem, are we Rogers," Graves sighed, "because I really do like you."

"As long as you don't continue to yank my chain, sir, we won't," Rogers returned, "and it's Sergeant, I work for a living."

"Fair enough," Graves nodded, finally backing down.

"Now that we're done measuring sizes, "shall we continue the tour?" Lady Tech inquired.

Once again, the two older men were at an accord, turning their disapproving gaze on a fresh mouth, Erica. She gave them a dismissive eye roll and her back as she continued the tour.

"As I was about to say, I constructed Purgatory with various unique holding cells capable of dampening EVO powers and abilities across the board regardless of power levels, all except for the Source that is."

"What's the Source?" Rogers asked.

Once again, his question stopped the procession as Graves grabbed his nose, feeling a migraine coming on. Lady Tech spun around on her heel in disbelief.

"You're joking, right? You don't know?"

Erica turned her disapproving attention to Graves and Dr. Alexander.

"Out of curiosity, what exactly did you tell the good Sergeant to get him to join this operation?"

"I'm pretty sure, Dr. Champion, you can, and will, update Sergeant Rogers on all EVO affairs later," Graves steely retorted. "Especially considering the Source is not an imminent threat at this time to National Security. Now may we continue the tour? I have other appointments to keep."

"I'll fill you in later."

Lady Tech's mental voice came like a whisper in Rogers's ear.

It made the old Marine wince as he narrowed his eyes at her. Clearly not accustomed to telepathy, he would talk with Ms. Champion later about invading his mind without permission.

"Anyway, to your left are the living quarters," Erica announced, continuing her tour, "and down this way is the Hurt Locker."

Graves paused again, raising an eyebrow.

"Hurt Locker?"

"A training facility for our new recruits to develop their **superpowers**," Erica answered with her trademark sarcastic tone.

The Secretary of Defense's visage revealed his patience wore thin from it. As they continued walking through the massive facility, a pack of miniature Doozers the size of small dogs scurried, disregarding them to get to their next project.

"Over there is the mess hall, armament, fabrication, and my lab, and over here is the central command."

Lady Tech gestured to a massive circular steel door with the symbol of a metallic eagle with its wings spread out with the letter 'R' etched into its chest covering the entrance. The insignia broke into two as the two halves of the door opened. As they walked in, aside from Lady Tech and Dr. Alexander, the look of awe broke through both Rogers and Graves's granite exteriors, while Mendes believed he was standing on the main deck of the starship Enterprise.

A gargantuan theater display screen wrapped around half of the room. In the center of the room, flashing pictures and identification of known EVOs worldwide were sorted and cataloged around a holographic globe that rotated as red lights popped up one by one, indicating their locations on the planet. The entire room had a sleek, clean look with its white on a black color scheme and steel blue accents—everything operated by voice command, touch screen, or holographic projection.

"Welcome home," Maxine greeted.

Her voice threw off men as it projected from inside the room, not over the speaker system like before. They turned to face the real Maxine, unprepared for what was before them.

Her hairstyle was similar to Lady Tech's but colored pink with white streaks. The pink lipstick she wore matched her hair and large pink glowing eyes, clearly not human. They also mirrored her body, which was also not human. Aside from her head, the upper thighs and shoulders appeared human. The rest of her body, from the neck down and legs and arms, were hard cybernetic metal in a pink and white color scheme. Blue lights glowed silently from different parts of her limbs, body, and neck, indicating an unknown power source allowing her animation. Mendes pinched his arm to ensure he was not dreaming.

"Thank you, Maxine," Erica smiled.

"I thought you said she was a computer?" a fascinated yet disturbed Graves snapped.

"The term is AI," Lady Tech clarified with an eye roll. "This is the cybernetic android form that she uploads into to do physical tasks when necessary, to assist me."

She walked up to Maxine, looking at her nearly six-foot form with motherly pride.

"Cybernetic battle chassis built out of dark metal," Erica explained.

"And her power source?" Graves inquisitively asked.

"Ionized liquid mercury, or what I like to call Liquid Ion," Lady Tech answered with a smirk, "a mixture of mercury, saline water, and compound gelatin that can conduct electricity on the level of a nuclear submarine. Several small pulmonary generators circulate the liquid through her circulatory and central nervous system, giving her a constant cycle of power."

"Like a human," said a fascinated Mendes, moving forward to get a better look, "is it a self-sustaining power source?"

"Not yet," Lady Tech replied, shaking her head. "The mercury eventually evaporates, requiring a transfusion every eight months, which is significant progress considering the first batch I made only lasted for twenty-four hours. Her eyes are constructed with microscopic solar panels providing her with a secondary power source, putting less strain on her main power supply. The goal is to make it self-sustaining once I find a bonding agent to prevent the mercury from turning to vapor or a replacement for it, capable of holding and cycling a charge of that capacity indefinitely. All in all, she cooks, cleans, and is proficient in all forms of combat. She is also an excellent pilot and driver."

"Why the human parts?" Mendes questioned.

"It looks cool," Erica answered with a shrug. "Not to mention, I'd get creeped out, always talking to something out of a Schwarzenegger movie."

"So why not make her look completely human?" Mendes asked a follow-up question.

"Because... it... looks... cool!"

Lady Tech finished her loud and slow response, glaring at Mendes as if he were deaf or mentally challenged. Mendes wore a face expressing that he, too, was tired of her displays of disrespect.

The round metal door parted again, forcing Mendes to spin around and jump backward, bouncing off a Rogers wall. The cause of his startle was two more female android creatures similar to Maxine. A bubbly one with long orange hair and big glowing orange eyes had a rustic red and orange color scheme to the metallic parts of her cybernetic body. At the same time, her molded bust was slightly larger than Maxine's metallic bosom.

The female droid adjacent to her wore a cynical look on her face with her arms folded. Her hair was cut like Erica's and Maxine's but dyed purple with black streaks matching her deep glowing purple eyes; her color scheme was gothic gunmetal gray with light yellow accents. Unlike Maxine and her companion, the bright lights on her limbs and body were orange. Her frame was slenderer with a smaller chest than her other two "sisters."

"You built more than one," Graves asked with a hint of displeasure.

"Well, I couldn't just build one," Lady Tech replied with a smile and shrug. "The one in orange with the fire top is Angie, and the brooding one in purple and gray is Jennifer, my lovely dolls."

"Dolls..."

Graves's tone became more displeased by the second, while Lady Tech gave him the same look that she gave Mendes as if he, too, was slow.

"Uh... yeah... I'm a girl. I like dolls. I specifically designed their AIs for each of their bodies, but they can also upload into the main system like Maxine or other bodies. Angie was designed for heavy lifting, while Jennifer was built for speed using lighter armor and ridiculously fast lightning speed processors."

"Again, using this facility as your little personal playground, Dr. Champion," Graves admonished her while frowning.

"Actually, I built them because I don't trust **normal stupid** people to work on my projects with me," Erica retorted flatly. "Considering all of their AIs were mapped from my brain. It's like having **three more** of me to execute the tasks I need to be done, so I'm not wasting your **little 2.5 billion** that I could make ten times over if I decide to rejoin the private sector."

The awkward silence returned as a new and old school locked eyes again, giving neither an inch nor a quarter.

"Why don't you stick your tongue down her throat, you perv?" The android, designated as Jennifer, asked, breaking the silence with her raspy voice. "Isn't that the reason you're staring her down so hard?"

"Jennifer! That's rude!" Angie scolded her sister with a high-pitched Valley Girl voice. "He's the Secretary of Defense!"

"Well, he's acting like Bill Clinton, damn lolicon!" Jennifer sneered.

The comment made Rogers grunt. Mendes forced himself to choke on his chuckle while Dr. Alexander shook his head. Graves slowly turned to the android, who looked disgusted as she glared at him and decided he had his fill, specifically of Lady Tech's company.

Graves dryly began his exit speech.

"I believe we've seen all we need to see of this facility, and I have more pressing matters to attend."

~~~~~~~~~~~~~~~~~~~~~~~~~~~~~~~~~~

Eight minutes later, everyone, excluding the androids, was again topside. Dr. Alexander and Mendes boarded the helicopter while the Secretary, now flanked by his agents, addressed Abe and Erica.

"As I stated earlier, Rogers, the rest of your team should be arriving tomorrow at 1100 hours. I'll take it. I don't have to worry about you getting them squared away in the six months' time required."
~~~~~~~~~~~~~~~~~~~~~~~~~~~~~~~~~~

"No, sir," Rogers answered, keeping it tight and formal with Graves.

The Secretary cracked a fake smile.

"I know we got off to a rocky start. But I have every faith that I have chosen the right man for this position."

Rogers's granite exterior cracked a fake smirk.

"I'll do my job, sir."

Before Graves could extend his hand for a shake, Rogers snapped a crisp salute, bidding him farewell. Graves smirked and nodded.

"Dr. Champion," Graves addressed Erica without making eye contact.

"Secretary," Lady Tech returned with a bright, cheesy grin.

Graves turned and walked up the steps, followed by his entourage with derogatory thoughts about jarheads and today's youth running through his mind, while Rogers watched him leave with demeaning thoughts of pencil-pushing bureaucrats. They observed as the Secretary's helicopter ascended and took off; neither cared where it went.

"So," Erica sighed, "Just you and me now."

"You know that thing where you were whispering in my head," Rogers said while looking at the sky.

"Don't do it again," Erica answered, still looking up.

"Also, if you think you're going to run roughshod over me like you did the Secretary, you will lose."

"Fair enough, care to return to the Batcave and get settled in?"

Rogers glanced at her before marching off back to the hangar. Erica turned and skipped, following him from behind.

~~~~~~~~~~~~~~~~~~~~~~~~~~~~~~~~

Another eight minutes later, they returned underground to the main central command accompanied by the android sisters.

"So, I can tell just by the look on your face, you have questions about the Source," Lady Tech deduced, "what do you want to know?"

"Everything," Abe answered.

"Maxine."

Upon Erica's command, an image of a prison record appeared on the theater-sized screen before Rogers.

"Sophia Dennison, formerly Sophia Matheson," Erica introduced, "widow, thirty-nine years old, United States Citizen born in Mount Vernon, New York, originally resided in Houston, Texas. She graduated from Texas Southwestern with honors, formally a licensed doctor and skilled surgeon. Sentenced to death by lethal injection, which was carried out in 2008 for the murder of her husband, a former highly decorated United States Marine veteran."

"I know her," Rogers said with a nod. "The superwoman from the incidents in Texas and DC back in 08."

"Very good; she is also the reason why you and I are the way we are now. She is the Source, the first EVO, or EVO Zero, and the cause of what we now call the Big Bang 2 incident. She was the one who stopped that nuclear warhead from wiping out the West Coast."

Rogers began putting the pieces together.

"A General went down for that, Bernard Matheson. He's…"

"Her father-in-law," Erica answered, filling in the blanks. "Don't know any of the stories between the two of them, but I imagine there was some pretty nasty family history there."

"How is she the reason we are who we are?" Rogers asked.
~~~~~~~~~~~~~~~~~~~~~~~~~~~~~~~~

"Maxine," Erica requested again, "please bring up sequence theory 091312."

The holographic globe disappeared in the middle of the room as a simulated projection of Sophia flying toward a nuclear warhead appeared, as Lady Tech explained.

"It's all just a theory, but when our girl slammed into that nuke, she must have taken considerable damage. I'm thinking deep tissue damage, maybe even more; however, those cells didn't burn up and die.

They regenerated into a viral form, multiplied, and went airborne, allowing the winds to take it to the Earth's four corners, contaminating our air, food, and water supply. As it infected a host, it either killed, remained dormant, or, in the case of you and I, systematically destroyed our normal cells while replicating new ones in its place, rewriting our DNA, turning us into who we are now. She is our 'mother,' so to speak, responsible for giving birth to the entire superhuman race."

The holographic image changed, displaying her abilities in detail.

"EVOs are designated classes one to ten based on their ability to cause destruction from a city block to an actual city with the scale being Manhattan; Ms. Dennison has no designated class since her powers can devastate on a continental, maybe even planetary level.

She is stronger and faster than any EVO on this planet, impervious to conventional firepower, including energy-based weapons and nuclear armament, immune to all diseases, and immortal for all intent and purposes."

"Where is she now?" Abe inquired.

Erica again pulled up the holographic globe and pointed to a lit-up blip.

"Right there, one thing she can't do is hide; she emits some kind of bio-energy signature that lights up like a dwarf star. She created her own island half the size of Brazil, which is located in the middle of the Pacific..."

"Wait, what do you mean, 'created?'"

"I mean, she descended to the deepest depths of the ocean, underneath the Earth's crust all the way down to the tectonic plates. She then physically began to move plates around while diverting a massive magma upward to erupt an underwater volcano." Erica slowly explained, "where she either plowed or blasted her way. Ms. Dennison then found a way to push the volcano to the top of the sea level, where the lava eventually cooled, forming a surface. Lucky for us, she created it in the most remote part of the Pacific. Most of Japan and the West Coast only felt some small tremors.

Then she started terraforming it. She began by swiping trees from different forests around the planet, especially ones that would have been big business victims. The process took about six to eight months to complete, which is nothing for someone who does not need sleep."

Erica projected a detailed image of the large ghost landmass. The first thought she could tell was swimming in his head based on his facial expression, which was why this was not headlining news anywhere.

"No one knows about this?" Rogers asked, looking at the globe.

"The **majority** of the general public around the planet does not know about this," Erica said. "Every government and scientist on the planet knows about this. They also attempted to show Ms. Dennison how unpleased they were with her little project."

The holographic globe disappeared again as another video began to play.

"Behold the ass-kicking never televised," Lady Tech narrated, "Russia and the US in a joint Co-Op mission sent in the Siberian Machine, the leader of the Russian superhuman unit Утюг Спецназ, which stands for "Iron Spetsnaz" and Captain Omega, who for some reason volunteered for this harebrained scheme, to either capture or terminate Ms. Dennison on sight.

Class 10 ranked Titans with exceptional durability, endurance, and strength, lifting within or above the eighty-five thousand to one hundred thousand-ton range. Parts of the footage were slow-moed over a thousand times to see what happened. Oh, by the way, I have it on good knowledge;

the fight started due to the Siberian Machine saying some very disparaging things about Ms. Dennison and her mother."

The audio system boomed with the sounds of gods warring.

Rogers watched as a woman with dreads in a black and yellow wetsuit was fending off two of the most powerfully recorded EVO Titans on the planet with a combination of Muay Thai and Krav Maga techniques.

"For a doctor, she has some moves."

"That's thanks to her photographic and muscle memory."

Rogers turned to Lady Tech.

"You mean…?"

"She can retain anything she sees, hears, or reads like a supercomputer, probably works with scent too. Anyway, this not only allows her to obtain a vast amount of knowledge and speak every language on the planet but duplicate a physical movement just by seeing it performed one time as long as it's within her physical capability, which, as you can see, are pretty vast. She's also immune to mental attacks and mind-reading."

Blows reducing a skyscraper to rubble, she blocked and defended, but that was not all Abe saw. Even the most trained combatant ducked or evaded a blow to get some breathing room or mount an offense. Sophia blocked every punch and kick thrown at her and stepped into the blows, which was an offense on its own as she knocked each man backward every time they struck her.

It was similar to watching toddlers playfully pushed around by a larger adult. Sophia was controlling the fight. Her defensive maneuvers positioned the Captain and the Machine where she wanted them to be.

As Sophia purposely allowed them to flank her on both sides, both men, with split-second eye contact, came up with the idea to shoot and tackle her simultaneously. That one unified attack defined the difference in power between the three combatants. Sand exploded into the air as Sophia charged the Siberian Machine, shattering his shoot attempt with an NFL-style shoulder tackle, which knocked a man twice her size backward almost six feet into the air and twenty yards across the three-day-old beach.

As the Russian crashed painfully and awkwardly, Captain Omega, who regained his footing after missing his initial shoot attempt, kicked up his own sand as he attempted another tackle. The former All-American from Virginia came in for a sack that could derail a freight train; Sophia dug her toes into the sand, assuming a football stance of her own. With a burst of force with a distance of only three inches per Erica's readings, she derailed the unstoppable force known as Captain Omega.

To Rogers, it was like watching a motorcyclist from one of those reality television shows slamming into a brick wall, going sixty miles an hour, and wondering how they survived. The Captain's neck snapped back violently as he was lifted off his feet before coming down on the upper part of his shoulders. As the rest of his body came down, he folded like a lawn chair. Erica, who viewed the footage multiple times, still winced from watching the brutal blow.

It was clear to Rogers what Sophia was doing. Her speed and apparent hand-to-hand combat skill could easily have dismantled the super-powered duo with a couple of well-placed strikes. She, however, was looking to etch this fight into their skulls.

Sophia continued her lesson on the slow-rising Russian as the Captain groaned, slowly unfolding himself from his painful position. This time, she took the offense, blasting across the sand with a sonic boom sprint on her newly-raised island, darting straight toward the Machine. Just before impact, she had to hop to hit her six-inch taller target. With a clothesline that would make the legendary Stan Hansen wet himself in Rogers's eyes, Sophia dismantled the Machine turning him inside out. He crashed back down to the semi-moist sand again, never rising. Only a fluttering groan signified that he was still breathing.

As Sophia looked down at the semi-conscious Russian, a roaring Captain Omega back up on his feet came out of nowhere, using his pistons for legs to propel him back into the fight, hitting Sophia across the face with an earth-quaking Superman punch. He followed up with a full-on assault of lefts and rights, delivering face and body shots and staggering her. Rogers knew it was not the case; she saw him coming a mile away and could have swatted him out of midair. Instead, she chose to drop her guard, allowing him to wail away at her. Readings showed that the Captain had struck Sophia over twenty times, raining down thunderous blows that could total a tank. It appeared as if the Captain was winning with each impact.

The grin on her face said otherwise.

Even with Sophia's tremendous durability and endurance, the sand she stood on could not hold her in place to withstand Captain Omega's devastating hits, causing her to slide around every time he struck her. The tale ended with her catching one of his missile blows in mid-strike. Sophia followed up with a brutal gut check on a man he saw single-handedly pull two aircraft carriers to shore with just a steel chain for a charity benefit a year ago. It echoed throughout the central command with the distinct sound of bone cracked by a sledgehammer.

The punch lifted him six feet off the ground, dropping him to his knees. Ms. Dennison grabbed him by the front of his leather red and blue cosmic-themed costume with one arm draping him up. She slowly ascended into the sky with him, kicking up a sandstorm partially covering the Machine. Sophia was sending a message to those watching aboard the U.S.S. George H.W. Bush.

The audio could not pick up what she was saying, but it was not hard to read her lips, "Don't come back."

Even with his regenerative healing being several times greater than Rogers, he could not recover from the fight-ending body blow. She could have done anything she wanted with him in his weakened state. Sophia decided on something a little humiliating. Rearing back her head, she cracked him in the skull with a nose-splitting headbutt that shook his whole body. The Captain went limp in her grip like a puppet on a string.

Sophia descended to the Earth to collect the downed Machine on his hands and knees, still shaken from the pro wrestling lariat she used to take him down. Sophia grabbed him by the pants of his red, white, and blue costume military attire and flew them back to the US aircraft carrier they sailed on. She gently dropped them onto the ship's deck in front of a shocked and terrified crew and Captain.

"They will recover," Sophia said. "The Captain's ribs are cracked, so keep him straight, so they have a chance to heal properly."

With no more words, she rocketed off; another view from a Russian class destroyer that accompanied the ship named Sovremenny caught Sophia grasping the rear of the 102,000 long ton vessel, performing a simple one-arm push, sending the carrier sailing like a paper boat back from whence it came never to return. At the end of the feed, Rogers stepped back. His face was the same impenetrable stone expression, but his body language revealed the footage rocked even him as he turned to Lady Tech.

"I don't understand; why did they send in a two-man team? The Russian team is a six-man crew alone."

"Yeah, that would be the logical response," Erica coughed, "but the speedsters would have just got in the way, and energy-based EVOs would only make it worse. She can absorb energy attacks increasing her strength."

"How does she possess this array of abilities?" Rogers bluntly asked.

"Ms. Dennison's primary talent, which no EVO on the planet has," Erica explained, "is the ability to not only regenerate when injured but to build physical defenses preventing her from being hurt the same way twice. The tradeoff is she sometimes acquires powerful offensive abilities."

"So, the more you try to hurt her," Rogers concluded, "the stronger she gets."

"Very good," Lady Tech said with a nod, "After the much-failed mission, an emergency UN Security Council meeting was called in secret. By a unanimous decision, they categorized Ms. Dennison as a 'force of nature,' advising no further confrontation with her under any circumstances. She can go wherever she pleases; war-torn countries hold a cease-fire whenever she is in town, and Al-Qaeda and ISIS scatter like roaches when she shows up in their region.

Her island will never be mapped, and a five-thousand-mile radius around it is designated as a no-fly and sail zone. Under their governments' advisement, almost every major news network has agreed not to cover her. She also keeps an ultra-low profile and has a cute knack for emitting a small burst electromagnetic pulse to ensure she doesn't become a YouTube or Vine exclusive. The woman loves her privacy."

Rogers nodded before turning back to the holographic view of her island.

"What does she do there?"

"As you can see, she's built an entire village and wildlife preserve for endangered species. She takes in and cares for anyone looking for sanctuary," Erica answered while pulling up a satellite view of Sophia's village, "the homeless, orphans, drug addicts, victims of white slavery, refugees from some of the vilest places on the planet. She takes them there, cares for them, and protects them."

"Doesn't sound like the actions of a cold-blooded killer," Rogers said.

"Yeah, the whole thing stinks about that," Erica scoffed. "If you remember, she made it all the way to CNN in Washington to declare her innocent and ratted out our nation's infamous unknown death squad known as the D.E.A.D. It's one of the reasons no one lifted a finger to bring her in, on top of the fact that no one or nothing on this planet can stop her."

"You keep saying 'nothing on this planet' as if you believe in something… off this planet."

"Due to my own personal studies, I've come to believe the EVO virus was not created or engineered by anyone on this planet. My theory is that it was reverse-engineered by Dr. Zimmerman and those from the original project, based on the virus's original blueprints. There are proteins and elements within it, which number in the trillions, that are clearly nowhere on any periodical chart. Unfortunately, the virus has successfully integrated itself into the human gene pool as a cell. The only way I can successfully decipher its origins is if I got a sample directly from her."

Rogers furrowed his brows.

"If you got a sample, what would you hope that it could tell you?"

She turned to him, locking eye contact.

"Who really made her who she is now, and us."

Rogers turned with narrowed eyes, staring at Sophia's profile on the big screen.

"Well, I guess you'll want to get settled," Erica huffed, "before the fresh meat arrives tomorrow, dinner is at 1800 hours. Maxine, what's on the menu?"

"Stir-fried night for you, and for the Sergeant's palette, I cooked up a prime rib steak with mash potatoes and greens," Maxine chirpily answered.

"Angie, can you please escort the good Sergeant Rogers to his new living quarters," Erica politely asked.

"Don't get lost," Jennifer said to her sister teasingly.

Angie smilingly gave her sister the finger as she strolled up to him.

"This way Sergeant Rogers."

Abe followed her, stopping to pick up his bag near the entranceway. He halted to ask Lady Tech one final question.

"How come the enrollment for this outfit was so low? I thought the US had the second largest population of EVOs to Europe?

"Aside from you and the other three recruits picked," Erica sighed, "the other six applicants that applied had psychological and personality problems that made them unfit for this team."

Rogers dawned an uncomfortable look.

"Ten in all? No one else applied?"

Erica took two steps toward him.

"People tend not to forget the treatment of others, and how our government dragged their asses to treat heroes who ran into the toxic rubble of fallen buildings to save lives at the risk of their own. They also did not forget the lives of servicemen and women lost for wars that did not need to be fought. Because of that, people don't really like our government very much these days and are less inclined to stick their necks out. That includes superhumans. The current hero community is willing to fight the good fight, just not under the banner of the US government."

"So, why are you doing this?" Rogers asked.

"I have multiple reasons," Erica answered with a smile. "One of them happens to be that, like it or not, we need to feel as if we can trust our government again. People need to believe that it will step up to protect us from the right people and the right situations. That's not done if everyone just sits on their asses."

Rogers nodded in agreement with her logic; he turned, following the orange-haired android leading the way to his new quarters, looking around again at his new home.

CHAPTER 6

Gatesville Women's Facility, Gatesville, Texas:

Sophia sat in the courtyard, examining her next move. It was her usual weekly visit. Sister Shareef had taken out her queen's knight and king's bishop in five movements. Her last defense for her king was her queen, a pawn, and a rook. Sister Shareef sat patiently across from her, awaiting her next move, attacking two bishops, a queen's knight, a king's rook, and two pawns. One was at the end of Sophia's board, ready to become a queen.

"So, twenty-eight girls," Sister Shareef sighed, glancing upward into Sophia's blue, glowing eyes.

"Twenty-eight girls," Sophia returned a steely tone, not looking up from the board, "and I got all of them this time. One was working with two cracked ribs, and one was pregnant and only fifteen years old; she wants to keep the baby, by the way. Two have Chlamydia, one so bad it may leave her sterile because it was left untreated for so long, and one is HIV positive.

Add on the mountainous psychological damage they will all have to endure for the rest of their lives. On day one, on the island, they asked to occupy four huts between twenty-eight of them. They sleep two to a bed and move in unison like meerkats. It's almost adorable if you don't know the story behind it.

What bothers me is watching them walk around with their heads down; they flinch and coil at anyone who comes near them. Every night, I hear one waking up screaming from night terrors. That son of a bitch didn't just break those girls… he shattered them, and now I have to put them back together."

Shareef leaned back in her seat, now less interested in the pending victory she had secured on the board and more in her friend's state of mind.

"When was the last time you slept, baby girl?" Sister Shareef asked with a head tilt.

"You forgot already, sis; I don't need to sleep," Sophia answered with a voice of frustration as she scanned the board. "I also don't need to eat, drink, or breathe air. I can survive the crushing depths of the ocean and the harsh cold atmosphere of space itself. If this godforsaken world ever ends, it'll be me and the friggin roaches that are left."

"Even with all you can do now, you're not…"

"I swear if you utter the word "super," I will slap the taste out of your mouth right here," Sophia sternly warned.

She moved her pawn forward in disgust, the only move she had to play as Shareef glared at her, none too appreciative of the verbal threat.

"I was going to say, God, queen me," she fired back, moving her pawn to the end of the board and turning it into a queen.

Sophia snarled as she took Shareef's pawn, replacing it with her captured queen rook, protected by her original queen. She moved her pawn forward again, only for it to be taken out by Shareef's king's bishop. Sophia's final attack was to remove the newly promoted queen, allowing Shareef to take down her lone queen.

"Check," Shareef snapped, now focused on the game.

Sophia had no choice but to move her king forward with her rook on the other side of her king. This allowed Shareef to move her queen across the board, taking out Sophia's rook.

"Check again."

Sophia's eyebrow twitched as she moved her king forward again, allowing Shareef to move her queen across the board to F8 while her king's rook sat comfortably on H1, flanking her on both sides, forcing her to move forward again. Shareef calmly moved her king to F1; Sophia's only move was to advance forward. Shareef then shifted her king's rook left to G1.

"Check," Shareef sighed, not looking up from the board.

Sophia returned a more profound sigh as she played her final move to H4, allowing Shareef to move her queen back to H8.

"Checkmate, and if you knock this board off the table, **I'm going to slap you**," Shareef sternly warned her.

Sophia glared at an unintimidated Shareef with folded arms, staring her down. Sophia's face softened as she looked down at the table, although the frustration was still there. Shareef leaned forward, resting her forearms on the table. She reached out, grabbing one of Sophia's locks and playing with it; her dreadlocked mane had grown even longer since her escape from prison almost seven years ago.

"Soph, talk to me. What is really wrong?"

"I had to fight two more superhumans," she finally said. "They were hired muscle."

"You didn't have to..."

"No," Sophia said, "I easily overpowered them, but they were there. They were there because of me."

Shareef let out a huff as she put her head down.

"Soph, if you're going to start with the 'Diary of an Angry Black Woman' pity party cliché shit, I can go back to my cellblock and take a nap," Shareef said with a steel-like tone to her voice.

Sophia raised her head, stunned by her friend's remark.

"You were expecting me to whip out a tit and nurse you?" Shareef continued before Sophia could say, 'Excuse me?' "You got a mama in New York that can do that for you, and I am personally getting tired of having to reaffirm for you every time you come here that nothing currently going on in this crazy messed up world today is your fault.

Greedy men searching for the power they had no business digging for is why the world has gone from zero to shit in overdrive. You were unfortunately caught in the middle of it, and considering that you could have been rotting in a six-foot grave for a crime you didn't commit, the world can kiss my ass! A lesser person would have let Oregon and the West Coast go up in flames after what you learned and endured, but you chose to take a nuke head-on despite it all and saved millions of lives. No one has the right to blame you for anything. The Judgment Day virus is not your fault, superhumans walking the Earth is not your fault, and what happened to Bishop's son is not your fault! You did not kill Miguel; the virus did."

Sophia's eyes poured glowing blue tears as she looked at her friend.

"I couldn't save him either."

Shareef leaned forward.

"And you weren't meant to, honey, but you gave them both something just as precious, a little more time to say goodbye."

"In medical school, they drill it into your head not to get attached," Sophia said while wiping her eyes, "never to make it personal, and accept the fact that sometimes people will die even under your watch. Knowing what dying feels like has changed everything; I can't 'not' feel."

Sister Shareef sighed as she placed her hand on top of her friend's hand to comfort her.

"A part of me wishes I died the day of my execution," Sophia admitted. "I accidentally remade the world, yet, I don't fit in it. I thought I could pre-occupy my time by helping people, but this isn't a stupid comic book! People's lives just don't miraculously get better because you swoop in and save the day!"

"Girl, don't you know comics ain't what they use to be?" Sister Shareef scoffed. "I just done heard on the news that they killed off Archie. Now you know it's some bull vine defecation when they decide to cut down little ole cute and indecisive Archie. Who's next? Snoopy?"

Her jest achieved the crack of a smile she was looking for.

"You're right; life is not like in the comic books," Shareef agreed. "And no one expects you to live as if you're in one. You, of all people, know that even before you gained these powers, you can't save everyone, no matter how hard you try. And maybe having them has temporarily blinded you to think that you should, but you're not all-powerful, Soph. Someone else still holds that title. I know that, and Bishop definitely knows that."

"How is she?" Sophia nervously asked.

"She's holding up," Shareef informed her. "She has to for Annabelle and Manuel. She calls me almost every day and drives up every month to come to see me. Shows me pictures of the latest custom she's working on."

Sophia managed a smile.

"I'm glad."

"She never stops talking about how her big sister gave her a garage with all the fixings," Shareef said sternly. "She keeps asking me the last time I heard from you and how much she misses you."

"Well, someone's dreams should come true; I'll make time to go visit her."

"Yeah, you will," Shareef ordered her.

Shareef spied the warden on top of one of the watchtowers. He nervously pointed to his watch, letting her know the time was up. She nodded in agreement before rising to her feet.

"Well, as much as I adore our weekly visits and chats, time for me to mosey on in."

Sophia groaned as she got up; once again, she looked up at Sister Shareef, who now towered over her a powerful four inches. Much of the signs of age and prison hardening no longer ravaged her face; the only thing revealing her actual age was her longer silver dreads.

"You know this is bull," Sophia informed her.

"I have to set a good example for the girls," Shareef answered with a shrug.

"But you don't have to stay here," Sophia said. "It's not like anyone can stop you if you decide to leave, especially considering what you did was justified."

"No, it wasn't," Shareef sternly returned.

~ ~

She remembered when her name was Agnes Shareef Wilcox-Miller, Mr. and Mrs. Wilcox's daughter, the youngest of three children, one eldest brother, and an older sister by a year. Her father worked on oil rigs, while her mother sold beauty products from door to door. Agnes grew up in as regular a household as one could have in Austin, Texas. She finished high school and was the second in her family to graduate from Community College. She met her husband, Derek Miller, on the way to work one day; three years later, she became a happily married woman, and four-and-a-half years after that, a mother of two, a son and a daughter.

Derek worked as a car sales representative; she worked as a social worker, keeping their roots in Austin.

She had a happy and everyday life, although her job was sometimes uneasy. It was a constant battle to help those unfortunate by birth and economic class or who took a wrong path by the fault of addiction or a criminal lifestyle. Sometimes, it entailed long hours at work, and during those days, she would ask her favorite fourteen-year-old niece, Rebecca, the eldest daughter of her older sister, to babysit her two children until she or Derek got home. Things in her simple life appeared okay until she received an alarming call from her older sister about her niece and an incident at school. A high school teacher had caught young Rebecca in a sexual act with two other boys from her class in the boy's bathroom. Rebecca led them into the bathroom from the boys' account to show them something cool.

Obviously, her parents had a conniption upon hearing the news. Agnes, however, had a gut feeling something else was wrong. She knew Rebecca from the womb to the crib to now. She was a shy young lady who covered her eyes when her parents kissed; her experience at work with sexual abuse cases regarding teens and minors told her she had to speak to her niece and understand what had happened.

Agnes prayed her naïve niece learned it from one of her female school friends, who was taught it from someone else; she prayed for her parents and her sake. Upon entering her older sister and brother-in-law's home, her first job became settling down the irate couple. Her older sister, Marcia, was in a rant, contemplating the only humane thing to do for her daughter due to the humiliating situation.

Marcia shook her head, pacing back and forth in her living room.

"I gotta kill her! I got to! It's the only way! I got to kill my baby!"

"Marcia, calm down… you ain't killing anyone," Agnes firmly returned, attempting to talk her older sister down.

"You don't understand, Agnes! You don't understand! Even if we transfer her to another school, this will follow her," Marcia continued, "and with two of them! Those nasty little bastards flanking my little girl in the boys' stall of all places with their… Oh god, I' ma throw up!"

Rebecca's father, Martin, tried to step in.

"Hey… look."

"Don't you say nothing!" His wife lashed out at him, "This is all your fault!"

"Whoa! Whoa! Hold your horses!" Martin angrily went on the defensive, "how's this all my fault?"

"I told you I didn't want those nasty videos up in this house! But nooooo! 'It's to liven the mood, baby' This is for being a lazy sum bitch and not finding other ways to turn your wife on!" Marcia spat hot venom at him.

"All that shit is under lock and key behind a combination safe in our bedroom, which she doesn't know, and I always put it away after we finish getting busy!" Martin bit back. "So don't blame me for this! How we know she didn't find ole Bugs Bunny up in your dresser draw?!"

Marcia looked at her husband as if he was crazy.

"What?"

Agnes palmed her face, wishing not to know about her sister and brother-in-law's love life right before them.

"Don't think I don't know why we keep replacing batteries in the remote every two weeks! I'm surprised you can feel "anything" down there!"

Agnes' eyes widened, wishing she were deaf at that point.

Marcia decided to hit low.

"Like I can't feel your little…"

"All right! Yawl needs to cool off and leave this house." Agnes ordered, stepping in. "Take the little ones out for about an hour, go for a drive, and leave me with Rebecca."

"Agnes…" Marcia dropped her older sister's tone.

"Marcia… you're my older sister, and I love and respect you, but for once, I am begging you. Take your husband and the kids… leave the house and let me talk to my niece. You both are all worked up, and you're not thinking straight right now. Go out… clear your head, come back, and talk to your little girl after I've spoken to her."

An awkward silence filled the room between mother, aunt, and father.

"Please. For me," Agnes pleaded.

"Well, why can't we just wait outside on the porch?" Martin asked, shrugging his shoulders.

"Because yall are gonna start up again, and the neighbors will be up in your business. You want that?" Agnes said, pushing back, "Just give me one hour… please. You called me here to help. Let me help."

Reluctantly, both Marcia and Martin caved into Agnes. They took their younger son and newborn daughter to get take-out. Agnes released a deep sigh of relief as she prepared herself to deal with another prickly situation. She could hear her niece's uncontrolled sobbing as she walked down the hallway to her room. She entered the young girl's room to find Rebecca curled up in the corner of her canopy bed with her arms wrapped around her legs and her face between them, weeping hysterically, remorseful and frightened about what she had done.

Agnes approached her as one would a timid little fawn.

"Rebecca?" she gently called her name.

"I'm sorry! I'm sorry! I'm sorry! I'm sorry!" Rebecca cried repeatedly.

Agnes hugged Rebecca tightly, kissing her on her forehead while stroking her back like her mother did when she was little.

"It's okay, honey," Agnes soothingly whispered, "everything is okay."

"Mommy and daddy hate me," Rebecca bitterly wept.

"Nooo… honey… no… they could never hate you," Agnes reassured her. "They love you dearly; they're just shocked and upset because they know what happened in school is not like you. They know like I know that you are a good… girl… and you always will be."

Agnes kissed Rebecca on the forehead again to calm the little girl down. She took a deep breath before coaxing Rebecca to tell her what had happened at school.

"Now I know, you didn't learn what you did at school by yourself, I know that… so I need you to tell me… who taught you. Was it a school friend?"

Rebecca meekly tried to coil away from her aunt.

"I can't…" her voice cracked.

Agnes held her hand, caressing it to calm her again.

"Honey, if it was a school friend, we need to talk to her and find out who taught her," Agnes gently pressed, "and if it's an adult who taught you, that person is not a nice person, and they cannot hurt you. I won't let them. Your mother and father definitely will not let them, but we have to know who they are to stop them from doing this to you and other girls. All you have to do is give me a name, baby… please tell me… who taught you this."

Her words only made Rebecca cry again even harder while fighting to pull away.

"I can't, auntie… I can't," she whimpered, "he said that you wouldn't understand and that you'd hate me… I can't!"

Upon hearing her niece's words, a cold, sick feeling came over Agnes.

"Honey… why would I… hate you?" Agnes stammered. "Who said I would hate you?"

The little girl did not have to say anything else as Agnes looked into her eyes; her shaking hand cupped her mouth as she felt like vomiting. Her whole body began to shake while tears no longer controlled ran from her eyes as she pulled her little niece closer to her to look into her eyes. She knew the truth; she just had to hear it with her own ears.

"When baby? When? Please. Tell me. When?" Agnes coaxed with a quivered voice.

The rest of her body trembled with a burning sensation running through her.

"Last year… when I started coming over to help watch Mike and Stephanie…" Rebecca timidly said. "One night, you were working late… he came home and saw I was sad because the girls were teasing me at school for having a small chest and the boys liking them more."

She wanted to stop, but Agnes's face begged her to continue.

"He said he could teach me a trick so that the boys would like me even if I didn't have a big chest," Rebecca began to bawl. "He showed me a cartoon with a schoolgirl doing it."

"Oh god… baby no… no," Agnes began to cry.

Her words, though unintentional, shattered her body and spirit beyond repair in one shot.

"He said I could practice with him… and that it wasn't sex because he wasn't sticking it between my legs," Rebecca squealed. "He said you and mommy used to do it, but you wouldn't understand because you were adults now… I thought I was ready."

"Oh, God! No! No! No!"

Agnes screamed, scaring Rebecca against the wall beside her bed.

Doubled over, Agnes could not stop screaming as she clutched her belly while stomping her feet, trying to break the floor beneath her. Her gut felt like someone ripped it open with a serrated knife right before her.

"Auntie! I'm sorry! I'm so sorry!" Rebecca cried, expecting her aunt to pummel her.

Agnes grabbed her as gently as possible, pulling her back, looking at her sternly with tear-drenched eyes.

"Don't ever… say you're sorry to me… you hear me?" Agnes gingerly commanded. "You did **nothing wrong**… **do you hear me**? You are… **a good girl** … and you will always be a good girl… in my eyes. **Don't ever** apologize to me again… is that clear?"

Rebecca nodded as she continued to cry. Agnes hugged her as tight as possible, emitting a gut-wrenching wail. Agnes released her, pulled herself together, grabbed her book bag, opened it, and pulled out a notebook and pen. Quickly, she jotted something down so her niece could not see, ripped the page out, folded it, and handed it to her.

"When your mother gets home, give this to her. Do not open it… just hand it to her and no matter what happens. I love you. Do you hear me? Stay here, and do not leave this room until your parents come home. Do you hear me?" Agnes sternly ordered.

Rebecca meekly shook her head in understanding while taking the note from her aunt.

Agnes got up in a daze, walking out of her niece's room into the living room. She looked at her mother's old grandfather clock, which read 4:45 PM. Derek got off at five; he picked the kids up at 2:30 PM, took them back to work with him, and would be coming home soon. Her sister begged her not to tell him what happened because of the embarrassment. She had to get home before he did, but first, she ran upstairs to her sister's bedroom.

Agnes did not know if it was God or the Devil himself that allowed her to drive home over the speed limit without being pulled over, but she got there before him and waited, sitting on the front porch steps of their house as he drove up with their children. The whole time, she just sat there looking at the ground. Derek stepped out of the car, concerned to see his wife in what appeared to be a state.

"Babe? Baby? You all right?" he nervously asked.

Agnes did not even have to look at him. His voice set her off as she raised a chrome Colt 1911 with a pearl grip handle and fired a shot, hitting him in the left shoulder. She remembered at one of her sister's many drunken bridge games, she showed it to her as one of Martin's brand new pieces he bought for his collection. He always kept a firearm out as his gun of the month while the others stayed under lock and key.

Agnes remembered Marcia showing her how to load and fire it. She prayed it was still out when she went into their bedroom, looking for it. It was a lucky shot; she had never fired a gun before, and the recoil was tremendous even from a seated position, but she still managed to hit him. Agnes did not hear the screams from the neighbors running for safety nor her husband's cry as the shot spun him around. All she could hear were the screams of her children in the car.

"Mommy! Daddy!" Little Michael bawled as Stephanie sobbed uncontrollably in the back passenger booster seat.

"Stay in the car and do not come out for anything!" Agnes screamed orders to her children as Michael cracked the door open to get out.

Agnes turned to Derek, who was attempting to get away with blood gushing from his left shoulder. This time, she took aim with two hands and fired three more rounds from the Colt. Two missed while one managed to hit him in his lower back; the children screamed and wailed as they watched their father go down, not understanding what was happening.

"Stay in the car!!" Agnes shrieked one final time to them.

She trudged over to Derek, lying in the dirty street covered in blood, sobbing as he now crawled to get away.

"Oh god… god… help me!" he cried as his wife stood over him with the gun.

"Turn over," Agnes ordered him.

Derek continued to crawl with snot and spit running from his mouth and nose. It mixed with the blood on the street as he searched for a sanctuary he would never find.

"I said, **turn over**!" Agnes screeched.

Reluctantly, Derek turned over to look at his heartbroken, enraged wife, pointing the Colt with three more rounds in it.

"Did you touch Stephanie?! Did you touch her?!" Agnes shrilled as her hand shook, aiming the barrel at his skull.

"No!" Derek wailed, begging for his life. "I swear to god, no! Agnes! Please! Please!"

"My niece?!"

Agnes's voice was almost half-gone, eyes bright red from the tears that would not stop falling.

"I gave you everything! My love! My body! I gave you children! I gave you everything! She's a child! My sister's baby! She trusted you! She trusted me! What didn't I do that you had to take her innocence?! What did I do?! Tell me, Derek! Tell me!"

With tears in his eyes and his body getting cold from the loss of blood, Derek Miller gave his wife of seven years an answer that would not only kill her but also change their lives forever.

"You… got old," he quivered.

It was not so much what he said but the look in his eyes when he said it. The look was as bright as day; he had done this before, well enough to never be caught.

Agnes had heard about these things and taught the signs to notice if one was in a house harming a child. She had the misfortune of running into two of them during her career, in which she had to notify the proper authorities. Right in front of her, one of those things was actually her husband. She allowed this thing to make her fall in love, get on top of her, slide inside of her, share her most intimate details, marry her, and take ten years of her life. Create a family with her while being a part of her extended family, only to destroy it. How could she miss this? How did she allow this thing to get past her?

Agnes did not know if she was laughing when she pulled the trigger; she remembers pulling it repeatedly, even when there was nothing in the clip. Old Mrs. Harper from across the street dared to hobble over, taking the gun out of her hand before the police finally arrived.

In the note that Agnes left with Rebecca for Marcia, Agnes wrote, "This is not Rebecca's fault. She is a good girl. I failed you. I am sorry for everything."

In her eyes, she had brought the monster into their family, she who had dealt with the redeemable and the unredeemable daily, she who trained to know the signs could not see the beast that slept in her very bed. She had to put him down; she had to make it right. The Austin, Texas, legal system did not see it that way. She might have gotten away with an insanity plea had she just shot him once while sitting on the porch, but the district attorney painted a picture of a cold and calculated execution.

He pressed that no act of vigilantism could go unpunished, no matter the justification. It also did not help Agnes's case that most of the jurors were male. The emotional testimony of her niece and family, coworkers, neighbors, and church parishioners speaking on her behalf about her character did not sway them a bit. All they saw was a woman taking the law into her own hands, killing her husband in cold blood, something best not to be encouraged. Despite the defense's best efforts, the jury found Agnes guilty of murder and sentenced her to forty years to life in prison with parole eligibility after twenty years for each extra bullet she fired into her husband.

When the judge asked her if she had anything to say, Agnes replied, "I only regret not taking that extra clip."

After four years in prison, Shareef converted to Islam after being recruited by Sister Ailia Assad, the original leader of the Sisters of Islam. Sister Ailia turned the mantle over to Shareef, making her leader after finally making parole for good behavior for a thirty-year prison term on a narcotics conviction. Her older sister, Marcia, willingly took in her two children, raising them as her own along with her husband, Martin. Michael, her oldest son, refused to forgive her for killing his father, especially in front of him. When he came of age, he stopped seeing her altogether and distanced himself from the rest of the family; he also refused to believe that his father had molested Rebecca.

Stephanie continued to visit her whenever possible; it became harder since she began attending Spelman College in Atlanta, Georgia.

As for Rebecca, she eventually overcame the ordeal. She graduated top of her class studying law, becoming one of the youngest district attorneys for Austin, Texas, and an activist fighting for better laws to protect women and children. Happily married, she had two children of her own. Every month, she took a day off to travel to Gatesville to visit her aunt.

~~~~~~~~~~~~~~~~~~~~~~~~~~~~~~~~~~

"I don't regret what I did, but it was not justified, and I am guilty. And the ones who paid the highest price for my actions were my own children. I murdered their father in front of them and left them without a mother. Don't ever tell me what I did was justified, ever."

Another uneasy silence came over the two as Sophia apologetically lowered her head in regret.

"I've been a real buzz kill this last visit," Sophia sheepishly admitted.

"Hell, yeah," Shareef snapped back, "but it's still great to see you."

Shareef pulled her in for a tight hug and a kiss on the forehead.

"You are not alone," Sister Shareef whispered, "you are never alone. How much worse would those girls be if you did not save them? And, yes, maybe people out there are doing bad things with their abilities, but what about those doing good?"

Sophia lowered her head again.
~~~~~~~~~~~~~~~~~~~~~~~~~~~~~~~~~~

"It just doesn't feel like the scale is balanced in our favor. And I didn't sign up for the never-ending battle between good and evil."

Sister Shareef placed her hands on her hips.

"Then, you should ask yourself why you became a surgeon in the first place, Dr. Dennison."

"To help people…" Sophia muttered.

Sister Shareef moved some strands of dreads from Sophia's face.

"You may think your yoke is a heavy one. But you were given the strength to carry it. And you got to believe there was a reason you did not die on that table that day. No matter how bad things get, you got to believe you are here to make a difference. No amount of pep talk from me is going to open your eyes to that. You have to see and believe it for yourself."

She appreciated the pep talk even though it did very little to help how she felt.

"Our next visit will be more pleasant," Sophia promised.

"I hope so," Sister Shareef huffed, "now go on. Get."

"You might want to stand…" Sophia began to warn.

Sister Shareef stopped her with the "You forget who you're talking to" look.

"Right," Sophia smiled. "Next week, then."

She exploded into the air with a mighty leap, kicking up dirt and small rocks leaving another sizable crater underneath her. After clearing a good thirty feet, Sophia ignited the nearly invisible propulsion at the soles of her feet, rocketing off into the skies.

CHAPTER 7

The following day, Rogers was up early at five in the morning. Not a morning person, Erica slept in until 9 a.m., going for 10 until Rogers repeatedly pounded on her door until she got up. He could hear the slew of profanity Erica muttered under her breath behind her room's closed steel sliding door; some of it was in Spanish. It continued until the door slid open, and she shot him a dirty look.

"Good Morning," Rogers smirked.

Erica rolled her eyes, walking past him, heading to the mess hall to get some much-needed breakfast and distance from the Sergeant.

Lady Tech found one, but not the other, as Rogers sat across from her sipping his extra black Columbia brewed coffee as she dined on a helping of pancakes, eggs, with turkey bacon, and a side of orange juice.

"I hope you enjoyed your long beauty rest," Rogers said between sips, "because that's the last one you will be taking as of today."

"Excuse you?" Erica asked, leaning back while munching on a piece of bacon.

Rogers took another sip before answering.

"The second the new recruits land, everyone will get up by five and down by nine for the next six months, no exceptions."

"But I'm a growing child," Erica shot back. "I need my beauty sleep."

"That's why I'm allowing you to get up at seven," Rogers said. "You want to be a part of my outfit; those are the rules."

"Miss, Sergeant Rogers, the new recruits, will be landing in ten minutes," Maxine announced.

"Thank you, Maxine," Erica said before giving Rogers a sardonic smile. "Guess we better get ready to meet the new fresh meat."

Rogers sat there, deflecting her smile with a dull look as he calmly sipped on his coffee.

~~~~~~~~~~~~~~~~~~~~~~~~~~~~~~~

Six minutes later, the two silently traveled to the surface, this time with Maxine's cybernetic form next to them. Erica glanced at the old soldier's stone demeanor and saw the wheels turning. Although she would never attempt it, she wanted to know his thoughts.

For her own personal moral reason and his warning about staying out of his head, she decided to remain in the dark. As the doors to the hanger opened once more, they stepped out into the light as a similar CH-46 Sea Knight descended from the sky, landing on one of the designated helicopter pads. As it touched down, the door opened, allowing the new recruits to step out individually. As they lined up next to one another, taking casual stances, Erica's expression revealed she was not too impressed with what she saw, even though she and Dr. Alexander handpicked them.

"Oh, joy," Lady Tech's sarcastic smile returned as she whispered, "our new team members are Will Smith pre-Fresh Prince, Pauly D, and JWoww."

"I seem to remember you being a part of the selection process," Rogers reminded her.

"Based on abilities, physical health, mental state, and stable personalities meaning the ability to work and play well with others. Not attitudes."

"Attitudes are easily broken," Rogers answered while walking toward the new recruits. "That's why I'm here."

Erica muttered a curse under her breath as she picked up the pace to catch up with him while Maxine kept in step with her. They both stopped a couple of feet from the new recruits as Rogers wasted no time facing the lightning-charged EVO, Blitz, who had a four-inch height advantage on him. He showed zero signs of intimidation with a smirk as he locked eyes with the battled-hardened Sergeant.
~~~~~~~~~~~~~~~~~~~~~~~~~~~~~~~

"Name," Rogers asked flatly.

"Blitz," he smirked, "I wanted to go with Black Lightning, but it was already taken."

Snickering came from the twins' direction, which Rogers pretended to ignore. He mentally marked it down as ammunition to make their lives a living hell later. He leaned in closer, asking him again.

"Guess I wasn't speaking English," Rogers's voice boomed full of bass, "real name… now."

"Oliver Brandon." Blitz coughed out as he quickly fell into line.

Rogers looked him up and down.

"Oliver Brandon, the next time I ask you something, I expect a straight answer. The next time you give me anything other than that, I will pull your jawbone out by the root, is that clear?"

Brandon straightened up more.

"Yes, sir."

"Sir, yes, sir, when you address me!" Rogers's voice sounded like thunder.

"Sir, yes, sir!" Brandon yelled back, snapping to attention.

He attempted to make his body as straight as a steel pipe.

Rogers nodded with satisfaction, sensing he had broken the will of the lightning wielder; he now towered over Ms. Esposito. Her smirk and gum-chewing vanished the first time Roger's voice boomed. She shuddered as she looked into the eyes of Abe, burning a hole into her very soul.

"Name," Rogers requested again with the same flat tone he addressed Brandon.

"Ro… Rosann… Esposito…" she stuttered.

"Why are you stuttering?" Rogers pressed her.

“Sir?” Rosann asked, clamming up.

“At least you know to call me that.” Rogers began the verbal pounding. “You and dumbass over here are snickering like a bunch of pubescent school girls when your mouths should have been zipped shut with eyes forward.”

“Hey, how about easing up, ‘Cap,’” her brother Adrian returned fire on his sister’s behalf.

Abe noted her brother’s comment, marking it down as strike two. He leaned closer to Rosann as if he was about to kiss her.

“That’s gum in your mouth, right?” Rogers questioned her.

“Sir… yes sir,” Rosann stuttered.

“Swallow it.”

“Screw dat Rosey… hey, yo pops,” Adrian snapped, scowling, “raise up out of my sister’s face! We ain’t sign up for dis shit!”

Rogers ignored Mr. Esposito, mentally marking his final offense as strike three. He waited for Rosann as she slowly swallowed the gum she had been chewing. The dark-haired, hazel-eyed Staten Island resident had stood up to some tough customers in the past, including her own brother and father, but staring back at the battle scars that ravaged the side of his face down to his neck told her this was not the type of man she wanted to mouth off to. She cursed her twin in her skull, praying for him to shut up. His back-talking did nothing but make the situation worse for her.

“Why are you here?” Rogers bluntly asked.

“Sir, to become a hero, sir,” Rosann stammered.

Abe tilted his head.

“You think this is one of them reality shows?”

“Sir… no sir,” Rosann answered, fighting the trembling of her body.

Rogers looked around.

"You see any cameras or film crew around here?"

"Sir, no, sir."

"No!" Rogers barked in her face, "And last I checked, I didn't come out here wearing my underwear outside my pants sporting a cape, and asking you for the secret friggin handshake! I am a United States Marine, trained to kill in my country's service, which means I train killers! Are you a killer Rosann Esposito?!"

"Sir, no sir…" Rosann stuttered, "but I can…"

"You had me at 'No sir!'" Rogers roared, rattling her spine. "It's obvious by your answers that you're in the wrong place! You're not a killer; you want to be a superhero! So why don't you take your French manicure, gum-chewing, disrespectful little ass back to that bird over there, go home, and go find one of them, leagues?! Go avenge something!"

Rosann fought through her fear of the Sergeant to answer.

"Sir, I wanna be here…"

"Why?!"

Her eyes became glassy as she got out her words.

"I got these powers for a reason. To help people, and I want to be taken seriously… not another joke from Staten Island."

"My asshole bleeds for you, girlie," Rogers sneered, "it really does."

Rosann lowered her head, wiping her eyes as Rogers looked up to the heavens, contemplating her fate.

"Seeing as how you refuse to leave, guess I'll take you in. See if there is a killer inside of you," Rogers sighed, easing up for a split second.

"But the second I hear a whimper, an 'I can't do it,'" he growled, "I will personally drag you by the roots back to Staten Island and dump you where that chopper picked you up from… are we crystal clear?!"

"Sir, yes, sir!" Rosann answered with conviction.

Rogers leaned in, making sure she smelled the coffee on his breath.

"You're on my shitlist, little girl. Don't expect to get clean anytime soon."

Rogers turned to don a 'pleasant' smile as he took one step and turned again to face Rosann's twin brother Adrian. He was an inch taller than Abe, wearing a blue and white Nike jumpsuit with a white wifebeater underneath two smaller sizes that his tan, muscular physique hid. With his spiked, gelled black hair, he was missing a Z-IROC or a tuner vehicle to finish his look. Mr. Esposito took the first offensive, leaning forward. Grasping the crucifix around his neck, he transformed into the metal element of Platinum, locking eyes with Rogers. Rosann lowered her head, wishing she was not a twin at that moment.

"Oh shit," Rosann whispered, "here we go…"

"Adrian Esposito, but you can call me 'Hard-On' soldier boy." He announced while cracking a smile. "Am I close enough for you to try to kiss me?"

A huge grin formed on Roger's face.

"Thank you."

It was the first one Erica had seen on the old man's face since meeting him. Without reading his mind, she could sense it was an omen of something terrible coming in a few seconds.

Adrian knitted his eyebrows, wondering about the Sergeant's game.

"Thank me for…?"

Rogers disrupted Adrian's question with the sound of a human skull smashing into his Platinum metal nose. Esposito's neck snapped back as he grabbed his nose, shocked that he was registering pain in his metallic form. It surprised him so much that he did not see the haymaker punch Rogers caved his chest in with, lifting him off his feet and sending him forty feet away.

"Adrian!" Rosann screamed.

Blitz turned, watching his new teammate go sailing.

"Oh shit."

Rosann watched in horror as her brother landed back first into the ground, creating a crash drag; he used the momentum to backward roll to his feet while digging his fingers into the dirt to brake. He shook off the cobwebs as newfound rage filled his eyes. As Adrian prepared to take on an advancing Rogers, Rosann went to reach for a tiger tooth necklace around her neck.

"I wouldn't do that," Erica projected her voice into Rosann's mind, stopping her.

Rosann whipped around, baring her teeth, turning to the culprit inside her skull.

"Get out of my head, you little…"

"Rogers is a professional, and your brother needs some schooling," Lady Tech returned, echoing again in her skull. *"So, stay out of it."*

"That's my brother, you, little bitch!" Rosann fired back.

"Tell me something I don't know," Erica scoffed. *"Transform or move from that spot, and I'll make you think that you're going blind with an itchy asshole that needs a good scratching."*

A frustrated Rosann reluctantly watched as her enraged brother proceeded to pick up speed, charging at Abe.

"You cock sucker!" Adrian howled. "You wanna go? You wanna piece of me? Let's go!"

Rogers did not bother to answer him as he continued to advance in his direction. Esposito went to shoot on Rogers for a takedown, but a more experienced soldier stuffed his shoot attempt with his powerful legs digging deep into the dirt. With no hesitation, he used one hand to keep him bent while raining brutal forearm blows down on his back.

"You old bastard," Adrian growled, "can't… hurt me…"

Hard-On roared as he powered out of Abe's grip and swung for the hills with a powerful right. A skilled Rogers stepped in, catching his arm. He hit a well-executed judo flip, slamming him into the dirt creating a small crater.

"My arm now…" Abe growled back.

Rogers sunk in a powerful armbar, forcing Adrian to his feet; Esposito was baffled that he registered pain in his metallic form. He proceeded to whip Adrian around into a giant swing, taking him off his feet before leaping a good thirty feet into the air. While in midair, Rogers delivered another judo throw, hurling Hard-On back to the Earth, creating a human-size crater with his body; before Adrian could recover, Rogers returned to Earth, delivering a boot to his chest, causing a mini dirt explosion, adding insult to injury. Rogers removed his boot from his chest and placed it on his throat, forcing him to gasp for air as he squirmed, trying to get free from underneath Abe's boot.

"Now that we've established that I'm not only stronger than you but can kick your miserable ass, hide three ways to Sunday and then some. Why are you here?!"

"Thought… it was cool," Adrian gasped, "to be a part of a real… superhero… team… sir…"

Rogers drove his boot even deeper into his throat.

"Same damn answer as your sister. But at least you're honest, and to answer your question why you lost, it's because you're an ignorant dumbass. I know all about your power; just because you can transform into properties like metal or stone doesn't mean you're not human. Blood still courses through your veins and your nervous system lights up, so if I hit you hard enough, you can still feel pain. Now you got five seconds to tell me why I shouldn't send you home with a permanent limp?

"I… can… be… better," Adrian gurgled, "sir… give… me… a chance…"

Rogers savagely twisted his boot to silence him.

"Chance? Before, you were a badass. Big dick wily swinging with your bra shirt, all "blinged" out looking to show me something, now you want a chance? Well, let me think about that."

Rogers looked to the heavens again, scratching his chin as he contemplated the male Esposito's fate.

"Okay, Limp, I suppose if I can throw your sister over there a bone, I can throw you one too. Aside from being a total waste of human excrement… you got guts."

Rogers scowled, driving his boot deeper into Adrian, forcing him further into the dirt.

"But you so much as look at me sideways, I'll pop you like a Pepsi can, you hearing me, boy?"

"Sir," Adrian gurgled, "yes… sir!"

Rogers finally released Esposito, allowing him to struggle to his feet; he powered down and stumbled back to the line, standing next to his sister with his head down. The Sergeant calmly strolled over and stood before the completely humbled new recruits.

"Now that I know who you really are," Abe's voice boomed, "allow me to introduce myself! My name is **Sergeant Abraham Rogers**, and you will all address me as **"Sir, yes sir,"** calling me anything else to my face will make you subject to cruel and **unusual punishment**!"

"Sir, yes, sir!" all three managed to sound off in unison.

Rogers began to pace.

"My job is to take you three pieces of turds out the crack of God's ass and turn you into a fighting force capable of defeating and killing the Devil himself! And I will have you know that I have never failed when a mission has been presented before me. The only way this will fail is if you fail me. Are you going to fail me?!"

"Sir, no, sir!"

"No, you won't, because I will **physically kill you** if you do. Each of you had a chance to opt-out," Rogers continued to bark. "You didn't take it, so now you belong to me… heart, body, mind, and soul. **Rule number one,** obey me as if your life depended on it… and it will because to not obey me means I get to **physically kill you**… is that understood?!"

"Sir, yes, sir!"

"Rule number two, no one is allowed to use their powers and abilities unless ordered to do so," Rogers howled, "you were shit before you had powers, and you're still shit with them! My job is to pound you worthless pieces of shit into fertilizer so that you can grow into the most feared and respected fighting force this country has ever seen!

To do that, you all must become human beings before you can become superhuman beings, and you're not human beings! In my eyes, you're nothing but a bunch of freaks of nature taking up God-given Earth, air, and space… If you want my opinion to change… then it's your job to prove me wrong… failure to follow rule number two means I get to **physically kill you**… is that understood?"

"Sir, yes, sir!"

"Now, allow me to introduce you to your other teammate."

All three turned their attention to Erica, stepping up with a bright smile on her face to stand next to Rogers.

"This here is Lady Tech; she is responsible for designing and building this facility and all of the tech and gear needed to both train and prepare you for future missions should you survive me," Rogers roared, "which means she's got more brainpower in one strand of her hair than all of you combined! I am God… she is Jesus Christ… which means despite being half your age, you are to give her the respect of someone twice your age because she knows damn well what she is talking about! Failure to do so means I get to **physically kill you**. Is that understood?!"

"Sir, yes sir!" all three shouted in unison one final time.

"Now that you understand," Rogers said, nodding with approval, "get your shit, and get ready to descend into hell."

~~~~~~~~~~~~~~~~~~~~~~~~~~~~~~~~~~~~

Ten minutes later, the twins and Brandon all wore similar faces of disbelief as they looked around at the massive facility, vehicles, and independent automatons moving about the base. They all looked like they had descended into another world or centuries into the future.

"This is the Ranch, our base of operations and training ground," Rogers began his introduction, "here you will eat, piss, shit, and learn to be a proper soldier … on my level… and it's a very high-level people… I'm talking looking God in the eye type of level… Lady Tech."

"Sleeping quarters are this way," Erica announced, pointing out, "each of you has been assigned your own quarters."

"Sweet," Adrian whispered.

"Mess hall is here, central command, which you will see soon, is down that hallway," Lady Tech continued, "and over here… is what I'd like to call the Hurt Locker."
~~~~~~~~~~~~~~~~~~~~~~~~~~~~~~~~~~~~

The twins looked at each other in bewilderment as Blitz swallowed, anxious to see what awaited him on the other side of the steel doors. As they entered, they found a massive, bare room.

"Looks like they forgot to put in the 'hurt,'" Adrian whispered.

"Shut up, Adrian," Rosann harshly whispered, "not trying to catch shit again…"

"This is a multi-scenario combat room, built for training in multiple combat situations," Lady Tech explained. "Here, we can upload holographic environments from jungle…"

Out of nowhere, a deep forest jungle area similar to Vietnam appeared around them with fantastic realism.

"To urban."

The environment switched to downtown Times Square with people walking around them.

"The environment and civilians are created by a holographic force field generated simulator. As you can see, it is realistic, sensitive, and made to interact with your actions creating combat scenarios that you can learn from."

"So, we're supposed to train off of some ghosts?" Adrian inquired with a raised hand.

"Adrian!" Rosann growled.

"What?" he shouted, "I can't ask a simple question?"

"No, you're expected to train off these," Erica answered.

The floor opened up in front of them, creating a gigantic square opening as a platform rose in the place where the ground was. Standing before them were six human beings of various sizes, shapes, and ethnicities wearing similar outfits to Lady Tech; they appeared asleep on their feet. The Japanese woman in the front was the first to awaken, revealing her green eyes. She raised her hand, which began to spark. It erupted from a spark into a giant flaming sphere, which she controlled, causing Rosann's eyes to widen.

"Whoa."

A stunned Adrian reacted with a head tilt.

"Holy…"

"They're called Replicators, cybernetic androids underneath a synthetic organic grown skin. They can imitate regular humans or, in this case, EVOs."

"EVOs?" Rosann raised a hand.

"You, you're brother, and Mr. Brandon," Lady Tech answered while motioning to the trio of new recruits, "it is the government classification for "superhumans" such as us. People infected by the EVO Virus, which you know as the Judgment Virus, after the Big Bang II incident. The sub-classification is Prometheans like me, Moleculars, or Elementals, like you two, extremely rare.

Apollo types like Mr. Brandon. Mercurians, which are the speedster class."

A small yet ripped male Latino Replicator exploded into a run, creating a sonic boom and forcing everyone but Abe to cover their ears as he moved and turned at blinding speeds through New York City's imaginary street before returning to his spot again.

"And Finally, Titans like Sergeant Rogers," Erica said while pointing to him, "by training with them, you will learn how to combat various types of EVOs on different power levels and in different environments. Here you will be able to hone your abilities and hopefully increase them and learn your limitations. Being superhuman does not mean you are invincible. Understanding that will teach you to rely on other tools aside from your abilities."

"How come there aren't any Replicators with our powers?" Adrian inquired while raising his hand again.

"Good question," Erica addressed him. "I have not been able to develop the technology to replicate your abilities. Yet. Molecular types' cells are highly evolved to the level of being almost sentient, which is how you are capable of transforming the way you both do."

A broad smile appeared on Adrian's face, then vanished when Rogers stepped over, getting nose to nose with him again, looking him up and down.

"Your bodies may be evolved. But not that pebble rattling around in that skull of yours."

Adrian swallowed while standing at the stiffest attention again.

"Sir, yes, sir."

"Anything else, Lady Tech?" Rogers asked while burning a hole through Esposito.

Erica smacked her forehead.

"Shoot, how rude of me. Let me introduce you to the rest of our family. Maxine, please call in Angie and Jennifer."

"Yes, Miss," Maxine acknowledged.

Less than a minute later, Jennifer and Angie walked through the door, gabbing with one another.

"Holy smoke, there's three of them," Oliver swallowed.

They walked over to their sister, standing nonchalantly next to her, ending their conversation as they turned to look at the new recruits before them. Jennifer appeared disinterested, while Angie wanted to zero in on a specific recruit. With a bright smile, she waved and gave a wink.

Adrian furrowed his brows, realizing she was addressing him.

"Maxine, you have already met," Erica began to properly introduce, "she is not only an android but the main AI computer for the entire base. Next to her are her sisters, Jennifer and Angie. They will also be your instructors and sparring partners from time to time. All three possess a well of knowledge that you can tap. So if you pass them in the hallway, and have a question, don't be afraid to ask."

During Erica's introduction, Adrian began to uncomfortably fidget as Angie continued to make flirty suggestive advances toward him from afar. They mainly were puckered kisses, lip licks, and eye winks.

He lowered his head, pretending not to see and to avoid getting on Rogers's bad side again. Jennifer, catching her sister's antics, gave her a sharp elbow. Angie retaliated with an elbow of her own.

Before it turned into a full-blown fight, Maxine, showing emotion for the first time, glared at her two younger sisters with bright pink glowing eyes, ending the disagreement. After finishing her tour and introductions, Lady Tech stepped back, allowing Rogers to step in again.

"Now that we've all been properly introduced, the schedule for the next six months is pretty damn simple. Asses up at 0500 for breakfast, training from 0600 to 1200 hours, and then lunchtime. Training begins again from 1300 to 1900 hours, after that is chow, and the rest of the night to do as you damn please, which should be getting rest to do it all over again the next day and then the next. Do I need to send you an email or text message about this schedule?"

"Sir, no, sir!" the trio yelled.

"Good, because the dumbass that shows up one second late will suffer, and the ones that show up early will suffer twice as worse."

Rogers's threat made Oliver and Rosann turn their eyes to Adrian standing in the middle. He answered the non-verbal accusation with a dirty look.

"Now, I would like you three to get the hell out of my sight till tomorrow," Rogers ordered with a grin. "Maxine will escort you each to your new quarters. By all means, explore and take in this grand facility, because come tomorrow, each of you will wish you took that chopper ride home. Dismissed!"

"This way, please," Maxine requested, gesturing with a smile.

The trio grabbed their duffel bags and followed Maxine out of the Hurt Locker with Angie sashaying behind in tow until her sister bounced her in disgust. The two sisters began arguing again, exiting the room and leaving just Rogers and Lady Tech.

"Is that going to be a problem?" Rogers inquired.

"Nah, they argue all the time," Lady Tech snorted.

"I was implying to the orange-haired one giving Esposito ammunition for a sexual lawsuit," Rogers elaborated.

Erica innocently shrugged.

"That's what happens when you build highly evolved artificial intelligence; it's just a harmless schoolgirl crush; you want me to reel her in?"

Rogers shook his head.

"Nope, let's continue to make Mr. Esposito uncomfortable for now. See which one makes him break… her or me."

"So, what do you really think of our new recruits?"

"My true opinion is not for young ears such as yours," Rogers answered, "six months will tell me if this is or isn't a waste of our time."

~~~~~~~~~~~~~~~~~~~~~~~~~~~~~~~~~

Three months later, Rogers made good on his promise of breaking the trio's will. The first day of training told him what he already knew. Despite their impressive physiques, both Adrian and Oliver's stamina and endurance were not only subpar to Marine standards; they barely met the criteria of children, while Rosann failed to meet both standards altogether. Although he already knew what he was working with, it did not stop him from tearing into them. And so began the task of breaking their bodies to rebuild them. From morning till noon, he drove them into the ground until they puked their entrails out, and then after lunch, he did it again for another five hours before handing what was left to Erica.

Some nights for almost a month, he'd walk past Rosann Esposito's room with her door partially open and hear her crying to herself, wishing to go home. Every day when they fell in, he waited for her to raise a hand, giving her resignation and request to go home. Every day, she never uttered a word. During the two hours in the Hurt Locker, Erica taught the trio EVO physiology 101 to better understand, control, and employ their abilities in combat situations.

Oliver had more practice and control over his abilities than the twins. He had already mastered flight and energy manipulation. Unlike his other counterparts who wielded electricity, Oliver could use his powers in various ways. By focusing, he could envelop his body in a greenish-white electrical plasma form without harm to himself. This apparently bolstered his abilities to an even greater level.

Oliver had two problems. The first one that Erica saw was that his emotions affected his abilities. Emotions such as anger and frustration brought him to uncontrollable levels, especially in battle. Left unchecked, he could accidentally unleash a multi-directional electrical nova blast devastating a two-hundred-mile radius.
~~~~~~~~~~~~~~~~~~~~~~~~~~~~~~~~~

Erica created a special suit and boots to regulate his powers until he could consciously control them independently. His second problem, which Rogers caught due to his first, was that he hesitated in combat situations. Even when civilians were not present in combat scenarios, Oliver hesitated because Rosann and Adrian were in the area. His main tactic was strafing and evading, searching for an opening while using concentrated attacks to bring his opponents down.

In Roger's eyes, prolonged fights did not need to be stretched out, leaving the team to further unknown dangers. He always pushed him into heavily populated scenarios, especially those where civilian lives were lost. Abe had to make him understand that if he hesitated, lives would be lost. And even if he did not hesitate, lives could still be lost. He had to live with it if he wanted to be an effective soldier.

For Adrian, it was learning the properties of different metals and other noncarbon-based materials and how they would affect both his strength and durability. Aside from his antics that frequently bore him to the wrath of Rogers, Esposito proved to be a quick study with great potential to be a skilled soldier. His problem was both overconfidence and an eagerness to prove himself a capable soldier. Because of this, he performed some dicey acts. Some were successful, while others badly backfired. In the first, he found no praise from Abe. The second found him dragged through the seven levels of hell and back after Rogers was done with him.

Rosann's training was similar, except hers consisted of getting used to her hybrid transformations, which were painful for her, and a Zoology course. Through practice, Erica revealed that transforming into mammal hybrids was easier on her body because their and human physiology were somewhat similar, and repeated transformations were vital to them becoming easier. She taught that it was akin to stretching a muscle. With training, it would become both painless and second nature to her. Human and EVO transformations proved to be much easier for Rosann as the only thing that changed was her skin, hair, eye color, and sometimes muscle physique. When duplicating other EVOs' powers and abilities, her feats were similar to her brother's when she copied his ability. However, when she copied Rogers's Titan abilities or Oliver's electrical powers, she was slightly weaker than her male counterparts.

Erica explained the reason for this was based on compatibility. Because she and her brother's DNA was virtually the same, it was easier for her cells to accept her brother's cells and all of their properties. However, when it came to others whose DNA was not similar to hers, some coding would be lost or discarded, allowing her to duplicate whoever she touched powers, but not at the same strength or intensity as the originator.

Erica also pointed out to both twins that the properties they absorbed did not disappear when they returned to human form but reverted to dormancy. Once they absorbed a property, it remained within their cells; touching the element again only triggered and activated their abilities. In time, with training and concentration, they could morph without a trigger. Rogers stood before the observation training window with Lady Tech, watching the twins and Oliver participate in a fierce simulation battle with three Replicators.

The purpose of the training session, which he explained before it took place, was for the team to learn to deal with fighting in single combat situations while figuring out how to get back to their teammates in order to fight as a unit. They were placed in an urban city scenario several blocks from one another. One stipulation enforced on Rosann was that she could not borrow her brother's or Oliver's powers during the battle. She had to rely on her own abilities to help her team win. In a female humanoid cheetah form, Rosann tried her best to match speed with a Mercurian Replicator, while her brother Adrian in Titanium form took on a Titan Replicator. Blitz battled against a Replicator who could unleash intense heat and flame.

"They're not doing too bad. Oliver is showing great control over his power." Lady Tech said while observing. "The twins' combat prowess is getting better. Adrian's using more of what you taught him and less brute strength."

"Yeah," Rogers sighed. "Now, let's throw in the wildcard."

The wildcard was a fourth Replicator with the power to manipulate water. Powering up, it pulled air together, focusing and channeling a massive amount of H20. Its first act was to team up with the fire Replicator. They purposely crossed streams of fire and water to create a steam smoke screen.

"Guys!" Oliver yelled. "Could really use some help here!"

Seeing Blitz being double-teamed even through the thick, steamy mist, Adrian sidestepped the Titan Replicator, slamming its gut with a knee and then booting it to the side of its skull, knocking it down.

Turning on his heel, he rushed to Oliver's side only to run into an ambush from the flame-wielding Replicator, blasting him with a total dose of plasma heat. His titanium physiology saved him from fourth-degree burns, but he choked and gasped within the airless environment. With a fist cocked and charged with electrical power, Oliver dived down to his teammate's aid clobbering the Replicator with enough force to send it crashing into a concrete building.

There was no breathing room as the water-wielding Replicator unleashed a hurricane-force stream on a recovering Adrian and an electrically charged Oliver. The blast shorted out Blitz's powers and sent him flying along with Adrian. He crashed through the window of a Walmart while Oliver smacked up violently against a parked Honda Civic.

A feral Rosann barely took down her Replicator speedster. She landed a lucky open-handed slash to its face. The Replicator's synthetic body and reaction were incredibly realistic as it hit the pavement in writhing pain, with simulated blood pouring from the four gashes made by her claws across its face. It caught her off guard a bit. Even though it was not a real person, the scene was too realistic for her. Her hands trembled at the sight of the blood on them.

"She's freezing up again," Rogers exhaled.

Rosann's feline senses detected an incoming attack, forcing her to leap back as the recovered Titan Replicator came down with both fists, looking to hammer her head off. It ended up cratering the concrete instead. Twenty feet up, it left Rosann open to a midair attack from the water wielder, blasting her with the same powerful stream it hit Oliver and Adrian. She slammed violently against the simulated concrete wall of a building, but her feline reflexes allowed her to get her feet underneath her.

Rosann recovered quickly enough to see the water wielder using water as jet propulsion hovering over her, the Titan flanking her left, while the recovered speedster flanked her right side. She roared, preparing to fight when the simulation came to an end. The Replicators went into standby mode as the force field generated holographic buildings, and cars disappeared, leaving an empty room again. A soaking-wet Rosann reverted to human form as her drenched brother got back to his feet and transformed. He walked over, grabbed Oliver's hand, and helped him up to his feet.

"Where should I begin," Rogers's voice boomed over the audio system, "Esposito… and I mean the male Esposito… you once again failed to neutralize your target with a neural damper. Knocking him down does not mean that he's out, especially when he possesses regenerative healing. So your sister can thank you for getting her triple-teamed and possibly killed."

Adrian bowed his head and nodded, acknowledging his screw-up.

"Mr. Brandon, you've been told a million times your electrical abilities only stun fire-wielding EVOs," Rogers admonished him.

"Sir! I was attempting to do that, sir!" Oliver answered.

"You also know the heat does not have any effect on you," Rogers continued, "so why didn't you bum rush that Replicator and beat the hell out of him instead of getting into a damn dog fight with him?"

"Sir… I," Blitz stammered.

"You froze again, Brandon, relying once again more on your powers and not your physical abilities and training," Rogers sternly said, pointing out his flaw. "Had you done so, you could have bagged and tagged him and then dealt with Mr. Super Soaker. FYI, water is a perfect conductor of electricity, which means a concentrated blast from you would have dropped him and not the other way around. You would have known that had you not gotten rattled by being double-teamed."

"Sir, yes, sir," Brandon acknowledged.

Abe sucked in some air and then exhaled before addressing Rosann.

"Female Esposito, mind telling me why you froze again after turning that speedster into a scratch post?"

Rosann lowered her head.

"Sir, no sir," "I… don't."

"Yeah, you do," Rogers shot back. "You froze at the sight of fake blood on your hands. You froze because the reactions of that dummy standing before you were all too real for you. Am I right or wrong?"

"Sir..." Rosann said, hesitantly nodding, "you are… correct,… sir."

"Now answer this rhetorical question," Rogers continued, "if this was a real-life situation, and the other way around, do you think your opponent would hesitate or finish the job?"

"Sir, finish the job, sir," Rosann answered.

"Esposito, the only reason you're still standing there with your brother and Brandon," Rogers said with raw iron sternness, "is because I lost a fifty-dollar bet with Champion here that you wouldn't last a week. You have proven me wrong about whether you have the physical and mental aptitude to be here… so far. Psychological-wise, it remains to be seen.

This is not the Peace Core, Esposito; this is a superhuman combat unit, which means there will be times when you must fight, draw blood, and possibly kill. Actions needed not just to save your life but the life of your team that you will be fighting next to. You need to come to terms with the hard truth and decide if you can and are willing to do it or not, and you need to decide quickly, Esposito, or else I will decide for you. Is that clear?"

"Sir, yes, sir!" Rosann acknowledged.

"The purpose of this training is to see how you all do in individual combat situations and as a team," Rogers addressed all three of them. "There may be situations where you begin fighting as a team and end up separated. Where the odds will not be in your favor. Where you must think on your own and battle to get back to your team. Failure to do so will result in a certified ass-kicking and a possible toe-tag. Do we understand one another?"

"Sir! Yes sir!" they all howled in unison.

"Dismissed then," Rogers barked, "get out of my sight and get some food in you."

Rogers watched all three leave, reading their body language. With her shoulders hunched over and clutching her right bicep, Rosann glanced at the Replicator speedster she clawed down with trouble plastered all over her face. Oliver's shoulders were not hunched, but his head was lowered. A look of disappointment was written all over his face. Adrian yawned and stretched, seemingly without a care in the world. Rogers came to learn it was the opposite. As annoying as Esposito was at times, he had a hard work ethic. He did not dwell on his mistakes; he worked hard to do it better the next time.

"Well, they didn't do too bad," Erica sighed.

"They didn't do well either," Abe grunted, "and I need perfect."

"You can at least say we're doing well with three more months to go," Lady Tech snapped, glancing his way.

"No," Rogers flatly answered.

He turned, walking out of the observation deck as she shook her head, blowing blue-dyed bangs out of her face.

~~~~~~~~~~~~~~~~~~~~~~~~~~~~~~~~~~~
~~~~~~~~~~~~~~~~~~~~~~~~~~~~~~~~~~~

Thirty minutes later, Rogers sat at the desk of his quarters, examining video images and Intel of superhuman combat units already established in several countries. Russia had a six-person team known as the Iron Spetsnaz; the United Kingdom had a five-person division known as the Lions of Elizabeth. China had an eight-person squad known as the Order of the Dragon, while in North Korea, there were the Guards of the Republic.

It was unknown how many EVOs were a part of their team, but intelligence guessed there were possibly six. South Korea countered with a five-person team named the Heroes of the Republic. Teams were also being formed in Iran, Israel, Australia, and possibly Japan. Russia had the strongest team, all class ten, followed by the UK with the second strongest, while China possessed several heavy hitters and the numbers game. Russia and North Korea maintained the most experienced superhumans with military combat backgrounds. Rogers leaned back, regretting he did not have more of a say in the team's selection process before taking the position to train and lead it.

"Maxine," Rogers called out, "Are you there?"

"Yes, Sergeant," Maxine responded, "how may I help you?"

"Other than the battle with Captain Omega and the Siberian Machine, how many other combat situations has Ms. Dennison been in against other EVOs?"

"I calculate six different confrontations," Maxine confirmed, "two within Ukraine, three within the continent of Africa, one in Mexico, and one within the Middle East."

"Where in the Middle East?"

"She defeated a class eight Titan by the name of Alborz Mahmoudieh near the border of Iran and Afghanistan," Maxine reported.

"What happened there?"

"Alborz Mahmoudieh, a low-ranking member of Al-Qaeda, apparently became a top lieutenant when his abilities activated. On March 11, 2013, he marched into a small town with a regime of thirty men looking to set up a temporary camp. Unbeknownst to him, Ms. Dennison was also there bringing medical aid to the villagers," Maxine explained. "Ms. Dennison asked Mr. Mahmoudieh to kindly leave the village and set up camp elsewhere. Mr. Mahmoudieh did not take kindly to being ordered by a woman and attempted to assault Ms. Dennison. She soundly defeated him in three seconds."

"Send me all the footage you have of her in combat situations." Rogers requested while leaning back in his chair. "And any stats currently compiled on her."

"Certainly," Maxine complied. "Shall I include the Miss in your research?"

"Negative, this is my own personal research. But inform everyone to show up in the debriefing room at 2200 hours tonight."

"Yes, sir," Maxine acknowledged, "compiling data."

Rogers leaned forward as Maxine created a folder, assembling the video footage and data he requested.

~ ~

Debriefing, Room 2200 Hours.

The trio wore the same faces they had on after leaving the Hurt Locker. Sitting next to Adrian, Erica leaned back in her chair, reading updates from a well-known comic book news website, Comic Vine, from her tablet as they waited for Rogers.

"So uh," Adrian inquired while fiddling, "do you know what this is about?"

"Nope," Erica sighed.

"No clues," Adrian pressed, "none?"

"The only thing I know is Wolverine dies," Lady Tech answered nonchalantly while reading her tablet, "and Tom Hardy just got signed for the Captain Omega movie. He is so hot."

He slowly leaned over to check out the content on her tablet when Rogers entered the room, making him stiffen up with his sister and Oliver. Erica continued to scan through her tablet. As Rogers neared the center of the room, he did a quick scan, looking into their eyes. No one wanted to go home.

"You're not diamonds, but I bet I can trade you all for a three-piece and a Happy meal," Rogers huffed. "Top brass wants you ready within the next three months. I say you all need at least six more months to get your balls up. Unfortunately, orders are orders, so it's time to switch things up to some on the job training."

The trio glanced at one another with both confusion and eagerness. Lady Tech lifted her head from her tablet, glaring up at Rogers with uneasy, narrowed eyes, wondering what he was up to, especially since he did not debrief her privately on his plans first.

"Maxine, bring up the file," Abe requested.

Lady Tech's eyes bulged while almost falling backward out of her chair. Oliver and the twins glanced her way before turning back to the mug shot and rap sheet on the screen.

"Her name is Sophia Dennison," Rogers began debriefing them, "an immensely powerful EVO, probably the most powerful one on the planet. She's currently located on a remote island in the Pacific, which we will visit tomorrow, where the word of the day will be 'recon' people.

This is an information-gathering mission only, with the emphasis on 'information gathering.'"

He scanned their faces to ensure they understood what he was saying.

"Any questions?" Rogers asked.

Erica's arm shot up into the air. She violently waved it, demanding his attention.

"Dr. Champion," Rogers recognized her with narrowed eyes.

"Exactly what type of intel are we expected to gather on this 'recon' mission?"

"I will be the one actually gathering the intel," Rogers informed her, "you four will be providing backup, and that is all you will be doing. Any more questions?"

No one else had questions, but they were all uncomfortable at the sudden tension between Lady Tech and the Sergeant.

"So tomorrow, make sure you're suited up and on the deck by the bird no later than 0900 hours," Rogers ordered, "anyone late for our little field trip will be subjected to cruel and unusual punishment, and those that are early will get worse."

Oliver and Rosann's eyes turned to Adrian again, who returned their glare again with a dirty look.

"Dismissed."

Rogers exited the debriefing room, leaving the twins and Brandon perplexed. Erica shot up to her feet, going after him.

~ ~

As Rogers entered the hallway, walking off, Erica followed him with an irate, rabid ankle biter's demeanor.

"Permission to speak freely, sir!"

"As long as you keep it G-rated," Rogers returned dryly.

"What the hell are you doing?"

Her high-pitched, stern voice echoed the anger and frustration on her face.

"Close enough," Rogers sighed

He halted, turning to face her.

"Why the hell are we going to Dr. Dennison's island tomorrow?" Erica yelled. "And why wasn't I debriefed?"

Rogers tilted his head, unimpressed by her temper tantrum.

"I just debrief you. For a college grad with a list of degrees longer than my arm, I think you'd understand the meaning of the word 'recon.'"

"This is more than a reconnaissance mission, and you know it," Erica sneered at him, "and what part of her island being a 'no-fly zone' did you not get?"

"I'm banking on her being such a humanitarian that she wouldn't bring down a vessel with no hostile intentions," Rogers scoffed. "And any additions to this mission is on a need to know basis, which at this time you do not need to know."

"As co-leader of this group, I demand to know," Lady Tech said.

Rogers sighed, stepping forward now, towering over her with a stone-cold look, making her feel smaller than she already was. As intimidating as the Sergeant was, she tried to stare him back down.

"Let's get something straight." Rogers brought out his instilled fear bass voice. "There is no co-leader; there is only one leader. Me. I'm the adult; you're the child… I run this team… you're part of the team. I give some extended authority because your brainpan is much bigger than our current Three Stooges.

However, you still do what I say, and if you don't like it, you can take your toys and your gadgets and get off my base… and the next time you decide to grow a pair and challenge me like, I put a ring on your finger. I will personally throw you off this base… are we clear?"

"Sir… yes sir," Erica snarled.

"I don't give a damn if you're Spock smart; you ain't grown," Rogers nipped at her, "now we leave at 0900 hours tomorrow morning. I'm giving you the authority to make sure everyone is up, in gear, and on that deck by that time. If they're not, it's on you. Are we clear?"

"Sir… yes sir," Erica answered with grinding teeth.

Rogers marched off, leaving Erica with anger and hurt feelings. She stormed off in the opposite direction, muttering something unkind about the Sergeant.

CHAPTER 8

0500 hours the next day:

Rogers rose out of his bed as if it was another day and hit the floor, executing his routine of two hundred push-ups. By right, he no longer needed to do any push-ups based on his physiology that would allow him to do them into the next week without tiring; push-ups kept him disciplined, reminding him that he was still human. He rose back to his feet, walked into the bathroom of his quarters, and ran ice-cold water over his face. He then took a razor to his skull and mug for a quick cleanup. He finished off his regimen with a thorough brush and floss.

After a last rinse and spit, he returned to where he placed his fatigue and gear after checking it the previous night, only to find that it was gone and replaced by something else. His military fatigues and flak jacket were replaced by a black bodysuit with an armored body look to it. His rank as Sergeant was embossed on the front right breastplate, while both shoulders bore the Regulator Eagle symbol. Rogers narrowed his eyes in bewilderment as he ran his hand over the material. Aside from the breast and spinal plates, which had a rubber-like feel, the rest of the suit seemed constructed from a light and soft fabric.

"Maxine!" Abe barked, looking around.

"Good Morning, Sergeant Rogers." She greeted him over the audio system in his room. "How may I help you?"

"What the hell happened to my gear?!" Rogers yelled.

"The Miss had it replaced last night while you slept."

"What?!" Rogers barked. "How?!"

A holographic image beamed down from one of the micro-cameras in the room, replaying the comical event that went down under his nose as a duo of miniature Doozers snuck into his room. At the same time, he slept, taking his uniform off the table and replacing it with his new uniform before scurrying out as he turned over during mid-snore.

"Where is it?!" Rogers howled.

"She had it incinerated," Maxine calmly responded.

"Incinerated?!" Rogers roared in disbelief.

"Yes, sir, incinerated."

"Where is she?!"

"She has instructed me not to give you her location," Maxine informed him. "She will meet you at the expected mission time with the team up and ready. She has also instructed me to play her recorded message to you. Shall I play it now, sir?"

"Play it!"

"Good Morning, Sergeant Dooshbag," Erica's voice rang over the audio system. "By now, you're probably throwing a hissy fit because I got rid of your old duds. Get over it. You may run this team, but I am still in charge of facilities, tech, and equipment for all operations, and I'm sorry, gramps, your gear is severely outdated... Desert Storm was last... last year.

Before you is the latest in high-grade bodysuit protection designed by yours truly that I like to call IMPACT armor. It's a million times stronger and more resilient than the stuff you're used to wearing. It can withstand a direct hit from a 120mm KEW-A2 cartridge and is resistant to sub-zero freezing and 6.6 million degrees Fahrenheit. Considering who you are sending us against is a bazillion times worse, it would be in your best interest to suit up. Sorry about torching your other gear, but I didn't want you to have another option... at least I made you a new matching beanie... see you at 0900 hours... sir."

Abe ran his mitt down his face.

"She's just a child. She's just a child... she's just a child."

~ ~

0845 hours:

Rogers marched into the hangar, all business decked out in his new gear. He wore his new black military beanie hat low as his team stood in line, minus Lady Tech, for inspection.

Hard-On stood at attention wearing a similar outfit to Rogers in blue, black, and silver with the Regulator symbol also imprinted on his outfit's shoulders. His boots were identical to Rogers but in a deep blue color. Around his waist and right leg, he wore a belt and holster system that housed his sidearm. Next to him, Rosanna was wearing a blood-red and purple leotard version of their outfit, also bearing the Regulator symbol on both shoulders. She also wore matching fingerless tactical gloves, a sidearm, and a belt similar to her brother's outfit. On her feet, she wore an open-toe shoe system in purple and red that covered a portion of her shins, ankle, and foot up to her toes, which made Rogers look her in the eye.

"Sir, Dr. Champion said it was so I would not have to compromise the use of my abilities, sir."

Rogers nodded as he walked up to Blitz, wearing a different version of their outfit with a glowing green and white electrical grid pattern. Like everyone else, the shoulders of his uniform were adorned with the Regulator emblem. He wore black metallic bracers and boots with the same glowing grid pattern as his outfit. They were used to assist him in regulating his power output. Unlike his teammates, he did not carry a firearm. His abilities would cause either damage or render them useless in combat.

"Where's…?" Abe began to ask, looking for Lady Tech.

A sizeable booming sound interrupted him and made all three facing him step back and look up.

"Right behind you, old man," Erica's voice rang out.

Rogers turned around to another booming sound, forcing him to look up as well. Erica sat in its three-fingered and thumbed left palm as it carried her. It stood a humongous sixteen feet tall with two hind legs, similar to a cat or a dog. Like the android sisters, it had white lights pulsating a powerful energy source; unlike the sisters, a large one glowed from its breastplate. Its armored plating was a shiny chrome black with neon green flames like one would see on a supped-up tuner car; Erica's personal touch as she wore a skintight gray and silver plug bodysuit one would see in an anime cartoon. Like the rest of her teammates, each shoulder displayed the Regulator emblem.

Adrian was the first to break the silence.

"What the hell is that?"

"This people is SAM," Erica introduced, "SAM wave to everyone."

The Goliath machine gave a cheerful wave with its free hand, unnerving everyone except for Rogers.

"Okay," Rosann said, "what the hell is SAM?"

"SAM, my good people, stands for Synthetic Armored Mech," Erica said. "He's my personal armored mobile suit."

"You mean you can ride inside of him," Oliver asked, "like in Gundam?"

"I do love a man who knows his anime, but you are correct. SAM here adds exponential muscle and firepower to our little team, which we desperately need."

Rogers donned a sardonic smile as he gestured for her to come down so he could speak with her.

"Down, please, SAM," Erica nervously coughed, knowing the conversation would be unpleasant.

The hulking armored mech slowly dropped to one knee, placing its creator gently to the ground. Lady Tech gradually strolled over to the Sergeant as if bracing for a switching. He leaned forward, forcing her to recoil backward.

"I warned you if you try to test me… you're going to lose," Rogers calmly whispered to her. "Torching my uniform was strike one, your fashionably late grand entrance was strike two… you want to break Limp's record over there?"

"Sir… no sir," Erica swallowed hard.

"Then move your tail and fall in."

Erica quickly scurried over to Oliver, standing next to him, and stood as straight as possible, fighting through the embarrassing lecture she received. Rogers took one last look at the gigantic armor whose chest expanded as if it was breathing as it looked back at him. He shook his head as he turned to address his team.

"Now that we're done admiring each other's Halloween costumes," Rogers began, "based on the debriefing which you all should have read, we are heading to an uncharted man-made remote island in the South Pacific. There are civilians on this island; some are American, which means we do not bring a firefight unless necessary. This is strictly a recon mission and nothing else... is that clear?"

"Sir, yes, sir!" all four howled.

"Alright then, get your gear, and let's load 'em up, five minutes, people, move it!"

Four and a half minutes later, Rogers boarded the Tornado, sitting in one of the swiveling passenger chairs, strapping in.

"Uh, excuse me, sir," Adrian swallowed, "shouldn't somebody be up there with her?"

"I can't fly a plane," Rogers answered plainly, "can you?"

Hard-On touched his cross, transforming into metal form, but not before Rosann quickly reached over, touching him. She then grasped a metal portion of the seat, changing her body to metal. Adrian looked over to see Oliver clutching his chair's armrests as if he was about to tear them off. A very ironic scene, considering the electricity wielder seemed so comfortable in the air.

"Bro," Adrian asked cocking an eyebrow, "you afraid of flying?"

"Dude, I'm afraid of crashing," Oliver got out.

Adrian took off his crucifix chain, handing it to him. Oliver quickly grasped it, kissed it, and then held it tightly as he again grabbed the armrest.

"Thanks, man."

"Alright, ladies," Lady Tech announced over the PA system, "normally, I would push this baby to get us there in under an hour. But considering it would be rude to show up unannounced during breakfast, we will be cruising the normal speed to get us there by lunch. So sit back and relax. Next stop, our funeral."

The hanger's roof opened as the Tornado was elevated to the topside via the platform elevator it rested on. Daylight shined through the craft's cockpit as Lady Tech went through final checks. The powerful engines whined and erupted, sending gusts of wind and dirt everywhere. Jay-Z's "Change the Game" featuring Beanie Sigel and Memphis Bleek filled the cabin. Everyone in the cabin looked at one another in disbelief save for Rogers, who leaned back and tilted his beanie down to get some shut-eye.

As the Tornado went vertically into the air, Lady Tech's head bobbed to the music. Dominant rear thrusters replaced the V/STOL as the Tornado rocketed toward its destination.

~ ~

1215 hours:

The Tornado entered the no-fly zone around Sophia's island almost four hours later. Erica quickly cut the music, getting everyone's attention while waking a slumbering Rogers, who was out for most of the trip.

"Look, alive people, we have reached the point of no return. We'll be coming up on our destination in five minutes."

Along with Rogers, the trio looked out their respective windows to get a view of the massive landmass that was an official ghost to the rest of the world.

"Holy," was all Adrian got out.

Rosann followed up with "Wow."

Oliver, who finally settled into his seat, just sat there, amazed at how beautiful the island looked from his viewpoint.

Sitting in the middle of the beach's snow-white sand that circled half the island like a crescent moon was a gargantuan, highly polished black granite stone with the words "Welcome to Sanctuary" etched deeply within it. Fresh tropical vegetation covered at least ninety percent of the island. Integrated within the forest and foliage were large, highly constructed huts the size of houses and mini-mansions with what appeared to be solar paneling on the roofs. The team could view specks of what appeared to be people, pausing to look back up at them.

Lady Tech's bio-signature tracking system pinpointed Sophia's location as she piloted the Tornado to the far side of the continent-size island's beach, where there appeared to be new housing being constructed. Children running around on the beach playing tag stopped to look up in wonderment as the Tornado flew over them, looking for a place to land. Many women of various ages, sizes, ethnicities, and backgrounds sat at the beach's edge to sunbathe and get their feet wet, looked up as well, and then at each other with worried looks, wondering who was coming to disturb their peace this time.

~ ~

A young, pale, slender male covered in tattoos with piercings through his lip, nose, and ears sporting a purple Mohawk ran through the new hut homes' construction site with a frantic look on his face. Some workers yelled at him, telling him to watch it as he almost bumped into people and knocked over some building material as he rushed up the stairs of one of the newly constructed huts.

"Sophee!! Sophee!" the panting young man hollered.

Today, she wore a bright yellow and black bikini top with blue daisy duke shorts, which displayed her extraordinarily toned and womanly features. Her eerie glowing blue eyes and radiant smile underneath her long jet-black dreads greeted the frazzled young man trying to catch his breath.

"Hey Zeek," Sophia chirpily responded.

"Soph," Zeek coughed, fighting to get air, "there's... a ship…"

"I know," Sophia chuckled, "just catch your breath and calm yourself."

"Never... seen anything like this before," Zeek gasped. "Looks like we're being invaded!"

"Doubt that, but why don't you do me a favor and quietly ask everyone on the beach to calmly head back to the village for me."

"You got it, Sophia," Zeek nodded, ready to help.

As she watched a hyperactive Zeek run out of the hut again to do her proud, an older man, fourteen years her senior and several shades darker with a cue ball look and peppered beard in a simple white tank top, jeans, and construction boots walked up to her holding a board in his hand.

"Trouble?" he asked.

"Don't think so," Sophia said, turning to him, "but why don't you take everyone back to the village as well for a break... just in case."

"We can stay and help you know," he gestured.

"If I need help, Earl," Sophia replied with a smile, "I'll scream."

Earl grinned at her little joke of reassurance before howling at everyone else to wrap it up.

"All right, people, lunchtime, back to the main village!"

As everyone departed, Sophia strolled to the hut's open door; she leaned against the entrance, watching as the now hovering ship descended on the remote side of the beach several yards away. Despite the great distance, the force of the VTOL's thrusts sent sand in her direction. Shaking her head with a smile still on her face, she returned to work.

~ ~

Back at the landing site, the Tornado's crew disembarked and began securing the perimeter around their ship. At the same time, Lady Tech scanned the beach for the location of the inhabitants and their target.

"Save for those two over there, everyone else is back at the village, and our target is still in the new construction."

"Doing what?" Adrian asked.

"Working," Erica answered with a shrug.

"So, what's the plan, Sarge?" Adrian inquired.

Rogers looked at him, wondering if he was sleeping during the debriefing.

"Recon. Which means you sit your tanned ass here, while I go have a conversation, and the next time you call me 'Sarge' instead of 'Sir,' I'm going to pound your sorry ass into the ground like a tent peg."

Rogers walked off as Hard-On glared at him, clutching his fists with sheer frustration.

"Is anyone else getting really tired of this shit?!" Adrian lashed out, looking around.

Rosanna answered her brother's annoying whining with an eye roll while Oliver shrugged his shoulders.

Rogers walked the beach nearing the two stragglers implied by Lady Tech; the younger was Zeek yelling at an older gray-whiskered dark-skinned man sporting a bare chest with a potbelly in some knee-high jeans shorts. He held onto a fishing rod, trying to cast his line while shooing Zeek away. Next to him was a bucket full of tropical fish he had captured before the team's arrival.

"Come on, Mr. Norton!" Zeek yelled, "we've got to go!"

"For the last time, Zeek, I ain't going anywhere!" Mr. Norton returned. "I'm trying to catch me some fish for supper tonight, and as you can see, I am on a roll!"

"Mr. Norton, we can go to the other side of the island and fish!" Zeek coaxed. "It's not safe here!"

"Today is not the day to go fishin on the other side! Today is the day to go fishin here! And what you talkin bout not safe, you can't get no safer than Sanctuary, except maybe Heaven itself!"

"Mr. Norton, do you not see whose coming this way?" Zeek snapped, losing his cool again. "It's about to be a warzone up in... oh... oh, no..."

Rogers walked past, tipping his beanie to a smiling Mr. Norton and a nervous and frustrated Zeek.

"Gentlemen."

"Hey... hey, I know you," Mr. Norton yelled with a beaming smile, "you're Abe Rogers, right? Da Wrassler! Tell me I'm right!"

Abe turned to address him.

"Yeah. I was."

"I remember you! You probably don't remember me! November 15, 2007, you were in Madison Square Garden. After the show, you were leaving and signing autographs... I had on one of your shirts I got at the Goodwill, and you signed it for me! Then you slipped me like a couple hundred dollars! You didn't even look to see what was in your wallet! You just pulled it out and gave it to me... told me it wasn't much but make sure I use it to get something to eat and stay warm... I would have been happy with just the autograph… I don't have the money, but I still got the shirt!"

Abe cracked a rare, genuine smile.

"I do remember you, sir."

"You ain't come to start no trouble, right? You just come to talk to our Sophie," Mr. Norton asked, gesturing, "cuz you just like her… a hero sent from God… to help people like me."

"I'm not all that," Rogers answered, "but I did just come to talk to her."

"Well, she right over there!" Mr. Norton informed him while pointing.

"Thank you, Mr. Norton."

Abe tipped his beanie again out of respect.

Rogers continued walking as Zeek gave him a nervous glare, making it known that he did not like him.

"What the hell, Mr. Norton!" Zeek began admonishing the old man, "Why'd you tell him where she was?!"

"Boy, hush yo mouth, and help me catch these damn fish here before I pull dat ring clear out of your nose!" Mr. Norton snapped while wagging a finger at him. "You look like a cracked-out bull!"

The two continued to argue as Rogers finally reached the construction site; slowly, he walked up the steps, viewing Sophia casually placing a piece of hardwood cherry panel next to the others she put up to create the final part of a wall. She began to push thick eight-inch nails into the board, attaching it to the beam on the other side as if they were thumbtacks.

"Welcome to my island, Captain," Sophia greeted him, not looking his way as she continued to work.

"Sergeant," Rogers politely corrected her, "Sergeant Abraham Rogers… former United States Marines."

"Figured you for a Marine," Sophia said as she ran her hand across the panel to ensure it was secure. "My apologies… I'm not up on all the latest superhero…"

"I'm not a superhero," Rogers corrected her again.

"Super Soldier?" Sophia innocently asked.

Rogers cracked a simple smile.

"Just a soldier, ma'am."

"Humble… nice; hope you don't mind if I talk to you while I work… I want to finish all these huts before tomorrow."

"Not enough room?" Rogers asked.

"Plenty of room," Sophia answered. "These are for new residents."

Rogers watched as she grabbed a larger board, laid it down, and measured it; she cut through it like a scalpel through paper, slicing it in half with her thumbnail. She then took the board, tacking it into the beam behind it as she did the last one.

"New residence?" Abe asked, looking around.

"Yep, whoever wants to come," Sophia sighed, motioning to the men he met, "Mr. Norton, who you just met, former Vietnam Vet… former alcoholic… homeless on the streets of Manhattan for twenty years ever since he was no longer able to work and lost his home and wife to cancer. Ezekiel Marsh from LA, which you also met, was a former Heroin and Meth junkie… before that, he was being beaten and molested by his father and older brother. We have people here from Cambodia, Iraq, Iran, Darfur, various parts of Africa, Europe, South, and North America… war refugees, homeless, drug addicts, rape victims, molested, oppressed… you name it… all get a chance to live and start clean life afresh here."

"Quite an admirable undertaking," Rogers said with a nod.

"Nothing admirable about this, Sergeant," Sophia sighed while cutting more boards. "Just good, clean common sense.

How often have key governments 'intervened' in war-torn and impoverished countries to bring liberty and peace only to leave, making things a thousand times worse than when they came in?

Then there are the people going in and out of drug or alcohol rehab because the poison they are trying to avoid is so easily obtainable when they reach a low point for any reason. Instead of being treated as sick people, they are locked up like animals, and their lives are forever destroyed by a system needing a severe overhaul.

One that fat geriatric bureaucrats are too lazy to fix. They can't get a job because they have a record, and the next thing you know, they're left to die on the streets and looked upon like garbage."

After cutting five clean new boards, she paused to give Abe eye contact.

"And that's just a couple of many stories taking place in the messed-up society of a world we live in. Here in my own backyard, I control the playing field. Other than medicinal, which certified others and I administer, illegal drugs and recreational alcohol are not allowed here, and everyone is perfectly fine with it. They can live without fear of someone raiding their village to rape and murder them or take their children away to be child soldiers. Here they can live as they were intended to live. Peacefully and like human beings."

"Mind if I ask how you're funding all of this?" Rogers asked, noticing that the oak wood she cut was expensive.

"You want to give me a donation, Sergeant?" Sophia inquired with a smirk.

It forced a simple smile on Rogers's lips as he playfully shrugged.

"Wouldn't want your money anyway," Sophia said, waving in jest. "Let's just say a woman with my 'skill set' can venture places mere mortals cannot go and make bank. Off the record, I have acquired more liquid assets to dwarf Mr. Buffet, Zuckerberg, and Ms. Winfrey combined, which is needed to run an operation like this. We use solar panels during the day and an industrial-sized electrical generator at night. I also plan to order some wind turbines in the next month. We also have satellite and fiber optic connections allowing us the creature comforts like television and the internet."

"What about education?" Rogers asked, remembering that he saw children as they flew over the island.

"New York State licensed teachers from kindergarten to high school. Personally interviewed and triple-vetted by me. They're paid their worth as long as they come with a passion for teaching, which children need. So far, who I have picked has not disappointed me.

But this is not a one-stop for everyone, Sergeant. Some people have made this place their permanent home and are welcome to stay for as long as they like. For others, it's a way to get back on their feet, and when they decide it's time to leave, I ensure they remain on their feet."

"And if they fall again?" Rogers asked.

Sophia smirked before she answered.

"Like my mom always says, you can always come home."

"Sounds like a model Utopia," Abe said with a hint of sarcasm.

"There's no such thing as a 'model Utopia,' Sophia responded, ignoring the tone. "No society is perfect, and there are rules implemented and enforced by myself and the council that I formed, and not everyone can come or stay here if they do not wish to abide by my rules. I don't know if it's a blessing, but I had to remove only two people from this island in the past three and a half years since I started this. One was personally difficult to do, one wasn't."

Sophia walked smiling with pride, gazing through the hut's open structure, still under construction, at the clear view of the village five minutes away.

"In that time, I've seen people from all walks of life, race, religion, and nationality that were cast away, beaten, broken, and scarred heal and band together. Forming not just a community but a family. People who just needed a real chance have risen to become teachers, nurses, electricians, and, as you can see, construction workers. Some have created their own online businesses while here. Here the only label that matters is one of being a human being."

"So down with religion and culture?" Abe asked.

"Quite the opposite," Sophia answered. "People here are proud of where they come from, free to practice their religion, and open to sharing their cultures with one another. That is because they don't have ignorant, greedy people whispering in their ears that they're poor because of 'those people' or 'remember 9/11.'

Treating good people equally and giving them the fundamental rights of decent shelter, good food, clothing, and the safety of not having a suicide bomber or drone dead leveling their home, or killing their loved ones. They have more time to learn and realize that the person sitting across from them who may be of different skin color, or maybe worship the same God just a bit differently or call Him another name, is not that different.

In the end, reasonable people want the same thing worldwide for themselves and their children. Greedy people with power and a sense of entitlement are the ones who make this world a darker place. They use their influence to turn innocent people against one another by exploiting their weaknesses and misfortune to fuel their agenda. Racism, corrupted use of religion, and fear are age-old business ploys people of power use to line their pockets."

"Greed isn't good," Rogers chuckled.

"I'd like to deck Oliver Stone for creating that stupid line," Sophia snorted.

She began to chuckle at her comment, waking Rogers to realize he was having a casual conversation with a woman he watched lay out two of the most powerful Titans on the planet. In a new world where the impossible was possible, it was still hard to fathom that so much unbridled power lay in a woman with such a pleasant, warm smile.

"So Sergeant," Sophia sighed, "let's cut to the chase, shall we? You didn't fly all the way here from the states to admire my artisanship or listen to my worldviews. I assume, based on whatever file you have on me, it's not to ask for my surrender, so it's either to enlist my services or for something else… which is it?"

"I did come here to enlist your services," Rogers respectfully answered, "but it's for something else."

~~~~~~~~~~~~~~~~~~~~~~~~~~~~~~~~~~

Back at the Tornado, a restless male Esposito paced the sand, contemplating what was taking Rogers so long as the rest of his teammates casually stood around, waiting for the Sergeant's return.

"What is this shit?!" Adrian snarled. "Standing here with our thumbs up our asses when we should be dragging this bitch out in restraints, not talking to her!"

"What part of a 'recon' mission do you not get, Limp?" Erica sighed. "And attempting to 'drag her out in restraints' would be just rude considering she extended us the same courtesy of not knocking us out of the sky before we got within a hundred miles of this place."

"I've read the debriefings," Rosann interjected in the conversation. "It's still kind of hard to believe… I mean… about whom she is."

"EVO Zero, also known as the Source and proverbial birth mother of all EVOs
~~~~~~~~~~~~~~~~~~~~~~~~~~~~~~~~~~

on the planet," Lady Tech recited, "possessing god-like superhuman strength, speed, durability, and stamina. She has the ability of flight and possesses energy on what is calculated to be on a bio-nuclear level that can sustain all her functions indefinitely, meaning she doesn't need to eat, sleep, or even breathe normal air… for all intents and purposes, she's a fully functional immortal."

"So she's a bit "tough," Adrian snorted with a dismissive gesture, "like the Sarge said, everyone has a weakness."

"And you've figured out how to take down 'Mom,'" Rosann scoffed, "in the thirty-five minutes we've been standing here?"

Hard-On gave his sister a look she knew, indicating that he had an idea, forcing her to run her hand down her face, meaning that whatever he was thinking was a bad idea.

"Adrian… no…" Rosann whispered, "no!"

"You haven't even heard my plan yet!"

"If your plan involves going against what the Sergeant told us not to do," Rosann lectured, "it's a **bad idea**."

Adrian walked up to his sister, attempting to reason with her.

"Recon means to gather information, correct? Which means we're eventually going to have to go to blows with her. So why not use the element of surprise to take her out while we're here? Based on what little Miss Poindexter…"

"Bite me…" Erica blurted out.

Adrian ignored her remark while continuing to reason with his sister and Oliver.

"Source or not, she's still an EVO just like us, no matter how powerful she is. What would happen if you were to touch her?"

The prospect of gaining the Source's power made Rosann pause and think her brother's idea was not too stupid.

"And how pray tell, do you intend to get her close enough to touch her 'genius'?" Erica butted in.

"With the help of our man Blitz over here," Hard-On answered while gesturing to Oliver. "Rosann touches him, gaining the ability to fly at the speed of lightning, and while we're distracting her, Rosann moves in close enough to touch her, gaining her powers, and then we just triple team and beat her ass into submission, dragging her home in restraints."

Rosann frowned, unsure of her brother's plan.

"Somehow, this feels more complicated than you're making it sound."

"Like the intel, you forgot about how she can drain energy wielding EVOs like me, increasing her strength," Oliver said, finally butting in. "I would be like a power bar for her."

"And I don't remember telling anyone I created anything that could restrain the likes of her," Erica snorted.

"Alright, let's cut the shit!" Adrian howled. "We got an opportunity to take down the most powerful EVO on the planet today! It all comes down to us, hitting her first!

~~~~~~~~~~~~~~~~~~~~~~~~~~~~~~~~

At the hut, Sophia leaned against the doorway with her arms folded and a raised eyebrow, attempting to wrap her brain around Rogers's request.

"You want **me**… to help you train your team?"

"Yes," Rogers said plainly.

She gave him a head tilt before she answered.

"I take it you didn't get authorization for this request."

"I didn't even ask for authorization to fly here."

"Why me?" Sophia inquired, narrowing her eyes.

"I am currently in command of a four-person team that is supposed to be the
~~~~~~~~~~~~~~~~~~~~~~~~~~~~~~~~

United States' answer to this new brewing Cold War if you want to call it that." Rogers snorted. "Our other job, which I was informed on the day of orientation, was to also handle domestic threats that arise."

"That's a lot of responsibility," Sophia nodded.

"Aside from me, all four of my other team members just came off the tit," Rogers sighed, "but despite being a bunch of snot-nosed brats, they're good kids with a hard work ethic. I owe it to them to equip them in any way possible to make sure they don't get killed."

"Then maybe you should advise them to quit, Sergeant," Sophia coughed, "if we're being honest, I'm not a real fan of my fellow superhumans and less of a fan of 'superheroes.'"

"Something we have in common," Rogers admitted, "but I'm not trying to create superheroes. I'm trying to make soldiers."

"Doesn't make your argument any better," Sophia sighed.

She turned to look out into the white sanded beach she created.

"I'm fully aware of what is going on in the world, Sergeant," Sophia said with a bit of sternness not directed toward him. "I choose not to get involved because I can't stop what's coming, and I honestly don't care. I was dragged against my will into the affairs of men looking to be gods. I paid a hefty price for that in more ways than you can imagine. I didn't just build this island to help others; I built it because I want no part of a world that has cost me so much."

"A lot of people paid a heavy price on that day," Abe coughed.

"Then they should take it up with their government, Sergeant," Sophia snapped. "This whole mess got started because 'Keeping up with the Kardashians' and 'Love and Hip Hop' won over 'What the hell is my government doing with my taxpaying dollars behind my back.' Governments no longer fear their people, especially those that are elected to office, because they sadly see the people for what they are."

"And what are they?" Rogers asked.

"A bunch of idiots," Sophia bluntly answered, "ignorant, self-absorbed, easily manipulated, and distracted."

"Kind of harsh," he scoffed, "don't you think?"

She turned to look him in the eyes.

"Really? Who the hell with any common sense pays for an eight hundred-thousand-dollar house with a thirty-thousand-dollar income? The world didn't just go to hell just because Big Business exploited the American Dream. It went the hell because ignorant people thought they could get away with partying like a rockstar on a poor man's salary without consequences. We live in a world where people put brakes on the second they hit the cliff and are shocked when they fly off it."

"You act like you weren't a part of that world at one time."

"I very much was so." Sophia willingly admitted. "Although I wasn't as ambitious. I wanted what every girl wanted. House with the picket fence, a loving husband to care for, and children to love. The house I wanted only cost three hundred and fifty thousand, and we bargained it down to three zero."

She let out a chuckle, lightening the heavy subject.

"I can say that it was all taken away from me in a night, but that's not true. My own ignorance blinded me to the signs in front of my face. I cracked my head a couple of times before I could see clearly. Now that I can fly, I see a world with both the power and potential to change but refuses to because the one percent is standing on the neck of everyone else to remain the one percent, while everyone else is killing one another to be the one percent. And amidst that chaos were those working in the shadows with deeper, darker ambitions to become actual gods. Because of me, they both failed and succeeded. So now I choose to stay out of the madness protecting those that wish to stay out of it as well."

An irritated sneer crossed her face as she continued to look out toward the direction of the beach. It did not make Rogers uneasy, knowing it was not directed at him. However, he could tell that this conversation took her back to places she did not want to go.

"The world got its wish," Sophia snorted, "they wanted to bring fantasy to life, a world where people had superpowers. Let them deal with the consequences."

A strange silence fell over them as they looked out onto the beach. It was as if the two were the oldest friends, and Rogers had popped in for a visit. His initial mission would fail, and his request would be denied, but it was pretty refreshing to stand and talk with someone over thirty. Rogers agreed with Sophia on some things; on others, he did not agree with her at all, but even with the reasons he disapproved of, he could respect her based on the intelligence behind her opinion.

She was not angry at the world but tired of its antics. She politely distanced herself from it so she could be left alone.

"Apologies if my tone was a bit abrasive," Sophia said sincerely.

"None needed," Rogers politely responded.

"Looks like your team is looking to do something foolish," Sophia sighed while gazing in the direction where the Tornado sat on the beach.

"Say what?" Rogers sneered.

Rogers pulled out a pair of binoculars from his pouch to view Rosann touching Blitz's hand, changing her hair into a black frizzed-out afro while her skin color and features also altered to match his. Her body began to emit a highly intense electrical discharge.

Abe shook his head, snarling.

"What are those idiots doing?"

"While we were here talking," Sophia answered, "I saw the hard body in blue rallying the troops with a plan to take me down."

Abe raised a perplexed eyebrow while looking at her.

"You can hear what he's saying?"

"If you're asking if I have 'super hearing,' no, I don't." Sophia bluntly answered. "But I do have keen eyesight… and I can read lips.

"That dumbass," Rogers muttered.

Rogers reached to contact Hard-On and the team on his headset but paused, looking at Sophia.

"Say, you wouldn't mind…?" Rogers began to ask.

"You want me to humble them for you," Sophia finished his request.

Abe's lips formed a devious smirk.

"Just a little."

Sophia gazed back at him with narrowed, unsure eyes.

"If I do this, I'm not going to see a bunch of warships at my front door, am I?"

"Like I said, no one knows I'm here. So, there's no one to complain to."

Sophia turned to look out at the beach again.

"So should I just walk out there, or do they need some motivation?"

"I guess some motivation wouldn't hurt," Rogers suggested.

"Then you owe me a new wall," Sophia sighed.

He cocked an eyebrow, unsure what Sophia meant by her statement.

"Huh?"

Despite him knowing it was a sell, Rogers was still surprised how easily Ms. Dennison snatched him up by the front of his combat harness, hoisting him effortlessly into the air, and then flung him through the brand new wall she built, launching him half a mile onto the beach he had trekked from. He did not need to sell the impact as his body bounced off the seashore several times, kicking up sand everywhere. He came to a rest in front of his team before they even put their plan into action.

"Holy...!," Oliver yelled.

"Sergeant!" Rosann screamed.

Sophia stepped through the large hole she created in the semi-built hut. She walked down the steps into the beach's warm sand, allowing the grains to sink between her bare toes.

"Let's get the bitch," Hard-On snarled.

Blitz and Rosann nodded in agreement. With knowledge of his abilities during training, Rosann powered up along with Blitz. The two of them took to the air, propelling themselves at Sophia while Hard-On transformed into metal form, darting across the sand toward her. Rosann swung a tight U-turn in midair to take Sophia from behind while Blitz barreled straight toward her. An onlooking Erica, staying out of the fight, shook her head.

"And the plan falls apart in five, four, three, two..." Lady Tech counted.

To the human eye, it was apparent they would overwhelm her. The trio, however, did not count on Sophia moving faster than the speed of lightning. She darted out of their attack path within nanoseconds, going straight for Adrian. Sophia slammed on the brakes, extending her right arm out. Unable to do the same, Adrian ran chest-first into an unbreakable arm, turning him inside out.

He crashed violently, sending sand spraying.

Not too far off, Mr. Norton, still on the beach, cackled insanely while a terrified Zeek ran his hands through his Mohawk.

"He gonna feel that for a while!" Mr. Norton hysterically laughed.

"Mr. Norton, we got to get out of here!" Zeek yelled.

"Boy, I ain't going anywhere," Mr. Norton said. "This is the best seat in the house!"

Hard-On groaned as Sophia sashayed over, grabbing him by one of his legs.

"Hope you don't rust," Sophia sighed.

She hurled him into the ocean half a mile off in one motion. She was sure he called her the B-word as he went sailing.

The first to recover, Blitz was on his feet, transforming his entire body into a plasma electrical form. He exploded across the sand while channeling energy into his right fist. On impact, it would deliver the force of two tons of TNT. Sophia allowed him to land it, tanking the building, demolishing blow, and causing a mini three-second sandstorm. The blinding spray died down to reveal her holding him high by his throat.

"Power down," Sophia ordered him.

"Screw you," Oliver groaned.

"Gotcha!" Rosann yelled.

Mimicking Blitz's plasma-charged form, she snuck up behind Sophia the second after Oliver delivered his seismic blow. Returning to her regular form, Rosann quickly grabbed Sophia's left arm and waited to take in her DNA and power.

A half-minute later, nothing happened.

"What the…" a startled Rosann stammered. "What the hell happened?"

"Let me guess," Sophia asked, "you're a morpher, right?"

"Yeah," Rosann answered with a lump in her throat.

"The plan was to distract me so that you could grab me, right?" Sophia deduced. "In hopes that you can take in my DNA duplicating my abilities."

Rosann slowly nodded as the sweat of fear washed over her.

"Yeah, see, although the barbs on your hands possess the strength and density to pierce most organic materials, some with the density level of steel or titanium," Sophia lectured, "**my skin** is denser than any material on the planet."

"Oh… I see…" Rosann swallowed.

"You probably chipped or broke a few grabbing me. Your barbs will eventually grow back, but if you want them to grow faster, Sergeant Roger's regenerative healing will speed up the process."

Sophia held Oliver high by his throat during this conversation like a rag doll in his plasma-charged form.

"Let me… go… you…" Blitz gurgled.

"Boy, if you don't want to be a sniveling drooling husk at my feet, you better not let that word slip from your lips," Sophia warned him. "Now power down, or I will power you down myself."

"Yes… ma'am."

Oliver obeyed, reverting to his human form.

"I'm going to put you down now. You going to behave?"

"Yes… ma'am."

She lowered him back to the sand. During this time, Adrian reverted back to human form to keep from sinking to the Pacific's bottom and managed to swim back to shore. He remained on his hands and knees, exhausted from the strenuous ordeal.

"Go help your friend," Sophia ordered Oliver.

"Yes, ma'am."

Oliver bowed, then trotted over to fish Adrian from the beach's shore; Sophia turned with a beaming smile to Rosann, still holding her arm.

"Soft to touch, isn't it? I lotion it with scented baby oil after I shower and cocoa butter at night, but it's crazy how it doesn't feel like a dry elephant or rhino skin."

Rosann finally pried her shaking hand from Sophia's forearm.

"We lost the second we got out the gate."

"Don't beat yourself up; it was a decent tactic. The problem was you used it on the wrong person. Your brother also talks too much."

Rosann turned to watch as Oliver pulled a drenched Adrian to his feet.

Rogers casually walked over, glancing at Oliver and a disheveled Adrian with a smirk and a head shake. His gaze then fell on Rosann, who lowered her head and quickly fell in line behind him.

"Hell of an arm you got there, Ms. Dennison." Rogers acknowledged while dusting himself off.

"Hope I didn't hurt you too badly," Sophia said while blushing.

"Think I got sand in places I don't want," Rogers sighed, "but other than that, I'm as right as rain."

"Well, I really appreciate the unexpected talk and the workout, Sergeant, but my answer is going to have to remain no. You and your team are more than welcome to stay for lunch."

"No, I think we've outstayed our welcome," Rogers said.

He took a minute looking around, absorbing all he saw, breathing in the fresh ocean air.

"You got a really nice set up here, Ms. Dennison. It's nice to know that these people you've taken in have someone like you to look out for them. If I didn't know any better, I'd say what you're doing here is almost god-like. You know, deciding who gets to live in paradise and who gets to rot in hell."

Sophia's face switched to an unpleasant look, read by Rogers that she did not appreciate his comment and had officially worn out his welcome.

"Anyway, thank you for considering my offer."

He turned away but stopped snapping his finger, remembering something else.

"Sorry, really sorry. Could you indulge me by answering just one question?"

Sophia's eye twitched, not caring for the apparent game Rogers was playing as he stood within punching distance of her.

"I was just dying to know, the day you decided to play chicken with that nuke, and basically turn our world into one nightmarish neverending Saturday morning friggin cartoon… did you…"

"No," Sophia answered with a slow headshake.

She read into his eyes why he came to her island to see her.

"I did not know all of this would happen."

Rogers nodded, knowing she was not lying.

"If you knew?" Rogers asked, looking out into the blue ocean.

"I would have definitely done it differently," Sophia answered, lowering her head.

"Well, at least you answer when I talk to you," Rogers gratefully said with a nod. "Thank you for your time. Sorry for disturbing you and starting a battle on your beach."

Rogers about-faced, walking off as Sophia stood there watching him leave. She left out a sad huff, placing her hands on her hips.

"Alright, children," Rogers barked, clapping his hands. "Tuck your tails in between your legs, and let's move out! Come on! We got 'superhero' shit to do! Move! Move!"

With wounded pride, his team, minus Erica, followed him back to the Tornado, dreading what was in store for them when they got back to the Ranch.

~~~~~~~~~~~~~~~~~~~~~~~~~~~~~~~~~

The flight home was dead silent and uncomfortable. No music played while the trio looked everywhere but at each other and Rogers's direction. The Sergeant sat in his chair with his beanie over his face. They did not know if he was actually sleeping or didn't want to look at the sight of them. The second the Tornado landed and was secured in the docking bay, the trio exited and lined up without being ordered to do so. They knew they were responsible for the storm coming and prepared in advance to accept the consequences of their actions.

Rogers strolled down the steps of the aircraft, followed by Erica. She chose to sit on the steps of the plane and watch him get Medieval from afar, seeing as how she had nothing to do with the harebrained scheme that she knew would epically fail in the first place. Rogers, heading to his room, looked as if he did not notice them. He then stopped in his tracks and turned in their direction.

"You're all waiting for me?" Rogers asked, bewildered.

The trio nervously looked at each other, then back at him, unsure how to answer, as he casually strolled over to them.

"I'm just a bit curious because from what I witnessed on that beach today, you three are apparently running this outfit. So why are you standing here waiting for me to talk to any of you?"

Adrian stepped up to take the heat.
~~~~~~~~~~~~~~~~~~~~~~~~~~~~~~~~~

"Sir, what happened was on me. I was the one…"

"I know what you did, Esposito. You know who else knew what you were up to before you put your dumbass plan into motion? The woman you tried to take down today. She could see you a mile away, flipping that slit on your face, and understood what you were saying."

Adrian lowered his head in defeat. His accomplices did the same, throwing in a headshake to express how much they knew his plan was terrible.

"What part of **'recon'** did you mental midgets not get?!" Rogers's voice boomed. "Am I at fault for not realizing that in the age of stupid war movies and video games, you three knuckle-dragging Neanderthals can't tell the difference between recon, short for reconnaissance, which is defined as an information-gathering mission, as opposed to a combat mission, which you each failed miserably to pull off today! You three could barely work together to take on a couple of life-sized Barbie dolls; what made you think you had what it took to take her on?!"

Erica scoffed, shaking her head, catching Rogers's attention.

"Dr. Champion, why aren't you standing over here with everyone else?"

A wide-eyed Erica looked around, thinking he was joking.

"Who me?"

Rogers turned, burning a hole through her.

"I don't see anyone else sitting their narrow ass on the steps of that goddamn plane."

"Whoa," Lady Tech snapped while coiling back, "what did I do?"

"Exactly," Rogers shouted at her, "what didn't you do? Get your ass up and fall in, now!"

Erica slowly got up, walking over. The look on her face asked Rogers what he was doing as she fell in, standing next to Oliver.

"On the flight back, I've been wrestling with what pissed me off more." Rogers began while towering over her. "These three ass clowns failing to follow orders, or you standing around while they got their asses handed to them."

"I told them it was a bad idea! How am I…"

"Sir!" Rogers roared at her, "you are to address me as sir!"

"Miss," Maxine interrupted, "Are you alright?"

Rogers turned to see Maxine, Jennifer, and Angie walking up with their eyes glowing extra bright, apparently locked on him.

"Your heart rate is elevated to the point of distress," Maxine indicated.

"I'm fine, Maxine."

Her face and mannerisms told a different tale. Erica felt small and embarrassed, while Rogers showed no compassion or letting up.

"You think because you make all these cool things and have your little degrees, you're so smart," Rogers scoffed, "but you're not. You're just book smart and world dumb, and that's because you're still a baby. You also showed me you don't know what it is to be a part of this team. Being a part of this team means standing by each other's side, possibly to the end, even if they make dumb decisions. Not standing around playing Candy Crush while your team gets a mudhole stomped into them. It's the only sliver of respect I have for dumb, dumber, and dumbass!"

"Uh… is that from me down or…?" Adrian inquired with his hand raised.

"You're **two seconds** away from getting shot in the face, dumbass!" Rogers growled.

Rogers's hand hovered on his sidearm within its holster to show he was dead serious.

"Sir, yes, sir!" Adrian yelled while straightening up.

Rogers gave her a face of complete disappointment. It hurt Erica more than his words.

"I expected better from you. Much better."

He backed up to address them all.

"I'm tired and can't stand to look at any of you. Make it your mission to stay out of my sight till tomorrow morning. Is that clear?"

"Sir, yes, sir!" the trio howled.

Erica did not answer as she looked down to hide her, forming tears while he turned away in disgust.

"Dismissed."

Rogers left them behind, each reduced to a microscopic state. Erica stormed off without a word, flocked by the android sisters. Oliver fell against the side of the Tornado, staring off into space, while Rosann turned to her brother with a look that said she wished she had a bat to bash his skull in with.

"I can feel your look, Rose," Adrian snapped. "You ain't got to tell me how I badly screwed up again."

He stormed off, leaving just her and Oliver alone in the hangar.

CHAPTER 9

A half-hour after Rogers's brutal verbal abuse, Adrian and Oliver stood at the door of Lady Tech's R&D lab. Her "do not disturb" red light lit up on the commlink. Adrian huffed as he pressed the notification button, letting her know they were standing outside her lab.

"Ms. has informed me that she does not want to be disturbed," Maxine spoke on her behalf from the audio speaker above the door.

"Maxine, tell her if she doesn't open up, I'll do my metal version of Sheldon," Adrian warned.

"I've seen him do it," Oliver said. "It's really annoying."

Instantly the door slid open, the sound of DMX's "X Gonna Give It to Ya" spilled out of the lab, assaulting them. They walked in, not knowing what was more humorous, someone of Erica's intellect listening to something so harsh, or Jennifer and Angie rhythmically nodding to the song as they worked along with Maxine at different tables assisting her in her projects.

She lowered the music before turning to glare at them.

"What do you two want?" Erica snapped.

"We were wondering if you cared to join us for some Mario Kart 8," Adrian inquired with a grin.

"We also intend to raid the fridge for some smores and ice cream," Oliver added.

"As you can see, I'm kind of busy here," Erica answered with a sardonic smile.

"No, you're not." Adrian huffed. "You're working because you're pissed; I have first-hand knowledge of doing that back home when it came to my GTO. A lot of love and anger when into that car."

He took an apologetic step to her with his head down.

"Look, what happened on that island was my fault. It was all on me. I didn't follow orders, I came up with that crazy-ass plan that could have gotten us killed if things were different, and I got you yelled at today. My bad."

Erica's eyes fell to the ground.

"Apology accepted. But, it's not your fault that our leader is an ass."

"Yeah, he is an ass."

Adrian quickly looked around to make sure they were truly alone.

"But at the end of the day, he means well; he reminds me of my old man back home. Old school guys like him will always be as hard as stone, and they have a weird way of showing they care, but they do."

"So, why do you find ways to annoy him?" Erica curiously asked.

"Because that's just me," Adrian snorted. "I'm always testing boundaries. He's also not right about everything. Just most things. So come on, let's go drive some video game go-karts on a sugar rush."

"I get Princess Peach," Erica muttered.

"Done." Adrian agreed while throwing up his hands.

Angie walked overcrossing into Adrian's personal space.

"Can I come too, baby?"

"Don't call me, baby!"

Adrian turned, scowling at Erica.

"You said you fixed her!"

"I did," Erica squeaked with an innocent shrug.

"You're the only one who can fix me, lover," Angie whispered with a sensual smile.

Oliver shook his head, fighting not to laugh as Angie pinned Adrian up against one of the lab workstations nuzzling up to him while using one of her fingers to trace a circle on his chest.

"Please, let me come with you. , Please… please…"

"Alright!" Adrian yelled. "But you got to behave yourself! No monkey business, and no invading my personal space! Like right now!"

"I'll behave," Angie promised while blowing an air kiss at him. "For now."

She eased up a bit, allowing him to barely slide from between her and the workstation. Adrian turned to Erica, desperately trying to hide her amusement under an innocent face.

"Fix her," he whispered.

This gave Angie the opening to cup his rear, making him jump. He turned, shooting her his trademark dirty look.

"We're not in the lounge area yet," she coyly reminded him.

Adrian stormed off with her sashaying behind him. Jennifer, with a sneer, shook her head, following behind her playful sister.

"They're going to have some ugly ass kids."

Oliver walked up, standing next to Erica, as they watched the comedy unfold.

"You're not going to fix her, are you?" he asked.

"Nope," Erica answered with a cackle, "he must suffa!"

They both broke into laughter as they exited her lab, followed by Maxine heading to the lounge area.

~~~~~~~~~~~~~~~~~~~~~~~~~~~~~~~~

As the trio, with androids in tow, ventured to find entertainment to blow away the gray cloud of the incident and aftermath of visiting Sophia's island, Rosann saw herself quietly walking into the firing range. She found Rogers discharging armor-piercing rounds from his modified M-45, tearing holes through steel structure targets. Two-handed was how he held it, just as he learned in the Corp, and how he taught them to do it.

Because of his strength, Rogers did not need two hands, but the old soldier stood for doing things the right way. Rosann stood at nervous attention, waiting for him to notice that she was in the room; then she glanced at three bottles of Jack Daniels among an M4 Carbine, an M16, and an M249 LMG. As he fired off his final round, he picked up a bottle and knocked it back as if it was water. He downed three-quarters of the Jack before pulling it from his lips.

"Use to be a time when five glasses of this would knock me on my ass," Rogers said while gazing at the bottle. "Now, all it does is give me bad breath and a gallon of piss. Damn regenerative healing."

Rogers placed the bottle back on the table mixed with weapons, grabbing a clip to reload.

"You gonna just stand there gawking at me," Abe asked, "or you gonna shoot something? Here..."

Rogers grabbed the M4 Carbine tossing it to her; Rosann caught it, checking for a loaded round as taught. She relocked and loaded, taking up a position in the firing booth next to him. She aimed and breathed, letting the Carbine rip as it tore through the steel target in front of her. The modified version still had a kick due to the powerful ammo it was loaded with. Rogers, now with M16 in hand, unleashed hell on a new standing steel target. Although she was hitting the target, Rogers's accuracy was far more superior to hers.

Rosann touched one of the bone fragments on her armband, transforming into a humanoid ring-tailed lemur, which allowed her the strength to hold the gun without it kicking back, as well as use her keen eyesight to hit the target more accurately. She smiled at her accomplishment but then turned to the feeling of eyes on her. Rogers looked at her with a blank expression that displayed neither anger nor disappointment.

"Cheater."
~~~~~~~~~~~~~~~~~~~~~~~~~~~~~~~~

She quickly transformed back into her human form.

"Sir, I just took what you taught me and used my abilities to improve upon it… sir."

Rogers did not bother to answer as he handed her a couple of more clips. She laid the cartridges down on her table, took one up, and reloaded her rifle. She lifted it to retake aim but ended up lowering it, turning her gaze to the Sergeant who let off a couple of more rounds.

"Sir, permission to speak freely, sir," Rosann nervously requested.

"Not if you going to turn back into a rodent Esposito," Abe answered.

She nodded, looking down at the floor.

"What's on that brainpan of yours?"

"Why are you here?" Rosann bluntly asked.

"I thought I told you," Rogers answered with a leery grin, "to try and turn you all into good little super soldiers for the US of A… make sure you at least don't get killed on your first two missions… don't ask me to see past that."

"I know we look like a bunch of screwups, but we're here trying to learn to take these abilities given to us and make some kind of difference in this world," Rosann pressed. "I seem to remember when I signed up for this that we're supposed to be a team. But it's like, yeah, you're training us, but you don't believe in us. You don't believe in this… so again, I ask… why are you here?"

Rogers turned, looking her in the eyes. It was not a straightforward look, more dismissive as he put down the M16 and began to reload the M-45.

"I was supposed to be retired… from all of this, on a porch watching the days go by, counting the expected grandkids … with my wife. The virus made sure that would never happen."

Rosann took a relaxed stance holding the rifle in her hand as she gave Rogers a listening ear.

"While you were still a tadpole in your pop's sack, I was on the other side of the world watching a landmine blow two good kids to shit. The rest of the blast filled me up with shrapnel and took the vision out of my left eye. Military career over, I came home as a typical vet with a purple heart to wipe my ass with, along with what little pension and disability Uncle Sam gave me for giving up my eye.

Took a job in construction to pay the bills, paid to go back to school and get a better paying job… as a teacher," he scoffed, "then an old buddy of mine talked me into a wrestling gig… being that it was all staged didn't matter too much that my eye was bad. Paid good money and, after 9/11, people would eat up the old soldier bit. I said, what the hell… quick fast dough… a couple of matches… nice stress reliever between working on houses for shit pay, or killing someone's kid over a spitball… who the hell knew it would take off like it did. Next thing I knew, I got the BWI calling me in for an audition, and a month later, I'm headlining."

Rogers motioned as if he was there once again.

"Once again, I was on the road, traveling from state to state and country to country, only, this time, I got sixty to seventy thousand people screaming my name or chanting "USA… USA… When I stepped onto that rampway and walked down to that ring, I was as high as a kite."

Rogers grounded his teeth while picking up the liquor bottle, giving it a look over as he continued his story.

"And night after night between all the promoting, endorsements, talk show interviews, and photoshoots; I went out and punished what was left of my body that landmine didn't take all for that drug. Then, after a couple of days on the road, I'd go home to my loving wife, who met me at the door with a hug and a kiss. She'd draw me a hot bath in our fully paid eight-point-five hundred thousand dollar house that she stayed alone in for most of the time. Pour me a drink and then talk to me about how she spent her days… till I fell asleep, which would be for a day and a half till I had to get back on the road and do it all over again… her name was Katherine."

A halfhearted smirk appeared on Rogers's lips at the mention of his wife's name.

"Sometimes I'd make holidays and birthdays… sometimes I wouldn't… she never complained… ever… but I never missed a Christmas… ever… and every Christmas I'd look at her and say, 'Baby this is it… I'm done.' And then she would look at me with a smile and say, 'You're so full of shit… you know you're not done yet.' And she was right… after about four years, it became a running joke. Finally, when the booze and painkillers couldn't keep me going… when it took five more minutes to get to my feet when it should have taken three.

On the seventh Christmas after coming home from the road… I looked at my wife and said, 'Baby… I'm done,' to which she replied, 'You're so full of shit… you know you're not done yet.' But this time… I held her hands, looked her dead in the eyes, and said, 'No baby… I am… done.' She just burst into tears… was like watching her again when I came back from Kuwait."

Rogers let out a heavy sigh.

"Legacy 6, the grandest Pay-Per-View of the BWI, was supposed to be my last match. Two months before that, the sky lit up on fire, and everyone thought it was the end of the world. But even with the possibility of doomsday, the show went on. As the weeks counted down, I didn't realize I needed fewer painkillers… that I was getting stronger, moving faster, going longer without tiring. Then it happened in the middle of my match at Legacy… it wasn't almost breaking a kid in half after I launched him into a nearby turnbuckle or putting a severe dent in a ring post… it was when I could finally see clearly out of my dead left eye… I had never been more terrified in my entire life until then."

Rosann flinched as Rogers let out a laugh.

"I don't know how I held it together. It was the fastest match I ever jobbed. Couldn't have gotten the hell out of there fast enough. All I wanted to do was go home. It was like a new lease on life. I went back to my wife, deterioration-free of pain, booze, and pills. The night I got home, we stayed in bed for two days and had to order a new one the next morning."

Rosann could not help but crack a smile. Rogers's stone exterior broke as well, remembering better days.

"A month after that, Katherine was diagnosed with the Judgment Virus. The same thing that was healing and strengthening this once broken down body that I willfully punished and abused till there was nothing left was killing and destroying my wife, who barely took a drink in her life and never smoked."

Rogers's stone-cold look reformed as he laid down the M4 next to the other guns on the table and leaned against the firing range divider taking a swig from the bottle of Jack in his grip.

"She held on for six long months after four, she asked me to take her home. We spent every day together, talking and laughing like we were supposed to. In her last two weeks, I took her up to our cabin that she loved so much. One day she asked to go out on the river in the canoe I made. She died falling asleep in my arms. I must have just sat there for hours, just talking and singing to her."

Rosann somberly lowered her head; Rogers did not shed a tear. It was clear whatever tears the old hardened Marine had shed were gone years ago.

"So to answer your question, when you're a bitter broken down old man… who's lost pretty much everyone and everything he gave a damn about… and now cannot just roll over and die; there ain't too many options for a son of a bitch in my situation."

Rogers displayed a toothy grin before taking another swig from the bottle of Jack. Rosann lifted her head to look at him. A part of her regretted asking her question, unprepared for the painful answer she'd received. The other part of her was glad she got a glimpse into his world. His face read that he did not care what she thought of his story, but Rosann's heart told her that he needed someone to unload the pain he still carried. She was glad to be that person.

"Rogers."

Lady Tech's voice came over the commlink.

"You and Rosann need to get up to central command like now… we've got a huge problem."

"On our way."

Rogers turned to Rosann.

"Guess it's time to prove to me you can make a difference."

~ ~

Five minutes later, the entire team was in central command facing Lady Tech; an uneasy tension filled the room like a chilling breeze. Lady Tech's big emergency eclipsed it for now.

"Midtown Manhattan is under attack!"

Erica pulled up a holographic image.

"Five minutes ago, Midtown Manhattan fell under attack to an occult terrorist cell known as the Zombie Nation."

"Wasn't that a house song way back?" Adrian asked.

"The Zombie Nation is comprised of five EVOs who have managed to keep under the radar for quite some time. They are wanted in connection with several kidnapping and murder charges throughout the US and Europe, among other things," Erica relayed. "They've uploaded several videos onto the web performing actual satanic ritual sacrifices on live people which, thanks to me, have been intercepted before anyone can actually see them. They've evened mailed some to television stations hoping they'll air them. They believe their powers are gifts from Satan himself so that they can usher in his rule on Earth… they are also cannibals."

"That's just messed up," Oliver sneered.

"We've been trying to block their sick messages in hopes of not alarming the public and catching these filthy bastards, but it looks like they've gotten frustrated and decided to do something drastic," Erica continued. "Causalities are in the double digits and growing. Captain Omega is reported to be on the scene along with two other heroes… Seeker and Lady Electrify."

"Great," Adrian muttered, "with those three, the fight will probably be over before…"

"Miss, Lady Electrify has been killed in action," Maxine reported. "Cause of death is impalement and severe blunt force trauma."

Rosann's eyes widened as she took a stunning step back.

"Oh my god."

"Suit up, people. Get locked, loaded, and ready to fly in four minutes," Rogers ordered. "Anyone not ready by then gets left behind."

CHAPTER 10

Five minutes later, the Tornado was again in the air, headed for Manhattan, moving at Mach 8. They would be in the combat zone in less than eight minutes. Rosann stared at the ground as her brother sat next to her, clutching the crucifix chain given to him by his mother for his sixteenth birthday. Sitting on the opposite side of Rosann, Oliver also stared at the floor. Every minute, he fidgeted with either the bracers on his arms or the straps on his boots.

Rogers sat there looking at each one with his modified M249 LMG rifle in his lap. In his eyes, these were just more children marching once again to hell itself, a nightmare he had never faced before. Rogers did not like it one bit. If he was not ready for this, they definitely were not prepared for this.

"Miss, reports indicated EVO known as Seeker has been killed in action," Maxine reported. "Cause of death is decapitation."

"Jesus…" Rosann uttered, cupping her mouth.

"Erica! What's our ETA?!" Rogers yelled.

"We just entered New York State," she barked back, "we'll be there in two minutes at this speed! Patching in Channel 11 News. They've got a reporter crazy enough to be on the scene!"

The sound of battle and the screams of one lone reporter telling the tale of the designated war zone within Times Square forced everyone to sit up within the Tornado.

"I report, Seeker has been killed," the reporter screamed. "The well-known superhero speedster of New York overwhelmed by a two on one attack has been decapitated! It has now become a three-on-one fight against Captain Omega and three out of the five members of this Zombie Nation! We have bodies of innocent men, women, and children littering the streets of Times Square! This is just too overwhelming, and Captain Omega is fighting like a madman to turn the tide!"

"Going to stealth mode folks," Lady Tech yelled, "hang on!"

"Oh, Jesus Christ," the reporter screamed over the audio speakers, "Captain Omega has just been killed!"

Dead silence filled the Tornado cabin as Hard-On, Blitz, and a shocked and teary-eyed Rosann looked at each other, then back at a stone-faced Rogers.

"I can't believe it," the reporter cried, "the Captain looked like he was going to turn the tide of the battle, and then he looked like he was blinded out of nowhere. Then the monster of a man who looks like an unholy Viking just started hacking away at him with that huge battle-ax of his… till he cut his head off… our greatest hero is gone, folks… he's gone… they're literally desecrating his body in front of us… it's horrific beyond imagination…"

"There's a goddamn Promethean down there," Lady Tech muttered with her head down.

"Erica, keep us up, and open the bay doors," Abe ordered.

"You gonna parachute into…?" she began to ask.

"Just open the damn door, and keep us up!" Rogers yelled, losing his patience.

Rogers quickly checked his M249 LMG, heading for the rear doors now opening; he stopped and turned, feeling three presences standing behind him. He turned to see Hard-On already in metal form, along with Blitz and Rosann, ready to go.

"Where the hell do you think you three are going?"

"Jumping out of a perfectly good airplane with you, sir," Hard-On answered.

"Cut the shit, Esposito," Rogers ordered, "wait till the ship lands then…"

"Excuse me, sir, but you can screw yourself," Adrian said.

"What did…?" Rogers snarled.

"We ain't got time to discuss this!" Adrian yelled back. "People are dying down there, so when you jump out of this plane… we're going to be following you… as a team!"

"Whether you like it or not," Rosann chimed in.

"We're ready," Blitz confirmed with a nod, "sir."

Abe Rogers narrowed his eyes as he looked at each of them. He turned, pulling his beanie down tight over his head.

"Keep your formation tight. Spread out… pick a target… go hard… and work together."

"You all be careful when you get down there! My readings tell me there's a class 10 Titan, a class 9 Apollo fire type, and a Mercurian also class 9," Lady Tech informed them. "I'm also pretty sure they got a Promethean, and I think he or she is pretty powerful too, so they're going to know you're coming the second you exit the Tornado!"

With no more words, Rogers and the team dived out of the back of the Tornado, rocketing into a war-torn Times Square like SCUD missiles.

~ ~

Below, the world was in hell, as a beast of a man in both size and demeanor held high the head of the fallen Captain Omega. Conversely, he had a massive double-bladed curved battle ax the size of an average man. His other weapon was a gigantic, sinister-looking broadsword that appeared to be a New York taxi's length. It stood standing as it impaled the headless corpse of Captain Omega and the concrete street of Times Square that it rested on.

"Where are your heroes now, piglets? Huh?!" the monster howled. "Where is your nameless god to save you?! Where are they piglets?! Tell them to come so that the Draugr can kill and fuck them like I did this worthless cunt!"

He was four times the size of four powerlifters combined and appeared as if he could block out the sun with his nearly nine-foot frame. He wore black pants, leather and gold plated bracers, and a belt with a fur skirt reminiscent of a Viking or barbarian. He wore heavy, dark black armor with detailed demonic skull etchings and orange flame accents over his boots, thighs, bracers, and shoulders. Armor that he appeared not to need after killing one of the most well-known and powerful EVOs on the planet.

Those people still alive, either injured or too terrified to move, watched as the monster tilted his head back, allowing the blood from the Captain's decapitated head to pour out into his mouth as if he were drinking wine. His long, brown, frayed beard matched the locks on his skull, covered by a demonic helmet resembling a skull. It mirrored the rest of the demonic Viking armor he wore. His mouth and beard were soaked in blood as he looked around with a wide-eyed, baseless, and inhuman expression, searching for more prey.

Above him hovered an Asian woman via a pinnacle of flames. Her entire face was tattooed with the visage of a demon, while large, colorful demonic tattoos adorned different parts of her body. She wore a long, scantily black leather dress with two long thigh-high slits. Her bone-straight black hair covered half her face on the right side. Though she was not as animalistic as the Draugr, she seemed also void of all emotion, compassion, or sympathy.

"All things must burn," she softly muttered in Mandarin. "All things must burn… all things must burn."

No scene was more gruesome and disturbing than the man in the middle of the street holding two long, thick, machete-like blades drenched in the blood of Lady Electrify. Her body was unrecognizable due to him hacking her to pieces during and after her death at superhuman speed. His entire face was also tattooed; the artwork appeared as if his face was peeled off by a blade. The gray hood of his long-sleeved top shrouded the rest of his head. Two huge tan leather belts covering most of his abdomen and matching suspenders held the top and matching gray pants he wore together. He cackled and swayed as he gazed upon Lady Electrify's savagely defiled body with pride as if he'd created a piece of art.

Standing in the middle of the chaos on top of the abandoned and destroyed police outpost was their leader. His pale, stark white skin and long black hair made him appear as if he stepped out of the 17th Century, while his faintly glowing purple and black eyes told of a dark power he held within him. His red and black ensemble made him look like a priest from an S&M club.

In his hand, he had a chain attached to the collar of a porcelain white bald-headed woman with a wild, insane visage on her face clinging tightly to his right leg. Headphones covered her ears as she clutched the tiny black iPod player for dear life. Her black top, shorts, and a long Goth trench coat with the front entirely gone gave her the look of a Valley Girl from hell.

To the man's left stood a big female bruiser with a Mohawk. She wore a beefy pink-chained bikini over a fishnet bodysuit, tight black leather shorts, and black steel-plated boots. Satanic and Neo-Nazi tattoos covered her left cheek, breast, abdomen, right bicep, and back. She calmly wiped clean the huge, jagged-edged knife she wielded with what seemed to be a bloodied shirt belonging to a child.

Sitting in front of her was a little person in a brown, ratty-looking monk's cloak drinking blood from the severed head of a male victim with a Slurpee straw... due to the massive size of the hood, one could not see their gender.

Their pale-skinned leader clapped his hands, getting their attention.

"All right, children, let us not lose focus as to why we are here. A Seal must be broken, and our father requires much more blood than this to do so."

With a calm, business-like demeanor, he first turned to the monstrous Viking to instruct him.

"Draugr, be so kind as to start tearing down buildings," he requested, "there are plenty of warm bodies hiding within them. Nachzehrer do help him."

The female powerhouse with a Mohawk nodded with a smile as she finished off her blade cleaning with a quick spit shine.

"Ghoul," he addressed the man with the machetes, "stop playing with your toy and start butchering everyone still around. Be sure, to begin with, those ridiculous individuals in Sesame Street and superhero costumes, not to mention the idiots dressed like the Statue of Liberty."

Teeth shined underneath the man's hood as he took a couple of swipes, flinging excess blood from his blades.

"Jiang Shi," he beckoned to the flame-wielding Asian woman, "help him by turning the remainder to ash; we'll start a path from here to Wall Street."

Screams and cries erupted from those too terrified to move as the Draugr laughed and howled while pulling his body-cleaving sword from the corpse of Captain Omega to begin the slaughter again.

Before the carnage could begin anew, the cloaked little monk stopped drinking from the head, looking upward.

"Revenant, someone is coming."

"Coming?" Revenant scoffed. "More heroes, Anchimayen? From where?"

Anchimayen pointed.

"Look up."

Revenant and Nachzehrer looked up to the sound of bombs dropping. Bombs with arms, legs, and rage in their eyes. There were no words, cool catchphrases, or battle cries as they descended into Times Square like avenging angels; whatever needed to be said was written all over their faces.

"You sick animals... we're coming to kill you."

The slow-witted Draugr finally looked up to see what got the attention of his teammates.

"Who dares?"

His words were broken as a freefalling Rogers without a parachute to slow him down slammed right into the Draugr at 614 miles per hour, creating a massive crater on impact, now covered by smoke and flying concrete. The next thing heard was the deafening sound of Rogers's M249 LMG being unloaded into the Draugr's helmet-covered face. The Ghoul sped out of the way as Hard-On created his own crater, slamming into the ground; Rosann forced him to move again as she touched a bone on her armband midair, changing into a humanoid Cheetah. She grabbed a lamp post to slow her falling momentum and to launch herself at him, roaring and slashing. The siblings wore pure rage on their faces as they readied themselves to take on the machete-wielding speed sadist.

"You will all burn," Jiang Shi sneered as she produced large flames from her hands.

Blitz hovered down behind her, engulfed in his greenish-white plasma electrical form.

"The only thing frying tonight is you, witch."

Before Jiang Shi could spin around for an attack, he unleashed a devastating lightning strike channeled through his hands; she barely conjured up a shield of flames, which did nothing more than weaken what would have been a fatal direct hit. She screamed as the current passed through her body, sending her reeling. She quickly recovered, turning her shield into a fiery blast, forcing Blitz to cover up as his plasma form protected him from the intense flames she unleashed, an apparent standoff as both glared at each other.

"Your power cannot burn me," Jiang-Shi snickered, "boy…"

"I don't have to burn you to kill you," Blitz returned, "you foul evil woman."

He roared as he unleashed another electrical charge that she barely evaded. The two began a fire versus lightning aerial battle above the streets of Times Square.

"Who da fuck are you two suppose ta be tin man?" Ghoul spat.

Hard-On responded with action as he pulled out his sidearm and unloaded on Ghoul, forcing him to dodge. Rosann sprinted, roaring and charging Ghoul, unnerving the blade-wielding murderer. He began to run as Hard-On turned on his laser scope, trying to get a bead on him.

"Nachzehrer," Revenant sighed, "they're not playing fair with Ghoul."

Nachzehrer licked her lips, smiling as she leaped off the outpost into the air. Hard-On, catching her coming at him from the corner of his eye, spun around, firing shots at her. Each round of his Desert Walter 01 delivered a velocity superior to a rail gun and could easily take down a Merkava Mark 4. He put two in her gut and one in her chest as she descended from her descent with her knife, held high. Her Titan genetics quickly healed her wounds, while her insanity kept a sickening grin on her face.

Hard-On braced for impact with his forearm up to block the attack as she crashed down on him in an attempt to drive her knife into his metallic skull. The hit sent them into a sizable crater, sending debris flying everywhere. Hard-On glared at Nachzehrer with a disgusted look as she grinned at him, running her blade across his forearm.

"I shall have fun masturbating with your cock tonight," Nachzehrer drooled.

"Wait, how are you?" Adrian asked before sneering as he comprehended what she meant. "Oh, you sick bitch."

Hard-On pulled his sidearm to his hip, still free to use his right hand; with his thumb, he flipped it to automatic mode and unleashed a volley of shots into her gut, forcing her to roll off him and cover up. Discharging his last round, he went to reload when a now livid Nachzehrer lunged, slamming into him and knocking the gun out of his hand. Hard-On, remembering his training, rolled through, flipping her over. He moved on top of her, going ballistic as he rained down thunderous lefts, rights, hammer fists, and forearm shots. On the other side of the war zone, Rosann sized Ghoul up, moving closer to him like an actual cheetah on the hunt with her fangs exposed, preparing to pounce while the Ghoul getting his nerve back, grinned while he wagged his tongue at her, pointing his blood-soaked blades at her with a sadistic gleam in his eyes.

"I'm gonna enjoy wearing your skin up and down 42nd street, like a pimp."

Rosann responded with a booming roar as she charged and leaped, cutting the distance between them, putting Ghoul on the defense again, realizing that she had some speed to her. He let his blades fly, looking to slice her in half; Rosann's feline instinct helped her evade strikes that cut the wind itself.

Back in the crater, the gunfire ended due to Rogers needing to reload; this gave a very ventilated, tremendously pissed off Draugr a chance he needed to grab his battle-ax and swing for the hills knocking Abe's M249 LMG out of his hand. Rogers dived out of the path of the second ax swing going for his sidearm and unloaded on the murderous Titan again; only Draugr used his massive left armored forearm as a shield, rolling to his feet.

Back out of the crater, as Hard-On hammered away at Nachzehrer, all he could hear was laughter bellowing from her as his metallic hands pounded her face into next week. With one eye the size of a grapefruit and her face painted in blood, she continued to laugh at him; he paused in disbelief at how much she was enjoying it.

"Are you… just going to keep… giving me foreplay," Nachzehrer spat out, "or are you going to fuck me?!"

Before a disgusted Hard-On could respond, she hacked a thick wad of blood in his face, blinding him.

"Dammit," he cursed.

Hard-On violated the code drilled into him by Rogers. "Unless they're in a coma or no pulse… you never let up." Nachzehrer's disgusting stunt allowed her to use her hips to buck him off her, reversing the position. On instinct, as she tried to reach for his throat, Hard-On instantly turned it into a triangle choke, but all he heard was that insane laughter again.

"If you wanted me to suck you off, boy," Nachzehrer gurgled, choking, "all you had to do… was ask!"

Through blood-blurred vision, Hard-On could see that the damage he had done to the female Titan's face had already healed as she dug her feet in, locked her arms, and hoisted him high.

"Oh shit!" Adrian yelled.

He kept the lock on, increasing the tightness, hoping to bring her down into a brain-dead state or snap her neck. Nachzehrer continued to gurgle and giggle through the hold as she hoisted him higher and drove him again into the street, creating another crater.

"What's that?! You like that?!" Nachzehrer screamed. "You want more?! Okay!"

Nachzehrer roared as she snapped, hoisting him high again, coiling her legs like a spring; she leaped into the air as if flying off with him. The force of her leap sent them several stories up before beginning a downward descent back down into Times Square. Hard-On rifled away at Nachzehrer, busting her open again, fighting to get free as she laughed at him, refusing to let go. Those still brave enough to be in the Square or too terrified to move ran for their lives as a freefalling powerbomb sent both Nachzehrer and Hard-On through the concrete. Debris flew everywhere as the two combatants disappeared into the depths and darkness of Manhattan.

High above, the Manhattan sky was ablaze with fire and lightning as Blitz and "fire witch" battled, jockeying for position in an attempt to bring one another down. Jiang Shi screamed a war cry as she unleashed a blast of metal-melting flames at him, which he easily evaded. He returned with an onslaught of electricity, which she quickly dodged, remembering that she was immune from the burn but not the jolt of his deadly lightning attacks.

Humans below ran for sanctuary as "gods" warred over their heads.

"It is only a matter of time before I turn you into ashes!" Jiang Shi screamed, "I'll drink your boiling blood from your charred skull!"

"Not if I take your head off first!" Oliver roared.

He charged Jiang Shi with great speed, remembering he could not go full power due to the people and buildings around him. She nervously unleashed a full blast of flames to stop him, but he barreled through it and came out on the other side, swinging at full force to take her head off with his fist; she barely ducked the electrically charged punch. The sheer force exploded bricks while melting the building's glass and metal behind her when she evaded the blow.

"You're… you're mad," a shaken Jiang Shi uttered.

"And you're a dead woman, you murderous bitch," Oliver bluntly informed her.

~~~~~~~~~~~~~~~~~~~~~~~~~~~~~~~~~

Back in the crater, Abe, losing his sidearm to an ax-wielding Draugr, now wielded a knife as he ducked and dodged the Draugr's chops and swings to slice the trained Marine in half. It was not the first time Rogers had someone swing a blade at him. Despite his massive size, strength, and berserker rage, the Draugr was not a trained Viking warrior reborn. Rogers proved he was a clumsy oaf who saw too many Conan movies as he found an opening and shot for his legs. Rogers did not need much strength to perform a textbook lift. He tried his best to ensure it hurt as he slammed him onto his back.

On his back again, the Draugr was on the defensive as Rogers began cutting, slashing, and stabbing any body part within the range of his blade. The Draugr's armor, which had the feel of tank metal, was no match against the highly tempered dark metal knife Rogers wielded. Rogers slashed and stabbed, looking for a weak point, but the Draugr's regenerative healing quickly repaired what he cut open. The blood that poured made the brawl slippery and sticky. Draugr roared as he found an opening with his right hand and palmed Rogers's face, looking to crush his skull. It would have worked with a less experienced man. Rogers retaliated by stabbing and pulling down, cutting the tendons in his arm. The Draugr roared in pain and rage as Rogers pulled his face from his mitt, locking in a side armbar in hopes of breaking the big man's arm, making it completely immobile, long enough to figure out how to kill him. It appeared Rogers did not cut deep enough because the stronger Draugr growled as he balled his fist and flexed to prevent his arm from being hyper-extended. He then fought to his feet, lifting Rogers, still attached to his arm like a tiny infant.

~~~~~~~~~~~~~~~~~~~~~~~~~~~~~~~~~

Back up top, Rosann was not faring too well; her heightened senses could barely keep up with the Ghoul's speed and viciousness. He would dodge and evade every lunge, swipe, and pounce she executed, coming back harder and faster.

"Here, puss puss! Puss puss!" he taunted her.

Toying with her; the Ghoul finally went for a blitz attack, coming in at blinding speed and swinging his razor-sharp blades at her. Her leotard bodysuit withstood the glancing blows that could have sliced her open; however, the Ghoul also targeted her exposed legs.

Her current dense animal physiology kept her standing. Rosann tried to go into a feral rage to fight back, but a faster Ghoul drove one of his fourteen-inch machetes into her gut. Rosann's eyes went wide with sheer pain; instinctually, she grabbed Ghoul's right arm and slowly transformed into her human form. A now stronger Ghoul grinned as he slowly hoisted a bloodied Rosann high into the air, causing her to sink deeper into the blade. Rosann spat blood into Ghoul's face as she gripped his hand to keep herself from being further impaled.

He licked some of the blood from his face.

"Mmmmm, my favorite BBQ sauces, now... what should I sample... first?"

Out of nowhere, Rosann began to giggle.

"Pray tell, what do you find so funny about me about to slice, eat, and then fuck what's left of your skewered ass, cunt?" Ghoul asked with a screwed-up face.

"Da fact... that I now have.... your abilities, ya dumb cazzo."

Ghoul wore a perplexed look on his face, not understanding her meaning.

"Wha... the...?"

Then, Ghoul noticed that Rosann's initial wounds were healing rapidly as her skin, hair, and eye color changed to match his own. Before he could react, Rosann, now with superhuman speed and strength at her disposal, used the seconds of advantage she had to drive a vicious foot into his face, shattering his nose while launching herself off his blade. The kick sent a completely stunned Ghoul crashing into a parked taxi, caving it in, while Rosann crashed into a heap onto NYC's streets. She spat up more blood while holding her gut, allowing the regenerative healing to repair the damage done. It was not healing fast enough as a now livid Ghoul pulled himself out of the cab, blowing a massive wad of blood from his already-healed nose. He now brandished his blades with murderous intent.

"I'm gonna enjoy cutting your twat out and eating it," Ghoul snarled.

"You couldn't handle my twat, speedy," Rosann sneered.

Ghoul roared, charging to slice her to ribbons only to freeze into place for some unknown reason; a look of fear now appeared on his face as she realized he could not move. Rosann finally reached her feet, giving him a sarcastically innocent yet devious look.

"Sumatta gov?" Rosann mocked his English accent. "Cat gotcha tongue?"

As a huge shadow cast over her and him, Rosann sped out of the way. The last thing she heard was Ghoul screaming as something massive came crashing down on top of him, creating another colossal crater in the street sending debris flying everywhere. Standing tall in the enormous cavity and on top of Ghoul was Lady Tech in her SAM battle-armored mech suit, ready to join the fight with the rest of her team.

"So, what did I miss?" Erica's voice emitted out of her SAM's audio system.

Rosann sped back to the crash zone, standing before her.

"What took you so long?!"

"I'm sorry!" Lady Tech yelled back, "I had a ship to pilot!"

"Hello?! Maxine is your autopilot!"

"Hey! I'm down here! You're alive, and this asshole is a pancake! Get over it!"

Rosann cut her eyes in disgust.

"Where the hell is Hard-On?"

A massive explosion shook the streets again as the ground opened up with a body flying past the two of them. They watched as it landed hard, taking out a cop car. The body belonged to a battered and pissed-off Nachzehrer. She slowly rolled herself off the destroyed police car. Out of the hole crawled an equally disheveled Hard-On, ready to brawl.

"Damn crazy psycho bitch," Hard-On snarled.

"Nice of you to come out of the gutter and join us," Lady Tech greeted him.

"Hell happened to you?" Adrian asked his sister, who was covered in blood.

"Where should I start?" Rosann sighed. "The part where the son of a bitch tried to slice me like an onion or when he stuck me like a shish kabob?"

"Say what?!" Hard-On howled. "Where da fuck is he?!"

"Tech's standing on him," Rosann answered, pointing.

"Oh… oh… god," Ghoul whimpered.

Hard-On spat on him.

"Good for ya, ya piece of…"

"Enough, I'm all right, thanks to that sick bastard's regenerative healing," Rosann reassured her brother.

She turned to Lady Tech.

"How'd you manage to stop him? I thought Mercurians were immune to mental attacks."

"Low-level mental attacks," Erica corrected her, "my suit boosts my abilities to the level of a pure breed; that's how they were able to kill Seeker and Captain Omega."

"But, that would mean they have a kid on their team," Adrian deduced.

"Exactly," Lady Tech said. "The creepy micro monk over there ain't a little person."

"That's some sick shit, man," Hard-On shivered, "how come he's not freezing us?"

"One, I'm mentally tethered to all four of you, allowing me to both block and jam his signal with one of my own," Erica answered, "and two, despite his vast power, he's obviously a noob. He has a basic knowledge of his abilities, but nothing advanced."

A loud booming sound cut the team's conversation short as debris flew out of Rogers' massive crater, and the Draugr waged their war within.

"Oh shit," Adrian snapped.

“We’re standing here, flippin our bicks, and the Sarge is fighting for his life in there!” Rosann yelled. “Wait, where’s Blitz?”

A high-pitched scream followed a fireball hurling from the sky that detonated on top of a white Mercedes-Benz, obliterating it. A badly battered, shaken, smoldering Jiang Shi rolled out of the flames unscathed as Blitz slowly descended from the skies. His outfit displayed burn marks from her flame attacks.

“Now dat’s gangsta,” Adrian acknowledged.

Jiang Shi spat blood at Blitz, shivering.

“You think I fear death, boy, I have a throne waiting for me next to my dark lord! And when I return as one of his concubines… I shall bathe in fire and your blood!”

Oliver charged his hands, causing the air in his vicinity to heat up to unbelievable temperatures. Glass from nearby windows cracked, unable to bear the heat as the concrete around him smoldered. Though Jiang Shi was immune to the heat, there was evidence of fear on her face, knowing what the electrical charge could do to her. Blitz’s plasma form and the electrical charge he emitted changed to a bright blue and white color that shattered glass and blew out any electrical device around him as he prepared to deliver a killing blow.

“That’s new,” Hard-On uttered with a cocked eyebrow.

“And very bad!” Erica yelled. “The fire witch’s cells are like nitroglycerin! At that power level, Blitz could ignite them, and…”

“Blow up all of Times Square,” Rosann finished her sentence. “Oliver, no!”

“Here’s a first-class ticket to hell!” Oliver howled.

Before Blitz could unleash the full force of his power on Jiang Shi, Rosann, using superhuman speed, darted into his path, holding her hands up for him to stop. She screamed and gyrated in pain, unable to withstand the massive surge of heat and electricity he was unleashing. Ghoul’s regenerative healing was the only thing that kept her from death by electrocution. Oliver powered down and grabbed her as she collapsed.

“Rosann!” Oliver yelled frantically, “What the…?!”

“Can’t… kill her…” Rosann stuttered violently, shaking, “like that… you’ll destroy city… if you do…”

Finding an opening, Jiang Shi screamed as she blasted them both with a stream of pure fire. Blitz quickly snatched Rosann, pulling her close while turning his back to Jiang Shi, trying his best to shield her from the flame attack. Hard-On yelled in rage as he rushed to his sister and Oliver's aid, while Lady Tech opened up a volley of concussive-type energy blasts that slammed into Jiang Shi, knocking her off the car and into a nearby wall. Knocked out cold, she hit the floor hard with a violent thud. The flames around Rosann and Oliver died down. Blitz, unscathed, held Rosann tightly as the parts of her he could not protect healed before his eyes. As they locked eyes, the world and all the madness around them disappeared for a second.

"Are you both alright?!" Adrian frantically yelled.

"Yeah," Blitz said.

"I'm fine," Rosann answered with a nod as she stared into Oliver's eyes.

"Seriously?!" Hard-On snapped at both of them.

"What?!" Rosann snapped back.

He was about to lecture them both about the ill timing of finding love on the battlefield when another eruption came from the pit Abe and the Draugr battled in, this time expelling a body. Rogers bounced violently off the concrete, creating smaller craters before coming to a rest. He sprung to his feet in front of his dumbfounded team. He looked like a man who had descended to the seventh level of hell, looking to return.

"Sarge!" Adrian yelled, "you alright?!"

"Don't call me Sarge," Rogers barked. "Someone give me a gun that blows big holes!"

The back of Erica's mech armor opened up and jettisoned a massive black rifle that looked like an amalgamation of a Barrett M82 and an AS50 sniper rifle. Rogers caught it as a savage, grinning Draugr crawled out of the crater for round two.

"M1 Ballistics rifle," Erica explained. "Basically, a compacted railgun with…"

"Don't care," Rogers yelled.

Figuring out where the safety was and how to turn it off, he took aim, pulling the trigger.

Parts of the rifle emitted a bright blue light followed by a whining sound. The shot sounded like it came from a tank; Rogers's strength handled the kickback but did not stop him from sliding back two feet. The round's velocity shattered windows before striking the Draugr dead center, sending him and his sword flying while producing a bullet hole the size of a human skull in his chest. The beast of a man roared as he crashed back into the crater Rogers had created.

"He'll be up in a minute," Abe spat. "If you all are done with your team poses, Hard-On, with me against Hagar, Rosann you got Ms. Neo-Nazi over there, Lady Tech after you've bagged and tagged the slimy sack of shit you're standing on, you and Blitz take care of the rejects on the police outpost."

"Sir, yes, sir!" all four sounded off to Abe's orders.

Adrian quickly returned to his human form, extending his hand to his sister, offering his DNA and power.

"Wonder twins time?" he asked, believing she needed extra strength to take on the sadistic female Titan.

"No, thanks," Rosann said with a grin. "I plan to put this asshole's power to good use."

She darted off, leaving the team. With a roar and Mach 3 speed, Rosann cocked back and delivered a superwoman punch taking Nachzehrer off her feet, knocking her into a nearby Sephora.

Nachzhehrer quickly recovered, exploding from the women's cosmetics store covered in makeup. She snatched up a heavy metal garbage receptacle, hurling it at Rosann, who darted out of the way. It went flying into the Hard Rock Café on the other side of the street. Rosann picked up speed once again, going on the offensive, whizzing in and out, finding openings to strike as the now frustrated female Titan tried to swat her like a fly.

Rogers and Adrian armored up again and went hunting for the Draugr, flanking opposite sides of the crater. This time, the monstrous Viking with a recovered ax in tow did not wait for the hunters to come as he exploded out of the hole with a bellow and a mighty leap, clearing four stories.

"Aw shit," Adrian growled. "It's on!"

The Draugr landed, cratering the streets. The impact launched large chunks of concrete like shrapnel. Roger's let off two rounds from the building leveling rifle. The Draugr quickly spun blocking both headshots with his armor-covered forearm. The armor-piercing projectiles tore through his thick armor like butter, stopping at his tree trunk for a forearm, which just healed in seconds.

The Draugr bellowed as he took another leap, aiming for Hard-On with his ax ready to fly. Adrian's metal form could have tanked the ax blow. He chose a tactical move, rolling out of the way, evading the Draugr's blade that dug into the concrete. Back on his feet, Hard-On leaped into the air, howling as he delivered a powerful haymaker caving in the side of the behemoth's helmet.

The Draugr answered his mighty blow with a forearm backhand, knocking him clear across the street. The strike buried him into the side of a building. With Adrian clear through unconventional means, Rogers let off two more rounds, which the Draugr blocked by folding his arms across his body and tucking his head to tank the shots. Hard-On groaned as he pulled himself out of his imprint in the building, dropping to the ground. He quickly snatched up an abandoned New York Taxicab, hurling it at the Draugr. The behemoth of a man cackled as he sliced it in half as if it were a grapefruit. The vehicle's front half crashed into a parked Mercedes, while the rear half shattered the restaurant's storefront.

Adrian turned to Abe.

"Ideas?!"

"Keep flanking him," Rogers muttered, "the head is the weakness. We either have to cut or blow it off!"

"Easier said than done," Hard-On returned.

"You got anything else better to do?!" Abe asked him.

"Nope," Adrian answered with a shrug.

The Draugr took the offensive, charging like a mindless bull going for Abe. As he shook New York streets with each stomp, Rogers opened fire with three more rounds from his rifle before ducking and rolling for cover as the Draugr howled, taking a broad swing with his ax, hoping to slice him in half. The only thing his weapon cut was the storefront of the building. Abe stood his ground. Before he could wrench his blade from the concrete he embedded it in, Hard-On leaped onto his back and began to rifle his helmeted skull with repeated shots. He was about to rip the helmet off when the Draugr spun around and threw himself back first into the building; he slashed, pancaking him between it.

Adrian held on as the Draugr, who showed great agility for a man so massive, executed a tumble roll to steamroll him into the concrete. Adrian refused to be bucked off until the mountain of a man reached up and ripped him from his back, hurling him into the concrete. Hard-On had seconds to cover up as the Draugr brought a boot down on top of him, driving him further into the street.

Abe drove the monster off his teammate with two well-placed rifle shots to the chest and skull.

Erica finally stepped off a broken Ghoul, palming his upper torso and pulling him out of the crater she created. Her armor's large palm shifted and cracked open, allowing a malleable device to wrap around his upper torso, locking it into place. He began to groan as the device glowed and hummed. Erica released him, letting the device take off with the Ghoul into Manhattan's skies back to the Tornado.

"Nerve Hammer sends a pulse of electric shock straight to his nervous system, causing a seizure and paralysis." Erica referred to the device. "Won't kill him due to his regenerative healing. The same power creates electromagnetic propulsion taking him back up to the Tornado. Maxine will lock him into one of the cyropods till we're done."

Oliver powered up, taking to the air again, hovering.

"Good, now, let's take care of the rest of this damn freak show."

"Anchimayen, my boy," Revenant sighed, "fetch Jiang Shi before that nasty machine decides to take her away from me. I still require her, and while you're at it, come close as well."

Obedient Anchimayen climbed to his feet, standing atop the police outpost. With an extended hand, the cloaked child deployed the power of telekinesis to lift his downed team member, quickly pulling her over to the roof of the outpost they stood upon laying her at Revenant's feet. He then scurried over, standing next to the sinister-looking man.

"Wendigo, my love," Revenant smiled, "time to go play."

Wendigo's eyes grew as wide as a full moon; the second Revenant removed the leash from her collar. She quickly rose to her feet and strolled forward while holding the volume button to her iPod, pumping the sound in her headphones. She stepped off the police outpost roof, causing the whole area to tremble as she hovered midair.

"Miss, detecting a massive energy reading from the woman in front of us," Maxine emitted from the inside of Erica's cockpit, "on a sonic level."

"How massive?" Erica asked.

"1,000 MHz and rising," Maxine indicated.

"Full shields up now!" Lady Tech screamed frantically. "Patch me into everyone! Guys! Run or fly, you've got to get out of the area now!"

"We're kinda busy here getting our ass kicked!" Adrian yelled. "Ooof!!"

Hard-On groaned again as he took a full ax swing to the chest, taking him off his feet and knocking him into a parked car. The impact sent him and the parked car into a nearby storefront. Before the Draugr could advance on a downed Adrian, Rogers stopped him in his tracks with several hammering rounds from his rifle.

"Guys, I'm telling you, you have to leave now!" Lady Tech screamed.

Still using the Ghoul's speed, Rosann quickly sidestepped a charging Nachzehrer. She grabbed and slammed her face-first into a parked car before spinning her around and launching her skull first into a brick wall of a building.

"What's the problem?!" Rosann asked, finally patching in.

"In about five seconds, we're about to witness death by stereo!" Lady Tech frantically responded.

"What, Ms. Cue ball floating over there?!" Rosann scoffed. "I can…!"

"No, you can't, Rosann!" Lady Tech forcefully yelled. "Run! Run like you have never run before! Run!"

Erica miscalculated by two seconds.

Pulsating through the woman's headphones was "Inbred Evil" by the rapper Boondox. Wendigo extended her left hand and opened her mouth, unleashing an attack that emitted throughout the city. Blitz dove into the streets at breakneck speed without hesitation, swooping in and snatching up Rosann, frozen with shock and fear, taking her to the skies with him. Though Oliver was fast enough to evade the initial blast, he could not outmatch the aftershock while holding Rosann. It clipped him in midair, separating both him and her. Blitz spiraled out of control, flying into an office where he smashed through several rows of cubicles, while Rosann knocked several blocks across and fell helplessly to the streets below. She cursed as she had no choice but to try her best to maneuver in mid-freefall and cover up as she came crashing down on top of an SUV, obliterating it on impact. She lay there writhing in pain, saved by the Ghoul's slightly dense physiology and regenerative healing, repairing her injuries.

The lucky ones were Rosann, Blitz, and those not in the blast zone vicinity. Those not of a superhuman level or wearing high-powered armor were killed instantly. The force of the blast sent both Rogers and a recovered Hard-On flying through several buildings; even Nachzehrer felt the wrath of her teammate sending her sailing from the sonic blast. Anything not bolted down was sent flying; whole sides of buildings were blown off, raining glass and rubble everywhere. The only ones left standing aside from Wendigo were Revenant and Anchimayen, who stood behind her in a strange purple energy dome shield generated by the sadistic leader, the Draugr now bleeding from both his ears and nose and Lady Tech in her high-powered SAM armor.

"Shields withstood near the point-blank blast," Maxine reported, "holding at forty percent, power reserves at eighty percent. Miss, you're bleeding from your nose and ears; scans show your vitals are elevated drastically."

"Prepare to retaliate," Lady Tech panted, "weapons set to deadly force… full power to weapons…"

"Miss… even with the SAM armor, you cannot withstand…" Maxine cautioned.

"Stop arguing with me, Maxine, and do it!" a frustrated Erica ordered.

"Weapons on full power…" Maxine obeyed. "Miss Incoming at three o'clock!"

"Say what?"

Erica turned to the sound of a war cry.

She raised a block in time to deflect a savage blow from the Draugr's recovered sword, sending sparks flying against its dark metal armor.

"You got to be freaking kidding me!" Erica screamed.

Lady Tech retaliated with a devastating left hook, staggering him. He, however, quickly recovered, swinging his battle-ax, which also sparked across Lady Tech's armor;

she did not even bother blocking as she followed through, caving in the mad Titan's chest with a right haymaker, lifting him off his feet and through the window, of a nearby Duane Reade. Lady Tech would find no breathing room, now back on the defensive as she barely dodged and evaded Wendigo's vicious sonic attacks backed by energy strikes from a now airborne Revenant joining the battle. She returned fire, unleashing powerful ionic plasma rounds from the gauntlets of her SAM.

Revenant grinned as he evaded two of the volleys and swatted the third one away with the help of the protective purple energy shielding that looked like an aura bathing him. He returned fire, which Erica tanked with her own shielding and armor. However, each hit she took weakened her own energy shield.

"Magnetic deflector shielding at eight percent," Maxine relayed, "power levels at…"

"Maxine, I love you, but I need you to shut the hell up!" Lady Tech yelled. "Just keep the display up and let me fight!"

"Incoming vehicle at nine o'clock!" Maxine blurted out.

Erica spun around quick enough to punch a flying squad car in two, only for the monstrous Draugr to tackle her, lifting Lady Tech off her feet and slamming her into the street. He followed up by raining down thunderous blows, eager to crack the armor shell protecting her. Erica was rattled back and forth in her seat by the earthquake-like impacts.

"Get this son of a bitch off me!" Lady Tech screamed.

"Yes, ma'am," Maxine complied. "SAM, take over and protect her at all costs."

The SAM armor emitted an animal-like growl as it took over its body. It coiled its legs and fired them like twin pistons, kicking the Draugr in the midsection sending him through a building on the other side of the street. As a shaken Erica fought to keep it together, it sprung back to its feet. Within the cockpit, she sat in waist-deep blood with the severed heads of her fellow teammates floating around her while snakes hung about the place—the psychological work of the one named Anchimayen attempting to break her will.

"Get out of my head, you little shit," Lady Tech ordered.

"You know you're going to die here," Anchimayen hissed, ***"you and your friends are all going to die… and waiting for you in hell is an infinite number of***

demons and beasts waiting to…"

"The only thing waiting for me is the chance to put my foot up your scrawny little nasty ass," Lady Tech responded, *"and cram a bar of soap down that filthy little mouth of yours. Now get the hell out of my head!"*

Pushing her mental abilities to the max, she forced him out of her psyche, removing the disturbing illusions.

"Incoming attacks from all sides, unable to evade," Maxine indicated.

Fighting to defend its creator, the SAM began to map out the best attack plan to deal with the incoming threats, while inside, a battered, bloodied, and drained Erica recovered from the exhausting mental battle. The shoulder compartments of the SAM opened up, unleashing a barrage of mini concussion missiles targeting both Wendigo and Revenant. They were not enough to knock them out of the sky, but they drove them backward, scattering them.

It gave it breathing room to deal with the Draugr and Nachzehrer attacking from the front and back like mountain lions pouncing on a kill. It waited for the last second to move to perform a spinning technique, evading and ringing the Draugr's bell with a spinning hammer fist, sending him crashing to the ground. Nachzehrer managed to jump onto the SAM's back, but in one single motion, it jumped backward, falling on its back, crushing her in between it and the concrete.

She screamed, letting go as it rolled back to its feet. Painfully, she moved to her hands and knees as it now stood over her. Taking aim, its right forearm opened up, firing another version of the Nerve Hammer, hitting Nachzehrer in the back at point-blank range, pounding her again into the concrete. Four sides of the disk device popped open, revealing four malleable, mechanical limbs locked around her back and torso.

As she attempted to rise again, a needle from the disk pierced her back, touching her spinal column. The disk lit up as it channeled several thousand volts of current through her nervous system, sending Nachzehrer into eye-rolling writhing pain. Like its counterpart, it activated its electromagnetic propulsion, whisking her away into the skies toward the hovering Tornado.

~~~~~~~~~~~~~~~~~~~~~~~~~~~~~~~~

Fourteen blocks up from 42nd Street, Adrian finally came to with a groan on top of an abandoned Nissan Maxima he had totaled on impact. He pulled himself off it and staggered to his feet, still in his metal form, which saved his life. He now stood
~~~~~~~~~~~~~~~~~~~~~~~~~~~~~~~~

within the Upper West Side, a ghost town. Not a soul was on the streets. The innocent either fled for their lives or hid from the hell happening in Times Square that might come their way. The only things around him were abandoned vehicles.

He could hear the fighting still taking place and had to return to his teammates quickly. He looked around and found an abandoned red and black Ducati Monster 696.

Adrian walked over, pulling up the bike.

"Maxine, can you hear me?"

"Yes, Adrian," Maxine answered from his headset. "The Miss is currently in a battle with the members of the Zombie Nation by herself."

"I'm on my way," he said, hopping onto the motorcycle, "Can you hotwire this bike for me?"

Without answering, Maxine patched into the bike's computer, turning it on. Hard-On revved up and gunned the Ducati down the Avenue of America, making a quick right on 53rd Street to take Seventh Avenue back to Times Square.

~ ~

Abe came to clutching the M1 Ballistics rifle still in his grip. He stood up on instinct, aiming and scanning his surroundings, which appeared inside a Broadway theater.

Rogers shot up to his feet, looking for the exit.

"Maxine," he barked. "What's the situation?"

"Sir, the Miss, is currently in combat with three remaining members of the Zombie Nation," Maxine relayed. "Hard-On is en route, no response from Rosann or Blitz."

Rogers smashed through the theater's steel exit door, triple-timing it back to the heart of Times Square on foot.

"I'm on my way!"

~ ~

Erica was far from safe as Revenant evaded, destroyed, and tanked her missile attack with purple and black energy shielding. He returned with the same energy as an offensive weapon, firing volleys at her. SAM spun, ducked, and dodged the barrages that tore chunks into Times Square's streets and buildings.

"EVO is firing dark matter-energy," Maxine confirmed. "Shielding will not hold if hit by such an energy attack. SAM employing evasive maneuvers."

SAM's feet and back thrusters ignited, launching it into the air. It rolled and strafed between the buildings to evade his attacks. Able to maneuver above him, it opened fire with a full ion plasma stream from its gauntlets.

It put Revenant back on the defensive, throwing up another circular energy shielding to block the attack. SAM prepared to unleash another salvo of missiles upon him when it was viciously rattled from a long-range sonic attack from Wendigo.

"Shielding down to five percent…" Maxine indicated.

Before SAM could attempt to recover from the sonic blast, it was struck by a powerful direct hit from Revenant, knocking it into a tailspin out of the sky.

"Shields disabled… unable to recover… impact is imminent…" Maxine relayed.

Lady Tech hit the streets of New York hard, sending rubble flying everywhere. Her crash landing produced another large crater where she came to a rest. Red lights went off in the cabin as Erica sat barely conscious in her seat.

"Come on, big boy… get up and shake it off," Lady Tech commanded.

Obeying her orders, her armor fought back to its feet, where it found no breathing room as the Draugr came crashing down on top of it, driving it further into the crater. SAM swung for the hills, but a faster Draugr caught its right haymaker, holding it in his grip while using his right boot to pin its left arm. He drooled under his cracked helmet as he reached for the SAM armor's chest plate and proceeded to pull.

"Draugr attempting to breach the hull, armor's integrity is being compromised," Maxine reported, "SAM attempting to power Ion chest cannon."

Lady Tech braced herself for the worst; tears ran down her eyes as she fought not to cry or scream. Faced with meeting a gruesome end, she wanted Rogers to know that she did not run, Erica did not beg for mercy, and she was a soldier.

"Extremely high energy source inbound to our location!" Maxine responded.

"Blitz?!" Erica screamed.

"Negative," Maxine answered. "Something much more powerful."

Lady Tech rolled her eyes, wondering what next as a thunderous noise overtook Draugr's creaking sound, trying to breach her cockpit. The monstrous behemoth paused his dismantling of her mech just in time to receive a hit to the face with what appeared to be a golden staff charged with an unknown power source. The blow was deafening on impact, forcing Erica to cover her ears as it launched the blood-driven juggernaut into the air through several buildings sailing over the Hudson River. He crash-landed into a small Yacht on the New Jersey side.

Erica slowly opened her eyes, getting a visual of her savior.

"Oh my god…" Lady Tech stammered.

That is what she believed stood before her, Egyptian, to be more specific. His armor shined bright silver and gold with blood-red accents as he looked like an amalgamation of an Egyptian Pharaoh and a character from the 1994 Stargate movie. The long snakehead staff with an emblem of the sun shining behind it that he held in his hand matched the gold and blood-red parts of his armor. A bladed crescent moon capped off the end of his staff. Erica also noticed that his headdress's back had a long golden scorpion tail hung like a braid. His bright golden-brown eyes added to his demigod stature, while his humble dark brown smile made Erica's heart flutter amid the chaos around her.

"Status on the new player," Erica asked.

"Unknown," Maxine reported. "I am unable to get a reading on the individual, his armor, or weapon. Unknown energy shielding is deflecting my scans. From what I can diagnose, the energy he is emitting is on a cosmic level."

"You mean like a comic book," Lady Tech swallowed.

"I mean like remnants from the first 'Big Bang,' Miss," Maxine elaborated.

Revenant descended to street level, hovering. He clapped, bringing Erica out of her schoolgirl crush, and turned her golden prince's smile into a scowl as he turned to face the leader of the Zombie Nation.

"Bravo… Bravo… an imposing display of power," Revenant applauded. "And may I ask who might you be?"

He did not answer, gripping his staff as he stood between him and Erica. He could feel Wendigo hovering about to his right in a vibrating field of sonic energy, itching to attack.

"Let me guess, the strong silent type," Revenant scoffed, "you play it very well… but we all know this isn't a comic book. The Draugr will be back any minute now, more enraged than ever. Carving a path of destruction right to you for embarrassing him, and while you managed to take all of us by surprise with that little light show of yours, I highly doubt despite that lucky shot that you are a match for me, Wendigo, or worse all three of us combined."

In the middle of his speech, Rosann zoomed in, standing next to a recovering Lady Tech. Not far away, Hard-On sped through the streets of Manhattan on the Ducati he borrowed while Rogers sprinted at unimaginable speeds to get back himself.

"We're here to break the first of many seals which will usher in the new world order, and we will not be stopped," Revenant sighed, "…so please… just fucking die already."

The Egyptian warrior's staff came ablaze with raw power as he stood ready for Revenant while Rosann braced herself behind Erica's SAM armor, waiting for impact.

Rogers and Hard-On arrived only a block away to see Revenant unleash his attack on their teammates. Hard-On yelled as he gunned it while Rogers gritted his teeth, picking up speed and tearing concrete under his boots. A massive explosion forced Adrian to swerve to a halt while Rogers continued to run through the smoke hitting Times Square. He came to a halt when he realized the actual cause of the explosion.

The Egyptian never got the chance to test his might against Revenant. A stunned Revenant hovered in midair, but not by his own power. Gripping his neck was the mother of all EVOs, and she was none too happy.

"Dammit," Sophia muttered with a scowl, " I just bought this jacket."

CHAPTER 11

Sophia stood hovering in the middle of a devastated Times Square. The energies channeled through her feet kicked up dirt and debris around her, forcing those still alive within the vicinity, both powered and non-powered, to shield their faces to get a glimpse of her as she held the leader of the Zombie Nation by the throat. A purple aura of energy covering his body shielded his larynx from Sophia, crushing it.

"My… **you are** extremely… powerful," Revenant groaned, still wearing a grin.

"And the last person on the planet you want to piss off," Sophia's voice boomed, "power down... now, or I will turn you into a husk."

"I don't... believe so," Revenant wheezed. "You see, the energy I wield is not a part of your appetite."

Sophia increased her grip, putting a cracking strain on Revenant's protective construct.

"And what might that be?"

"I'm not a scientist," Revenant choked out, "But I am... pretty sure... it's in the realm... of... dark... matter. I have... a talent for absorbing regular matter... converting and manipulating it to wield as... I please... in either... an energy or solid-state... like right... now."

"How about we test that theory of yours?" Sophia growled.

Revenant managed to chuckle in between choking.

"As much as I…would like to, she might… have a problem with that."

Revenant pointed to Wendigo, who extended her hand, unleashing a vicious sonic attack on Sophia with no regard that Revenant was still in her grip. Luckily for him, he increased his shielding to weather the storm of his own subordinate's sonic blast, ripping him from Sophia's grip. He crashed through an office window while Sophia was driven through the brick wall part of a building one floor below him.

The sadistic sonic wielder turned to the Regulators and the Egyptian demigod powering up his staff to take her down. Blood-curdling screams froze everyone in their tracks, including Wendigo, as the bodies of almost thirty innocent bystanders were ripped from their hiding places and levitated nearly one hundred stories up.

The unknown source of the terrifying phenomenon was the cloaked child known as Anchimayen. He walked near the edge of the police outpost roof he stood on with his right hand slightly elevated to show he held the multitude of floating hostages in his telekinetic grip.

"I could snap their necks… like pigeons," Anchimayen warned them. "Ever see a dead body flop around before it hits the pavement? It's pretty funny. Would you like to see?"

Everyone stood rooted, mirroring sick, disgusted expressions on their faces. It was hard and revolting to see and believe that a child was carrying out such a heinous act and talking in a despicable manner.

"Now here's what we're going to do," Anchimayen began to dictate his terms.

Exploding rock and rubble interrupted him as Sophia, coming from whence she was buried, attempted to rush him.

"Careful lady!" Anchimayen screamed, backing up. "All I have to do is close my hand!"

The chorus of screams overhead stopped her in her tracks mid-hover.

"As I was about to say," Anchimayen continued, "my associates and I, the ones you have not captured, will be leaving right now. When we are at a safe enough distance that you cannot follow us, bodies will start dropping. Whether they're alive or dead when you catch them depends on if you stay put. So don't try to follow us. You hear me, bitch?"

He turned his attention to Erica, who had a look of disbelief that he actually called her the B-word in public.

"Don't try to send one of your stupid gadgets to follow us," Anchimayen warned, pointing at her. "I will know, and the blood of these people I now hold will be on your hands. Are we clear?'

"Crystal, you little inbred bastard," Lady Tech acknowledged.

"Revenant!" Anchimayen yelled out. "You dead?"

The leader of the Zombie Nation peered out of the office window; he went through dusting himself off.

"Why, no, my dear boy," Revenant replied, "and a spiffy little plan you conjured up on your own."

Revenant stepped out using the dark matter energies he controlled to hover. He turned to Sophia, a couple of feet off from him.

"It was the utmost pleasure meeting you. Hopefully, we will meet again under better circumstances."

Sophia glared at him while she wondered what he meant by his statement. Revenant and Wendigo took off first, followed by Anchimayen carrying a still unconscious Jiang Shi via telekinesis. Sophia and everyone else readied themselves to begin catching people. Hard-On looked around, realizing someone was missing.

"Where the hell is Blitz?"

In the mayhem, everyone had forgotten about their electricity-wielding teammate. A massive explosion caught everyone's attention on 42nd Street between 9th and 10th Avenue. A violent blue and white electrical discharge erupted in an attempt to keep something back.

Erica turned to Rogers while preparing her armor to take flight.

"Sergeant, I think you and Hard-On should back Blitz up. The four of us should be able to do this."

"Are you sure?" Rogers asked.

"I got a clear visual the second they start to fall," Lady Tech confirmed, "go."

Rogers nodded, hopping on the backseat of the Ducati. He held onto his left shoulder, still toting his large rifle as Hard-On gunned the bike heading to join the new battle between Blitz and the Draugr.

"Alright, people," Erica relayed, tensing up. "Get ready to go HAM."

The moment appeared to stand still forever until the screams erupted again while Lady Tech's sensors instantly detected the elevation change.

"Go! Go!" she screamed.

Sophia was the first in the sky, catching those who believed they would die that day. She did not have time to return them to the ground, so she dropped them off at the top of the buildings. The Egyptian followed her lead, doing the same. He pointed his staff that glowed, emitting a gold energy construct of a bowl he used to catch people. It moved about expanding as it captured more and more freefallers.

No one had time to be amazed as a few got by the faster of the four. Erica safely snatched up three before they hit the pavement while Rosann put the Ghoul's abilities to fair use. She darted about, leaping into the air, catching one. She pushed her legs to overdrive as the last two came down simultaneously.

"Erica! Get ready to catch!" Rosann screamed.

She leaped into the air, grabbing a bawling woman by her leg before she hit head first, swinging her back up into the sky. She then twisted and dived, snatching a twelve-year-old boy before he hit the pavement. She held him close as she crashed into the side of a parked car. Erica was there to catch the woman. Her heart quickened as she landed, setting the catatonic woman down, rushing over to her teammate, who struck the car brutally hard and seemed unresponsive.

"Rosann! Rosann!" Lady Tech nervously yelled.

Rosann groaned, cracking her neck as she came to. The first thing she checked on was the precious package she caught, still clinging onto her for dear life.

"You okay there, honey?" Rosann asked while stroking the top of his brunette-haired head.

The rattled boy shook his head, acknowledging he was okay. The additional silver lining was when the boy's mother ran up hysterically with tears taking him from her.

"Thank you! Thank you!" she cried.

She held her child with all her strength while he clutched his mother just as tightly.

Rosann nodded, slowly getting to her feet as the regenerative healing she stole from the Ghoul repaired whatever injuries she sustained.

"I don't ever want to do that again," Rosann exhaled, looking at Erica.

"Me neither," Lady Tech agreed. "And if it wasn't for Dennison and the Gold Lan…"

Erica paused her statement, looking around before turning to the sky.

"King Tut, where'd he go?! Maxine?!"

"Unable to detect him, Miss, I detect no energy or departing flight pattern."

"You mean he just vanished?!" Rosann asked.

"It appears so," Maxine confirmed.

A loud popping sound broke their attention on the mystery of the vanishing super-powered Egyptian as they looked up again to see Sophia jetting toward 42nd Street between 9th and 10th Avenue. Their eyes widened, remembering the rest of their team was in mortal combat with the Draugr. Rosann retook flight on foot as Erica powered up her thrusters, following her.

~~~~~~~~~~~~~~~~~~~~~~~~~~~~~~~~~~~

Sophia arrived in seconds to witness the beast of a man taking on the combined strength of Rogers, Hard-On, and Blitz barehanded. The Draugr's body smoked from the electrical attacks Oliver repeatedly rained down on him. Even with Rogers arriving on the scene, hitting him with high-powered energy rounds from his rifle, the Draugr would not
~~~~~~~~~~~~~~~~~~~~~~~~~~~~~~~~~~~

fall. Instead, he chose to rage and fight on as he attempted to swat a faster-moving armored skin Adrian with a New York Taxi.

Adrian ducked, dodged his first two swings, and then stood his ground, throwing a powerful right and destroying the vehicle's back half. The monstrous Titan once again revealed his incredible speed, smacking Adrian with what was left of the car. He flew like a long-drive baseball, crashing through a McDonald's front entrance, where he took out the front counter and then the soda machine.

Seeing enough, Sophia let off a powerful eye beam blast, blowing the rest of the taxi out of the Draugr's hand and staggering him. She then darted, slamming him into the side of a theatrical building, leaving a massive crater pattern where his back hit. Erica and Rosann arrived in time to see her pinning him by his throat against the side of the building. Despite her strength, the Draugr refused to surrender violently, struggling to break free.

"Give up," Sophia warned. "It's over!"

For the Viking Goliath, it would not be over; with a burst of strength, he powered out, knocking a surprised Sophia backward. The Draugr did not hesitate as he hauled off, cracking her with a vicious, quick, short left, ringing her eardrum and staggering. He followed up with a thunderous right haymaker to the face. The force of the blow, while she was airborne, sent her careening through the main glass window of a Madame Tussauds Museum, killing a Beyonce wax figure. Her back cratered against the wall, shaking the building and sending a wax figure of Dwayne "The Rock" Johnson falling flat on its face, separating its head from its body.

Sophia shook her head from the cobwebs as the ringing in her ear left as quickly as it came. She could hear the monster standing outside, laughing at her. Sophia could not call it a sucker punch as she walked into it. Despite his immense size, the Draugr was disturbingly fast and powerful as her jaw and skull radiated from the blows she took. Sophia had to end this fight quickly. The only upside to it was that she did not have to hold back for once, which was her opportunity to cut loose.

"Is this the whore everyone is afraid of?" the Draugr howled. "I'll split her in half with my…"

The Draugr never finished his vulgar statement because he never saw Sophia exploding from the museum, delivering a flying right cross to his jaw, almost taking his head off. Where he needed two punches to send her flying, Sophia only used one. The hit hurled the behemoth through the front entrance of a BBQ and through a wall dividing the restaurant and a Broadway musical stage. He totaled the stage on impact, obliterating it as it finally halted his momentum. Scaffolding and light fixtures no longer secure rained down on top of him, burying him.

Back on 42nd Street, Sophia stood waiting as the Regulator team watched from a distance. They began to move in to rally around her, but she held a hand out, motioning for them to stay back.

"It's not over yet."

As Sophia predicted, from the thundering footsteps getting louder, an enraged Draugr barreled through the BBQ with his pride wounded, creating a much larger exit. In his eyes was the intention to murder Sophia in front of a live audience with his bare hands.

Standing her ground as the immovable object, Sophia timed and tanked the unstoppable force with a devastating gutshot, halting him in his tracks. Staggering backward, Draugr clutched his abdomen, spitting up blood and bile. He roared in defiance, frothing at the mouth. He forced himself to stand tall despite possible torn muscles and shattered ribs. She doubled him over for a second time using her weak left hand for another body blow, causing more internal injury. The Draugr hobbled around on butter legs, unable to suck air into his lungs. Sophia got into a boxing stance, stalking him.

Sophia was quick and vicious, hammering both sides of his skull with a furious left followed by a right. It was a setup for a ground-shaking near head removing jumping uppercut seen in a popular video game minus the trademark yell. The devastating punch launched the Draugr into the air past many of Manhattan's skyscrapers. Sophia wasted no time going airborne after him. She purposely passed him on the way up to set up for the kill. As he came within range, she unleashed a right cross that sent a shockwave, shattering glass within her vicinity.

The Regulators watched as the one-man wrecking machine that gave them hell almost an hour ago flew lifeless across New York City via a devastating blow. The Draugr's point of impact was in the middle of Central Park. Not giving the Regulators a second look, Sophia flew to where the Draugr crash-landed. Rogers ran, heading for Central Park on foot, followed by Adrian in his metal form keeping up. Still wielding the Ghouls' abilities, Rosann sped ahead of them while Blitz took flight, followed by Erica in her battle-riddled armor.

~~~~~~~~~~~~~~~~~~~~~~~~~~~~~~~~~~~~

Eight minutes later, Rogers and Adrian were the last to stand by their
~~~~~~~~~~~~~~~~~~~~~~~~~~~~~~~~~~~~

teammates at the edge of a massive trench within Central Park. At the end of it, Sophia stood over a downed, defeated, and unconscious Draugr. Rogers ran and slid down to where Sophia stood. Nonchalantly, he stood next to her, looking down at the comatose, monstrous beast of a man. He appeared shaken from mortal coil if not for the shallow breaths and slight rising of his wall for a chest.

"Don't know what would have happened if you didn't..." Abe began his thank-you speech.

Choking and gurgling replaced it as Sophia grabbed him by his throat with a "slide of the hand" speed, lifting him into the air.

"What the?!" Hard-On yelled.

He slapped his right metal bracer, transforming again into his metal form to square off against the strongest EVOs this time.

Rosann and a powered-up Blitz prepared to attack as well. Rogers's hand-held high signaled them to stay back, preventing another battle. Sophia bared her teeth at Rogers as her eyes glowed brighter.

"You know, after you left my island, I came to have a sliver of respect for you, Sergeant. Until I realized you were just another bureaucratic lying sack of shit."

"Mind filling me in," Rogers got in between gasps. "On what the hell are you talking about?"

She tightened her grip on his throat.

"Don't play dumb with me, Sergeant. You're not smart enough to do that, especially with me."

Rogers was witnessing firsthand a sliver of the power the Draugr felt, and it was staggering. However, the old iron-forged Marine showed no fear and refused to back down despite his predicament. Abe bared his own teeth while fighting to breathe.

"No one's playing dumb with you, you psycho, and you can choke me till my head pops off. I still don't know what the hell you're talking about!"

Sophia pointed to Erica's still functioning battle-ravaged SAM armor.

"You think because seven years have passed, I won't remember that?! And put two and two together that you're working for them?!"

Erica wore a look as if EVO Zero was not addressing her. She contemplated opening her mouth or leaving Rogers to hang, not wishing to have Dennison's incurred wrath directed toward her.

"Again, you crazy bitch," Rogers bit back. "I don't have the slightest idea what the hell you're talking about!"

"Liar!" Sophia roared. "You can throw whatever fancy new name you have on it; you're still D.E.A.D scum! And I will bury you like I did them!"

"Sergeant Rogers is not a part of, nor does he have any prior knowledge of, the Disavowed Extermination Assault Division!" Lady Tech yelled from her cockpit. "He also does not know anything about the Biological Assault Mechs you fought seven years ago. I do."

Everyone, including a wide-eyed Rogers, turned to Erica, whose stomach was now in a knot as all eyes locked on her.

"We are not D.E.A.D. I can and will tell you everything you want to know about them, Project EVOlution, and Director Rosen to prove that," Erica said.

Sophia lowered Rogers back down to the ground, releasing him. He breathed in much-needed air before hacking a spit as he glared at her. Erica's confession did not dissipate the newly formed tension that an ax could cut.

"Excuse me!" Hard-On yelled, raising a hand. "Might I suggest we begin this much-needed Q&A session later and get that big ugly son of a bitch to lock-up before he finally wakes up and realizes he got knocked the F out by a chick?"

Adrian's crude yet logical statement forged a temporary truce between Sophia and Rogers. A dire matter had to be attended to before questions could be answered.

CHAPTER 12

Four hours after the battle that turned Times Square and other parts of Manhattan into a war zone ended, the Regulators stood in the Ranch's central command with their guest being debriefed by Lady Tech about the first three permanent residents of the Purgatory prison facility.

After the battle, the Draugr, with Sophia's aid, was locked into gravity field restraints. For extra insurance, Lady Tech attached every ion body damper within the ship to keep him subdued during the flight home with the captured Ghoul and Nachzehrer.

Rogers sent her by herself to process them into their proper cells. It was tactical as the team stayed behind along with Dennison to help search for the missing, assist the injured and dying, and collect the dead bodies. Dennison and Rogers, hardened by past experiences, were used to the sight.

The young Regulator team officially baptized in battle on that day was not. The aftermath of the horrors did not halt them from doing their duty; it just made it harder, especially when the victims' age became younger and younger. Sophia remained off the side, leaning against an empty wall with her arms folded under her chest. At the same time, the Regulators, still in their gear that reeked of combat and blood, stood together as Lady Tech updated them on what information she could gather on the three new inmates as well as the remaining four members of the Zombie Nation that needed to be hunted down.

Erica began with the Draugr, pacing in his new, positively reinforced cell.

"His name is Thomas Brennan, born March 19, 1973, in Providence, Massachusetts. There is no prior criminal record that we know of. Both parents are deceased; he's the eldest of two younger brothers. He's had no place of residence or job since the age of twenty, which is why he's been off the grid.

Draugr's name comes from old Norse mythology. It stands for 'one who walks after death,' they're said to be the walking dead possessing superhuman strength, capable of increasing their size at will and carrying the unmistakable stench of decay. They exist to guard their treasure, wreak havoc on living beings, or torment those who wronged them."

"So he's officially bat shit crazy," Blitz blurted out.

"Clinically, yes," Erica answered. "He's a textbook sociopath in stereo and one of the most powerful Titans I've ever seen. His skin and bones are denser than the hardest metals on the planet, carried by his muscle fibers that are just as dense and packed like steel coils, which also explains his freakish size of eight-foot four inches. Add his exceptionally high regenerative capability. All you need to do is paint him green. I had to get inventive with his cell, and in a hurry. It's a twenty-by-twenty-foot box with the walls twenty inches thick of pure dark metal coated with an anti-friction film to prevent him from gripping and tearing at the walls. Micro cameras monitor his every move. I then dropped it into this tank of Zero-G gelatin. It's similar to water, only a bit thicker. If he attempts to charge the wall, the cell will just spin and float, negating his momentum."

"What if he has to take a dump?" Hard-On asked.

Rosann shot her brother a dirty look.

"What?" Adrian snapped defensively. "It's an honest question!"

"No worries," Erica said. "The cell descends and docks with the port at the bottom when he has to use the facilities and ascends docking with the port at the top when he has to shower. Air blowers and heat dry out the inside of the cell. They also detach automatically if he steps out of line. The cell also dry docks to the port to the right to get fresh clothes, food, and water via a small security lockbox in the cell. The whole thing is powered by solar energy by day and our reactor by night. The cell also charges up every time it docks with one of the ports."

"What about our other residents?" Rogers asked.

"Our second fellow resident with the career killer tattoo on his face is Edmond Wallace, a.k.a Ghoul," Erica elucidated, "from Liverpool, England. Mr. Wallace is of Jamaican and Scottish descent and one of England's most wanted with a rap sheet taller than me. Seven charges of sexual offenses, five charges of assault, four of the assault charges have a weapons offense tacked to them, and two charges of murder. Who wants to bet his activities tripled the second he gained his abilities."

"And what about… uh," Oliver fumbled with his words.

Blitz attempted to get his words out while motioning to an imprisoned Nachzehrer sitting in the buff on her prison cell's bed. She had torn apart the orange prison jumpsuit given to her to wear, leaving it on the floor. Realizing she had an audience, she leaned back and slowly spread her legs, putting on a show. Oliver lowered his head, pretending not to look, while Adrian tilted his, unsure how he should feel about the situation, until his disgusted sister popped him in the arm. Lady Tech sighed, shaking her head as she shut off the video feed to her cell before her show turned from R to X-rated.

"Lurleen Magnilda Schlesinger, a.k.a Nachzehrer the name for German vampire although it's more associated with zombies," Erica indicated.

"So what part of Germany is her nasty ass from?" Rosann sneered her inquiry.

"Actually, she's a United States Citizen." Erica turned to answer her. "Born and raised in Chicago, and from a very prominent family of socialites. She's the second youngest of four children. Her father is a well-known exporter and importer of rare diamonds and artwork."

"So she's a Kardashian on steroids," Adrian confirmed.

"More like a Hilton," Lady Tech corrected him, "but instead of sex tapes, this one decided to join her local Nazi skinhead Chapter. She's wanted in connection to multiple hate crimes in the US and Europe, assault and battery, possession of drugs with the intent to sell, and four DUIs. She's got several bench warrants in four different states. Some of these charges were dropped due to her daddy's connections."

"Well, he ain't bailing her out of this," Abe growled. "What about the other four that escaped?"

Erica threw their images on the screen.

"Revenant, Wendigo, Jiang Shi, and Anchimayen. Surprisingly, Fredrick Stockholm, a.k.a Revenant, has no criminal record until today."

"You're joking, right?" Oliver asked in disbelief.

"I wish I was," she answered him. "He's also a United States citizen, but he lived the majority of his time between England and South Africa. He graduated at the top of his class from the University of Cambridge, majoring in Criminology and

Biochemistry while minoring in art history."

"So he's a brain," Rogers concluded.

"A massive brain, which is why he probably has not been caught until now."

"What was that weird power he was wielding?" Adrian asked.

Lady Tech switched to video footage of him wielding the purple and black energy.

"Believe it or not, that really is dark matter energy he is producing. It appears he can absorb regular matter and convert it into dark matter. Readings show he can absorb the very air around him, making his abilities infinite. His dark matter constructs are also attributed to him controlling the energy on a molecular level. Not only is he extremely dangerous, but he's also rare. There is no other EVO currently on the planet that has his abilities."

"What about Sinéad O'Connor dark?" Abe asked.

Erica pulled up a missing children's profile, flooring everyone within the room except for Rogers and a silent Sophia listening from the corner she stood in.

"Facial recognition matched her to Angela Waters," Erica said, "reported missing in 2008 at the age of fourteen by her parents John and Alannah from Boston, Massachusetts. She was last seen waiting for them at the Boston Higashi School."

"She's autistic?" Rosann asked in disbelief.

Erica's visage revealed it to be a touchy subject with her.

"Yes, she is. Her entire body is similar to a tuning fork or audio speaker, allowing her to manipulate sound waves. I don't believe she has the same ability as other energy manipulators to store it, which means if you destroy either the headset or her iPod Touch, you can render her powerless. The problem is the sonic field she generates to protect herself is so powerful that I can't get a signal through to do it even if I wanted to shut off her iPod remotely. Next, we have Meiying Kwan, age twenty-five, from the Hunan providence of China. She used to work at one of K-Marts' many sweatshop factories."

"What turned her into a fire breathing, Kabuki Dragon Lady?" Oliver asked.

"Kabuki is Japanese, not Chinese," Sophia sternly corrected him.

Her tone of irritation forced everyone to turn her way.

"Sorry," Oliver nervously apologized.

"Not sure," Erica sighed, continuing her report." Her name Jiang Shi stands for a "hopping" vampire or zombie from Chinese legends and folklore. It's depicted as a stiff corpse dressed in official garments from the Qing Dynasty, and it moves around by hopping, with its arms outstretched. It kills living creatures to absorb their qi, or "life force," usually at night, while in the day resting in a coffin or hiding in dark places such as caves."

"Well, she's got her folklores all mixed up," Adrian scoffed.

"I believe their names were selected more so to fit the theme of their group," Erica responded, "as for our mysterious little Jawa."

Erica brought up a still of Anchimayen, whose entire face and body were cloaked in a long brown monk-like robe.

"I was unable to get any facial recognition concerning him. It could be because of the massive amount of psionic energy emitting from him. What I can tell from mentally communicating with him is that he is between five to six years old, which means he's under the classification of a True EVO."

"Which means he's extremely powerful for his age," Abe clarified.

"Extremely," Erica agreed, "someone twisted this poor kid's mind to the dark side. And I mean Pinhead dark. Inexperience is probably his only weakness. Maxine is currently searching missing and exploited children's databases to find a match to his profile. As for the name Anchimayen, it's the name of a mythical creature in Mapuche mythology. Anchimayens are described as little creatures that take small children's form and transform into fireball flying spheres that emit bright light. They are the servants of a kalku, a type of Mapuche sorcerer, and are created using the corpses of children."

"We have to find these four," Rogers declared, "by any means necessary."

"Miss," Maxine politely interrupted. "Secretary of Defense Robert Graves's helicopter is hailing for permission to land."

Both Rogers and Erica looked at one another with mirrored looks of disgust.

"Grant permission, and then head upstairs to escort them down," Erica commanded.

"Yes, Miss."

~~~~~~~~~~~~~~~~~~~~~~~~~~~~~~~~

Eleven minutes later, Graves stormed into the central command, escorted by Maxine's android form along with Mendes and Dr. Alexander. He spied the room, reading the expressions on everyone's face. Erica's and Abe's faces both wanted to know what the hell he was doing there. Along with Oliver's faces, the twins wanted to know why he walked in with an attitude. Sophia's face dared him to say one word to her.

Graves pointed in Sophia's direction.

"What the hell is she doing here?"

Rogers stepped forward to answer.

"She's a guest who saved our asses in Times Square. Is there a problem?"

Graves took a step forward to correct Rogers.

"She is an escaped fugitive on government property."

Rogers took another step, staring down Graves.

"Last I checked, the crime she was "accused of" happened in Texas and occurred when she was a human and alive. Lady Tech, Ms. Dennison, was reported dead at the time of her execution, correct?"

"That is correct," Erica nodded with a smirk.

"And how many times has Ms. Dennison been in the state of Texas since then?" Rogers asked.

"Since I've been tracking her movement," Erica replied, pretending to guess. "Ninety-one times, eighty of those times she visited the Gatesville prison for women."
~~~~~~~~~~~~~~~~~~~~~~~~~~~~~~~~

Abe nonchalantly shrugged his shoulders.

"See, if the state of Texas ain't looking to bring her in, then why should I break my neck doing it?"

Graves glanced over at Sophia, narrowing her eyes at him. He turned his attention to Rogers, brandishing a toothy grin.

"May I speak with you in private, Sergeant?" Graves whispered.

"As long as the kid can come," Rogers requested, motioning to Lady Tech. "I need her to translate big words for me."

~~~~~~~~~~~~~~~~~~~~~~~~~~~~~~~~~~~~

Two minutes later, by the platform that housed the Tornado, Abe stood again with Erica at his side, staring down at Secretary Graves flanked by Dr. Alexander and Mendes.

"You disappoint me, Sergeant." Grave shook his head, mirroring his words.

An unshaken Rogers folded his arms.

"How so?"

"I breathe life back into you by giving you this opportunity." Graves snapped at him. "You promised me you would have this team ready in six months…"

"First of all, it's been only three months," Rogers cut him off.

"Well, if your team wasn't ready," Graves demanded with an elevated voice showing his displeasure, "then why the hell was they in Times Square creating a PR nightmare?"

"Because the only three other individuals who had the balls to do what we did down there **are dead**," Rogers said. "My team handled themselves exceptionally well, considering they only had three months of training and were outgunned. And I am exceptionally grateful for Ms. Dennison and our mystery golden boy for showing up to give us some backup. So excuse me if I don't give a shit about PR, especially when they're still counting bodies."
~~~~~~~~~~~~~~~~~~~~~~~~~~~~~~~~~~~~

"Language," Lady Tech warned.

"Sorry," Abe responded with eyes still locked on Graves.

Graves glanced at them both and decided to temporarily change the subject.

"What is the status of the four EVOs also responsible for the destruction in New York that escaped?"

"Currently, they're off the grid," Lady Tech answered. "I suspect using the same tactics they've used to remain hidden until now. However, I'm employing every form of tracking I can find or invent to hunt them down. We'll find them eventually."

"Since you both decided to throw yourselves prematurely into this game," Graves declared, preparing to issue a command, "I expect them to be found, captured, or otherwise."

"Any other orders you'd like to give us?" Abe dryly asked.

Graves displayed a false smile before he answered.

"Only for you to kindly remember that all of this is not yours, this belongs to the United States Government, and you are all its employees. And if I continue to see a lack of productivity or growth of insubordination, I will shut you down, take all of your cute little toys, throw you out on your ear, and stretch the budget to pay someone a lot more to replace you. Do we have an understanding?"

Both Rogers and Champion wore mirrored looks of displeasure toward Grave's polite and professional threat.

Graves sardonically snapped his fingers, remembering something.

"Oh! You do know divulging information of national security to a civilian is treasonous and punishable by a very long federal prison sentence."

Erica smacked her lips, knowing the comment was aimed at her.

"I really hate him," Erica mentally whispered to Abe.

"Me too," Rogers thought back, *"and stay out of my head."*

"No need to see us out," Graves said with a smirk, "we know the way. You need to get back to your 'guest.'"

He turned, strolling off, not even giving them a second look as he, Mendes, and Dr. Alexander followed him back to the lift. Rogers noticed Lady Tech narrowing her eyes further as she locked onto Graves.

"What is it?" Rogers asked.

"I don't trust Graves," Erica sneered.

"You didn't go…?" Rogers began to ask with a disapproving tone.

"Of course, I did," she snapped back, "but I didn't pick anything up… his thoughts mirrored his words, which means he has a device on him that can block me."

"How do you know?"

"Usually, when we talk, we're sometimes subconsciously thinking about something else," Erica explained, "taking out the trash… the movie we saw the other night… all I picked up from what he was thinking is what he was actually saying. Also, even though they said nada, I couldn't read Mendes or Dr. Alexander's thoughts either."

Abe narrowed his eyes, mirroring Lady Tech's eyes.

"All three?"

"Somehow, they were shielding their thoughts from me. Which means there's something they all know that they don't want me to know."

Rogers furrowed his brow.

"Let's keep that between ourselves for now, till we know what's up."

"Mums the word," Erica answered with a nod.

Rogers watched as the lift took the trio back up to the surface.

"And Dr. Champion, real solid work out there today."

"I had a tough teacher; that's why I'm still alive."

The two briefly glanced at each other before returning to the central command to deal with more pressing matters.

~~~~~~~~~~~~~~~~~~~~~~~~~~~~~~~~~~

Several thousand miles away, Graves sat in his government-issued private helicopter across from Mendes and Dr. Alexander.

"We're clear now," Dr. Alexander indicated.

"Finally, I can take this damn thing off," Graves sighed.

He pulled off a patch of "skin" from the side of his head; underneath it was a small silver disk that he laid on the table before him.

"I do hope this device of yours did its job, Dr. Alexander."

"As I said it would, it only emits thoughts of what you are saying at the time; all of your other thoughts were cloaked from her via a psionic jamming frequency."

"Can't take the chance of that nosey little brat digging into any of our skulls," Graves huffed. "They're not the figureheads I want, but they will have to do for now."

"Sir, is it really a good idea to start this over again?" Mendes asked. "Considering what happened last time, and if Ms. Dennison finds…"

"That overpowered wench will never find out," Graves dismissively interrupted him. "My predecessor failed by making it personal and forgetting about his first duty, which was to his country. I won't make that same mistake. There will be no paper trail to follow because, as usual, none will be created. The only good that came out of the disaster in 2008 is now we have ample raw material to work with to do it better."

"But, sir," Mendes hesitantly asked, "Is this really necessary now that the Regulators are online, even if premature?"

Graves leaned forward to look Mendes in the eyes.

"Mendes remember this," Graves sternly said, "this country has remained great by the "heroes" created in the light to keep the masses' mind at ease… and the monsters created in the dark that do what needs to be done no matter how unsettling it is… that is why project D.E.A.D… must be rebooted."
~~~~~~~~~~~~~~~~~~~~~~~~~~~~~~~~~~

"Should I begin the profiling for a new team?" Mendes asked, finally falling in line.

Dr. Alexander adjusted his glasses while Graves let off a low chuckle.

"Candidates will not be necessary, Mendes," Graves answered, leaning back in his seat. "As I said, no more mistakes… no more breaking in wild horses… this new team will be homegrown."

"Sir," Mendes inquired with a lump in his throat, "you're not talking about cloning?"

Graves lazily turned to look out the window of his helicopter.

"Sir," Mendes stammered, "you do realize both the legal and ethical implications of this, not to mention how this looks from a religious standpoint."

Graves continued to stare out of the window.

"Mendes, do you remember why I hired you?"

Mendes swallowed the lump in his throat before he answered.

"You said you weren't just looking for the best candidate capable of doing the job, but someone who shared your views for what was best for our country; you said I met both qualifications."

Graves looked at his fingernail, flicking dirt from underneath it.

"Did I make a mistake?"

Mendes slowly shook his head.

"No, sir, not at all."

A simple smile formed on the Secretary of Defense's lips as he finally turned to make eye contact with his Executive Assistant.

"Good, because I like you, Mendes, I really do. I would so hate for that to change. Dr. Alexander, enlighten me please, how long before we begin production?"

"With our new process and samples, we will be able to produce full-grown subjects in two and a half years," Dr. Alexander verified. "Actual production can take place in the next six months."

"Shoot for the six months, but if you need additional time, do take it," Graves advised, "zero mistakes can be made this time around. Zero."

CHAPTER 13

Rosann, Adrian, and Oliver departed to get cleaned up and recover from the hellacious battle in Manhattan. Leaving Rogers and Lady Tech to deal with an overly defensive Dennison still standing in the corner waiting for answers. Rogers gave her a dull look before turning to Erica.

"So, how do you want to play this?"

"How about we just do this girl to girl?" Erica answered. "She's not exactly your biggest fan right now, and it'll take away a lot of this tension."

"You sure you want to be left alone with her?" Rogers asked.

"Dude, I'm a child, and I'm cute. She's not going to do anything to me."

Rogers nodded to her logic.

"You girls have fun."

As he walked off to find food and clean up, Erica turned to display a bright Lolita smile toward an annoyed Sophia. It did not chip her hardened visage.

"Okay," Erica whistled with a gesture, "this way, please. It's time to tell you everything that I know."

~ ~

Fifteen minutes later, Sophia's lousy mood softened slightly as she was fixated on the Regulators' base's technological advancements. Her head could not stop moving as she looked around at the various types of Doozers moving about the place, either doing repairs, maintenance, or builds. She picked up a mini quadruped that waved at her before scurrying up her arm and jumping off her shoulder back down to the floor to go about its business. The act briefly cracked a smile on her face until she came upon the SAM unit without its armored shell standing dormant in the form of a docking station. It underwent repairs by mini Doozers similar to the one she picked up, scurrying up and down its frame.

Clearly, it was not like the ones she fought seven years ago. Seeing it, however, brought back bad memories she had chosen to suppress, leaving a nasty taste in her mouth.

Erica broke the ice with an introduction.

"It's called a SAM, which stands for Synthetic Assault Mech, similar to the first generation ones you fought in DC seven years ago. He's a second-generation that I built from scratch. Unlike the ones you fought, he has his own AI so he can operate independently, lessening neural link injury when I hook up to him."

"Neural link allows for it to mimic your movements by connecting your neural synapse to its own." Sophia deduced.

Erica nodded while revealing the neural link on her neck.

"The originals were called BAMs, Biological Assault Mechs, they were a fusion of cybernetic skeletal structure and shell, with a cloned organic muscular and nervous system. The idea behind the concept was to create machines similar to tanks that not only possessed raw strength but speed and agility while requiring very little maintenance or fuel."

"So that red liquid I saw back then was blood?" Sophia asked.

"A type of blood protein," Erica explained. "A rich mixture of oxygen and adrenaline saturates the muscle during high combat situations to give it additional strength and speed. SAM here is one hundred percent cybernetic down to the muscle, skeletal, pulmonary, and nervous system."

"Let me guess," Sophia formulated, as she got closer, "you were able to reverse engineer the human body to fabricate its structure. What material did you use to construct the skeletal muscles?"

"A special blend of carbon fiber that can mimic the expansion and retraction of an actual muscle with strength greater than Graphene; it took six fabricators and four days to create the whole system intricately. The rest was pretty easy and overall less creepy, making him far stronger and superior to his predecessors, like his sisters, he runs on Liquid Ion."

Sophia raised an eyebrow with a smirk.

"Liquid Ion? Like liquid electricity? You actually turned fantasy into reality?"

Erica nodded as she looked up at her mech with pride.

"Shaves off the reaction time by picoseconds. Delivering a nearly infinite supply of power with three-quarters the output of a nuclear power plant."

A look of impressiveness appeared on Sophia's face for a split second. Her eyes narrowed as she turned to Lady Tech, looking for more answers. Erica knew what she was thinking just by the expression on her face.

"Let me guess, you thought you obliterated everything at Mount McLoughlin."

"Didn't I?" Sophia asked with a head tilt.

"You were successful in wiping out the base and everything of value," Erica answered. "Except for the upper half of a badly damaged BAM."

Sophia breathed a sigh of relief.

"So, there was no data or samples left."

"None that could be found," Erica confirmed, "and from what I know, every inch of that base was combed."

Sophia continued to look at the Doozers, working on the SAM.

"I'm a bit surprised, Dr. Champion. I would not expect someone of your vast intelligence to be trolling around as a superhero."

Her remark made Erica blush as if her hand was caught in a cookie jar.

"I keep up to date with what's happening in the medical community," Sophia continued. "Your breakthroughs in Stem Cell and Cybernetic Genetic Research should have you in grant money until your retirement age. It's also a lot less dangerous."

"We all know the military grants better access to toys for R&D and less red tape. I could have Bill Gatesed it but, I don't have the stomach for business, nor the desire to be a suit," Erica answered with a smile. "I just got tired of sitting behind a lab desk just working on experiments. It started to feel like my old life."

Sophia looked her up and down.

"You sound like you're forty years old."

"Actually, as you already know, I am autistic."

"You have Asperger syndrome," Sophia confirmed.

"I had a knack for numbers and puzzles but not very much else," Erica sighed, watching the Doozers work on her armor. "I can't speak for others with my condition, but for me, it was like that scene in Man of Steel when young Clark Kent was sitting in the classroom overwhelmed by his powers. Only my situation was a billion times stronger. That's why a lot of us are viewed as idiot savants or the PC term autistic savants. We can receive data and information faster and better than anyone else. However, our current processor cannot keep up with the continuous waves of information, causing us to crash repeatedly to the point where we can barely function. The EVO virus gave me a better processor."

"So the real reason you became a dog of the military," Sophia deduced, "was to further your research with the virus to find a cure?"

"Dog of the military," Erica recited with a beaming grin. "I love that; it makes me feel so much like Full Metal."

Sophia motioned to her massive, armored suit.

"Well, you built your own Alphonse."

The humorous anime references severely lightened whatever tension was floating about; a sternness fell over Erica as she glanced up at Sophia.

"Seriously, if being a dog of the military will allow me to give others like me the gift I received, then slap a collar on me."

Sophia turned, sitting on the guardrail, separating them from the repair bay giving a listening ear.

"One day, I was banging my head against walls and throwing things in temper tantrums because I had run out of puzzles to do. I remember my mom crying in a corner because she could not help me. Then, the noise stopped one morning, and the world became clear and bright.

I got up out of my bed, walked into our kitchen, and made breakfast for my parents and three other siblings. Everyone woke to the smell of food, walked into the kitchen, and stared at me. All I said was, 'Good Morning,' and my mom fainted before us."

Erica leaned forward, placing her forearms on the guardrail, looking down as a little Doozer scurried past her onto its next job.

"After going through a series of tests to clear me to attend regular school, I went ballistic. I blew through school, high school, and college like a whirlwind. A part of me also had a chip on my shoulder as I did it. Eventually, the world around me began to feel small and primitive. I started to view everyone around me as my former self before the virus… even my own family."

Erica's smile dropped a bit.

"What should have drawn us closer ended up making us distant. It wasn't their fault. My dad is first-generation from Ecatepec de Morelos, México. He worked in construction for eight years while getting his degree in IT. He's now the CEO of his own IT company; that's where I got my love for tech. My mom was a junior analyst for a hedge fund. They met while my father pitched her company a new protective firewall.

She climbed up the corporate ladder to be a senior executive and was one year from making partner before she decided to resign to spend more time taking care of me. But even though I never said it to their faces, I saw them as slow and stupid like everyone else. I think they saw it in my eyes when I looked at them. It also didn't help that I could read their minds, and I started doing this."

Erica extended her hand as another Doozer with a red and black color scheme ran by. It stopped in its tracks as it began to levitate off the ground. The curious little machine waited while looking around, attempting to comprehend the phenomenon. As she lowered it back to the ground, it took a minute to recalibrate before heading about its business again.

"I'm not as powerful as, say, Mind Blast from the Defenders of Justice, but it was enough to scare the hell out of my mom. She called my abuela and both my aunts, who came armed to the teeth with crosses, incense, candles, and a live chicken. When I turned thirteen, I asked to be emancipated from them, and they both agreed and granted it. Been on my own ever since, which is for the best."

"You don't miss them?" Sophia asked.

"I check in on them from time to time," Erica said while shrugging her shoulders. "Usually just to know that they and the family are okay and healthy. It's usually an uncomfortable five to ten-minute conversation. This may be the coldest thing I will ever say, but it's a small sacrifice to pay to get rid of the hell I was in and feel normal. Everything else I've obtained is just a bonus. I wouldn't wish that existence on my worst enemy."

"I'm glad the virus was able to do that for you," Sophia exhaled, "but if I knew my actions on that day were going to result in what is going on in the world today, I definitely would have taken a different route."

Erica turned, looking up at her.

"You don't like what you've created? Do you?"

"I didn't create anything," Sophia said flatly. "My actions spread a highly aggressive virus that selectively killed a large percentage of the Earth's population while turning another sizable percentage into superhumans. That is all."

Lady Tech dropped her head, looking down at the floor.

"Excuse me if I don't share your views, and not because I won the golden ticket. Evolution can be messy, but it's necessary. Especially in these times, we're living in."

Sophia half-heartedly smiled.

"You believe in the ends justify the means?"

"I believe that the human race needs to move forward," Erica bluntly replied. "Thousands of years later, and how advanced are we? We've built airliners to crash into buildings murdering thousands of people for a belief system. We invented the Internet and created YouTube to broadcast beheadings and twerking videos. We use Facebook and Twitter to post pictures of us murdering our spouses and to cyberbully those that are different than us to the point of suicide."

"You forgot about rotting our brains to reality television," Sophia added.

"We're quicker to upgrade our iPhones than ourselves and our way of thinking," Erica concluded. "In every experiment or invention ever created, there is a particular form of risk. For us, it's the fact that there will always be evil people who will abuse their powers and abilities. But the trade-off is people like us. Around the globe, as we speak, there are people from all walks of life, race, creed, and color who do use their abilities to do good, inspiring others around them to be better human beings to themselves and each other. When do we stop fantasizing about what we read in a comic book, or watch on a silver screen, and aspire to truly race toward the sun?"

Sophia smirked with a nod.

"Out of the mouths of babes, cute reference at the end."

"I try," Erica acknowledged with a smile.

"I have to ask," Sophia inquired, getting serious again. "Is the price worth subjecting yourself to what you saw and went through today?"

Erica smiled, looking off into space, as Sophia moved closer with concern.

"You saw things that no one should ever see. Especially at your age. I don't see the scale balanced, especially when it comes at the expense of you enduring something like today."

Erica lowered her head, keeping her smile.

"I do, and yes, when you leave later, and everyone around here turns in to get some sleep. I will sit under a hot scalding shower for about half an hour. I will then put on my PJs and go to my room, which is soundproof. I will lay in my bed and clutch my stuffed rabbit BoBo like my life depended on it, and bawl hysterically until I pass out. Sucks for me, but a small price to pay to fight for a better world, that I believe can be achieved."

Sophia touched Erica's back for comfort, feeling the motherly instinct building within her. She extended her hand, keeping Sophia at bay. It violently trembled as Lady Tech held her bright, masking smile.

It was a plea that she was not ready to break down yet. Sophia respected her wish.

Erica pushed off the guardrail, stretching.

"How about we take this conversation to my lab, Dr. Dennison? We can swap notes, and I can show you some of my R&D."

"I would like that, Dr. Champion," Sophia agreed.

~~~~~~~~~~~~~~~~~~~~~~~~~~~~~~~~~~~~

During the five-minute walk to their lab, the two discussed their findings regarding the virus over the years. Many of their results were similar, from the main blast point, to whence it traveled outward, going global. The strength of the virus became weaker the further it traveled from its point of origin. The closer to the blast, those infected became stronger or died faster, while those further away had weaker abilities or lingered longer before death.

Sophia chose to withhold two critical forms of information that happened that day. One of them was that she was not alone in the heart of the nuclear explosion. Neither had yet to diagnose why some humans died while others gained powers and abilities, and the rest of the world remained dormant aside from cases of birth. The two did share two sentiments that they derived during their studies. The virus possessed near-sentient properties, and they did not believe it was created in a human lab.

Lady Tech had one theory about its selection process, which she projected via her lab's holographic imagery.

Sophia broke down the data floating before her.

"So, you're saying it has a hive mentality?"

"Exactly," Erica said, expanding on the topic. "All living organisms, no matter how big or small, have two prime directives. Survival and reproduction, we're like towns or cities that these things chose to set up shop in, and as we all know in society, one needs a military for protection."

"So regular humans are the worker bees, and we're the drones," Sophia concluded.

"Actually, you're the queen bee, and we're the drones," Erica corrected.

"Hate being the center of attention," Sophia sighed, "it still doesn't explain why some humans obtain abilities, while others have died from this, and why it's suddenly tapering out."
~~~~~~~~~~~~~~~~~~~~~~~~~~~~~~~~~~~~

"Can I ask how you got your abilities?" Erica asked nervously.

"I acquired the virus from my late husband," Sophia hesitantly answered. "It was sexually transmitted to me."

Sophia's face had liar written all over it. Erica knew it without even reading her mind, which she was incapable of. She decided to not bring back the tension by reframing from pressing the issue as Sophia changed the subject.

"What can you tell me about Dr. Archifeld Zimmerman and his studies?"

Erica nodded, pulling up his file.

"Ah, Dr. Zimmerman. He became the fourth lead scientist on Project EVOlution in 1971, originally from Germany; his specialty was genetics and cloning. Zimmerman was at the top of his field in both. Off the record, he is responsible for creating the original BAMs and the D.E.A.D project."

"Him, Arthur Rosen, and my stepfather," Sophia sneered.

"The other half of the coin," Erica sighed, pulling up Rosen's file. "Author Rosen was the third head director to take over the project and the man who selected Zimmerman. Originally he worked in the private sector of weapons manufacturing, jumping from one company to the next, climbing the ladder like bankers and brokers do on Wall Street. Rosen was the Steve Jobs of innovating military combat today behind the scenes. Our government presented the project to him, and he grabbed at it. He was also the first non-military person to direct the project."

"When did General Matheson become head of this project?" Sophia asked.

Erica bit her lip before she answered.

"Around the same time, he came up with the concept for the D.E.A.D."

Sophia wore a face as if she was hit with a punch to the stomach. Very little surprised and shocked her these days, especially regarding the General, but this information caught her off guard.

"I thought you said Rosen and Zimmerman created the D.E.A.D?"

Erica exhaled before pulling up the General's file.

"They created the D.E.A.D. based on the ideology birthed from your stepfather. It's what also earned him his four-star General rank. As you probably already know, the original concept was to take hardened criminals, namely sociopaths, conditioning and training them to create this country's own death squad. To give birth to demons in human skin.

Impressed with his "forward-thinking," he was made the EVOlution Project head to take his concept to the next level. It was also an easy way to test and ensure that the EVO Virus could be made weapons applicable without the scandal of risking the lives of actual soldiers. If you ask me; honestly, your father-in-law was given the position to be more of the fall guy in case this went sideways, which it did."

"Well, I never planned on being the X-Factor," Sophia snorted.

"Whether it was you or someone else, this wasn't the type of project anyone with any two cents about their career and reputation would want to be attached to," Erica returned. "The atrocities the D.E.A.D project are allegedly linked to run neck and neck with the Tuskegee experiment. And once it was up and running, it left a trail of blood over several countries, mostly third world nations, to be the third-largest act of evil this country has ever done next to the enslavement of African Americans and the Native American Holocaust. Guess why it will never come to full light?"

"Because no one really cares about criminals nor what happens in third world nations," Sophia sighed.

Her face became a scowl as she glared at the monster she once was related to by marriage. Erica swallowed as a nervous chill ran down her spine. Her confirmation of the bad history between Sophia and the General was dead-on accurate.

"How did this all start?" Sophia finally inquired. "The virus, everything?"

Erica exhaled while leaning up against one of her stations.

"Honestly, to this day, I do not know, and I've been searching for the answers. Whatever data was divulged to me on a clear need to know basis starts after President Harry Truman authorized the secret creation of the EVOlution Project."

"The same time he authorized the Manhattan Project," Sophia confirmed what Rosen told her seven years ago.

"Yep, President Truman realized before he authorized the strike on Japan the dangerous legacy he had left the world regarding nuclear weapons. The EVOlution project was his atonement for that decision. He knew wars would always be fought; this was a way to develop weapons that delivered nukes' effectiveness without the catastrophic collateral damage of August 6th and 9th. His final executive order was the continued secret funding of this operation to be hidden from even future presidents until the project was completed. That's how much he believed this had to be done."

"Where do you think this all leads?" Sophia bluntly asked.

"I think you know as well as I do," Erica said. "For a country well known for accidentally divulging secrets, this was one of their best kept until you blew the lid off of it."

"Not by choice," Sophia returned.

"Again, off the record. I've hacked every government database ignoring the possible threat of treason to find something that tells me the true origin of the virus only to come up with a dead end. Whatever this is, I think the reason they're hiding it so deeply is that they're afraid it will scare the crap out of the general public if it was ever to be revealed."

Sophia nodded in agreement. Believing that Erica honestly divulged everything she could possibly tell her about Project Evolution, she began to walk around her lab, marveling at the tech. Erica sat back, watching her look to her heart's content.

"What's this?"

Sophia motioned to the large glass cylinder attached to what appeared to be metal caps connected to the floor and ceiling.

Lady Tech walked over to where she stood.

"That is my fabricator. Basically, I develop a design that can be displayed as a 3D holographic projection in the cylinder. Size it, edit it and change the style and color. Sign off on it and let the fabrication process do its thing, bringing my design to life. I can make anything from machine parts, synthesized chemicals, and our uniforms. Anything."

A bright smile popped as she looked at Sophia's ragged battle-worn outfit.

"Say, can I make you an outfit?" Erica blurted out with nervous excitement.

Sophia raised an eyebrow.

"Excuse me?"

"An outfit, for like when you go out, the material I use is like a billion times more durable than leather or Kevlar, and although the barefoot look is adorable and bohemian, it's also very Omni-Man 2003. I can modify and style a version of Blitz's absorption boots to withstand your thrusts' output giving you coverage and better flight control. Please! Please!"

"Two conditions," Sophia sighed. "No stupid symbols, and no capes."

"Okay. What about…?"

"No capes and no symbols. Period," Sophia repeated.

She held up her hands, conceding to Sophia's wishes.

"No problem. Maxine, can we please get a body scan?"

On request, the pink-haired android strolled over.

"Please remain still," Maxine instructed with a smile. "Commencing body scan."

Green and red lights blazed from her eyes, forming a grid over Sophia's head. It slowly lowered, flowing from the top of her head to her feet.

"Official height is six feet one inch; official BWH measurements are 34D-20-38," Maxine reported.

Sophia caught Erica's grinning nod of approval.

"What?" Sophia snapped.

"Nothing! Just… very impressive. The standard suit, please, Maxine."

The cylinder came to life as beams from the top and bottom of the cylinder constructed a holographic faceless mannequin dummy with Sophia's height and measurements adorned with a skintight blue bodysuit and absorption boots with a red and silver color scheme. A closer look at the suit revealed a carbon fiber chainmail pattern.

"First of all," Sophia said, "get rid of the blue. Let's go with a black and red color scheme."

"Got it. Maxine."

The suit's color scheme changed before their eyes per Sophia's specifications.

"Darker red, like blood red," Sophia instructed. "And how about a silver pattern on the upper body?"

Erica's grin grew more profound as a once apathetic Sophia entered the design process.

"Can we add a big hood to the top?" Sophia asked.

"Why a hood?" Lady Tech asked while turning to her.

Sophia narrowed her eyes while inspecting the design.

"I like the style. Not to mention, people forget things. A child murdered by a punk just for rocking a hood is not something that should be a passing phase."

The fabricator added a hood to the design while giving the boots a blood-red color to match the outfit. Sophia slowly nodded with approval.

"Maxine, begin fabrication, please," Erica instructed.

"Total fabrication time forty-five minutes," Maxine calculated.

"Well, that should give you time to get cleaned up," Erica sighed. "Maxine will escort you to our showers."

"Should you really have me running around your base like this?" Sophia sneered.

"We have nothing to hide," Erica answered with a shrug, "and if we did, could we really stop you from prying?"

Sophia nodded in agreement and followed Maxine out of her lab to get cleaned up.

~ ~

Minutes later, she was showering in a foreign place for the third time in years. The open gym locker room shower concept felt less uncomfortable than Mountain View or Mount McLoughlin. She realized it was because she was a prisoner in the last two places.

She washed off the funk of battle and destruction before toweling off. Maxine took her old outfit for incineration. She did not want to bring it back home with her. Fewer memories of what happened in Times Square were better for her. It would be another ten minutes before her new outfit was finished; Maxine left a sweatsuit to wear until then.

She walked out into the locker room area to change, only to see Rosann, also in a towel, hunched over, gripping the long steel bench she sat on. She trembled as silent tears ran down her face.

"You okay?" Sophia gently asked.

Rosann sat up, wiping her eyes. Sophia casually strolled over, not bothering to get dressed.

"Sorry," Rosann sniffled. "Didn't know anyone was here."

Sophia sat down on a bench across from her.

"It's okay. First time in a real combat situation?"

"I'll get over it."

Sophia slowly shook her head.

"No, you won't."

"Those animals downstairs should be in a shallow ditch," Rosann said plainly, "not in a cell."

"Yes, they should be," Sophia agreed.

Rosann waited for the 'but.'

"You were expecting some moral high ground speech from me?"

Rosann looked down at her feet.

"I'm not naïve. I know there are evil people out there who do cruel things."

"It's a whole different story when you see that actual evil face to face," Sophia finished her following sentence.

Rosann wiped away her misting eyes.

"They just killed them, without even a thought. Like their lives meant nothing."

"A while back in Sudan," Sophia sighed, "there was a known warlord known as the Sand Lion. Like all warlords in that region, he raided villages, raped women and little girls, murdered the men, and recruited the children, mostly the boys, as soldiers in his army. Usually, the Sand Lion would force the children to shoot their parents as a display of allegiance to him. During one of his raids, he tried to force a twelve-year-old boy by the name of Pubudu to shoot his mother. Pubudu's mother, full of tears, told him to kill her so that he would live. Pubudu refused, throwing down the AK-47 and stood up to the Sand Lion in front of his entire village and regime."

Rosann turned to Sophia, listening attentively to the heroic tale.

"Now, normally, the Sand Lion would answer such an act of brazen defiance by shooting or beheading with a machete; instead, he decided to get creative on that day and send a very lasting message. He took four of his American and Soviet Cold War jeeps, tied them to each of Pubude's small limbs, and proceeded to draw and quarter him in front of his mother and everyone else still alive. He and his regime then raped and sodomized his mother into madness for almost six hours straight in front of his dismembered corpse."

New tears fell from Rosann's eyes as she cupped her mouth after hearing the horrid tale. Sophia's visage did not even flinch after telling it.

"Those animals downstairs," Sophia said, "are still a rarity in this world. Monsters like the Sand Lion have been walking this Earth for centuries. And the only time we give a damn is when it's happening in our own backyard."

"What happened to Pubudu's mother?" Rosann's voice quivered.

"I had to pry her son's dismembered corpse from her arms and bury him," Sophia answered. "Then I hunted down the Sand Lion, destroyed his entire regime while liberating the child soldiers under his captive. I then broke both his arms and legs and shattered his rib cage, collapsing his lungs. I left him to die in agonizing pain, either choking on his own blood or succumbing to pneumothorax. Six weeks later, Pubudu's mother succumbed to her madness and was found drowned in a nearby lake bed."

Rosann shook her head.

"How do you keep doing this?"

"If you're looking for superhero advice," Sophia sighed, "again, you're talking to the wrong person."

"You don't like superheroes."

Sophia cut her eyes before she answered.

"I think many of them are glorified fanboys and girls living out their wet dreams in real life. The world doesn't need people like us, causing mass destruction while fighting for peace, justice, and the American way."

"What does it need?" Rosann asked.

Sophia charged her right hand until a blue glow of pure energy formed around it. She used it to stroke her braids, drying out their excess water.

"You may not know this, but I have a younger brother, growing up, he was known as the 'little gentle giant.' He was tall and a bit heavy set. He loved dinosaurs, comic books, and things that had to do with science fiction like Star Wars and Star Trek, and he loved to read, even to this day. He was just an all-around geek at a time when being one wasn't cool."

Sophia sighed as she checked her hair for dampness while continuing her story.

"The thing that was adorable about him made him the subject of ridicule in school, especially at the hands of this one kid named Mitch Jackson, who was half my brother's size. Every day he would find a way to taunt my brother, who was not violent by nature, saying some very nasty and hurtful things to the point it would bring him to tears. My brother would go to the teacher and principal, who did very little to stop the obvious bullying. It would stop for a day or two, but then Mitch would start again with a vengeance because my brother told on him."

A hint of anger appeared on her face, which made Rosann a bit nervous, but it quickly disappeared as she went on to tell her story.

"One day, my brother came home and asked my mother what a faggot was. My mom was shocked that he knew such a word, explained what it meant, and then asked him where he heard it. He then told her how Mitch would call him this name several times, especially during lunchtime, because he was always reading his novels. Now, my mother, being a God-fearing woman, always encouraged us not to fight, but the nasty Jamaican side of her awakened on that day.

And she instructed my gentle yet large brother that the next time Mitch Jackson dared open his mouth and call him that name again, he would ball up his fist and deck him right in the face. She told him that he might hit him back, but to make sure he got one good one in so that the next time he even thought about uttering that name, he'd think twice."

The smirk on Sophia's face told Rosann what happened next.

"The next day, ole Mitch walked up to my brother after school in front of my little sister and me and said, 'What's up faggot?' To which my big, gentle little brother who had never thrown a punch before, balled up his near man size fist, and decked that little shit dropping him on his ass."

Sophia laughed.

"Both he and Mitch were taken to the principal's office. My mother came to find my little sister and me crying because we thought Anthony was in big trouble. When we told her what happened, she did not even bat an eyelash. She walked right into the school, into Mr. Callahan's office, looked at my younger brother who sat quietly waiting for her, and a sobbing Mitch who had a black eye the size of a baseball; the first words out of her mouth in front of Mr. Callahan to my brother was, 'You got him good, right?'."

"Doesn't sound any different from how I grew up," Rosann grunted. "What does it have to pertain to what happened today?"

"I think it's fairly obvious," Sophia said with blunt sternness, "to obtain absolute peace, to really stop evil from running rampant, people have to be broken and humbled. History has dictated that the only time humans take each other seriously is through a show of decisive and brutal force. Sometimes we shall overcome is not enough, sometimes you got to clobber them with some 'Fight the Power' for them to understand not to screw with you."

"So why haven't you decided to make that permanent change?" Rosann asked. "You have the power."

"I do have the power; I just don't want the headache that goes with it. People constantly trying to find a way to kill me, going after people I care about, I'd end up dead leveling the planet. Who wants that drama? I prefer the hidden, silent truce I have with myself and current world leaders. They leave me alone, and I leave the world alone. I help who I want, when I want, my own way, and the rest of the world is left to its own devices to figure their crap out amongst themselves."

Rosann's eyes revealed she was begging for some guidance.

"So, what should I do?"

Sophia shrugged, giving Rosann the answer she was not expecting.

"What you feel is in your best interest, and whatever consequences you think you can handle. Walk away and never have to see anything like what you saw in Times Square ever again, and no one would blame you for that. Stay, knowing that you are forever locked in the 'Neverending Battle' and with the knowledge that there could quite possibly be more scenes like what happened in Times Square and maybe worse. The question that only you can answer at the end of the day, 'Is what I am doing making a difference, and is it worth it? Do the ends justify the means, and can I sleep at night knowing that.'"

"Does it for you?" she asked.

"Honestly," Sophia bluntly replied to her. "I really don't know. Like I said, I'm no hero, so my actions are usually decisive and brutal, and I don't need to sleep."

Maxine's android form strolled in, interrupting their conversation.

"Ms. Dennison, your new suit is ready. I will take you to one of our vacant rooms to change."

"Thank you."

Sophia sprung to her feet. Stretching, she adjusted her bath towel before it slipped as Rosann looked down at the floor again, processing what she had said to her.

"What I want you to take away from Pubudu's story," Sophia began to say without looking at her. "Is not his tragic end, but his courage to take a stand at such a young age and face such a horrible death. He could have shot his mother like other children did and lived; no one would have blamed him. He did not have any powers or abilities like we do, but he took a stand nonetheless. I honestly don't think I would have had the guts to do what he did, especially at his age. How sad is it that people like Pubudu with no power have that type of courage, and people with real power don't? We pick and choose fights to get into because it's profitable or because someone attacked us in our backyard. We compromise with monsters because they're the enemy of our enemy. I don't know if anything I do these days makes any difference. What I do know is I owe it to that kid to at least try."

She walked away, following Maxine to get dressed. Rosann watched her leave and then sat there, contemplating the next steps of her own life.

~~~~~~~~~~~~~~~~~~~~~~~~~~~~~~~~~~

Her brother sat on a similar metal bench within the men's locker room with the same transfixed stare she had before Sophia walked in on her. Unknown even to himself, he had transformed into the metal composition of the bench. He sat crushing parts of it that he clutched in his grip. Oliver walked in on him, dawning a face of concern.

"Adrian. Adrian, are you okay? Adrian!"

Esposito woke up from his daze, looking up.

"Huh?"

"Dude, you okay? You're transformed and destroying the bench."

Realizing what he was doing, Adrian released the bench and reverted to his regular form.

"You okay, man?" Oliver pressed. "You want to talk?"

"I'm... uh... fine," Adrian said while shaking out the cobwebs. "Just need a shower."

"You already took a shower. You came out before me."

Adrian sprung to his feet, looking everywhere but Oliver's eyes as he adjusted his towel.
~~~~~~~~~~~~~~~~~~~~~~~~~~~~~~~~~~

"I'm going to take another one. I'll see you in a while."

Oliver stood there, respecting his teammate's wish not to pry further, knowing he was not all right. None of them would ever be all right after what they had witnessed.

~~~~~~~~~~~~~~~~~~~~~~~~~~~~~~~~~~~

Back at Erica's lab, Rogers walked in, still wearing his battle-worn bodysuit as she sat in her chair, studying holographic analyses of Sophia.

"Is that what I think it is?"

"A sub-atomic scan of Ms. Dennison," Erica confirmed. "I got it while Maxine took the measurements for her uniform."

"Isn't that kind of underhanded?" Rogers asked with a semi-disapproving tone.

"Technically, I've been studying her from afar for a while," Erica answered. "She leaves a biosignature every time she takes flight. This is just confirming my suspicions."

"What's that?"

"Our girl runs on a form of bio nuclear energy," Erica sighed. "Each one of her cells is outputting enough energy to light up New York City for a decade, maybe even more."

"All that from one bomb?"

"Nope, the bomb was one of the catalysts transforming her into an energy feeder. The upper layer of her skin's cell structure is similar to chloroplasts in plant life, creating photosynthesis, but at a much high rate, like a trillion times more. Physical contact with raw energy works just as well; she's like an energy vampire. As I suspected, her immune system is monstrously second to none. Zero radiation emission, her blood is the closest thing to Red Mercury that I've ever seen."

"Packs the same amount of power without the fallout," Rogers simplified.

"Padawan is learning."

"So her main power source is solar, nuclear, and electrical," Abe concluded.
~~~~~~~~~~~~~~~~~~~~~~~~~~~~~~~~~~~

"Correction, her source of energy is anything within the thermal, electrical, electromagnetic, and nuclear family. And she's been packing on the calories for a good five years. I calculate she's generating an output akin to a blue star."

"Would it be stupid for me to ask how is that even possible?" Abe asked.

"In this day and age, yeah," Erica chuckled. "But for the scientific answer, why does a lioness hunt and eat wildebeest, zebras, buffalo, and warthogs?"

"Because food is food in the animal kingdom," Rogers answered.

"Give the man a gold star."

"What about our golden friend?" Rogers asked.

Erica shook her head while bringing up his image.

"The Egyptian, no damn clue."

"He's not a superhero?"

"I can't pull a video, news, or even YouTube footage of him from anywhere. I don't even think he's an EVO."

Abe moved in closer.

"Say what?"

"From what I can determine," Lady Tech explained, "the energy I picked up was not coming from him but the staff and the armor he wore."

"Maybe he's a Promethean like you," Rogers deduced.

"I would believe that if this didn't happen," Erica smirked with a bit of nervousness and fascination in her voice. "In the time we had before all hell broke loose again, Maxine tried an intensified scan of his armor and got this."

A holographic wave file played as the audio system within the lab emitted a disturbing voice that did not seem human, speaking a language Rogers had never heard before.

"What is that?" Rogers asked.

"Breaking it down, each word comes from languages that have not been spoken in centuries. I'm picking up Ancient Egyptian, Sumerian, Akkadian, and Q'eqchi'. Maxine was able to lock onto where the sound originated from, which was the staff."

Rogers tried to wrap his brain around what she was saying.

"The staff was talking? What did it say?"

"End communication, or suffer the consequences," Erica translated. "Maxine decided best to heed its warning."

"Who or what the hell are we dealing with?" Rogers asked while staring at the visual of the Egyptian.

"The only thing that I can wrap my brain around that comes even close to this is an Ancient Mesopotamian religion, that's also been the discussion and wet dream of every UFO chaser and sci-fi conspiracy theorist."

With a wave, she threw up various pictures and texts for Rogers to see.

"They're called the Anunnaki," Erica explained with a face of disbelief. "Some believe they are deities, others believe they're an ancient race of aliens that came to Earth to study and intermingle with humans."

"You're joking, right? Tell me you're joking."

Erica turned to Rogers with a face that showed no shred of jest within her.

"I've got master's degrees out the wahzoo, and I deal in facts. The fact is the energies Mr. Dark and Golden was channeling and manipulating based on these readings are on a cosmic level. I'm talking 13.8 billion years old Big Bang theory level. We have ways to detect and study such energy and create theoretical models of it, but to harness and channel it, especially in such a small package? I can't do that. I couldn't even come up with a theory of how to do it either."

They both wore looks of mirrored concern.

"Miss," Maxine announced, "I am escorting Ms. Dennison back to your lab in her new suit. We are nearing the doors."

With another swipe, Erica quickly closed her screens as Maxine escorted Sophia back into her lab. The newly created outfit appeared as if it was a second skin. Rogers, who usually kept a titanium military demeanor, bowed his head, looking the other way to not seem like he was ogling her. Sophia also looked the other way, blushing. Erica glanced at one and then the other and then cracked a smile.

"I just remembered I have some work to do," Rogers coughed, "we can continue our conversation later."

He marched out of the room, continuing not to make eye contact.

"Dr. Dennison."

Rogers respectfully acknowledged with a head nod before exiting.

Lady Tech clapped with a smile.

"Congratulations. That's the first time I've seen the Sergeant uncomfortable about anything since I've gotten to know him."

"Not as uncomfortable as I feel," Sophia stated, looking herself up and down again while touching the fabric.

Erica's face turned to disappointment.

"You don't like it?"

"No, I like it," Sophia answered, "but it feels like I'm wearing nothing!"

"The plus side to being almost indestructible is it is lightweight with zero drag. Your speed will increase without you even trying," Erica returned with pride, "and here are some accessories."

Erica pulled out a set of bracers comprised of metal and cloth material similar to Sophia's new outfit's red color.

"Wonder bands?" Sophia sneered.

"Uh, no," Erica said. "As you can see, your outfit doesn't have any room for pockets."

Lady Tech slid open one of the panels on the left bracer, revealing a compartment.

"Right-arm can hold cash, credit cards, etc., and the left…"

Erica slid back the panel on the left bracer.

"Is basically a mini supercomputer with your own personal AI. You can synchronize it to all of your devices. It has GPS, land, sea, aerial, orbital navigation, web browsing, you name it. Made of nearly indestructible materials, it is waterproof, can function in the lowest depths of the ocean, in extreme heats and subzero temperatures, basically can take a licking and keep on ticking… to a point."

"To a point?" Sophia inquired with a smile.

"Yeah, it's not going to survive planetary level roughhousing or trips to the surface of the sun."

Lady Tech pulled out an earpiece in the bracer next to the mini-computer.

"One push to activate, and the earpiece expands and locks into your ear," Erica instructed. "I put it through a wind tunnel test, and it'll stay locked in up to speeds of Mach 30. It also operates in space and underwater; however, you can only hear people. You'll have to use the digital keyboard to text and send messages or emails to communicate in those environments. Enjoy."

Sophia gratefully took them, sliding one at a time, completing the look of her outfit.

"So, what is this luxurious gift going to cost me?" Sophia asked, looking them over.

"Eh, your money's no good here," Lady Tech dismissed. "But if you've got a couple more minutes to kill, I'd be happy if you tested out my new strength tester."

"Strength tester?"

"Yeah, I was going to have Rogers and Hard-On have a go at it tomorrow, but since you're here, it would be nice if you would do the honors and break it in."

Sophia grinned, seeing through her innocent request.

"You're also curious to get a baseline reading on me."

"Well, we are women of science!"

"It's okay. I'm a bit curious myself," Sophia agreed. "Just one thing. Someone has got to tell that boy that 'Hard-On' is a horrible name."

"Sounds like a name for a dirty-looking crackhead porn star," Lady Tech responded with a dull look, "I mean like… Ron Jeremy dirty… in his elder years."

"Young lady!" Sophia laughed.

"I'm just agreeing with you!" Erica answered with an innocent smile.

~~~~~~~~~~~~~~~~~~~~~~~~~~~~~~~~~~~~

Rosann walked the hallways in pink sweats and yellow flip-flops, heading back to her room. She turned the corner to see Oliver wearing a blue sweatsuit with the Regulator symbol on the right breast coming from the opposite direction. She lowered her head, pretending to be invisible. He turned, looking at the wall to do the same as they passed each other.

Oliver turned to find the courage to say something to her at the last second.

"Hey."

Rosann froze, took a big swallow, and slowly turned to face him. He nervously strolled over to her, taking a throat gulp himself.

"I… wanted to thank you for what you did in Times Square."

Rosann shook her head.

"I… didn't do anything."

"Yeah, you did; I was going to kill Jiang Shi, I really was, and I'm not just thanking you for stopping me from killing a lot of people. I know the Sergeant trained us to be soldiers, but I can't lose sight of who I am, and why I got these powers… to be a hero."

Rosann rolled her eyes.
~~~~~~~~~~~~~~~~~~~~~~~~~~~~~~~~~~~~

"Heroes don't exist. And people who pretend to be one die; we saw that today. We lived because we're soldiers."

"We lived because of our training." Oliver disagreed while moving closer. "That shouldn't define who we aspire to be. I joined this team because I wanted a better understanding of my abilities to help people. When I tried to hone my skills myself, I almost burnt down a neighborhood. Here I can learn control to both be and do better."

"That's all nice, Oliver." Annoyance filled Rosann's voice. "But, the truth is…"

"The truth is we all saw some horrible things today," Oliver cut her off, "Things that are going to haunt me for a long while. But I won't let that shake my conviction, just like it didn't shake Captain Omega's, Seeker's, or Lady Electrify's. I'm not naïve; I know that there may come a time where I may have to cross that line to protect people. I just hope that when that time comes. I used up every alternative option in my arsenal before that happens."

"Anyway," Oliver sighed while running his hand through his white afro, "thank you."

He turned, moving in the direction of his room.

"Can you stay with me tonight?" Rosann blurted out with eyes closed.

Her words froze him in his tracks. His face said he must be going deaf, and he was unsure if he should turn around to clarify what she said.

"I'm going to scream… in my sleep tonight," Rosann explained tremblingly. "I know it. I don't want the embarrassment of people running into my room when I do. If someone is sleeping in my room tonight, I won't scream. I'd ask Adrian… but I don't want to worry him."

"I'll get one of the duffel bags and sleep on the floor. As long as I leave before five hundred hours, it shouldn't be a problem."

"Thank you," Rosann exhaled.

"Rosann, Adrian, Oliver, and Sergeant Rogers!" Erica's voice boomed over the audio system, "can you please join me on the observation deck of the Hurt Locker. Thank you."

A perplexed Rosann turned to Oliver.

"Now what?"

Oliver, standing in the dark with her, shrugged.

"Better go find out,"

They both walked side by side in the same direction.

~~~~~~~~~~~~~~~~~~~~~~~~~~~~~~~~~~~

In the Hurt Locker's observation deck, Adrian was the last to appear as everyone else stood looking through the window. He walked up to see what everyone else was looking at.

"What's up? What'd I miss?"

He and everyone else looked into a transformed Hurt Locker where most of the ceiling and floor were removed. In its place was a large circular platform connected and held up by a massive piston attached to a gigantic energy generator at the bottom of the floor's opening. Standing on the podium was Sophia in her new outfit. Suspended over her head was another large circular disk attached to a piston connected to another generator within the ceiling.

"No fair!" Adrian whined and pouted, turning to Erica. "You said I could test it first!"

"Stop being a baby," Rosann reprimanded him, "you can play with it later."

"Adrian, I'll make it up to you," Erica promised before addressing everyone else. "But, it's not every chance you get to test the strength of EVO Zero."

"So, that's the strength tester?" Rogers confirmed.

"Oh yeah," Lady Tech gleefully answered.

"How does it work?" Oliver asked.

"The strength tester works via a quantum gravitational field generator of my own design," Erica explained. "The plate she is standing on continuously simulates
~~~~~~~~~~~~~~~~~~~~~~~~~~~~~~~~~~~

baseline Earth gravity as if standing on normal solid ground, while the plate on the top when magnetically polarized simulates the weight of whatever structure I punch up."

The bottom and top plates lowered and rose to meet each other. As they locked into position, Sophia raised her right hand, bracing the top plate.

"Are you ready, Dr. Dennison?" Erica asked, projecting her voice through the Hurt Locker's audio system.

With a nod, Sophia stood ready as Erica punched the first test on her tablet.

"Let's start with the Empire State building."

A holographic image of the iconic building projected on Lady Tech's tablet, the plate that Sophia held up with one arm made a thunderous booming sound. At the same time, the hydraulic platform she stood on was slightly lowered. She, however, did not budge an inch.

"She is now holding up 392,942.25 tons," Erica announced, "with one arm."

"Ain't that kind of easy?" Hard-On scoffed. "I could probably lift that in a transformed state."

Rosann rolled her eyes in mocking disgust.

"No, you can't."

Hard-On sharp-elbowed his sister in her arm; she retaliated with a smack to the back of his skull. Rogers ended it with a glare.

"Okay," Erica exhaled, biting her lower lip, "let's make this a little harder. Let's drop the total mass of Earth's atmosphere on her."

The plate made a loud earth-shaking booming sound this time. With lightning-quick speed, Sophia had to adjust to holding the plate with two hands. Her arms buckled, bringing the plate to the top of her head. She pushed back with an inhale and a slow exhale, lifting the plate over her head. The hydraulic platform she stood on groaned as it lowered closer to the floor.

"She's now holding 5.5 quadrillion tons or roughly one-millionth of Earth's mass."

"You can do that in your transformed state?" Rosann sarcastically inquired.

Hard-On politely responded with an arm-folded middle finger. Rogers turned to Lady Tech.

"That's a huge leap from a building. How did you know Dennison could take it?"

"Remember what we discussed earlier?" Erica reminded him. "Trust me, she can take it."

Rogers nodded, continuing to look on as everyone else wondered what they were discussing while Lady Tech thumbed her nose, preparing for the next test.

"Alright, time to bring the rain. Maxine, let's start with one hundred sextillion tons and increase it from there."

"Polarizing platform with equal anti-gravity force to neutralize the effects of planetary weight," Maxine informed everyone.

The platform Sophia stood on raised back out of the floor, returning slightly to its position before the first test.

"One hundred," Maxine announced.

No sound could describe the sound that hit the plate, only that it made Sophia's arms buckle while forcing a groan out of her.

"Two hundred."

Sophia's legs almost went out underneath her as she fell into a crouched position. They shook violently as she struggled to hold up the weight.

"Three hundred."

Sophia groaned again as the plate lowered near the top of her head while her shivering left knee slowly neared the platform.

"I think she's reached her limit," Rogers advised.

"Tests ends when one of her knees hits the platform," Lady Tech told Rogers.

"What do you say, Dr. Dennison? Want to stop?"

"Keep… it… coming," Sophia growled.

Her body violently shook as she was hit with another hundred sextillion tons, making the total four hundred she held over her head. Her left knee was now an inch or so from the platform.

"She'll be done after this next one hundred," Lady Tech declared. "It's still pretty impressive considering…"

"Subject's bioenergy levels increasing," Maxine informed everyone. "By one percent… two percent."

Sophia's eyes blazed as she gritted her teeth, emitting a groan. First, she began by straightening out her torso. She then got both of her legs underneath her in a squatting position. With another deep inhale and a slow exhale, she began pushing back again, forcing the plate up as she got to a standing position. With another inhale and exhale, she pushed the plate back over her head, locking it out.

"Current bioenergy levels are at one hundred and five percent," Maxine notified the team of onlookers.

Everyone wore a thunderstruck look on their face except for Rogers.

"Five hundred," Maxine proclaimed.

Another near-white noise-like boom came. Sophia was once again unmoved as yellow lights flashed inside the strength-testing chamber.

"What the hell is happening." Hard-On nervously inquired.

"Systems reaching their limits," Lady Tech exhaled.

"Shall we initiate shutdown?" Maxine queried.

"Let's take it to the fail-safe," Erica commanded. "What's her output reading?"

"Current levels still at one hundred and five percent, administering another hundred sextillion tons."

Another white noise booming sound hit the plate; this time, the chamber's lights turned orange. Sophia's hands began to imprint into the nearly impenetrable slab while her feet sunk, imprinting into the platform beneath her. She remained the immovable object.

"Current levels still at one hundred and five percent, administering another hundred sextillion tons."

Another white noise booming sound hit the plate. Sophia's eyes blazed brighter as she remained immovable. Lights within the chamber became a fiery red as a siren went off.

"Systems have reached their limits at seven hundred sextillion tons. Administering the failsafe shutdown. Final bioenergy level readings are at one hundred and six percent."

As the fields shut down, the platform lowered, locking back into its piston base while the plate above her head retracted to the top of the cylinder chamber.

"Ladies and gentlemen," Erica exhaled, "we've officially recorded our first planet mover."

Hard-On looked at Lady Tech as if she was crazy.

"Planet mover? You're joking, right?"

"Nope."

Erica projected the reading on her tablet into a holographic image for all to see.

"Ms. Dennison's baseline strength while functioning at one hundred percent is about one hundred sextillion tons, give or take. She, however, has reserve energy that her body stores. She can involuntarily tap into the reserves for additional strength if her body is being overexerted by the extra output that Maxine was detecting. A five percent increase in reserve energy allowed her to lift five hundred sextillion tons.

Her output increased one percent for every additional two hundred sextillion tons added before the strength tester gave out. The Earth's mass is calculated at about 6.580 sextillion tons. Suppose her reserves are equal to her base energy levels. In that case, she'd only need to exert one hundred and sixty-eight percent of the bioenergy-powered force to move the planet, if possible, without breaking apart."

All eyes were on Sophia as she stood tall; her eyes slowly reverted to their usual glowing hue, indicating that her power levels were normal.

"Planet mover, people," Erica cackled to herself. "Planet mover."

~~~~~~~~~~~~~~~~~~~~~~~~~~~~~~~~

Ten minutes later, Abe and Erica escorted Sophia topside, where she extended a hand apologetically to Rogers.

"Sergeant Rogers, sorry for trying to choke you in New York."

"Not the first time a woman's attempted to strangle me," Rogers stated, shaking her hand. "Thanks again for your help."

"You have a good team," Sophia informed him, "you don't need my help to make them better."

Rogers respectfully saluted before walking back to the hangar, giving Erica and Sophia some space.

"Doctor," Sophia addressed her.

Erica respectfully bowed her head to her.

"Doctor."

"My parents to this day are unable to comprehend anything about my profession," Sophia sighed, "in fact, they stopped helping me with my homework the minute I hit the fifth grade. But they had wisdom that I could not find in books, and as powerful as I am... I can't hug myself when I am at my lowest."

Erica looked down, kicking her boot into the tarmac.

"I guess it's not too late to go home."

"If they love you like I know they do," Sophia reassured her, "it's never too late, but till then if BoBo is not enough. You know where to find me."

She tapped her new left bracer. Erica giggled while pulling strands of windblown blue hair out of her face.
~~~~~~~~~~~~~~~~~~~~~~~~~~~~~~~~

Sophia took a few steps backward and exploded with a mighty two-hundred-foot leap into the air. She channeled the energy within her, forcing it down through the soles of her feet for propulsion with a thought. Her new boots absorbed the energy, regulating and focusing the power like thrusters from a jet, giving her more controlled precision. Even though she mastered barefooted flight, it was nice to have boots on; she was tired of repainting chipped toenails every week as she soared through the stratosphere for home.

~~~~~~~~~~~~~~~~~~~~~~~~~~~~~~~~

Within twenty minutes, Sophia returned to her island, touching down on the tarmac of her airport. The first to greet her was Earl with a look of concern.

"Girl, are you okay? What went down in New York is all over every news station worldwide! And what's with the new look?! You went shopping?!"

"I'm fine," Sophia sighed, "three out of the seven bad guys are locked in deep dark cells where they belong. And **this** was made by **a brilliant** young woman as a gift for helping put those people there."

"Looks good on you," Earl confirmed with approval. "So, how bad is it?"

Sophia solemnly lowered her head before answering.

"It's not good. I think we should have a town hall meeting so that we can address everyone's concerns about what happened, especially those originally from the area, who might still have family there."

"I'll relay it to the council members. Here's your phone."

Earl pulled out her gold iPhone 5, handing it to her. Concern appeared on her face as she saw a series of voicemails and text messages from the same person.

"You stormed out of here so fast you forgot it at the construction site. It's been ringing off the hook an hour after you left. The name Michelle kept popping up."

Sophia quickly punched in her passcode, turning her back to Earl, listening to the first voicemail message. An expression crept onto her face that had not appeared in years.

Fear.
~~~~~~~~~~~~~~~~~~~~~~~~~~~~~~~~

Sophia quickly handed her phone back to him.

"I have to go."

"What? Wait… what's going on?" Earl stuttered. "Where are you…?"

"I have to go, Earl!" Sophia yelled, taking a few steps. "Tell everyone I will be back soon!"

She launched into the air, almost knocking him on his rear from the aftershock. Flying faster than she'd ever flown, heading back to the States.

CHAPTER 14

Washington DC, Sophia made the flight in less than five minutes, tearing through the sound barrier at an incredible speed. Her heart pounded as she slowly descended and landed in front of the small Victorian-style home. It was an evening with most residents inside. Those who saw her land glanced and went on about their business, now used to people flying. Nonetheless, she pulled the hood to her new outfit, covering her identity.

Sophia never visited at this time. It was against the rules—against her laws. Her feet felt like lead with every step she took. Her insides became red hot the closer she got, and she had not even reached the steps yet. Sophia forced herself to trot up the steps to the door. If she lingered any longer, she knew she would have just taken off and never returned.

Her stomach groaned and churned as she stood staring at the doorbell she did not want to press. Commanding her hand to raise and point her finger, she laid into the buzzer and then stopped. A cold shiver ran down her body as she lowered her head. In less than a minute, someone came to the door and opened it. Sophia raised her head to look into her eyes. Michelle Armitage stood at the door barefooted in a simple red and white plaid dress with her long brunette hair tied back into a ponytail. Her left arm was in a sling with a small cast wrapped around the forearm.

"What the hell happened to you?!" a wide-eyed Sophia blurted out.

"Hairline fracture," Michelle snorted, "nothing to worry about. Get in here."

She grabbed Sophia's hand, leading her into the house, shutting the door behind her. Sophia's heart quickened again as she looked around the house she had been in over a dozen times, just not during the evening. The cream walls looked darker with the lights on. She felt like she was having an anxiety attack until Michelle came into view again.

"I saw you all over the news." Michelle began. "Is everything…?"

"Don't want to talk about New York, Michelle," Sophia nervously cut her off.

"Okay, um, we have a small problem."

Sophia frantically held up her hands.

"Michelle, freaking out here. To the point. Please."

"She got hurt," Michelle swallowed, "and then she changed."

"What do you mean she got 'hurt?'" Sophia asked with nervous irritation.

"She was rollerblading with some of the neighborhood children at the park," Michelle explained. "Apparently, she was showing off and duplicating moves that she saw on television. One of the stunts happened to be a jump from some stairs, sliding down a guardrail, and jumping off, landing again."

There was an eerie silence as Sophia stood there, stuck, fighting to process what she just heard.

"Say what?!" Sophia's voice boomed.

"She misjudged the last jump and went crashing onto the pavement. She got scrapped up really badly and broke her arm. One of her friends came and got me; I put her in my car and hightailed it to the hospital. Halfway there, she started to scream and cry, saying that her body was on fire, and then she collapsed and passed out in the back seat. So, I pulled over, and when I looked in the back seat… she started to grow."

"Define 'started to grow.'"

Sophia's tone now had nervousness to it.

"She's taller than me," Michelle answered with a boulder in her throat, "maybe four inches shorter than you. She's now a ten-year-old… in the body of a sixteen-year-old… at least."

Sophia swayed and stumbled as if she was about to faint from the news. Michelle instinctively attempted to catch her. She held a hand up, signaling she was all right as she stabilized.

"Her RDH forced puberty on her," Sophia blurted out.

"Her what?" a bewildered Michelle asked.

"RDH, regenerative defensive healing," Sophia anxiously explained. "The same ability that changed me, her cells can both heal her and then build defenses against specific injuries. Especially those that entail a foreign body piercing her skin. Stone or sand must have got into her wound and bloodstream. Her cells then analyzed and determined whatever got in as the cause of her injury—a threat. The first line of defense is to increase the density of her skin to be stronger than whatever pierced it in the first place. So her cells accelerated her growth process to make her bones and muscle stronger to carry her now denser skin. This entails the increasing of IGF-1, testosterone, and progesterone while significantly lowering her myostatin levels to achieve maximum strength levels."

Michelle slowly nodded. Being a high school teacher and a mother, she knew a bit about biology but was still amazed by the phenomenon's breakdown.

"Goddammit, Michelle!" Sophia flipped out. "Why would you let her do something so reckless?!"

"Hey! I didn't let her do anything!" Michelle defensively shot back. "You're the one who bought her the skates for Christmas last year, remember?! She's also a ten-year-old child that I cannot watch or hover over all the time! Children play, and sometimes they do stupid things and get hurt!"

She coiled back and nodded in agreement. While Michelle instantly forgot about their minor disagreement.

"We have a bigger problem. The bone did not set right. First of all, Kimberly tore through her clothes, so I had to run back to the house and redress her. The poor thing was in so much pain she accidentally smacked me off my feet, and that's how I got this."

Michelle motioned to her sling.

"I drove her back to the hospital…" Michelle continued her story.

"And no one can pierce her skin or rebreak the arm to set her bone," Sophia finished her sentence.

Whatever fear or anxiety she had vanished instantly as she made her way up the steps with Michelle following her. The sound of soft weeping guided her to the right room. Placing her hand on the doorknob of the shut door, there was a split second of hesitation. Only a split second as she flew it open and walked in. Within the primarily white and pink bedroom designed for a ten-year-old girl sat at first glance a teenager in a baggy dark blue FBI sweatsuit clinging tightly to a giant pink "My Little Pony" teddy bear clutching her trembling left arm. Her wild, curly hair was similar to hers when she was her age. She also had dark golden skin color, but her brown eyes that ran with tears belonged to someone she loved long ago.

She was not alone in the room. A black and white male spider monkey was standing on the bed, attempting to console her with its screeches. It turned curiously, looking at Sophia standing at the door. Sensing someone was now in the room with her, she looked up. They both wore a look as if they had seen a ghost at the sight of one another. The dead, awkward silence could go on for days as they gazed upon one another.

"What is **she** doing here?!" the child stammered while getting up. "What is she doing here?!"

Her words broke the silence and made Sophia retreat back a bit. Michelle, seeing this going downhill, took charge, stepping in.

"Kimberly, calm down," she gestured. "This is your…"

"I know who she is! What is she doing here?!"

Unable to control her new superhuman strength, the child backed up into the wall, caving a part of it in.

"Kimberly, calm down!" Michelle yelled.

Sophia came to her senses after the sting of the rejection. She walked into the room, grabbing the frightened child before she ended up in the bathroom.

"Let me go! Let go of me!" Kimberly screamed, struggling to get free.

"Look at me, look at me!" Sophia sternly raised her voice.

They were not the first words she wanted to say to her, but they were enough to quiet and calm her down. She trembled in her grip like a bunny.

"Your forearm bone has not healed correctly," Sophia said softly. "If I do not reset it properly, the pain you are feeling will not go away."

Kimberly reluctantly nodded in compliance. Sophia grabbed the left sleeve of the sweatshirt, tearing it up to the elbow. As clear as day, there was a jagged bulge underneath her skin.

"The ulna did not set right," Sophia sighed. "I'm going to have to rebreak it."

"Rebreak it?!" Kimberly screamed, struggling to pull away again.

"Look at me! Look at me." Sophia's stern voice came back again. "This is the only way. I won't lie to you, it's going to hurt a lot, but once I reposition the bone, the pain will disappear in a matter of seconds. I promise. Okay?"

Tears poured from her eyes as she nodded again.

"Hold onto my arm, and squeeze as hard as you want," Sophia instructed. "We will go on three, okay?"

The child timidly grabbed her arm and braced herself with a fretful look on her face.

"One," Sophia began.

The next thing to follow was a snap. The pain did not register initially, but the child squealed and screamed, fighting to break free. Although her face did not show it, she was amazed by how powerful the child's strength was as she dug her fingers from her right hand into her left bicep. Kimberly stomped down hard on the floor, putting her heel through it. Sophia's powerful grip was the only thing keeping her from tearing the room apart.

"You said on three!" Kimberly cried out. "You said on three!"

"I know," Sophia said with a consoling tone. "I know, we're almost done."

It was a clean break; Sophia knew whatever small bone fragments left in her body would be absorbed by her cells. Quickly repositioning the bone, she waited as her regenerative healing activated. The cells bonded again, mending the two halves to form one solid bone. As promised, the child calmed down again as her excruciating pain quickly disappeared.

As the awkward silence returned to the room, the child slowly pulled her hand away. Sophia lowered her head and backed up, giving her space. She about-faced with a timid nod, walking out of the room, leaving just Michelle and the child. Sophia headed back downstairs in a glass-eyed daze and found herself walking into the living room, standing there with her arms folded over her chest and her chin tucked in. She would have dropped to the floor, curled up into a fetal position, and remained there if she could. Sophia wandered over to the fireplace mantle, where she gazed upon pictures. They were of Mark, Michelle, Annie, their late daughter Penny, and Kimberly.

Slowly, she walked by Christmas, Thanksgiving, wedding, and Halloween pictures. She stayed longer, looking at those who had the child upstairs within them. Sophia stopped, standing in front of a particular one with a retired Mark Armitage with a big smile on his face, holding a five-year-old Kimberly at a baby animal ranch as she cuddled a white baby bunny rabbit. Her glassy eyes ran as she smiled while running her hand against the image of Mark, making her mind wander. Mark, a man of his word, not only made good on making her daughter disappear to protect her after the events at Mount McLoughlin seven years ago. He also found a way to adopt her, raising her as his own. He believed with all his heart that Sophia would somehow cheat death again and come looking for her little girl. She ended up proving him right.

Reconciling with his wife, they remarried, caring for Kimberly while their daughter Annie treated her like a little sister. Mark retired from the FBI, no longer respecting the agency and what it stood for. He also departed for health reasons, being one of the first people to contract the Judgment Virus.

Although Sophia returned, she realized she wanted her daughter to have an everyday life, and Kimberly would never have that if she was with her. After secretly discussing it with Mark and Michelle, they reluctantly agreed it was best Sophia remained dead to Kimberly. Behind the scenes, Sophia made sure her daughter wanted for nothing. She quickly acquired her now vast wealth through treasure hunts, mining for precious stones and minerals such as gold and diamonds in areas of the planet that had not been touched and reached only by her. Michelle or Mark would call her, or Sophia would visit during school hours to check on her. She hovered from afar every night, watching her window until her bedroom light went out.

Sophia also cared for Mark and Michelle's finances by paying off their house and medical bills. She appointed herself as his secondary doctor, working feverishly to find a cure and to prolong his life. Her treatments and Mark's iron will gave him five more years. Her mind went back to his final days.

Sophia visited every day. One gray Monday, she stayed for almost the whole day talking, laughing, and holding his hand. His condition severely deteriorated. He refused her treatment a month prior, telling her it delayed the inevitable. That he was both tired and ready. A teary-eyed Mark smiled and thanked her for giving him the best five years of his life. Four days later, he passed away peacefully in his sleep. As her mind came back to the present time, so did her hatred for a deity whose existence she always wrestled with. If God did exist, she hated Him for taking away her friends and people she loved. She hated Him for leaving her alone in the world with a hole in her heart that she could not close.

The law of action and reaction dictated her sad fate if He did not exist. Michelle nonchalantly walked down the steps with a sigh. Sophia quickly swatted away, her tears readying herself to leave.

"Well, she's finally calm," Michelle huffed, "her poor room is wrecked…"

"I can come to fix it tomorrow," Sophia gestured.

"It's a wall and floor," Michelle said, waving her off, "a fun DIY project for me."

"Okay," Sophia exhaled quickly, "I should be…"

"You're not leaving here without your daughter," Michelle sternly cut her off.

"I… I don't understand." Sophia stammered.

"The jig is up," Michelle informed her while walking into the living room. "The rules have changed. It is time."

"She still has school, and…"

"School ends in a month, and we both know she's a straight A+ student on the Principle's List." Michelle stopped her. "Right now, she doesn't need school… she needs you."

"Right now's not a good time," Sophia said dismissively.

"Sophia…" Michelle's tone became stern.

"I have a lot of things to do," Sophia said firmly. "I don't have the time…"

"Make the damn time; she needs her mother."

"I am her mother!" Sophia lashed out. "Every sacrifice I've made was for her! I've made sure she's never wanted for anything since coming back! I even bought this damn…!"

Sophia quickly halted, cupping her mouth. She shamefully shook her head, regretting what she was about to say and to whom she was about to tell it. Michelle walked up to her with a calm smile, gently holding her hands from her mouth with her uninjured hand.

Sophia's eyes glowed as they became glassy again.

"I… I didn't mean."

"Shhhh, I know the talk of fear when I hear it," Michelle calmed her. "There's no need to apologize."

"I'm not ready," Sophia whispered with her head lowered. "Michelle… I'm not ready…"

Michelle lifted the chin of the most powerful woman on the planet with a smile, looking at her with tear-drenched eyes.

"You're ready. You've always been ready. Every day when you're about to leave here after your visits, I can see it in your eyes how badly you wanted to take her. How much it killed you every time you had to fly away without her. I love her the same as I love Annie and Penny, but if you were to ask me to give her to you on any of those days. I would have packed her up in a heartbeat and with a smile… because she **belongs to you**."

Her words brought Sophia to sobbing fits. Michelle consoled her as if she was a child wiping her eyes.

"You have suffered enough," Michelle affirmed. "You have sacrificed enough. Your baby needs you, and you need her."

"I'm scared," Sophia whimpered, "I'm so scared…"

"You wouldn't be human if you weren't scared, and you're not alone. You are never alone."

"Shouldn't we wait," Sophia meekly asked, "like… give her tonight, and I can pick her up tomorrow?"

Michelle gave her a dull look.

"You want her to possibly run after I tell her. And then have to go through the pain of hunting her down?"

Sophia nodded in defeat.

"I'll call Benji."

"I'll go back upstairs and break the news," Michelle sighed, "get ready to chase her if she bolts."

Michelle smiled, rubbing her arm, and then turned, taking in another deep breath of air. She readied herself for more fireworks and marched out of the living room and back upstairs.

A timid Sophia slowly walked out of the living room and sat on the steps to listen. She listened as the child screamed, not wanting to go, refusing to go, while Michelle told her to calm down with motherly sternness. She threatened to run away, as predicted, but Michelle warned her that her mother downstairs was stronger and faster than her with the ability to fly, so there was nowhere to run. Bawling and pleas followed with incoherent words.

"Please, Michelle! Please!" Kimberly bitterly wept. "Please don't make me go with her! I'll be good! I promise! I'm sorry I hurt you! I didn't mean to! It was an accident! I won't do it again! I swear! Please don't send me away! Please! Please!"

"Honey, it's not about that," Michelle said softly. "You got to calm down and listen."

It was the crying that got to her. She was the reason for her tears. Sophia slowly covered her ears, tucking her head between her legs on the steps, fighting to drown it out. She wanted to run. She wanted to run someplace deep and dark so that she could die.

CHAPTER 15

Eight hours and thirty minutes later, Sophia came into view of her island. Her usual flight time was between fifteen and twenty minutes. She kept cruising speed with the private jet carrying her precious cargo.

Sophia flew ahead, touching down on the landing strip where a waiting Earl trotted onto the tarmac to greet her. His smile had a nervous twitch, reacting to the second time he saw borderline fear on Sophia's visage. He put two and two together, realizing it was coming from the approaching plane.

"Welcome home… again. You didn't tell me you were bringing home new arrivals."

"One new arrival," a hesitant Sophia answered, "my… daughter."

Earl wore a stunned yet calm mask as the plane came down for its final descent, making a perfect landing. As the plane rolled to a halt, parking in front of them, Earl appeared more anxious than Sophia, wondering if the child exiting the plane would be ordinary or a super-powered miniature similar to her mother.

"How old is she?" Earl innocently asked.

"Ten," Sophia said bluntly.

The door to the Embraer Legacy 500 opened as Benjamin, the pilot, came to the entrance with his carry-on luggage in one hand and a red suitcase in his other hand. He waited as a tall young woman in her teens with Sophia's complexion wearing long, curly, wild black hair timidly stepped into the entranceway, gripping a pink My Little Pony teddy bear. A spider monkey perched on her shoulder, looking at his new surroundings. The gray jumpsuit she wore belonging to Annie was too small, while the green flip-flops belonged to Michelle.

"That's a very big ten-year-old," Earl muttered, running his hand across his skull.

Earl quickly noticed that Sophia remained rooted in place. Her eyes fixated on the young woman who buried her face in her plush toy with fretting eyes. Earl took the initiative, trotting over to grab the rolling steps, docking it with the plane's entrance. He stepped down hard on the braking mechanism, locking it into place.

"Hello, young lady," a chirpy Earl greeted, "welcome to Sanctuary! Come on, don't be shy."

Benjamin gingerly gestured to Kimberly to go first. The child timorously advanced forward, grabbing the railing as she slowly walked down the steps. Her eyes glanced between the steps and her waiting mother, who fought to hide her trembling.

"Hello, there!" Earl said with a beaming smile. "Can I ask your name?"

Kimberly did not answer as her doe eyes locked with her mother's. It was the longest two minutes as they stared at one another. Earl looked at Sophia, subtly gesturing and snapping her out of her trance. Sophia straightened up, walking briskly toward the trio, which made Kimberly look down at the tarmac as if she had done something wrong.

"Thank you, Benji," Sophia said with a grateful, forced smile. "I really appreciate you doing this at short notice."

"Not a problem Soph," Benjamin replied with a nod. "This is the one place I enjoy flying to."

The awkwardness came back again for another minute. Earl never saw Sophia; this rattled and lost. He made a fake cough to break the silence again.

"So Benji, you up for some barbecue pork chops?" Earl innocently asked.

"As long as it comes with a couple rounds of checkers," Benjamin said, taking the subtle hint."

"Yes… I need to…" Sophia nervously coughed, "get her home."

Benjamin nodded, handing her daughter's suitcase to her.

"Well, we'll leave you ladies to settle in," Earl nodded. "It's nice to meet you…"

"Kimberly," Sophia tensely answered, "her name is… Kimberly."

Earl smiled, waving to her.

"Very nice to meet you, Kimberly."

Sir George waved goodbye for her as she continued to look down at the ground.

"Nice flying with you, Kimberly," Benjamin said, waving goodbye to her.

He nodded to Sophia before walking off to follow Earl for rest and relaxation. She knew their topic of conversation once Benjamin got settled in would be about them.

Sophia huffed. The two of them were finally alone, and she could feel the eyes once again on her.

"Uh," Sophia motioned while stumbling with her words, "so my house… is this way."

Butterflies abused her stomach as Sophia slowly turned to walk. The sound of flapping flip-flops meant she did not have to turn around, but she could still feel those eyes locked on her, making the hairs on the back of her neck stand on end.

~~~~~~~~~~~~~~~~~~~~~~~~~~~~~~~~~~~

A couple of minutes later, Sophia slowly walked with a stranger following behind her, who had been in her belly for nine months, tightly clutching her stuffed animal. Sir George, the spider monkey, sat on Kimberly's shoulder, absorbing his new surroundings. The evening moonlight shined high above as they walked through a village. Some people were outside sitting or standing on their huts' porches; others walked by, heading home. Everyone acknowledged Sophia. She could also feel them staring silently at the person following her.

For those who looked like they wanted to start a conversation, Sophia quickly waved to them or said she would talk to them later, sometimes in their own language. Sophia exhaled, glancing up at her house, which she had been away from for almost twenty-four hours.
~~~~~~~~~~~~~~~~~~~~~~~~~~~~~~~~~~~

The honey-varnished cherry oak two-floor hut-styled house was the first constructed home on the island. Built by herself with her own hands, it fit the climate while providing all of the modern world's amenities. Unlike the other residential huts, she added a one-car garage and a paved driveway.

"You have a car?" Kimberly innocently asked.

In her daze, she forgot the garage door was up. Halfway out of it was a fully restored 1969 ZL1 Camaro with a metallic sea blue paint finish. It stopped Sophia in her tracks. She slowly turned to the classic relic sitting in her driveway.

"Yes, I do," Sophia calmly responded.

"Why?"

"It belonged to your father," Sophia blurted out.

The silence was long and awkward. Sophia did not know why she quickly divulged that information or if she should say something else. She did know that she was fearful of turning around and looking into the face that had her late husband's eyes. The hairs stood higher on the back of her neck, feeling her daughter's eyes on her. This was not how she imagined motherhood to be. It was clear that they were both afraid of each other.

Sophia took a breath and continued to walk; the sound of flip-flops following her meant she did not have to stop again. She walked up the steps to the porch and turned the unlocked door, walking in first. Quickly flicking on the lights, she held the door open while fighting to keep from trembling as Kimberly slowly walked through the doorway, looking around.

The outside was exceptionally deceiving as she scanned the modern open floor plan. She spied a large sunken living room to her left with a full-size light tan sofa couch. In front of the sofa, Sophia built a stone fireplace. Hanging over the fireplace was a sixty-four-inch plasma screen television. Also within the living room was a Mason & Hamlin upright piano acting as a separator between it and the dining room.

The dining room was simple, with a large black table with seating for eight. Next to it was an open kitchen with a granite island, a chef-style stove and oven, and a large stainless-steel refrigerator freezer matching the other appliances. The kitchen cabinets adorned a rich cherry Oakwood with silver flower-styled knobs. Steps lead up to the second floor with an open view of what appeared to be four other rooms. To Sophia's right were double frosted bay doors and what seemed to be an office.

"Uh… welcome to… my… home," Sophia stuttered as she began her introduction. "As you can see, the living room, dining room, kitchen, small half bathroom, and my office."

Kimberly, along with Sir George, gave the place another look around. The monkey appeared to be more excited to be there than she was.

"Uh… upstairs are the bedrooms and bathrooms," Sophia continued. "Three bedrooms, and two full baths… one is an en-suite in my room, but the other bathroom is just as nice, and yours. Would you like to see your room?"

"Yes, please…" Kimberly meekly said, still looking around.

Sophia swallowed air into her lungs, nodding before leading her daughter up the stairs to the second floor. They passed one room and a bathroom to a smaller bedroom. She fought to control her hand from shaking as she opened the door, flicking on the light. Kimberly slowly walked into the room as if heading to the gallows. Once inside, her face changed to one of bewilderment.

Everything was styled and updated for a young girl. Even the Mac computer on the tan wood desk had a pink custom back attached. It was as if the room had been readied for years, waiting for her to arrive. Sir George leaped off her shoulder, running up to the desk where he climbed up, making himself at home. Kimberly walked over and sat down on the bed. It felt comfortable but was meant size-wise for the body of an ordinary ten-year-old.

"I will have a new bed in here tomorrow morning," Sophia promised." If you want, I can switch out the bed in the other room…"

"No,… this is fine," Kimberly answered, her face still buried in her pony.

"I will also get you some clothes that will fit you tomorrow," Sophia added. "I have some bedclothes you can wear tonight that should fit you."

"Can I just sleep in this, please?" Kimberly asked, referring to the sweatsuit she had on.

"Sure," Sophia nervously replied. "It's not a problem. Are you hungry? Do you want something to eat?"

"I'm tired," Kimberly responded. "I'd like to lay down, please."

Her request and tone caused Sophia to drop her head.

"Sure. It was a long flight. I'll be outside if you need anything."

Kimberly said nothing more as she rolled onto the bed, turning her back to her. She grasped her teddy bear tightly while wrapping her legs around it. Sir George leaped from the desk to the bed, stroking her hair for comfort. Sophia backed out of the room, leaving the light on. She closed the door, leaving it slightly cracked so she would not feel as if she was imprisoned. It began anyway; though faint, she could hear slight sniffling and whimpering coming from her.

Instead of going to her room, Sophia walked down the stairs. Her body shook violently with each step as her heart and stomach became tightly wrenched with knots. It was too overwhelming. She walked out the front door to her porch as her tears started to fall; hurrying down the steps, she ran around the side of the hut where she clutched her mouth. Collapsing in the sand, she bitterly wept, praying no one heard her. A flood of emotions and memories bombarded her weakened state. Joy, sorrow, fear, and anxiety assaulted her at once. In her mind, she begged them to stop, but they continued to have their way with her.

"I'm not ready for this… I'm not ready," Sophia sobbed. "What do I do? What do I do?"

Sophia knelt in the sand and leaned against her home, clutching her chest to keep her heart from popping out of it while muffling her cries as she endured the ordeal throughout the rest of the ending night into the early morning.

CHAPTER 16

The following day, Kimberly woke to the scent of freshly cooked food. She sat in bed, looking around at a room that was not hers, still clutching her teddy bear. The digital clock on the desk read 11 a.m. On the dresser, she spied a stack of neatly folded clothing. Her ears picked up the traitorous Sir George downstairs, chirping away, no doubt being fed by the woman who brought her to the strange island last night. Finally, releasing her grip from the pink pony, Kimberly set it on the bed and slowly rose to her feet. Taking a deep breath, she crept over to the full-body mirror to look at herself for the first time since yesterday. What she thought was a bad dream was a living nightmare for about a split second.

The initial shock of going from four-foot-five to five-foot-eleven inches startled her at first until she began examining the benefits of being a full-grown teenager. As Kimberly twisted and turned to check out her new physique, a devious little smile grew.

She looked around to ensure she was alone before peeking inside her sweatshirt.

"Ginger Fletcher is going to be so jealous," Kimberly whispered under her grin.

She looked around again, pulling up the bottom of the sweater shirt to reveal her abdomen, and shuddered, almost falling backward. Kimberly was a very active child. However, she had never done a sit-up or crunch religiously in her entire ten years unless in physical education. Kimberly ran her hand across her well-defined and shredded abs. It did not end there as she felt up her newly toned arms and powerful legs.

"I'm Peter Parker," Kimberly swallowed, addressing her reflection in the mirror.

She remembered the smell of food coming from downstairs. Sooner or later, she would be coming upstairs to get her. Although Kimberly would prefer to spend the next few days locked inside her new foreign bedroom, examining herself and away from the person downstairs, she knew that would not happen.

Kimberly glanced at the clothes on the dresser and decided to change. Her outfit consisted of a sports bra, underwear, a loose white t-shirt, and a pair of jean shorts that covered most of her thigh. Overall, it was an effortless and comfortable outfit for the tropical weather.

She scowled at her reflection in the mirror.

"Total dorksville," Kimberly snorted.

Closing the door for privacy, Kimberly looked around the room, pulling open the drawers to the desk and finding school pens, crayons, and notebooks. Eventually, she found what she was looking for.

Taking the shorts off, Kimberly went to work with the pair of scissors, cutting them a little shorter to the point of borderline Daisy Dukes. Putting them back on, she tied her shirt into a belly shirt. With one quick look in the mirror, she ran her fingers through her curly hair and then attempted strutting out of the room. Her grand, defiant entrance was railroaded when she grasped the brass doorknob, crushing it in her bare hand.

"Oh!" Kimberly yelled. "Oh, no!"

Like clockwork, she could hear her footsteps rushing upstairs.

"Is everything okay?" Sophia nervously yelled from the other side of the door.

"I'm fine," Kimberly stuttered.

Her mind raced, trying to figure out how she would explain the door. It was too late as the woman on the other side attempted to turn it.

"What's wrong with the door?" Sophia asked.

"Nothing!" Kimberly yelled back.

"Then why won't it open?" Sophia's voice grew higher with concern. "Did you lock it?"

"No! I… I think I broke it…" Kimberly finally admitted.

Without a word, Sophia pulled the entire doorknob and locking mechanism from the door, allowing it to open. She walked in, first noticing the doorknob that had been crushed to paste.

Next, Sophia noticed her daughter's changes to the outfit she laid out for her. Kimberly lowered her head, waiting for the stern lecture from her absentee parent on how inappropriate she looked.

"You're wearing it wrong," was all that came from Sophia's lips.

As Kimberly raised her head to ensure she heard correctly, her mother walked past her, placing the broken doorknob on the table. The next thing she felt was the knot she tied in the back, positioning the shirt right under her newly developed chest like a bikini top become loose and brought down. Sophia then pulled the shirt up, tying it in the back over her belly button.

"Nothing wrong with wearing a little belly shirt," Sophia said with a nervous smile, "especially in this weather, but I think this is the look you were going for… cute."

It was simple reverse psychology, especially in this fragile glass-shattering stage of their relationship.

"Thanks," Kimberly dismissively said.

"Don't worry about the door," Sophia reassured her. "I'll have it replaced by today. Now when you're ready, I have breakfast downstairs."

Sophia lightly patted her shoulder and quickly left the room, heading back downstairs. Kimberly narrowed her eyes at her as mixed emotions swelled up within her. She went to undo the knot she made until she took another look in the mirror and decided to leave it.

Kimberly slipped on Michelle's flip-flops, heading for the door. She stopped turning around for one last thing. Walking back to the dresser, she picked up the mangled doorknob and placed it between her hands.

She pressed her hands together. The metal of the abused knob crunched and groaned as she flattened it to a near pancake. Kimberly looked at one hand and then the other. Not even a scratch or blister appeared on them. A bright smile appeared on her face again as she examined the doorknob, now rendered useless.

"Forget Peter Parker, I'm Clark Kent."

Kimberly placed the knob, now transformed into a disk, back on the table, heading out the door. She wanted to stomp down the steps to annoy her but feared being childish would bring the entire structure down. The bone she had to pick with her birth mother did not have to entail demolishing her temporary residence.

As Kimberly slowly walked down, minding her steps, she looked over the inside of the home under the shine of natural sunlight. It was warm and cozy, the near-perfect merger of a regular house and a tropical bungalow. The smell of good food directed her attention to the dining room. The table was filled with everything from pancakes and toast to scrambled and fried eggs. She narrowed her eyes in disappointment at Sir George, already seated on the table, munching away on a banana.

A nonchalant glance into the kitchen turned into a two-minute-long stare on the steps as she watched Sophia moving about, preparing the last bit of breakfast. Kimberly realized one of the reasons she disliked her so much. It was hard to hate her when she looked so beautiful. Memories from birth to their second meeting at the mountain flashed before her, and she had not changed since then.

The advantage of possessing a superhuman memory was that Kimberly had an eternal reminder of who she came from. The double-edged cut of the sword was that she also remembered who did not want her. Sophia looked up long enough from placing her homemade biscuits on a plate to see Kimberly staring at her.

"Is everything okay?" Sophia nervously asked.

Her voice pulled Kimberly out of her trance. Her indifferent face was back on again as she continued down the stairs.

"I'm fine," Kimberly dismissively said.

She could feel her birth mother's eyes watching her as she descended the rest of the stairs. It did not stop until she sat at one of the chairs at the head of the table. Kimberly snuck a dirty look at Sir George, who continued to chomp away on his banana.

"Sellout," Kimberly muttered under her breath.

The enemy noticed how large the table and the distance were between the two of them. She adjusted, moving the food closer to her before sitting at one of the side chairs. Kimberly then noticed that all the plates and cups on the table were made of very thick metal, from what she could determine, made to withstand whatever punishment she might accidentally administer to them. She was not sure whether to be appreciative or insulted.

"I didn't know what you wanted, so I made a variety of things. I hope you like it."

"Thanks."

"Please, dig in," Sophia gingerly said to her.

Kimberly took her fork, stabbed at a couple of pancakes, placed them on her plate, and then some sausages. She took her spoon and scooped scrambled eggs from a bowl, plopping them into her dish. The food smelled good, but she had no appetite. Kimberly focused on the woman sitting across from her, attempting to act like this was a regular thing for them.

"So you own this island?" Kimberly blurted out while slouching in her seat.

"Uh, yes, I do," Sophia answered slowly, pouring tea into each cup.

"So, you're rich?" Kimberly fired off another question.

"I'm well off," Sophia politely responded with a smile minus eye contact.

Kimberly folded her arms, playing defensive while verbally going on the offensive.

"Did you buy this? The island?"

Nervous sweat ran down Sophia's back as she almost doused her cup of tea with too much sweet milk. This blatant interrogation out of nowhere, though not as verbally abusive as when she was arrested for Robert's murder, still rattled her. Sophia took a shallow breath, deciding to do exactly what she did then. Speak the truth and nothing but the truth, no matter how crazy.

"I… didn't buy this island," Sophia said, slowly swallowing. "I… made it."

"You made this island?" the ten-year-old asked, narrowing her eyes.

Sophia nervously nodded while sipping her tea, hoping it would settle the violent churning in her stomach.

"How?" Kimberly leaned in, asking.

She placed her arms and elbows on the table, hoping she would say something. Her one-word question unsettled Sophia's stomach again. No one ever asked her in detail how she made the island. Everyone just accepted the fact that she created it.

"I… uh… dove into the ocean," Sophia fought to form her words, "then I burrowed into the ground…"

"You burrowed through the Earth's mantle," Kimberly finished her sentence.

Sophia took another sip of tea.

"Uh… yeah, I then did some things… to force a large amount of lava along with an underwater volcano to the surface. It eventually hardened and created this."

The answer pushed the child back into her seat as she stared at her birth mother. Sophia's eyes focused on the table as her mind wandered back to the four straight days she spent under the upper mantle of the Pacific Ocean. With singed hair and a heavy-duty wetsuit slowly being scorched from her body, she carefully blasted rock. She moved tectonic plates, forcing enough magma to the ocean's surface to cause an underwater volcano to erupt to create her paradise. The hardest part was lifting a volcano while ensuring it did not crumble from the force she exerted to push it to the surface.

By right, Sophia could have commandeered any uninhabited islands within that area regardless of who had territorial rule over them. She wanted something she built with her two hands, something she did not have to fight for or dispute her claim over.

"Did you get in trouble for it?" Kimberly sneered.

The question jarred her back from her thoughts and memories.

Sophia looked around, scratching the side of her neck.

"Not really."

"So, why'd you do it?" Kimberly asked while sucking her teeth. "Create an island?"

"I guess I was bored," Sophia blurted with a smile.

Once again, Sophia sat there with her foot in her mouth, wishing she could rewind and take back what she had just said. It was Robert's PTSD all over again. She was capable of dealing with people's problems who were neither close nor family to her, but when it came to her own family, she was a bumbling buffoon. She second-guessed if using textbook psychological tactics to communicate with her offspring, who clearly did not care for her, was the best way to go.

She put her cup down, sitting up with her head shamefully lowered.

"What I just said did not come out right," Sophia apologized.

What she said came across as she occupied her time with other things instead of her flesh and blood. The scowl Kimberly tried to hide as she sat up signified how it was interpreted and received.

"So… what am I suppose to call you?" Kimberly inquired with an eye roll.

She decided to change the conversation before she slipped and said something she might regret. Sophia kept her eyes down at the table. In her mind, she did not earn the right to be called mom or mother.

"You can call me… Sophia, if you like."

"Fine…" Kimberly acknowledged.

She took her knife, cutting and slapping a piece of butter on her pancakes. She then grabbed the maple syrup, dousing them with it. She picked at the food a bit before taking a bite. She was unsure if it was hunger or the food tasted delicious, but she dug in. Unbeknownst to her, Sophia raised her head, watching a simple act that made her heart swell and her eyes glass over. Kimberly caught it mid-munch of a sausage link and gave her a disturbing, perplexed look.

"You alright?" Kimberly sneered with food in her mouth.

Sophia quickly swatted her eyes.

"Uh… yes… I am."

She collected herself, getting to her feet, as Kimberly wondered if she was trapped with someone with mental or emotional disorders.

"Um…, I… have some quick rounds to make around the island. You might want to get your room situated. You can do anything you want to it; everything in there is yours. I should be about an hour, maybe less. If you want, when I get back, we can go shopping and get you some more suitable clothes for your size."

Kimberly nonchalantly shrugged.

"Sure."

Kimberly hid her relief that she was leaving. She did not have to endure faking to be around her or attempting to get to know her.

"I'll clean up when I get back," Sophia said with a timid smile.

Kimberly no longer looked her way.

"Later."

She cut another piece of pancake, stuffing it in her mouth. Kimberly's mind became preoccupied with Sir George, who had finished his banana and now moved over to pick from her plate. She cut him another dirty look, remembering his treasonous act. He ignored her, munching away on a piece of her pancake. Sophia nodded, giving her a final look before slinking away. The rounds she had to make were not really important. Earl and the council members could have covered it. The questions were just too much for her. Sitting there and looking at her was too much for her. The woman who could bring down mountains was a sniveling psychological wreck before a ten-year-old.

What made it worse was, despite the indifferent mask Kimberly put on to hide her real feelings, Sophia knew that the child she bore hated her, did not want anything to do with her if she had it her way, and was justified about how she felt. She walked out the door, putting on her own mask so no one could see the heavy heart she carried.

With her birth mother gone to handle matters in the village, Kimberly finished her breakfast and took the time to explore the home in further detail. She started with her mother's bedroom, which was extremely large, housing an en-suite bathroom, a walk-in closet, and double glass doors that led out to a balcony with two regular seating chairs, a lounge chair, and a handmade wooden round table with an enormous tan umbrella attached to a stand that went right through it. Entering the walk-in closet, she ran her hands, looking through the various clothes and shoes neatly hung up or placed on shelves, until something caught her eye.

Kimberly reached up, pulling down a wedding photo album from a top shelf. She sat in the closet, flipping through it, viewing pictures of her mother and father on their special day. Besides making out who her grandparents were on both sides and other people she guessed were related to her, she could tell they were happy and in love. It brought a slight smile to her face to put actual faces into her imagination. It did not erase the resentment and desire not to be there. Tired of flipping through pictures, she got up, putting the book back where she found it. Kimberly walked out of the closet and over to the king-size canopy bed, plopping down. She ran her hand across the softness of the sheets the fluffy pillow, and breathed in the air where she slept. The cherry Oakwood dresser draw caught her attention and curiosity.

Nonchalantly, Kimberly pulled the drawer door open. At first, she did not believe what she saw lying at the bottom of the drawer. Her trembling hand reached in as a sick feeling crept into her stomach. She pulled out a full-size picture, her school picture, taken earlier that year. Her eyes welled up as she looked at herself before her transformation. Before Kimberly could wonder how and why she had that picture, she reached in and pulled out more photos of her. There was six years' worth every year that she attended school in Washington. A wave of anger she never knew she had before sparked inside her. It tempted her to tear the pictures to shreds and dash them across the bed for her to come back later and see.

Kimberly realized she would have to talk to her if she did, which she did not want to do. She wanted to leave the island and get as far away from her as possible. She could only plan her escape without knowing by remaining distant without acting like a problem child. Placing the pictures where she found them and smoothing out the bed and pillows to cover her tracks, she decided to leave the house to think.

Kimberly walked back downstairs, heading for the door.

"Sir George, let's get out of here."

The little monkey scurried from the kitchen room table, leaping onto her shoulder as she flew open the front door and walked out. She carefully closed it behind her, remembering the doorknob incident in her temporary room. The bright sun and warm, intoxicating air calmed her as she stepped off the porch.

Her first stop was the garage, which housed the metallic sea blue 1969 ZL1 Camaro. Kimberly stood there, imagining the man in the wedding pictures sitting behind the wheel of it and probably underneath its hood working on it. As she ran her hand across the car's hood, she imagined the rides he would have taken her on.

Memories she would never have brought forth tears and more anger. A form of hatred developed for the woman who bore her, subjecting her to these painful visuals that felt torturous. Another evil thought crept within her to smash the car to bits out of spite. Remembering her plan stayed her hand as she stormed off to get away from the house altogether.

As Kimberly walked through the village, she felt the eyes on her. They varied from nervousness to kindness to curiosity. Through her disinterested glances, she became aware of the various races and ethnicities around her. For the most part, she could pick up within earshot that the majority spoke English or a form of English, but some had learned to speak other native tongues. She was sure she heard a woman with a thick Russian accent speaking Chinese or Korean to an Asian woman who responded to her in Russian. An Arabic man addressed a husband and wife who appeared to be Mexican in their Spanish tongue or his best rendition.

All of their conversations became quiet as she passed by. It was evident that they all knew who she was. The village, though sizable, was not that big. She could tell some villagers wanted to approach and greet her.

Her evil demeanor was the perfect shielding, making her unapproachable.

To her relief, it protected her until she got out of the village, where she trekked to a remote side of the island to be alone. Kimberly sat cross-legged in the sand, collecting small pebbles. Looking to be helpful, Sir George leaped down and scurried about picking some up as well, handing them to her. Sometimes, he would come back with seashells, which she gratefully took, putting them off to the side.

After collecting a fair amount of pebbles, she began flicking them from a seated position. Her memories of watching people perform the action allowed her to execute it on the first try. At the same time, her newly acquired superhuman strength allowed her to fire the pebbles like bullets from a high-powered rifle. Each throw sent the stones tearing through the water a hundred yards at a time, depending on how hard Kimberly threw them. Unbeknownst to her, the anger within her slowly faded as she repeated the act. It also helped that every time she flung a stone, Sir George would screech, clap at the feat, and then scurry off to find more stones for her to do it again.

As much as Kimberly hated to admit it, the island was beautiful. She ran her hand across the warm white sand, wondering if she was too hard on the woman who had given birth to her. If she was being unfair and not giving her a chance, Michelle asked that she give her.

"Hey! Where'd you learn to throw like that?" a young boy's voice howled.

His voice was not only irritating; it brought back the anger and all of the reasons she wanted to get off the island. Kimberly turned, glaring to find not one but two of them.

"Oh, my bad." The boy backed up with a concerned look along with his friend. "We're not bothering you, are we?"

From what Kimberly could tell, he was about her age, maybe a year older. Like her, he was clearly from the States with his carrot-colored fade and freckles. His friend looked to be the same age as him and from the Middle East with dark brown skin. He wore a similarly faded haircut with a little more hair on the top of his head. They both were wet and wore black fishnet tank tops with colorful board shorts. Under their arms, they held boogie boards with anime character graphics printed on them.

Kimberly quickly fixed her face, throwing on a fake smile. The last thing she needed was to be told she was mean to the local brats.

She got up, dusting herself off.

"No, that's okay. I wasn't really doing anything."

"My name is Kyle."

He grinned from ear to ear before motioning to his friend.

"This is Akram, my best bud. He lives next door to us with his mom. They're from Iraq. His English is not so good yet, but he's cool."

"My name is Kimberly. And this is Sir George."

Sir George, formally known as Cornelius, gave a big wave while standing beside her. Akram smiled, waving back at him.

"So, do you have family here?" Kyle curiously asked.

Kimberly's smile slightly disappeared as she hesitantly responded.

"Ms. Dennison is my mom."

Kyle and Akram gave her skeptical looks. Kyle cocked an eyebrow before pressing the issue.

"Seriously?"

"Yeah." She said, looking down at the ground, "She is."

"So, you like got powers like her?" Kyle asked, scratching his head.

"I think I'm strong like her," Kimberly replied, shrugging her shoulders.

"Can you prove it?" Kyle enthusiastically inquired. "Can you pull up that palm tree?"

Kimberly thought about it for a second.

"Okay."

She walked over to a tall palm tree with a fat base. She gripped the trunk and took a deep, nervous breath. As Kimberly did it, she realized she didn't need both hands. The tree groaned with a simple pull as she uprooted it with minimal effort from the sand. Kyle and Akram's eyes widened at the impressive feat as a now fascinated Kimberly held up the one hundred ninety-six pound sixty-foot tree.

"Wow, it's not heavy at all."

"Put it back!" Kyle yelled, snapping out of his amazement. "Your mom will kill us if she sees this!"

Kimberly nodded. She quickly slammed the tree back into the hole she pulled it from; Kyle and Akram dropped their boards and hurried over, filling it with sand with Sir George's help.

"That was close." Kyle exhaled, wiping his brow. "Wow, she really is your mom. How come your eyes don't glow like hers?"

"I don't know," Kimberly replied with a shrug. "A day ago, I wasn't even strong like her or even this big."

"What do you mean?" he asked, perplexed.

"Yesterday, I was about your height, then I got hurt rollerblading. Next thing I knew, I turned into this." Kimberly said, motioning to herself.

"How old are you?" Kyle asked.

"I'm ten," she said plainly.

Kyle shook his head in disbelief.

"You're a huge ten."

She kicked around the sand as the sadness returned to her face; Sir George scurried over to her, climbing back on her shoulder to stroke the side of her head.

Kyle rubbed his chin, thinking of an upbeat topic.

"Maybe you have powers like a mutant. In the X-Men, the mutant's powers develop at certain ages."

"Do they come out during accidents?" Kimberly asked, interested in the topic.

"Sometimes, Cyclops' powers manifested when his parents had to throw him and his brother out of a plane to save them. He ended up using his optic blasts to slow his descent to Earth to save himself and his brother," Kyle said.

"Mines activated after I got hurt. I wiped out on some concrete while skating down a guardrail."

"First of all, that reeks of awesomeness," Kyle replied, pointing to her. "Secondly, how you get your powers isn't an exact science if you know what I mean."

"Supaboy," Akram said, trying to join the conversation.

"Hey, you're right, Akram!" Kyle yelled while snapping his fingers. "You could be like Connor Kent!"

Kimberly stood there with a cocked eyebrow, confused.

"Who?"

"Kon-El? Conner Kent? Superboy? Superman's clone? Well, actually, he's part Superman's clone and part Lex Luthor's clone," Kyle explained to her.

"I thought Superman was Superboy?" Kimberly inquired.

"That was during the Silver Age era, in the modern age, Superboy is a clone. The point is, Superboy originally didn't have all of Superman's powers due to his human DNA and the fact he didn't have long exposure to the sun like Superman did. He was super strong and could jump really far like the Hulk."

"You talking about de Young Justice Version," Akram corrected him.

"Dude," Kyle bit back, "she's obviously not a telekinetic, so her powers fall in line with the Young Justice Version. They still have the same premise."

It was unclear if Akram understood all that Kyle was saying. Kimberly, however, was getting bored with the talk of comic books.

"So, how did you all get here?" she asked, changing the discussion slightly.

Kyle halted his debate with Akram to answer her.

"Oh, well, Akram's dad died in Iraq, and his house was destroyed. Your mom found him and his mom homeless on the streets. His mom was really sick, so she brought them here, made her better, and gave them a new home. She did the same thing for my family and me."

Akram nodded in agreement with Kyle's explanation of how he became a resident of Sanctuary.

"My dad was an accountant for a big company in New York," Kyle said. "He got laid off and tried to get a new job but couldn't find one. For a while, we were okay, but then we lost our house. We started living in hotels and motels, but even that got too expensive. We started living out of our SUV, but then one night, some guys came and robbed us at gunpoint and took it. We were out on the street for a while, and when it got colder, Dad managed to get us into a shelter.

That was really scary. Then, one day, your mom walked into the shelter and announced to everyone that she had a large island, homes, and food for anyone who wanted to come and live with her. Many people thought she was nuts; plenty were afraid of her. I think my folks were both, but they decided they would go with her for some reason. My dad said it was because he prayed the night before about it.

Anyway, she brought us here and gave us a cool new house with everything our old house had. She even gave my dad a job. He helps manage the finances of the island. My mom is a part-time English teacher for those who want to learn English and helps maintain our vegetable crops. Akram's mom teaches Arabic and is one of the town's seamstresses. She made me these cool board shorts for my birthday last month."

As Kyle showed off his orange board shorts with Goku's symbols from Dragon Ball Z on each of the pants legs, Kimberly looked around with a mixture of wonder and resentment. Was being a hero and savior to other people and children more important than being her mother? She thought.

"So, she built all of this?" Kimberly snidely asked while looking around.

Kyle cocked his head, not catching the snideness. He was more perplexed that Kimberly knew nothing about her mother.

"Well, yeah. Your mom is, like, loaded. I think she's like Tony Stark/Bruce Wayne combined loaded. She also got this cool superhuman memory that allows her to do almost anything."

"How do you know that?" Kimberly sneered.

It was irritating for her that he knew more about her biological mother than she did.

"I watched her one day," Kyle nonchalantly explained. "She was on her iPad looking at a video on how to build a concrete foundation and some other stuff about houses. Next thing you know, she was doing it. She didn't even refer to the video."

"Oh, mimicry," Kimberly scoffed, rolling her eyes. "I can do that."

Instantly, she got into a Jeet Kun Do stance, mirroring Master Lee. Her voice and mannerisms changed, mimicking the final fight scene from "Enter the Dragon." Kimberly exploded, throwing powerful kicks and punches, cutting the air and spraying sand as she barked and howled like the legendary martial artist, causing Kyle and Akram to back up in amazement. She then did the unexpected.

Switching styles, her voice mirrored Street Fighter Chun Li's voice as Kimberly mimicked her video game version of the Hyakuretsukyaku "Hundred Rending Legs" technique. Her new, long, powerful legs sent shockwaves, cutting the air. Akram covered his ears while looking on with Kyle, who was awestruck by the display of power. After completing one hundred kicks in less than three seconds, she held her stance like the famed anime video game character. A bright smile beamed across her face with her own personal amazement. She performed the move before but never that fast and with that much power. She was now drunk off curiosity with the need to test her limits.

"Marry me," was all Kyle could say.

"Ew," Kimberly replied, coiling back with a grossed-out expression.

"Hancock!" Akram screamed with an epiphany, jolting both Kyle and Kimberly. "She can do Hancock!"

Kyle's eyes widened with excitement.

"Dude! You are so right! That's why you're my main man!"

The duo started with a fist bump into an explosion, switching to "The Whop," and then finished with the "Kid and Play," leaving Kimberly standing there rolling her eyes at the antics boys do.

"What's he talking about?" Kimberly asked, confused about the impromptu celebration.

"I think we know how to teach you to fly," Kyle grinned.

CHAPTER 17

The following early afternoon, Kimberly stood huddled on the beach around Kyle, Akram, and a couple of other kids from the village, viewing the scene where superhero Hancock, played by Will Smith, took flight after his strength returned on Kyle's iPad Mini.

Their plan from yesterday was to meet back in the same area to see if Kimberly could mimic the feat with her new abilities.

~~~~~~~~~~~~~~~~~~~~~~~~~~~~~~~~~~

Kimberly went home to a waiting Sophia, trying to mask her concern that she went out by herself without allowing her the chance to formally introduce herself to everyone.

Sophia asked how her day went, only for Kimberly to respond that it was okay and that she met some friends. She remembered she had to keep from being the problem child while maintaining an aura of indifference. Not outright hating her but not caring about her, as well.

It was a quiet dinner between the two, followed by Kimberly asking to be excused because she was tired. Sophia knew it was a lie. Her new abilities prevented normal human fatigue. With a timid nod, she allowed her to leave. After cleaning up, Sophia snuck up the stairs to her room with the newly fixed doorknob, bearing witness to a private conversation she wished she did not hear.

"Kimberly, you have to give this a chance," Michelle responded over Skype.

Kimberly sat pouting with her arms folded.
~~~~~~~~~~~~~~~~~~~~~~~~~~~~~~~~~~

"But I want to come home."

Tears ran from her eyes as she fought not to break down so the woman downstairs could hear.

"That is your home and your mother," Michelle reminded her.

"She's not my mother; she's someone who gave birth to me…!," she snapped back.

"Young lady! That is not how I raised you!" Michelle scolded her.

"That's right!" Kimberly answered back. "You and Mark raised me! The Stones raised me! She didn't! And the only reason I'm here is that I look like this! Please… let me come home… please… I don't want to be here."

"Kimberly, no."

Michelle firmly put her foot down.

"You don't understand now, but your mother loves you so much, and she had her reasons for not being there, which, trust me, are harder than you will ever know. She's hurting too. You have to give her a chance because right now you need her more than you need me."

"I don't." Kimberly whimpered, shaking her head.

"Yes, you do," Michelle assured her, "now try and get some sleep, honey. I love you."

Kimberly wiped her eyes, unable to muffle her cracking voice.

"I love you too."

Sophia crept away before she knew she was outside her door and spent the night in her own silent tears.

The following day, filled with shame, Sophia left early, leaving a fresh batch of assorted clothes her size outside her door in a basket and a warm breakfast waiting for her downstairs. Kimberly, needing something more durable, raided her closet and found one of her spring wetsuits in a blue and yellow color scheme. Glad to be alone, she munched on the breakfast as Sir George ate his daily banana, threw out the rest, cleaned up, and then headed out to the beach to see if she could learn how to fly.

~~~~~~~~~~~~~~~~~~~~~~~~~~~~~~~~

"You see," Kyle explained, "Hancock's flight, as shown here, is based on a feat of strength. He uses his super-strong legs to escape Earth's gravity and fly."

"Yeah, but," Kimberly said with a tone of uncertainty, "this is still a movie, not real life."

"Dude," Kyle persisted, "a lot of our real-life concepts come from movies! Hello, Star Trek, where do you think Steve Jobs got the idea for the iPad?"

"I'm not a dude," she snarled.

"Anyway," Kyle continued, "based on this, with those pistons you got for legs, you should have no problem getting airborne. Worst case scenario, you crash and burn in the ocean and swim back to shore."

"Gee, thanks." Kimberly snorted while rolling her eyes.

"Best case scenario," he reminded her, "is that you're up there flying speeding bullet style with ma-dukes."

The prospect of being airborne kept her interested in this hazardous, harebrained scheme, but not for the reason of just being able to fly like her mother. In her mind, achieving flight was her ticket off the island and back to Washington, DC, with Michelle and her friends where she belonged. She was willing to take the risk and overcome her fear.

"Okay," she exhaled with a nod. "Let's do this."

Kimberly took a deep breath, rubbing her hands together, before crouching down and positioning herself as Mr. Smith did in the movie for his final aerial lift-off.

She stayed in that position for about a minute.

"Nothing's happening," Kimberly snapped at them.

Akram gave a suggestion to Kyle in Arabic.
~~~~~~~~~~~~~~~~~~~~~~~~~~~~~~~~

"He says you need to tighten up, like a coil, and bare down into the ground," Kyle relayed.

With an irritated sigh, she stood, loosening up, and then got back into position, coiling up and bearing down as advised. She growled as she tried to squeeze every muscle in her body. Her actions caused the ground underneath her to tremble.

"Okay," Kimberly nervously uttered. "Something's happening!"

"Something's definitely happening!" Kyle yelled, waving his hand and motioning to the other kids, watching in amazement. "Everyone back up!"

Sir George quickly scurried away, climbing up a palm tree to watch at a safe distance.

"Should I go now?!" Kimberly asked.

"Try bearing down some more!" Kyle shouted. "Remember, you're gonna need a lot of power to get airborne!"

"Okay!"

As Kimberly pushed down harder, the ground shook more violently as she created a mini earthquake with the force she generated.

"Everyone get way back!" Kyle screamed again, backing up himself, "whenever you're ready!"

~~~~~~~~~~~~~~~~~~~~~~~~~~~~~~~~~~~

Back at the new huts' construction site, Kimberly's mother, carrying several tons of construction wood on her shoulder, paused as her ears and feet caught a sound and vibration that made her uneasy. She was not the only one to hear and feel it as everyone on the site halted what they were doing, wondering what it was and where it was coming from.

"Earl," Sophia said nervously.

"Sounds like it's coming from the other side of the beach." He speculated while rubbing his chin.
~~~~~~~~~~~~~~~~~~~~~~~~~~~~~~~~~~~

~ ~

Kimberly exploded with a leap, leaving a crater in the ground where she stood while sending a shockwave of sand spraying everywhere. Kyle and Akram shielded two smaller kids with their backs while others scurried away screaming. Sir George screeched insanely from his palm tree lookout as he watched his owner, now airborne, rocket away.

~ ~

Now, looking up, her mother dropped her hefty load, shaking the Earth. She stood dumbfounded with everyone else, watching her daughter rattle the sky with a sonic boom while achieving near hypersonic speeds as she soared to the heavens; it was barely a full two days.

"Oh, dear God," was all Sophia uttered.

Earl now stood next to her. Looking up, he wasn't too sure what to say at that point. Not every day one watched someone's kid physically propel him or herself into the sky with the velocity of a space shuttle.

"Wow, she's really high up."

Sophia slowly turned to Earl, narrowing her eyes. He didn't even bother to look at her, feeling her gaze upon him as he kept his eyes averted to the disappearing flyaway girl. With three giant steps, Sophia exploded into the air, taking flight to chase after her daughter.

~ ~

"Oh, god! Oh god! Too high! Too high!" Kimberly screamed.

Her voice disappeared as the sheer force of the winds turned her tears into ice, blinding her. In her mind, she contemplated how she planned to kill both Kyle and Akram if she survived. She tried to remember the video, hoping it would help her maneuver, but her body would not mimic what she saw. The sky became colder and darker all around her as stars began to appear. Her breathing became difficult as she looked down to see the landmasses shrinking while something came barreling after her.

Sophia chased after her daughter with thrusters blazing, or so she thought. She was cruising at supersonic speed, drunk with amazement that her daughter got this far, this fast, with just her leg power. She realized that fascination made her move at only half speed while her only offspring was probably terrified beyond belief.

She picked up speed to catch up with her. She matched her speed to witness the child trembling like a leaf. She grabbed her daughter, holding her tight. She realized they successfully escaped Earth's atmosphere. For her, it was the umpteenth time visiting outerspace.

After a moment, Kimberly no longer shook. Sophia looked her over, realizing she was adjusting quickly to the harsh atmosphere of space. Her color returned while her skin became warm, signaling that her core temperature was returning to normal. She looked into her eyes and saw a flicker of something she did not want to be there. Holding her close, she quickly changed trajectory, taking her back home. The descent back to Earth and the flight home was a quiet one. A mile off the island, Kimberly tightened her grip as she nuzzled close to her mother for comfort.

It took a couple of minutes in space, she thought, to break down the uncomfortable barrier between the two of them. She treasured the moment until they landed in the middle of the village, where the concerned residents flocked around her and her daughter.

Instantly, Kimberly released her hold on her and made distance between the two of them. She looked down at the sand, trying to hide the emotions building up within her. Catching it all, Sophia attempted to calm the crowd and disperse them quickly.

"Everyone, please," Sophia pleaded, "thank you, but she's fine! No need to worry! I just want to take her home now!"

Akram and Kyle ran up to her with looks of concern for their new friend.

"Kimberly, are you all right?!" Kyle asked.

"We were very worried," Akram threw in.

"I'm fine," Kimberly snapped while glaring at them. "Now get away from me."

Both boys looked at each other with sad looks, not understanding the meaning behind her sudden hurtful words or her apparent dislike for them.

"Kyle McArthur!"

His mother stepped out of the crowd of villagers.

"What did you do?!"

"We were just trying to teach her how to fly, Mom," Kyle nervously answered.

"Akram!"

His mother furiously stepped out as well.

"Did you have something to do with this too?!"

"Everyone, please calm down!" Sophia begged. "No one was hurt."

"No, I didn't get hurt," Kimberly snapped. "I can't get hurt, and it's good to know that I got to shoot myself into space for you to notice me."

Dead, unnerving silence took hold of the crowd from Kimberly's remark. Sophia was now on auto-control as she reached out, grabbing her daughter's arm to calm her down.

"Honey," Sophia stuttered, trying to find words, "that's not true."

"What's not true?!" Kimberly's voice rose as she snatched her arm away from her. "I had to grow like some freak for you to come running to see me! All this time you've been alive! I knew you were alive! Who'd you think you were fooling?! Collecting pictures of me, so you feel like you don't suck as a mother! While this whole time you've been here on this stupid island, taking care of these stupid people! When I was the one who needed you! Well, guess what 'Mom'?! I don't need you anymore!"

Her words made Sophia weak and small; she felt naked in front of onlookers who all wished they were not there to hear what was being said.

"I want to go home!" Kimberly demanded, "take me back to Michelle! She's my real mom! Mark was my real dad! He was dying, and he was still there for me! Both of them were doing your job! You didn't even have the guts to show up at his funeral!"

Her words eviscerated her in front of everyone. All Sophia could do was stand there.

"Kimberly…I…"

"I what?! I'm sorry?!" Kimberly screamed. "I don't want your stupid sorry! I don't want to be on this stupid island! And I don't want to make new stupid friends! I don't want to be with you! I want to go home! Take me home!"

"Honey… please."

Sophia reached out again to draw her in and calm her down.

"Don't touch me!"

Kimberly hysterically slapped her hand away.

"I hate you! I hate you, and I want to go home! I want to go home!"

Kimberly violently stomped, creating a vast crater sending sand spraying everywhere. Everyone in the vicinity yelled and screamed, covering their eyes, except for Sophia, who stood there like a statue. A distraught Kimberly bawled as she backed away from her.

"I'm a big girl now! I'm a big girl!" Kimberly sobbed. "I can take care of myself! I don't need you! I want to go home! I don't want to be here! Send me back home!"

Kimberly turned on her heels and leaped toward the jungle. Sophia stood, watching her leave. She slowly turned to realize everyone was watching her. Heads quickly went down or turned away, making her feel a billion times worse. It was clear everyone was embarrassed for her. She turned and timidly crept away in the opposite direction with her head down, her dreads covering her face as she wrapped her upper body with her arms. Those who stood in her way quickly moved out of it. With a hand motion, Earl dispersed the crowd as he watched her head back home.

~~~~~~~~~~~~~~~~~~~~~~~~~~~~~~~~~~

An hour after the incident, Sophia sat quietly in Robert's Camaro.

95.9 FM "The Ranch" played soft country music as she zoned out. This was her alone time away from the world on some Sunday afternoons or Saturday nights. Everyone knew that when the music started playing unless it was a dire emergency, not to bother her. It was actually Earl who put that rule into effect.

Being the first to break his rule, Earl strolled up to the car, casually running his hand across the passenger side.

Without her permission, he opened up the passenger door, hopping in. This was not the first time Earl had been inside of it. Being a car enthusiast, he could not help but
~~~~~~~~~~~~~~~~~~~~~~~~~~~~~~~~~~

admire its beauty whenever he got around it. Earl turned to view what Sophia was spacing out to; from their vantage point, they had a beautiful view of part of the village, the beach, and the clear blue ocean that went on forever.

"I know what you're thinking," Earl broke the ice, "you are not sending that child back to where she came from."

"I have no right to keep her here." Sophia cleared her throat. "If she does not want to be here."

"She's a child," Earl fired back. "She doesn't know what she wants."

"Earl…" Sophia sighed.

"Before you tell me this is none of my business, you remember the first time we met? There I was at Port Authority in the blazing summer heat, sucking on a bottle of Old Turkey. I reeked of booze and urine soaking through the pants of my old fatigues, which didn't matter to me, and here you come walking up with those creepy glowing blue eyes of yours, asking me if I'd like to come home with you to your island and get cleaned up."

"You said screw me and my island," Sophia said with a smirk, "that you were fine right where you were."

"Thank you for using the PG version of my comment." Earl chuckled with a bowed head. "Your smile never broke on that day. You then asked me my name and told me to take care of myself. This went on for about six months. Every four days or week would go by, and you'd show up, always with clean clothes and something for me to eat. We'd talk for a while and, just before you left, you'd always ask me if I wanted to come home with you."

"And you'd say, 'thank you kindly, but I'm good right where I am,'" Sophia responded.

"You knew that was booze and stubbornness talking." Earl sighed while glancing at her. "You know what did it for me? Grandpa Chip."

The mention of his name created a mist around Sophia's eyes as she stared into space.

"Back then, we called him Crazy Chip," Earl continued. "He'd walk around PA in all four seasons with just a torn white ratty shirt and a pair of jeans two sizes bigger than him. He stunk to high heaven from soiling himself all the time; feet were as black as tar because he wore no shoes. He went into fits where he beat his chest cursing and yelling, usually saying, 'I ain't gonna take this f'n shit no more.' It used to be a good ole joke for us hanging around there. We'd chime in sometimes."

Earl's face changed as he zoned out, returning to that time.

"I remember that hot ass day in August. Chip went into one of his fits, but it was worse than usual. He was screaming and banging his chest, saying the same thing over and over again, 'I ain't gonna take this f'n shit no more.' It became so annoying, we started to move away from him. He kept going till he was frothing at the mouth, and then… you showed up."

Earl lowered his head, losing his composure. Sophia held his hand, rubbing it to comfort him, as his lips trembled while tears fell from his eyes.

"You just walked up to him, and without a word, just threw your arms around him and held him. And I watched that screaming fit… turn into crying sobs. And he held onto you… Lord, he held onto you. And I realized, all that time, he was trying to say 'I can't take it anymore… help me… someone, please help me.'"

~ ~

Sophia remembered that day and the rest of the story. It was the only time she took a plane ride to her island. Chip held her hand during the flight as he rocked back and forth in a daze. Once there, she cut his hair and beard, stripped him of his soiled rags, and washed him from head to toe. Treated his scalp for lice, groomed and cut his overgrown yellow nails, and then went to work slowly removing the black callus from his feet.

He was the only other person to live in her home. Sophia worked on him for two days, nursing him with soft foods like porridge and liquids. His fits would come now and then, minus the profanity. During those times, she held and sang to him songs her mother sang to her until they subsided.

She did not know his story, and she did not care.

Sophia began addressing him as Grandpa Chip, and eventually, he began to respond to it. In time, he answered her with three words. The only three she would hear him speak, "God bless you."

When Sophia was on trips or missions, he would sit on the beach's edge, watching the waves roll up to the shore as the sun shined on him. She took him on routine strolls around the island and observed the lost life for decades return to him. He liked strawberry ice cream and his head to be rubbed. The first time he laughed, her heart filled, and her eyes burst.

Sophia enjoyed his company for eight long months.

One Friday night, when she put him to bed, he smiled at her and said, "God bless you, my child."

On Saturday morning, she went to get him for breakfast, she found him peacefully sleeping in his warm bed.

Sophia placed him on the beach to always look out, watch the ocean run up, and feel the sun on him.

~ ~

"That day, you didn't have to come over to me and ask if I wanted to come home with you," Earl continued. "Needless to say, my first three weeks here weren't heaven when you're trying to get clean for the umpteenth time. And my disposition wasn't the best stuck on an island where I couldn't run to a liquor store or cop some heroin or crack."

"There was a tribal vote to kick you off after the second week," Sophia interjected.

Her remark caused Earl to crack up laughing. His laughter was contagious as she cracked a smile.

Earl turned to her with glassy eyes.

"I'm going to die on this island. I and everyone else with my disease have come to terms with that, but we're alive because of you. And I would like to think that one of my purposes in this life is to be sitting in this car talking to you right now and helping you out for a change."

Sophia's smile trembled as her eyes became glassy.

"I know when people have really given up on you," Earl nodded. "When they've thrown in the towel and written you off as dead. My wife and kids did it, and I deserved it. That's not what's going on here today. As we speak, your little girl is sitting in the animal preserve waiting for you. Zeek and Oz took the ATVs to look for her and radioed in her position. She's out there angry, hurting, and waiting for you to weather that storm built up in her. You know it, and I know it."

"I've failed her, Earl," Sophia whimpered. "I wasn't there for her... I don't know how to be a mother..."

"BS," Earl fired back sternly. "You damn well know how to be a mother, even to a big baby like me! You didn't hesitate the second you saw her shoot up into that sky today. You went after her, and God help anyone or anything that got in your way. That is the building block of a good mother... a great parent! You just got rattled because she cracked the chink in your armor. You're human. It happens to the best of us."

The human part made her break down; Earl placed a fatherly hand on her shoulder.

"If she really wanted to leave, I doubt there's anything that could stop her. She would have swum, leaped, or whatever her way back to the states. She is out there waiting for you. All you've got to do is go get her."

Sophia gave him a daughterly hug, which took him back a bit. He embraced her as he would his own.

"Now, the price for my advice is..."

"You're not getting my car, Earl."

Earl chuckled, which made Sophia laugh again. Breaking up their hug, they sat there a little longer, enjoying the view and listening to the radio.

CHAPTER 18

Twenty minutes later, Sophia flew over her wildlife preserve, searching for her daughter. She had sectioned off a good portion of the island, creating habitats for endangered species to thrive and multiply. One section was for apes and monkeys, another for larger animals such as elephants and rhinos, and another for big cats. Sophia taught herself to care for each species, considering their environment, health, and dietary needs. Occasionally, she would fly in a specialist to assist in giving them regular checkups to ensure they remained healthy. She hoped to replenish the population under her protection and reintroduce them someday to the real world where they belonged.

Sophia slowly descended into the big cat section of her preserve. Not long before, a young male South China Tiger walked up to her, growling. He playfully jumped up, placing his massive paws on her shoulders while trying to sink his teeth into her impervious skin. Sophia patted his back while scratching his ear.

"How are you doing, Butch?" she spoke baby talk to him. "You being good?"

Sophia pulled him off, setting him back down on his feet. He, in turn, rolled on his back, where she rubbed his belly.

"Head on back to Gloria, big boy."

She gave him one final pat.

"I'll see you later."

Sophia walked off as he lay there, purring, watching her leave. She tried her best to stay detached to prevent domestication. However, her big heart gravitated toward beautiful things. Just as Earl confirmed, Sophia found her daughter sitting underneath a tree. Two young cheetah cubs lay beside her as their mother watched from a protective distance. She rubbed the male's belly as it playfully clawed at her hand while the female found its head resting on her lap. Sophia slowly strolled over, catching the attention of the cubs. Though her back was turned, Sophia felt her daughter rolling her eyes in disgust at her presence. The male pup sat up as she neared the tree and sat beside her daughter.

Neither one said a word nor looked in the other's direction. The young male Cheetah finally stood up and walked over, placing its paws in Sophia's lap, curiously sniffing her. She scratched his chin, which got him purring as she fought to form the words she wanted to say in her head.

"There's this nasty habit in the Caribbean and Latin American cultures that I've always hated," Sophia softly spoke. "It's actually prevalent in a lot of other cultures, but, in my opinion, it is the worst in those two. When something horrible or traumatic happens to someone, especially children, you're expected to get over it somehow and sweep it under the rug. To talk about it is to bring shame to the family or opening old and unnecessary wounds. I always thought it was a horrible and detestable way to live, and I was never going to partake in that aspect of my heritage."

The young male cub rested half of its body on Sophia's lap as she gently scratched his ear and neck, causing his hind leg to rapidly kick. She slightly closed her eyes as she continued.

"I don't expect you to get over this or forgive me for what happened to you. You have every damn right to be angry and furious because I'm furious too."

She paused a minute, expecting her daughter to say something. Sophia slightly braced herself to hear, "I really don't want to hear what you have to say." instead, she felt Kimberly shifting where she sat, attempting to be more attentive.

"I always wanted a baby," Sophia continued. "I had two Barbie dolls growing up and twenty different baby dolls. Cabbage Patch, you name it. I used to run up to pregnant mothers and ask to touch their bellies. I wanted to hold little infants but was too young, and when I was old enough and could hold them, a part of me didn't want to give them back. I was so baby crazy. I think I scared my mom. I overheard her one day telling a friend she was scared I'd get pregnant once I hit puberty. Probably the reason I was never allowed to have a boyfriend until I was seventeen."

Sophia smiled a bit, finding the memory amusing now that she was older; the male cub copied his sister and had now fallen asleep in her lap.

"Thankfully, that never happened; as much as I loved babies, I also wanted to be a doctor. I graduated top of my high school class, again in college, then too in medical school. While doing that, I met and married a wonderful man who loved me and wanted a simple happy life with children just like me. It was as perfect a life as anyone could have. Then it all went to hell in one night."

Sophia sighed, correcting herself.

"Actually, it was more than one night. There were signs that things were not right, and something bad was coming, but I just didn't see it, or I just refused to see it. Then during my trial, I found out I was pregnant with you. I couldn't decide if it was a blessing or the cruelest joke ever. Here I was carrying a new life that I always wanted, and my life was about to be over."

Her eyes glowed brighter as tears welled up within them.

"I decided then and there that I didn't give a damn about the trial," Sophia's voice crackled. "That for the next nine months, I was going to find a way to enjoy being pregnant and preparing for your future even if I was not there. I would cherish rubbing my belly every day as it got bigger, singing to you, and feeling your little kicks. And when you finally came out, and I got to hold you in my arms and kiss your little nose, it felt like it was just you and me and no one else in the world… until they took you away from me."

Sophia's glowing tears fell from her face as her voice got raspy; the male cub slightly opened an eye and cocked an ear as he felt his human pillow tremble.

"I am forever furious because you were mine. It was supposed to be my breasts that nursed you, my hands that burped and cleaned you. I was supposed to hear your first words, see your first steps, take you to your first day of kindergarten. And it was all taken away from me. I will never have those experiences or memories. And I am so friggin angry!"

"Then why didn't you come for me?!" Kimberly's own voice cracked as her tears fell. "When you came back, why didn't you come to get me?!"

"I did, I really did," Sophia earnestly said. "You were the first thing on my mind when I awoke, and nothing on Earth was faster than me on that day getting to DC. But as I hovered a mile up from the house, I realized I couldn't take you. I couldn't destroy your world for the third time. I couldn't give you a normal life."

"But I was never normal!" Kimberly shot back. "I remembered seeing you as a baby! I knew you were my mother from then! When I was old enough to talk, I'd tell people in front of the Stones that they weren't my parents! I'd describe you in detail! I'd hear Ms. Stone crying in her bedroom sometimes after I said it. I wasn't trying to be mean… I didn't know what I was doing!"

Sophia fell silent as she allowed her daughter to unload ten years of pain.

"I would go to school and get bullied and teased for being a know it all and acting so perfect," Kimberly rambled on. "No one wanted to play with me or be my friend. I was all alone until I saw you at that mountain. I knew who you were the second I saw you… and I thought my mommy came back for me. I'm not alone anymore… but then you flew away with that woman… and never came back."

Kimberly rocked as she cried uncontrollably. It awoke the female Cheetah resting in her lap, who looked up at her purring.

"I knew you were alive. Mark and Michelle never said anything, but I knew it. My mommy is the strongest person in the world; nothing could hurt her. She's going to come and get me. All I wanted was for you to come and get me. But you never came. So I started to think you didn't want me that you were ashamed of me because I wasn't strong like you.."

"No, baby, no," Sophia cried.

Sophia got to her knees and crawled over to her daughter, wrapping her arms around her. Frantically, she kissed her forehead as she sobbed. Kimberly wailed uncontrollably as she clutched onto her mother's arm. The cheetah cubs, now fully awake, lazily watched with curiosity the heartbreaking scene.

"I didn't know," Sophia wept. "I didn't know. I don't care about powers and abilities. I just wanted you to have what was taken from me… something normal. I didn't think I could give you that! If I knew all you wanted was me, nothing in this universe would have kept you from me."

Gently, she wiped Kimberly's eyes and raised her chin to gaze into them as she held her.

"Sometimes adults don't make the best decisions," Sophia explained. "Especially for their children. I chose for you, and I shouldn't have. I should have had the courage to come to you and ask you what you wanted. And in that, I failed you, and I am so sorry. I don't expect you to forgive me. I'm just asking for a chance to make things right. Let's start with any questions that you have bottled up inside you for so long. I'll answer it truthfully and honestly."

Kimberly nodded in agreement. Sophia let her go, allowing her to sit cross-legged in front of her. She mirrored her as they held each other's hands. Kimberly wiped her eyes and took a deep breath as she contemplated her first real question to her mother.

"What am I?" Kimberly finally asked.

"You are the first superhuman ever born."

It flowed from Sophia's lips as natural as breathing.

There was a bit of pride in her tone that was never there before, the realization that she had given birth to someone so magnificent and beautiful.

Kimberly's face had an expression of confusion and fear.

"I thought you were…?"

"No, I'm not; you know what DNA is, right?" Sophia hesitantly asked.

"Deoxyribonucleic acid," Kimberly recited. "They are the building blocks of all life."

"Very good, your father became an enhanced human due to experiments done on him by the military when he was a soldier. Enhanced meaning much stronger than normal humans, but nowhere in the ballpark of you and me. When I became pregnant with you, the DNA in his gene, which is the molecular unit of heredity of a living organism, became a part of you and turned you into what you are."

Kimberly tilted her head, still a bit confused.

"You weren't a super or enhanced human?"

"No," Sophia answered, shaking her head. "I was a normal human being."

Kimberly leaned in, still a bit bewildered.

"Then, how?"

"You… you turned me into a superhuman."

Sophia's eyes became glassy as she explained her transformation to Kimberly.

"When you were in my belly, you somehow passed your genes onto me and changed me from the inside out."

"So how come I wasn't strong like you?" Kimberly sheepishly asked.

"You are very strong. You are immune to all forms of sicknesses and diseases, so you can't get sick from anything. That kind of sucks for you because that means you can't fake an illness to get out of school with me."

Her poor joke brought a small smile to Kimberly's face.

"You have a super eidetic memory, recognition memory, adoptive muscle memory, and vocal mimicry," Sophia explained. "The first two mean you can remember and recall everything you've experienced in your life in detail. A book you have read, the movie you watched, a song you have heard, a flower you've smelled, or a food you have tasted. Adoptive muscle memory means that you can perform any physical action after seeing it performed once as long as it is within your physical capability. Those cool moves you were able to duplicate just from watching TV is because of that. You fell after your jump because the terrain was different, and you did not learn to adapt. Real-life is not as controlled as what you see on a screen; sometimes, you will have to use common sense and judgment to adjust and adapt to situations like that."

"Why am I bigger?"

"Our bodies heal differently than normal people when we get hurt; we don't only heal really fast, our bodies create self-defenses so that we don't get hurt the same way again."

"So if I get hurt again, I'm going to grow more?!" a panicked Kimberly asked.

Sophia patted her hand, calming her down.

"No. That's not how it works. Something foreign to your body has to break your skin open, entering your body, most importantly, your bloodstream. When you fell, some rock and stone got into your wounds. Your cells absorbed and studied the small fragments. They then made your skin denser so that rocks won't pierce it and hurt you again. The rest of your body had to mature and go into puberty early to help support your heavier skin weight. Your muscle and bones became stronger and longer, as well as your internal organs. God forbid, if it happens again, you'll probably only get as big as me. The tradeoff is you're now stronger, faster, and more durable."

"Is that how you got stronger?" Kimberly asked. "Did you get hurt?"

They were simple words that took Sophia back to bad times for an instant, enough for her to wipe tears again from her eyes as she nodded.

"Yes, I got hurt a couple of times."

Kimberly saw that her question was taking her mother into a sad place and decided not to press further.

"What was my father like?" Kimberly asked.

"A wonderful man with a big heart that could make you laugh for days." Sophia beamed as she answered. "You have his eyes and ears. Everything else, including the hair, is me. He would have so loved you. It wouldn't have mattered what you were, but I think he always wanted a little girl."

Sophia moved closer, running her hand through her daughter's thick, dark curls. Her heart quickened, realizing this was her third time touching her offspring since being with her. Kimberly closed her eyes as if she were one of the cubs.

"How did he really die?"

Kimberly let the question slip out before looking up at her mother.

Sophia did not flinch or break at the question. Instead, she drew her daughter close, holding both her hands. She leaned in with a smile, resting her forehead against Kimberly's.

"Let's make a deal, whether you decide to stay here or not, on your sixteenth birthday… if you really want to know… I will promise to tell you how he died. Right now, I just want to tell you… how he lived."

Kimberly's smile mirrored her own as she nodded in agreement.

"I'd like that."

The mother cheetah barked in the middle of their moment, signaling for her cubs to come to her. Obediently, they ran back, licking and nuzzling against her.

"I'm surprised they took to you so well," Sophia observed.

Kimberly bit her lip while raising her right arm.

"Actually."

The right forearm of her wetsuit had teeth and claw marks that went down to her unblemished skin. Sophia let out a laugh, shaking her head.

"Which one?"

"The girl," Kimberly chuckled, pointing. "She held on just hanging from my arm for, like, five minutes before she gave up. The other one ran up, stopped, and just sat there watching."

Sophia doubled over, cackling, which became infectious. They sat there talking and laughing into the night.

CHAPTER 19

Sophia took an official day off to spend with her daughter the next day. Earl and everyone else gladly stepped up to take over daily responsibilities as she and Kimberly spent time getting to know each other.

They made and ate breakfast together. Sophia took her for a proper tour of the village and island. Everyone they met greeted them with a hug and smile; yesterday's events were forgotten as if it never happened. Some shared stories about how they met their mother and what she had done for them.

They went on a tour of the island's essential parts from the other sections of the animal preserve, the harbor built for their fishing boats, and the enormous electrical generator that ran the town.

In the afternoon, they made lunch and ate. Sophia told stories and showed her family pictures comprising Jamaican, Belizean, and Texan heritage. She purposely left out General Matheson's evil actions, leaving it for when she was older to understand the truth about her grandfather.

Kimberly asked about her eyes and her ability to fly. Sophia first made her swear never to attempt to duplicate the process. Her daughter reluctantly agreed before she explained her current state of evolution. After lunch, she took her to the island's far side to display some of her abilities.

The more her daughter watched her, the more she saw the timid little girl melting away in her eyes, embracing the being that she was. Mixed emotions of pride and concern swelled within Sophia. Although she wanted her daughter to accept and embrace who she was, she also tried to keep her grounded and on the road to everyday life. The problem was that even Sophia did not know what daily life was anymore.

Later in the evening, they had a girl's night in. They gorged on smores, popcorn, and other sweets while watching Kimberly's favorite new movie, "Frozen."

Sophia enjoyed the movie until Anna turned to ice while protecting her sister. Kimberly, who always became emotional over the scene, was shocked to see her mother's eyes well up.

Kimberly smiled, wiping her eyes.

"Uh… you okay there?"

Sophia came to her senses, quickly swatting her eyes.

"Huh? Oh, a breeze just now blew in some sand into my face."

Kimberly slowly nodded and turned away to giggle; her mother retaliated by tossing a pillow at her.

At the end of the movie, Kimberly energetically began to sing the main song, mimicking the voice of Idina Menzel. Her mother stopped her solo.

"Sing it with your own voice."

Kimberly coiled back in her seat.

"I've… never…"

Kimberly had mastered her vocal mimicry ability to copy the voices of other famous singers. It was a great icebreaker to meet new friends and win some school talent shows, but she had never tried to sing in her own voice.

Sophia grabbed her hand.

"You will tonight."

A reluctant Kimberly followed her mother to a Mason & Hamlin upright piano. Sophia taught herself to play because she always wanted to learn. Her cognitive abilities helped her replay the song via keystrokes. She then began to sing the first part of the music in her own voice. Kimberly started the second part using Idina's voice, but Sophia stopped her again.

"You know the lyrics and the melody. All you have to do is channel it through your own voice."

Kimberly lowered her head.

"I don't have…"

Sophia gently raised Kimberly's head by her chin to look into her eyes so she could see her mother's smile.

"Yes, you do; you've just never used it before. Remember what I said about adjusting to your environment? It's just you and me, so have some fun with it."

Sophia began again and waited. Her voice was small and cracked at first. Little by little, Kimberly's voice gained strength as she sang a duet with her mother.

Sophia kept nudging her to loosen up. Eventually, Kimberly did, no longer caring if her voice was perfect. Their voices soared higher and higher, taking them to the end, where they sang the last line as arrogant as Elsa.

Like deer in front of headlights, they froze to the sound of applause and claps outside. Mother and daughter slinked down, giggling and dying of embarrassment, not remembering that their windows were open and their voices carried.

~~~~~~~~~~~~~~~~~~~~~~~~~~~~~~~~

The next day, early afternoon, Sophia stood on the airport runway with her daughter and Earl, wearing the outfit constructed by Lady Tech.

A disappointed Kimberly lowered her newly braided hair as her mother held her right hand, rubbing it while making a promise.

"I will be gone three hours tops. I have one errand I have to run, and your grandmother gridlocked my voicemail with messages ever since the incident in Times Square. If I don't go and see her, she will swim over here and kill me."

Kimberly finally raised her head.

"She has abilities like us?"

"No," Sophia chuckled, "but she comes really close. I also want to tell her
~~~~~~~~~~~~~~~~~~~~~~~~~~~~~~~~

about you, so that she can get ready to meet you... like, maybe tomorrow."

Kimberly's face brightened at the prospect of meeting more family.

"Really?"

"I promise, in the meantime, look after the island and make sure Earl doesn't get into any trouble."

"I'm standing right here, you know," Earl scoffed.

"I know," Sophia replied while looking at him. "I wanted you to be in earshot when I said it."

"I'll hold the fort down, boss," Earl grinned.

"You know how to reach me if you need anything."

Sophia backed up a couple of steps, then paused, wagging a finger at Kimberly, remembering something.

"Oh, while I'm gone, you might want to go and apologize to your two buddies. I think they're still a bit hurt over what you said."

Kimberly knew she was talking about Kyle and Akram. She lowered her head again, nodding in agreement that she needed to make amends.

Sophia took to the skies with a mighty leap, soaring high and fast, skimming Earth's atmosphere, propelling herself toward the United States.

~~~~~~~~~~~~~~~~~~~~~~~~~~~~~~~~

Minutes later, Sophia soared over her hometown of Mount Vernon, heading for Seventh Avenue. Children coming home from school flocked around, yelling and cheering as she descended, landing in the streets. They attacked her with questions about the battle in Times Square. Her answers to the sea of questions were, "Yes, he was big," "Yes, it hurt when he hit me," "Yes, I put his lights out," and "No, he won't be coming back."

She raised her head to see her mother standing on the steps of their house with her godfather, Uncle Mac, their conversation interrupted by her entrance.
~~~~~~~~~~~~~~~~~~~~~~~~~~~~~~~~

"Lawd god," Uncle Mac cackled, "Nopel look pon dis! Ah, supawoman descend pon us!"

Ms. Dennison scanned him up and down with a glare on her face.

"And what? Ah, my pickney dere. Me suppose to be impressed every time she swoop in and swoop out? You move."

With three loud claps and a whistle, she got the attention of the crowd of children holding her daughter hostage.

"All right," Ms. Dennison yelled with motherly authority. "All you pickney gwone ah ya yard! De Q&A session is over! Don't make me say it twice!"

"Yes, Mrs. Dennison!" the children obediently yelled in unison before dispersing.

Sophia slowly walked to the front gate as her mother stood there waiting with her hands on her hips.

"Well,... well," her mother huffed, "look what de cat dragged in?"

She gave her a sheepish smile.

"Hi, Mummy."

Ms. Dennison motioned with a head gesture.

"Yuh nuh see yuh Uncle Mac standing over here?"

"Hi, uncle Mac," Sophia greeted him, waving.

"Hey, baby girl!"

He gave her a bright smile, revealing a missing top and bottom tooth.

"What yuh standin out dere for? Bring ya self ina de yard!" Ms. Dennison commanded.

Obediently, the most powerful woman on the planet entered the gate of her parent's home, standing before her. Mrs. Dennison grabbed her and gave her three hard slaps on her rear. Sophia squirmed around, pretending it actually hurt.

"Low her, Nopel!" Mac busted out laughing. "Low her!"

Mrs. Dennison continued to spank her.

"Me half fe hear bout you fightin in ah de news! And you can't pick up de phone fe call ya mada?"

"I'm sorry, Mummy! I'm sorry!" Sophia yelled, laughing.

Her mother gave her one final slap for good measure.

"When dat big ugly bastada lick you, and you clout him back?" her mother asked, wagging a finger. "Him look worst dan you?"

Her daughter answered with a head nod.

"Good," Mrs. Dennison said with an approving nod.

"Well, me half fi run." Uncle Mac continued to laugh as he descended the steps.

Sophia met him, giving him a big hug and lifting him off the last set of steps.

"Lawd god, you strong!" Sophia's godfather hooted with amazement.

As she put him down, he quickly put an arm around his goddaughter's back, leading Sophia away from her mother.

"Hey Sophia, me have some barrels me need fi send down ah yard to me sista," Uncle Mac asked seriously.

Mrs. Dennison walked over, ending the transaction. Although she was five inches shorter than him, she grabbed the back collar of his shirt and draped him up.

"You fasty wretch you!" Mrs. Dennison shouted. "You see UPS written on my pickney's forehead?

"Wha ya do, Nopel?" Uncle Mac yelled, struggling to get away. "Ah me good shirt dis!"

"Gwone ah yah yard!" Mrs. Dennison ordered, finally releasing him. "Before me, report yuh missing."

Uncle Mac nodded while straightening out his wrinkled shirt.

"Talk to ya lata."

Exiting the gate, he slipped in a "Call me later" to Sophia about his favor. She responded with a head nod as he walked off, heading to his car.

She turned to her mother and knew what she was thinking.

"I'll call up Benji; he'll be happy to make the run."

"God bless you, child," Mrs. Dennison said while gazing her up and down, "now what dat you have on?"

Sophia knew her mother was referring to her new attire. She gave a twirl, showing it off.

"You like it? It's my new flight outfit."

Mrs. Dennison tugged at the midsection of the bodysuit.

"Flight outfit? Looks as if yuh comin from dance hall."

The clucking of the family rooster strutting up to her saved Sophia from going into depth about her attire.

"Hey, Tooni!"

Sophia happily called out the bird's name as she petted it.

"How are you?"

"Rude as eva," Mrs. Dennison answered, "he should have stayed gone."

Knowing her mother was only jesting, Sophia smirked as she remembered the "Great Tooni incident of 2011." Two weeks later, her mother got Tooni from a friend closing up his live poultry store to retire in Jamaica; some juvenile delinquents stormed the Dennisons' garage roof, tearing off the shingles and throwing them into the yard. To add insult to injury, they climbed down, cornered, and made off with poor Tooni minding his own business.

Sophia came home to her mother, distraught with tears, and decided to do what any child defending their parent would do. Retaliate.

Two powerful fly-bys shattered every glass window within the projects near Third and Fourth Avenue, forcing its residents into the quad, where a furious Sophia gave an ultimatum. Return the rooster alive and intact in one hour, or she would destroy every vehicle within the project's parking lot. She also made it clear that every hour the rooster was still missing, she would turn her attention to the cars parked on the street.

Tooni was returned within fifteen minutes. The juveniles were dealt with by their parents.

Her final warning was that all homes, cars, and Seventh Avenue residents between Fifth and Sixth Street, especially her parents' house, were a nation unto itself, and she was their nuclear weapon. Natives of Mount Vernon got the hint and passed the word to leave Seventh Avenue alone.

"So you eat yet?" Mrs. Dennison inquired as she continued to touch and inspect her outfit and hair.

"Nope."

Mrs. Dennison released her and turned, heading for the steps of their home.

"Come, me just made some stew fish, wit dumpling, rice and peas, and callaloo fi ya poopa when him come home."

Sophia raised a brow, searching for her father's car.

"Where **is** dad?"

Mrs. Dennison cut her eyes with irritation before she answered.

"Where you tink him is? Down ah, the shop cutting Joe's hair. Ever since you fix him knee, dat man can't stay put."

Sophia rolled her eyes, equalling her mother's annoyance.

"I didn't replace his knee so he could wear it out again. I did it so he could retire and walk without pain."

"Him don't do it often, baby girl," Mrs. Dennison defended her husband a bit, "him need something to do from time to time, and when him home, de house don't stay clean, so dat's fine wit me."

Sophia sighed as she followed her mother into the house. While her mother prepared her plate, she walked around, inspecting it for any possible repairs she may have to do in the future.

~~~~~~~~~~~~~~~~~~~~~~~~~~~~~~~~~~

The day she awoke from the bottom of the ocean floor, she made a beeline for home first to see her parents before going to DC for Kimberly. Sophia was amazed at how neither her mother nor father flinched on the day she showed up stark naked with glowing eyes on their doorstep. They only cared that she was alive and finally home.

After coming to the decision that her daughter kept believing she was dead, Sophia stayed home in her old room for almost two months. Her mother, who only had limited patience for pity parties, gave her the ultimatum to get up and do something or get doused with ice water every morning.

A reluctant Sophia decided to fix their house. Several "step by step" do-it-yourself videos on YouTube had her do everything from tiling and plumbing to masonry.

Within less than a month, she restored her parents' home, which looked better than the day her father finished renovations on it.

Bored again, Sophia started working on their neighbors' homes, taught herself to do automotive work, speak every language in the world, and read every medical journal she could access. After upgrading her parents' entire block within two months, she set out every morning at eight to test her other limits. Sophia traveled to different countries, some war-torn. At five o'clock, she always returned with a souvenir for her parents, ate dinner with them, and talked about her day.

Her mother's only real fear concerning her was when Sophia finally mustered the courage to fly into space. The combination of boredom and lounging around watching the old Christopher Reeve movie made her attempt the feat. Wearing just a thick black insulated wetsuit she purchased for her deep diving adventures, she remembered the Friday she took off into the sky and kept going straight up.
~~~~~~~~~~~~~~~~~~~~~~~~~~~~~~~~~~

Five seconds before she was supposed to break through the atmosphere, she almost lost her nerve the second she started to see stars.

Her desire to brag about being the first woman to fly into outer space under her own propulsion made her stay the course for those last five seconds.

Sophia, still to this day, could not determine what overwhelmed her most. The fact that she possessed the power to fly into space or that she could survive within its harsh atmosphere without the need for air.

Returning with smoking burn marks on her diving suit from the reentry, Sophia acted like a child who had just ridden her bike for the first time without training wheels. So caught up in her tale, she did not realize until the end the fear her mother fought to hide with a smile.

Mrs. Dennison was used to her daughter being superhuman; they were all over the news and television. At that moment, it set in that her daughter was beyond a superhuman level. She also saw recklessness in Sophia's eyes that day. She feared what this near-godly invincibility would do to her.

On that day, Sophia decided to make plans to set out and live on her own once more. She did not want to see that fear again in her mother's eyes.

~~~~~~~~~~~~~~~~~~~~~~~~~~~~~~~~

As Sophia sat down at the granite island in the sun-yellow colored kitchen, she watched the older woman she was forged from with a sentimental smile. Her cocoa-brown African skin and slightly broad English nose came from her mother, while her once curly brown hair, light brown eyes, and Latin features were a gift from her father.

Sophia could not find a speck of gray hair on her mother's head at sixty-two. She found it amusing how her parents became a mesh of each other just as she was. Growing up, she thought both her parents were Jamaican. The truth was her mother came from Kingston, Jamaica, while her father was the first generation born from Belize City in Belize. She started as a bus driver, eventually getting a position as a secretary in a purse and luggage company until she was promoted to office manager, working there until her early retirement.

Her father opened his own chain of barbershops, learning his father's skills passed on by his grandfather. Her brother, Anthony, took over the chain five years after graduating college. Due to the constant standing, her father continued to cut his personal clients and friends occasionally until his right knee went out on him. Sophia performed
~~~~~~~~~~~~~~~~~~~~~~~~~~~~~~~~

the operation to replace it and helped him with rehabilitation herself.

Aside from their children, they shared a love of music, God, and a deep love for one another, even when they bickered.

Two minutes later, they ate early dinner together. Ms. Dennison filled Sophia in on who passed away, who got married, who was pregnant, and who was asking for her. Sophia shared the goings-on at her island and briefly talked about the events at Times Square, not wanting to bring up any gory details at the table. She rolled her eyes when asked if she was still single.

Sophia maneuvered through the trenches, searching for an opening to drop the bomb that there was a granddaughter Ms. Dennison had not known about for the past ten years.

Finished with their dinner, her mother made peppermint tea while Sophia cleaned up, throwing out the scraps and washing the dishes.

Sophia sat down again as Mrs. Dennison placed her hot piping tea in front of her, along with some sweet milk. She also sat down, opting to put honey in her own tea.

"Oh! Before I forget," Sophia said, slowly stirring the milk into her tea, "you're a grandmother."

She braced herself while fidgeting in her seat.

"Say it again?" Mrs. Dennison asked. "Me hearing not too good dese days."

Sophia knew her hearing was perfect; she just wanted to hear her repeat it again.

"You have… a granddaughter," Sophia emphasized each word.

"You're pregnant?" was her mother's first obvious question.

"No."

Sophia lowered her head, running her finger in a circle pattern on the table.

"I never miscarried during the trial. I gave birth, and Charles helped me to fake her death. She was adopted by a family in Boston."

Awkward silence held the kitchen captive as her mother tried to process what her daughter had just said.

"Why?" was her mother's next question, encompassing a series of questions.

Sophia sighed, beginning her explanation.

"I did it to keep her away from the General; I knew he would try and take her even if I left her with you. I didn't want him to do to her what he did to Robert. Those evil people who killed Robert I told you about also killed the adoptive parents and kidnapped her because she's just like me.

Actually, she's the reason I am still alive. She's the first superhuman, not me. Somehow, I inherited her powers when she was in my womb growing inside me. She's why I survived the lethal injection chamber and everything else."

It was far more complicated than that, but her mother was a simple woman who did not need to hear the technical jargon, just the truth.

"I hate dat man." Mrs. Dennison muttered with a scowled face. "God forgive me, yuh not suppose fe hate, but I hate dat man for what him did to you, us, and his own family."

~~~~~~~~~~~~~~~~~~~~~~~~~~~~~~~~~~

Sophia slowly nodded in agreement. Although she and her family had survived and recovered from the events almost ten years ago, the General's actions shattered the Matheson legacy he tried so hard to build and protect with his family. After her final tour, Alexis left the army, not wanting to deal with anything military again.

Her relationship with her husband, who was still a Navy Seal, had not been the best because of it. Mrs. Matheson went into a deep depression, rapidly increasing her Alzheimer's. She passed away in her sleep a day before her birthday.

The General appealed his case for only four years and was executed via lethal injection at Leavenworth.

Sophia never attended his execution, but she went to see him three months after Mrs. Matheson's death. With full knowledge of who she was and what she was capable of, the warden did not stop her visit. She remembered the General shuffling in his seat with head bent and eyes on the floor. The once-proud Marine General was a broken down, terrified old man in her eyes that day.
~~~~~~~~~~~~~~~~~~~~~~~~~~~~~~~~~~

They sat there for almost five minutes, not uttering a word to each other.

Sophia looked at him with evil thoughts running through her mind. He just looked at the floor.

"Look at me."

He did not obey as he continued to look at the floor. Sophia's voice made his body violently quake. He uttered a whimper, shifting in his seat.

"Look… at… me!" Sophia's voice boomed while her eyes blazed.

A now teary-eyed and sweat-drenched Matheson raised his head, gazing at the consequences of his actions.

He saw rage, hatred, hurt, and sorrow in Sophia's glowing eyes that poured with tears. He saw his loss and shame.

"Was all of this… worth it?" Sophia's voice quivered as she demanded to know, fighting the urge to tear him apart. "Was it?"

"No," General Matheson answered, breaking down. "It was not."

Sophia stared at him for one more minute, ensuring her image was burned into his last memories. She left, not uttering another word, as he sobbed controllably at that table.

~~~~~~~~~~~~~~~~~~~~~~~~~~~~~~~~

"Where is she now?" Mrs. Dennison asked.

"With me now, before that, she was staying with a friend in Washington," Sophia sighed. "She didn't know I was still alive until a couple of days ago. Not until an accident activated her abilities, and she got stronger. I stayed away from her because I wanted her to have a normal life, and I didn't tell you until now because if people found out who she was, they would come looking for her, which would put you and everyone I know and love in danger."

"Okay," Mrs. Dennison said, leaning back in her chair, "so what now?"

"Aside from finally telling you the truth," Sophia answered with an earnest
~~~~~~~~~~~~~~~~~~~~~~~~~~~~~~~~

shrug, "I don't know."

"Of the three of my children," Mrs. Dennison began to speak, "you were always the most independent and intelligent. Not dat your brother and sister are stupid. But where Anthony and Gemma would give me a one-word answer, you would go into detail and say, 'Well, Mom, I think you should do dis and dat for dis reason.' I use to call you, Miss professor."

Sophia nodded as she waited to hear where her mother's story went.

"I pray daily for good things for all my children," she continued, "but for you, I knew I did not need to pray too hard because you were destined for great things. My one fear is that your independence would keep you from looking to the family for help."

Sophia, now annoyed, half rolled her eyes, not liking where this story was going.

"Mom," Sophia sighed, "with all due respect, I had no choice in my decision. This was the General we're talking about, a powerful man with a lot of influence, and I highly doubt a prayer group session would have stopped him from taking my child from you. This wouldn't have been some normal custody battle. This was a man with the power of the United States government in his back pocket, and who was creating death squads."

"Yeah, and normally you should be dead," Mrs. Dennison said.

Her comment stunned Sophia. She waited for her to take what she had just said back.

"Yeah, I said it," Mrs. Dennison scoffed. "Wha you gonna tell me? A science save your life? You can say it if you want, but I know it was a praying mother and father bowing and scraping to the Lord every day and night that released..."

"Oh Lord, another sermon!" Sophia snapped while tossing up her hands. "I get it. God is good, and hallelujer! Why are you even going there?"

Her mother clasped her hands together, placing them on the island's surface.

"Okay, you don't want a sermon. Then tell me what you want me fe say."

"Nothing, Mom." Sophia said with a huff, leaning back in her seat, "Nothing."

"Alright, you did what you did to protect her; I probably would have done de same ting. But what happen dese last seven years? Where was she?"

Sophia sheepishly lowered her head before she answered.

"At the Armitages'."

"Tu rass." Her mother cursed while shaking her head. "All dis time? Why?"

"I wanted her to have a chance at a normal life, Mom," Sophia answered with a tone of frustration.

"And we're not normal?" Mrs. Dennison asked while leaning back in her chair.

"I'm not normal, Mom!"

"You betta shut ya mouth before me throw dis tea inna ya face!" Ms. Dennison barked back. "Ah, me give birth to you! What is not normal about you? Huh? You have de same head, same skin, same nose, five toes, four fingas, and a thumb. What's not normal about you? Because you're taller, ya eyes have a glow? Because you can fly? So what? Enough of you is out dere flying, running, and breakin up tings! So don't tell me about not being normal!"

Sophia's eyes emitted a brighter glow, revealing her answer at a fever-pitched level as she sneered at her mother.

"You done? Because trust me, you can't make me feel as bad as I already feel. You want me to say what I already know?! I screwed up! I made a judgment call, and it was wrong. There is nothing you can tell me that I have not already heard from my own little girl! I thought I was giving her a chance at something that was taken away from me, but the truth was I abandoned her and left her alone! So don't think you can make me feel more shitty than I already am!"

"Ya betta watch ya mout," Mrs. Dennison warned her. "I am still ya mada!"

"Yeah, and I apologize for using that language around you. But don't think you know anything about me anymore, what I've been through, or the weight I have to carry. In this world of humans and superhumans, there is no one like me. No one has had to endure what I suffered and went through, no one. If I told you in detail what really happened to me… inside that mountain. What it felt like to be in the heart of a nuclear bomb! You would fold, crumble, and die."

Sophia's body trembled as her eyes blazed brighter from anger within her.

"I keep myself busy, sometimes going nights without sleep because I know the second I close my eyes, and I lose control, I can relive every one of those nightmares as if I was actually there. I'm surprised I haven't gone mad yet. And I was afraid of subjecting my child to that. I didn't think it was fair to do that to her because she had been through enough! So forgive me, dear Mother, if I did not make the 'right decision' concerning you and my child. You didn't have the opportunity to 'teach me' what to do in this type of scenario."

The kitchen became dead silent as sheer discomfort fell like a thick fog. Sophia knew it would not be a pleasant conversation, but she was not expecting to be judged so harshly for her actions, especially her mother. No one had the right in her mind, other than her daughter, to pass judgment on her. She prepared herself to leave while contemplating when she would return.

"Why ya decide ta build dat village?" Mrs. Dennison asked.

Sophia turned to her mother with her eyebrows furrowed, wondering where she was going with this inquiry from left field. Mrs. Dennison shrugged her shoulders as she continued.

"I'm just curious; you raised dat island and built your house to get away from people. Yuh didn't even have to raise an island, yuh could have went to de North pole, an…"

Sophia glared at her mother, signaling that she was not in the joking mood anymore.

"I'm just asking," Mrs. Dennison said seriously. "After all you've been through, why create a village? You don't owe anyone anyting, especially me, and you wanted to be left in peace. So, why create more headache for yourself? Why?"

She shifted in her seat as she fought to find the words to answer her mother's semi-innocent question.

"I had too much wood," Sophia huffed.

She leaned forward as her lips trembled, clasping her hands as she stared into space. Her mind recalled the day she had finished her new home.

"I finished the garage and backed Robert's car into it, and then I realized I bought too many supplies. So, I decided to build a shed to store the leftovers. But as I started building, I kept adding until I ran out again. And then I had to buy more supplies to finish it.

Next thing you know, I had built another house, but then I had more leftover supplies than I had before. I didn't want to be wasteful. So I just kept constructing, trying to use everything out. But there was always too much wood, or too much cement, or too much varnish left. Before I realized it, I had built eight friggin houses."

A smile formed on her mother's face as she bobbed her head.

"Then I was, like, great! What am I going to do with eight houses! Why didn't I stop?"

"Then something told you to fill them up," Mrs. Dennison answered.

Tears fell from her eyes as Sophia trembled like a leaf.

"Yes."

Mrs. Dennison reached over and grasped her hand, rubbing it to comfort her.

"You are right," Mrs. Dennison whispered softly. "I will neva know or feel what you have gone through. No one will eva know. And, honestly, I don't want to know because I'd probably go crazy if I did. Because when you hurt, I hurt, and I would go insane, knowing how much pain you had to endure, and I was unable to save or protect you from it. And that is what you will neva know, what it is to be a parent and powerless."

Sophia looked up to see her mother's eyes glassed over as she held tightly onto her hand.

"I gave birth to you," Mrs. Dennison told her with a crackling voice. "I raised you, watched you grow. I came to Ursuline school and threatened Principal Moore that I'd run my minivan through her school and over dat big fat McGrady girl, the next time, the teachers stood by and let her mess wit you. Not that you were a pushover, but because you are **my child**."

The memory of the incident brought a smile back to Sophia's face.

"And on October 15, 2004," Mrs. Dennison fumbled her words as her tears fell,

"I had to stand there and listen to Judge Kevin Coleman tell me that my child was guilty of a crime **I know** she did not commit and that he was going to kill her. And there was noting I could do about it."

The roles were reversed as Sophia now held her mother's shaking hand as she began to shrink right in front of her.

"I cursed God on that day, and I wished for that heart attack to kill me," Mrs. Dennison said, "the second-worst day of my life, and he would not let me die, guess what was the first?"

She lifted her gaze to the ceiling as her eyes blazed from falling tears. Her leg twitched as she groaned, imagining the ordeal her parents went through on that day.

"September 1, 2008. I didn't go to work the week before; I didn't go to church, didn't eat, couldn't sleep, and didn't answer the phone; I didn't pray. I sat upstairs in you and Gemma's bedroom, watching the clock countdown to midnight… just numb. My tears fell, but I could not cry.

Ya poopa downstairs started to bawl like a baby. Him cry so hard I don't know why he neva had a stroke. I had to run downstairs and hold him and massage him to calm him down. And at 2 a.m. in the morning, your brother drove us to de airport so that we could make de journey to collect your body, only to find out when we got there that you were very much alive and broken out of prison."

Mrs. Dennison shook her head and began to cackle, wiping her eyes as she leaned back.

"May he be resting in God's bosom, but I neva believed that foo-foo story Mr. Armitage tried to sell me about you joining some terrorist organization. I knew something was up, so I thanked him for telling me, brought yuh poopa home, and I waited. And on September 8, 2008, the plan was revealed to me.

The night before I saw you on CNN, this whole block was filled with police, FBI, you name it, with dem big guns, waiting for you. And when you shot into the air of Washington, DC, for all the world to see, I was the first to run outside yelling, screaming, and strutting up and down the block like I'd won the lotto! Every last one of them jackasses didn't know what to do with demselves!"

She nodded with pride while rubbing her daughter's hand.

"So you have to forgive me, my child," Mrs. Dennison said earnestly, "if what you went through has not only restored my faith a trillionfold but has turned me into a powerful prayer warrior because, by the laws of man, and by logic and science, you were supposed to be dead, and I, your mother, was supposed to be forced to bury you."

It was an argument Sophia could not refute as she lowered her head. With a smile, Mrs. Dennison leaned in and raised her daughter's head as she gazed into her eyes.

"You tink anyting is new about you, or anyting that is going on? God gave Samson strength to kill a lion, slay an entire army with only de jawbone of an ass, and destroy the temple of Dagon wit de Philistines inside of it. Him give Solomon great wisdom fe rule over de people of Israel, and my God sent Him only Son to walk on water, cast demons out of man, feed masses with a bit of fish and bread, and to die at the hands of man for the sins of the world only to raise again from the dead. Dat bwoy wit de hamma. What him name? Thunda god? Him have nuting on my Jesus Christ!"

A slight smirk appeared on Sophia's face from her mother's humorous yet profound remarks.

"And you can believe it's science or whatever that saved you, but I know…"

Mrs. Dennison paused as tears began to pour from her eyes again.

"That my God is Who saved you from death, to show the world that He is God, and only He has power over life and death! Hallelujah! Hallelujah!"

Mrs. Dennison clutched the table weeping; Sophia wiped away the tears from her eyes as she leaned over and gently rubbed her mother's back.

"And the ting those heroes of the Lord have in common is that in their weakest of moment dem called upon a Higher Power for help. Even the Son of Man Himself called for His Father," Mrs. Dennison said through her sobs. "You are not an island! You cannot keep holding tings like these inside and dealing with them on your own when you have a family and a God willing to share your pain and burden with you. **Dat is what makes you normal!** And then you just pop up out of nowhere and go 'by the way, I'm going through dis and dat.' Dat is unfair to us, and it is unfair to you! You ah doctor, and you nuh no stress kills? Family was created to ease stress and to carry each other's burden to make the load lighter! Dat is why we are here!"

She grasped her daughter's hand, holding it up tightly, and kissed it.

"Put your trust in God, yuh hear me? He bring you this far; He will bring you all of the way. Now," her voice gained strength again, "the next time I see you, I betta see me granpickney next to you. How old is she?"

"Ten," Sophia said meekly.

Her mother looked at her as if she wanted to take something and smack her. Sophia leaned back on instinct, fearing she would.

"I want to see her," Mrs. Dennison said again, "and don't you worry! Make whoever wan fe come, come! Dem tink you bad? Where dem tink you get it from? Ah, one mad Jamaican and Belizean give birth to you. Ah, lead soup we drink and our forehead we use fe cotch steel door. Make dem come!"

Her mother's odd, harsh humor had a way of bringing lightness back into a room. She could not help but laugh, which made her mother, attempting to be serious, laugh.

~ ~

The next twenty minutes before she left, her mother prepared a backpack filled with snacks such as Jamaican Bulla cake and Belizean style Gizzarda. She also threw in some lotion, a Gospel CD of her choir's latest concert, and some fingernail polish.

Sophia protested that she did not need to carry the items and that her mother would see the child tomorrow, but her mother demanded that she bring them anyway to her grandchild.

"And you make sure she gets these," Mrs. Dennison reminded her as they walked out the door.

"Yes, Mom," Sophia sighed.

"And remember!" Mrs. Dennison's voice got louder, "I don't want to just see her tomorrow! She's spending the weekend with me, so she better have a dress to go to church! If she don't have one, I will go out and buy one for her!"

"Yes, Mom," Sophia groaned.

"Now come give your mother a hug before you go!"

Sophia trudged over, wrapping her arms around her. She got back a kiss with a tighter hug and a ten-minute prayer filled with tears, giving thanks and asking for safe travels.

Sophia exited the gate, getting ready to take off, her heart much lighter than when she came, until a familiar vehicle pulled up, putting a scowl on her face. She threw on her hood, hiding her displeasure from her mother as her youngest sister, Gemma, stepped out of her vehicle wearing an edgy look.

"Auntie Sophee! It's auntie Sophee!" young voices screamed.

Spilling out from a jeep were her three nieces, Natasha, Joyce, and Anita, along with her nephew, Austin, the second eldest of the four, stemming from ages eleven, eight, six, and four years old. They swarmed Sophia, forcing her to throw a smile on her face as she knelt down to hug them all.

Showing her strength as a treat, Sophia lifted all four of them up as they held tightly. She gave them all kisses before setting them back down.

"Are you staying? Are you staying?" they all chimed in.

"No babies," Sophia answered with a smile. "I just came to visit Grandma. I have to leave."

"When are we going to see you again?" Anita asked.

"Soon, honey," Sophia replied, rubbing her head, "maybe this Saturday."

"All right, granpickneys," Mrs. Dennison yelled while clapping, "ya auntie half to leave, come inside the gate!"

They each gave her one last hug and kiss before entering the gate to greet their grandmother. Sophia walked away without acknowledging her younger sister. Gemma cautiously walked up to her, hoping not to make a scene.

"Hi."

"Mom texted you and told you I was here?" Sophia bluntly asked.

"No, I came to drop something off to her," Gemma defensively answered.

Sophia, with a disgusted glare, sucked her teeth.

"Yeah, right."

"Look, can we please talk," Gemma pleaded.

Sophia, towering over her sister, made sure her back was fully turned to her mother and the children so they did not see the disgust and contempt she had for her.

"About what, Gemma? It's been almost six years now. What exactly do you think is going to be any different from our last conversation, or how the hell I feel toward you?"

"I don't know how many times I can say how much I am sorry for what I thought and said about you," Gemma said with a quivering tone. "God, it was stupid, and I should never have thought or said those things."

"That's it? I'm sorry! I'm so sorry!" Sophia mockingly said with a sardonic smile. "And, magically, poof! We're all good, and everything is forgiven?"

Sophia gave her a scowl that would turn water to stone.

"You, my own flesh and blood, believed and told everyone I was capable of murdering my own husband, and you did it for a fifteen-minute spot on Fox News and then again on Season Five of "Snapped," you miserable bitch," Sophia growled. "Take your apologies and choke on them. What you did was unforgivable, and the only reason I'm even playing nice and uttering a word to you is because of that woman up there and our father."

"What happen?" Mrs. Dennison called out with concern, "you both all right?"

Sophia turned with a fake bright smile on her face.

"We're good, Mummy!"

Her face quickly returned to hatred when addressing her sister. But her mother already knew she was lying to her face. It was a charade they were putting on in the street. Things were still not right between the two of them. Knowing that made her smile drop and her heart sink.

"You can't keep this up." Gemma whimpered, shaking her head. "You can't keep hating me. I'm your blood; there are children involved."

"Don't you dare use your children as a bargaining chip against me!" Sophia slightly raised her voice, "from the hair clip to almost getting expelled from college to your friggin' first marriage, and everything else in between, I've been cleaning up your mess and standing beside you as an older sister, and the **one time** my world falls apart you join everyone else in sending me to the gallows. Screw you. We aren't ever going to be good. If those kids need anything from me, I will always be there, but you are dead to me as far as you and I go. By the way, you have a niece, and she won't need anything from you. Now move from me."

A hurt and stunned Gemma stepped back as Sophia, not giving her a second look, exploded into the air, rocketing off. She lowered her head, covering her face in the middle of the street so her mother and children would not see the tears she shed.

"Gemma! What's wrong?! Tell me what's wrong!" Mrs. Dennison yelled from the steps.

Gemma turned away to wipe her eyes.

"Nothing, Mummy! Nothing."

~~~~~~~~~~~~~~~~~~~~~~~~~~~~~~~~~~

Twenty thousand miles up, Sophia hovered and screamed her lungs against the cold, harsh air until she could no longer scream. She felt like bringing down another mountain to relieve her frustration. Looking at her bracers, she opted to do something more constructive.

Taking a deep breath, Sophia slid open the right bracer, revealing her new super mini-computer. She pulled out the earpiece and wrapped it around her right lobe, ensuring the listening part stuck into her ear canal. With a tap, the earpiece constricted, locking onto the ear. Placing the earpiece on also activated the computer.

"Hello, Ms. Dennison," a female voice spoke. "I am your personal AI. It is a pleasure to meet you."

"Female voice," Sophia said.

"I can also be a male voice if you desire."

The AI's voice changed into a proper-speaking male voice.
~~~~~~~~~~~~~~~~~~~~~~~~~~~~~~~~~~

"Let's keep you as a male for now," Sophia decided. "Do you have a name?"

"No," he cheerfully answered, "you can name me if you'd like."

She thought for a minute about using a particular name but decided it would be too weird, like attempting to bring back the dead.

"How about Vincent?" Sophia asked.

"I like Vincent," the AI responded.

"Then Vincent it is. Vincent, can you sync with my phone?"

"I can sync with all of your computer and communication devices if you wish," Vincent confirmed.

"What the heck, go ahead."

"Detecting an iPhone 5S, iPad Air, and an Alienware 18 laptop computer," Vincent verified, "syncing now. All devices synced."

"Wow, that was fast!" Sophia declared with widened eyes.

"Thank you, I try to be proficient."

"Vincent," Sophia sighed, "I need to relieve some stress. You have my music?"

"All eight thousand songs, including your twenty playlists."

"Need some flying music. Just so you know, I plan on traveling hard and fast."

"Anything in particular?" Vincent asked.

Sophia adjusted the straps to her backpack.

"Surprise me."

"I think I found something," Vincent chirpily responded.

Skrillex and Nero's Remix "Holdin' On" vibrated in her ear, drawing a bright smile on her face.

"Oh yeah, I can work with this."

Sophia exploded across the sky, soaring higher and moving faster. The wind was no match for her as she tore through it. All it did was boom out her location as she pushed her limits only to find that she had none.

Sophia pitched and rolled, executing every cliché flight pose she could imagine. She dove, skimming the ocean, creating her own waves with the force she generated, and then ascended to the skies, climbing higher. The song's hook was her trigger to push herself faster and faster.

While opening herself up, Sophia came across two superhumans streaking across the sky before her. She could tell they were not heroes, as they donned no unique letters, initials, or symbols other than Nike and Under Armor. They were just people enjoying the newfound gifts given to them.

The male in a blue and white compression outfit used powerful thrusts of plasma flames to propel himself through the air. In contrast, his female companion in a pink and black compression suit channeled air spinning around her body, similar to a mini tornado, to grant her flight. They both wore face masks and goggles that matched their outfits.

Feeling devious, Sophia increased her thrust, easing upright in between the two of them.

The two flying companions were shocked to see her; however, they gave her the race she was looking for with a nod.

Sophia made them believe they were her equal, soaring, diving, and strafing across the sky together. Then she revealed to them that they were not. Rolling on her back, she increasingly thrust to slowly pull away from them. They could not catch her no matter how much they pushed their powers.

She waved goodbye with enough distance between them and rocketed up to the heavens, forcing them to halt and hover, staring up in amazement as she disappeared.

Sophia continued, increasing her speed; her mission was to break through the Earth's atmosphere again. There was a chance the food would be inedible in her backpack, but she did not care. Sophia would quickly stop at one of the small islands if needed. She focused on reaching the stars she now saw before her.

Sophia tore through it like wet tissue paper, entering the coldness of space and becoming genuinely unbound. With her new target in sight, she extended her arms and let it go. She was a billion times faster, with no atmosphere attempting to fight against her. Meteors ranging from pebbles to baseballs capable of making Swiss cheese from an average unprotected human body crumbled to dust as they struck hers.

The endless Universe was vast as she streaked through it with the song pumping in her ear. It was all beautiful to her and tempting to explore, whipping asteroid belts, cannoning comets, spinning planets, with no fear of dying; for now, she just wanted to be the first woman to visit one place.

Sophia was amazed in the years after her reawakening; she never bothered to travel to the moon. She circled, slipping quickly into its orbit. Sophia could see the moon's barren surface without the sun's light. As she returned to its rays, she could see all five flags once, with the red, white, and blue colors now stark white due to the abuse of space.

"Maybe next time, I'll bring Kimberly, along with a Jamaican and Belizean flag."

Remembering she had a daughter to get back to, Sophia put it in warp drive, leaving the moon's orbit and heading back home.

~ ~

Back at Sanctuary, Kimberly slowly strolled, with Sir George walking beside her, onto the village boat harbor, where she tracked down Kyle and Akram.

She had not spoken to them since her blow-up in front of everyone in the village. She stopped by Kyle's home, where her mother happily told her what they were up to and could be hiding out.

They sat side by side with fishing poles, a six-pack of soft drinks, and a bait bucket. Without a word, she stepped out of her flip-flops and sat beside them while Sir George curiously peeked into the bucket, wondering what was inside. Neither boy looked in her direction to acknowledge her. Instead, they simultaneously scooted down, creating a gap between themselves and her.

For a minute, they just sat there, the boys staring off into the horizon while she looked down at the water that her toes nearly touched.

"Look," Kimberly fumbled with her words, "I'm really sorry about what I said the other day."

"Whatever," Kyle shrugged, answering with an irritated tone.

He had a face wishing she would leave. Akram slowly glanced her way while continuing to show unity with his friend.

"You guys aren't stupid," Kimberly said as she rocked. "I was just mad and really jealous of you guys."

"Jealous about what?" Kyle asked in disbelief.

"I only have like two memories of my mom," Kimberly sighed. "The day I was born, and the day she saved me from some, like, evil people. That's it; I didn't know anything about her until like two days ago. And you guys not only have your parents, but you had her. You knew almost everything about her, and I didn't, and she's my mom. It wasn't fair. But you guys didn't deserve that. You were trying to be nice to me, and I was a jerk."

"Nah, it's cool," Kyle said with a nod. "I guess I'd be jealous too if I had a cool mom like yours."

"So, are we good?" Kimberly asked, turning to them.

"We're good." Akram turned to her, speaking for himself.

"Yeah, we're good," Kyle said in agreement.

They sat there for another minute as Sir George pulled out one of the baits, giving it a sniff and lick test. In disgust, the Spider Monkey twitched and flung the bait away. He then returned to the bucket to see what else was in it.

"So, how high did you go?" Kyle coughed out his question.

"Really high," Kimberly answered with a smirk.

"Did you see stars?" Akram asked with a grin.

"Try floating in space for a couple of minutes."

"No way!" Kyle yelled.

"Way!"

Kimberly turned, sitting cross-legged to tell them in detail her first attempt to fly. The boys moved closer, listening attentively, no longer concerned about fishing.

CHAPTER 20

Thousands of miles away at the Ranch, Rogers granted a day of R&R for the team. Rosann decided to spend her day training in the Hurt Locker, honing her abilities and transformations.

Rosann started by touching a piece of bone on her armband to transform into a humanoid Bengal tigress; she then reverted back to human form and touched another bone slab to quickly change into a humanoid black-tailed jackrabbit. Remembering Erica's teachings, she conditioned her body to get used to the extremely painful transformations.

Rosann decided if she would remain on the team, fatal flaws, like discomfort, had to be pounded out of her. Remembering that every second counted in battle, her transformations had to be as simple as breathing.

As this was also the first time she used her rabbit transformation, Rosann took the time to examine herself, running her paw-like hands over her soft brown pelt and then her long ears. She then looked down at her massive feet and hind legs. With a mighty leap, she left where she stood, soaring across the floor twice the length of a basketball court. With another giant leap, she landed feet first against the wall on the other side of the room, backing and flipping off it for a somewhat graceful landing.

Satisfied with her feat, she quickly looked around to ensure no one watched her and then assumed the position using her hind leg to scratch the back of her ear.

~~~~~~~~~~~~~~~~~~~~~~~~~~~~~~~~~~~

Within the recreational room, Adrian and Oliver were going through another form of training as they squared off against one another. Feverishly clicking their controllers, they did battle as Marshall Law and Paul Phoenix in the video game realm of Tekken 6. The current score was two to one in Oliver's favor.

Oliver began his offensive, unleashing one of Paul's combo attacks, which Adrian weathered and sidestepped.

"I saw you coming out of my sister's room the day before at 0500," Adrian blurted out.
~~~~~~~~~~~~~~~~~~~~~~~~~~~~~~~~~~~

His remark caused Oliver to fumble with his controller, opening him up for a combo attack from Marshall Law, which Adrian controlled. Oliver quickly put the game on pause before turning to face him.

"Look, man…" Oliver nervously began to explain.

"My sister found our grandmother the day she passed away," Adrian said as he stared into space. "My folks didn't believe in those old folks' home crap because of all the evil shit they heard was done to the elderly while they were there. So when my dad's mom got too old to care for herself, she came to live with us. She was awesome and energetic for her old age, and we had a blast with her, especially Rosann."

Oliver leaned back a bit while listening to his teammate's tale.

"She was very old and had a bad hip, but she still showed up in time to have breakfast with us and see us off to school. One day, she seemed to take longer than usual, and Dad sent Rosann to check on her. Five minutes later, Rosann let out this blood-curdling scream.

When we all ran in to see what was the matter, Rosann was curled in the corner of the room crying hysterically, and my grandma was laid out on the bed with her eyes wide open and a painfully contorted look on her face. Doctors said it was a stroke. Every night for about a year, she'd wake up crying and screaming from night terrors. The only time it didn't happen was when my folks or I slept in the same room as her."

Adrian turned to place a firm grip on Oliver's shoulder, looking him in the eyes.

"Thanks for looking out for her. I really appreciate it."

"Anytime," Oliver said with a nod.

With no more words, Oliver unpaused the game, restarting the battle.

"So when are you really going to start dating my sister?" Adrian blurted out again.

Oliver fumbled again with his controller, opening Paul Phoenix up for another vicious sidekick from Marshall Law.

"Dude!" Oliver fired back.

Adrian was either nosey or using psychological warfare to get into Oliver's head to win the game, as he shrugged while tapping the buttons.

"I'm just saying, man, it's clear as day that you two had the Jones for one another since you met. Stop all the games, and make something happen already. Like my old man would say, 'Life is short and so is Happy Hour.'"

"What the hell does that mean?" Oliver asked while desperately attempting to recover from the beating he was taking.

"I don't know, my old man's always saying some crazy shit."

Another vicious combo attack secured Adrian the win.

"Son of a…!" Oliver yelled in frustration.

"Oh yeah!" Adrian yelled, wearing a savage grin. "That's tied at two, ready for the tie-breaker?"

"Hard-On's an idiotic name," Oliver blurted out, turning to him, "and doesn't do you justice."

Adrian wore a look as if he was hurt and offended, which made him almost regret saying it.

"It really is a stupid name," Adrian nodded.

"It is, man," Oliver said, laughing, "It really is."

Adrian screwed his face up.

"It sounds like a bad washed up gonzo porn name."

"It sounds like a low budget porn name, where it's like done in a dirty motel room with a camcorder," Oliver added. "So you see like every imperfection in both the girl and the guy while they're doing it."

"Like a Hunts Point motel," Adrian said as he shivered.

"I don't know where that is," Oliver chuckled, "but by the look on your face if it's one of those places where you can catch an STD just by walking into the room, then yeah."

"I don't know what I thought when I came up with that name," Adrian exhaled with a headshake, "all the good ones were really taken!"

"How about this one?" Oliver proposed "Heavy Element."

He sat briefly, thinking about the name, and then smiled.

"Heavy… Element," Adrian let it roll off his tongue, "that sounds hot, it's not stupid, sounds really badass, and covers all the basics regarding my abilities. Thanks!"

"No problem," Oliver said with a cracked smile. "Now, let's do this tie-breaker."

Oliver selected Brian Fury as his character, while Adrian picked Kazuya Mishima as they prepared to square off again.

"Seriously," Adrian asked, throwing the first punch, "did you at least kiss her before you left her room?"

Oliver fumbled again, allowing him to open up with Mishima's Electric Wind Godfist attack, knocking his Brian Fury character off its' feet. He gave Adrian a dirty look while getting back into the game.

~~~~~~~~~~~~~~~~~~~~~~~~~~~~~~~~~~

Within the central command, Rogers sat alone in his old Marine military fatigues at one of the consoles watching CSPAN, where various news anchors, reporters, and experts weighed in on Times Square's battle. Though people mourned the loss of Captain Omega and the other heroes who fell that day fighting to protect the city, the death toll on the human side tipped the scale as an example of what kind of threat the superhumans posed regular humans if left unchecked. This matter did not just divide the country but the world.

Areas like the Midwest and the Middle East saw them as abominations and demons, while New York, California, and Japan, to name a few, viewed them as celebrities.

Abe did not care about politics; his mind was on ensuring Times Square never happened again in any part of the country under his watch.
~~~~~~~~~~~~~~~~~~~~~~~~~~~~~~~~~~

He glanced at the surveillance monitors housing the three captured members of the Zombie Nation within Purgatory.

"Rogers, you there?" Erica's voice emitted over the audio system.

"Yeah, I'm here."

"Need you in my lab ASAP. We have a problem."

"Will be there in two minutes," Rogers nodded.

He sucked in some air and then blew it back out. He had hoped the day would have ended as it started. Peaceful.

Two minutes later, Rogers walked into Erica's lab. The expression on her face said it all as she flailed her arms.

"We've got a huge problem. I just finished watching the Draugr beheading Captain Omega…!"

"Why are you looking at something that gruesome?" Abe sneered, cutting her off.

"Because that whole incident has been stuck in my mind!" Erica shot back. "Captain Omega was a class 10 Titan who tanked armor-piercing rounds! The Draugr cut his head off with two strikes! Even if he got ahold of tank armor to forge his weapons, there's no way he should have been able to pierce his skin, especially with two strikes."

"But you said he's above a class 10 Titan," Rogers pointed out.

"Based on the density of the Captain's skin, the Draugr's weapons should have hit him like a Porsche hitting a brick wall doing eighty! Nicked him at best! I just finished doing an analysis of his weapons and armor. They're not forged from ordinary commercial or military-grade steel."

Rogers furrowed his brows, stepping forward to know more.

"What are they forged from?"

Erica turned to pull up the scans and data from the weapons and armor.

"The only type of metals that, when properly forged, can pierce Titan skin, Iridium blended with Maraging steel. The first is near impossible to find because it comes from space, and the second is extremely difficult to forge. Combined, it comes an extremely close second in strength to my dark metal formula. There's no way that lumbering mental midget down below had the brain cells to find and combine these two materials to create these weapons."

"How were they made?" Rogers asked.

"My guess," Erica swallowed, "a machine similar to my fabricator. The sword was also folded two hundred times."

"Folded… like… samurai sword folded?"

"Uhuh," Erica said while violently shaking her head. "Yoshida Yasutaka could not forge this type of metal. The edges weren't hand or machine sharpened either. They appear to have been heat-treated… like by a laser. The same process was done to the Ghoul's blades as well. It doesn't end there."

Erica quickly punched up scans of the Ghoul's outfit.

"The Ghoul's outfit is constructed from an experimental polyurethane material called Zero Drag and coated with hydrophobic nanoparticles. The combination creates a frictionless surface; the military has been testing it for new suits for Halo Jumpers. Once again, none of those idiots downstairs would know how to properly use this stuff to construct this type of outfit."

"So you're saying, this stuff was created in a lab," Rogers swallowed.

"An R&D military lab."

A sick feeling went from Rogers's stomach and onto his face.

"Maxine, give me a visual of all the inmates in Purgatory," Rogers ordered.

Holographic displays appeared within the Ghoul, Nachzehrer, and the Draugr cells. All of them sat calm and quiet in their cells with devious grins on their faces as if they knew they would not be there long. Rogers quickly turned to Erica.

"Do the other members of the Zombie Nation possess abilities to locate us or break through our defenses?"

"The kid in the robe may have the ability to create a mental tether to the ones downstairs," Erica answered, "to pinpoint our location. But there's no way they could blast their way down to our level before we responded with heavy retaliation. On our turf, we could bring them down in a matter of minutes."

The sick feeling was still with Rogers like a parasite, and Erica saw it all over his face. It said something or someone worse was coming.

"Tell everyone to suit up. Put the base on high alert and lock everything down," Rogers ordered.

"Yes, sir," Erica complied.

~~~~~~~~~~~~~~~~~~~~~~~~~~~~~~~~

Five minutes after Rogers gave the order, something fast and powerful struck the Ranch's main hanger entrance, popping it like a balloon. Shrapnel rained down everywhere as whatever demolished the hanger in under a second tore through two and a half miles of rock and steel down to the base with no sign of being stopped until it hit the hanger section where the Tornado rested, severing the ship in half, bringing down structures and destroying any Doozer within the vicinity of the impact.

The entire base violently shook as explosions erupted. Black smoke bellowed, and debris rained and sprayed everywhere.

Rogers covered Erica as heavy ceiling tile rained down, striking his thick frame.

"Maxine!" Rogers barked, "Have we been breached?"

"Confirmed," Maxine reported, "intruder has breached the base. The defense system was unable to detect an approach before impact due to immense speed and velocity. Attempting to bring up visuals."

A holographic image of the destroyed hanger appeared as the smoke within was thick as molasses. Yellow, sinister glowing eyes sliced through it like butter. The owner stepped through the smoke with a grin that said she had conquered hell and was ready to bring down heaven.

She wore long, filthy, matted blonde dreadlocks; her red and brown leather biker-styled outfit consisted of a red tank top, halter top, pants, and high heel boots; A red three-ring choker wrapped around her neck, while tan leather wristbands and a matching
~~~~~~~~~~~~~~~~~~~~~~~~~~~~~~~~

belt tightly encircled her arms and hips.

"Fee. Fie. Foe. Fum," were the first words audio picked up from her.

Rogers leaned in, squinting his eyes inches from the screen to get a look at the invader through the smoke.

"Maxine, what are we dealing with?"

"Energy readings are on a bio-nuclear level," Maxine confirmed. "Base readings are off the chart and unreadable."

"Oh god," Erica quivered.

She went limp in his arm. He lifted her up like an infant, holding her close.

"Going into full defense mode," Maxine declared.

All Doozers, both large and small, went into combat defense mode. The lights on their bodies went from blue to red as their backs opened up, unloading two shoulder-mounted ion plasma cannons. They all moved to converge on the location of the mysterious female EVO.

With no warning, they all powered up and laid down a salvo of firepower, striking her from all directions. Some smaller Doozers hung from walls and ceiling structures, unleashing their plasma rounds to bring her down.

Neither Abe nor Erica was surprised as the mystery woman tanked the murderous assault with minimal discomfort. Having her fill of being pelted, her eerie yellow eyes blazed as she returned fire with powerful eyebeam blasts, cutting down Doozers big and small.

"Maxine," Erica asked, finding her nerves again, "where is the rest of the team?"

"Rosann is in the Hurt Locker suited up," Maxine answered. "Oliver and Adrian were en route to their rooms before the attack."

"Tell Rosann to get to the central command, send Jennifer en route to back her up," Lady Tech commanded. "Send Angie to the guys and tell them to forget about suiting up and get there as well! Patch me into Dennison ASAP! Rogers put me down."

"What are you doing?" Rogers asked, setting her down.

"You know who she came for." Lady Tech said while grabbing her earpiece and putting it on. "She could be down there in less than a minute. We are currently outmatched in every way possible, and once she breaks those lunatics out, they will overrun us. We need to fall back to the central command."

"Massive energy buildup coming from the female EVO," Maxine reported.

Rogers and Erica turned back to the screen to view the mysterious female still taking fire from the surviving Doozers, powering up her right fist.

"All communications are officially down," the woman announced with a savage grin.

She slammed her fist into the ground, unleashing a shockwave-type energy discharge that swept through the entire underground facility, shutting down everything electrical. The bigger Doozers collapsed while the smaller ones fell from their perches or the rafters, crashing into the floor below. Maxine's android form also crumpled, hitting the floor with a hard thud as the power and lights went out in Erica's lab. Red-colored lights from the backup generator booted up within the lab and the base, providing light and energy to the facility.

"That was an EMP," Rogers noted.

"And a powerful one," Erica said with a shivering nod. "Maxine, the girls, along with the Doozers, are all built with anti-EMP shielding to defend against such an attack. She'll reboot in five minutes, the Doozers in ten, and the entire base within twenty. Until then, everything, including communication, is down."

"Enough time for her to get down to Purgatory," Rogers concluded, gritting his teeth.

"The security Doozers down there are still operational due to the distance between them and the blast," Erica informed him, "but they won't be able to slow her down, much less stop her."

~~~~~~~~~~~~~~~~~~~~~~~~~~~~~~~~

As Erica had predicted, the extremely powerful blonde dynamo extended her right hand, focusing. Her veins glowed as an orange-red electrical discharge poured from the pores of her skin, dancing around her hand, forming a baseball-sized ball of energy in
~~~~~~~~~~~~~~~~~~~~~~~~~~~~~~~~

her palm. As she unleashed it, it expanded to twice the size of a manhole cover in circumference, burning through the floor down to the Purgatory prison unit.

With no fear, she walked right into the hole, dropping a half-mile down, hitting the prison's ground floor, where she was met by two large and heavily armored Doozers with midnight blue and black color schemes opening fire on her. The powerful volleys from their shoulder cannons and four-finger mitts were ten times more powerful than their counterparts upstairs as Lady Tech equipped them with a quadruple Ion core system. They were able to knock her backward, taking her off her feet. She rolled to one knee still brandishing the evil grin she wore upstairs.

She answered the security Doozers' attack with another powerful eyebeam blast, burning a vast gaping hole through one of them, igniting the ion cells within it. The explosion tore through the prison hallway, sending shrapnel flying everywhere. Its brother, standing behind it for backup, took the brunt of its detonation, displaying superficial damage. It opened fire as the last line of defense between her and the prisoners.

Employing superhuman speed, she darted toward it. Now ready for it, she tanked its powerful shots, slamming right into it. The Doozer fought to stop her forward motion by using its back legs to put on the brakes, but she proved to be far too powerful.

She continued to push the behemoth of a machine backward. The back rear legs gave out simultaneously as she drilled it into the steel wall at the end of the hallway, crushing its upper torso on impact.

Badly damaged, it attempted to follow through with its prime directive to defend the prison by grabbing her. She tore it's right arm off, followed by its head, taking the last bit of fight out of it. She tossed the arm but paused to examine the skull.

"New model. Same old junk."

She casually chucked it to the floor as well. Her arms folded behind her, she strolled back to the occupied prison cells. Ghoul and Nachzehrer each lowered their head to her disapproving glare.

She shook her head with a motherly huff before tearing open each prison cell with one bare hand. The Ghoul was the first to exit, while Nachzehrer took a minute to come out, fashioning her torn prison garb into a skimpy makeshift bikini top and bottom.

Their apparent leader did not wait for her, heading for the tank that held the Draugr. She created a sizable hole in the tank with a powerful energy blast from her hand, shaking the facility. The thick gelatin liquid spilled onto the floor, violently crashing the floating cell to the tank's bottom. Her eyebeams cut through the dark metal-fortified cell like a dense frozen cheesecake.

It was all the monster needed to smash through his prison. The burn marks on his body from her eyebeams healed as he towered over her. He dropped to one knee without hesitation, bowing his head in servitude. She patted the top of his long brown mane skull and motioned for him to rise.

"Back out the way you came, huh, boss?" Ghoul asked.

The woman glared at him, causing the Ghoul to back up.

"Do I look like the type to walk?"

She raised her hand, forcing everyone, except for the Draugr, to run for cover.

~~~~~~~~~~~~~~~~~~~~~~~~~~~~~~~~~

Abe carried Maxine's android body up top, following Erica to the central command. She placed her hand on the hand imprinting panel, activating the manual override system to open the doors.

"You can put me down, Sergeant," a rebooted Maxine responded, "detecting Angie and Jennifer also affected by the EMP rebooting. Doozers will reboot in five minutes, all other systems in ten."

"Maxine, where the hell's everyone else?" Rogers asked.

"They're all en route here, they should be…"

She paused as her eyes went wide, bringing a sickening amount of dread to Erica and Abe.

"Detecting a massive power buildup coming from the Purgatory prison," Maxine informed them.

"Hit the deck!" Rogers screamed.

He grabbed Erica, wrapping his arms around her and using his back to shield her just as an energy blast the width of a train with force and heat equivalent to the sun
~~~~~~~~~~~~~~~~~~~~~~~~~~~~~~~~~

tore through the facility, engulfing everything in its path. The attack was so powerful it cut a route back up to the surface, ripping through the destroyed hanger.

It also started a chain reaction of explosions, bringing down solid rock and structures.

Rogers got to his feet and picked Erica up, checking to see if she was all right. Maxine, also knocked off her feet from the blast, stood before them.

"Maxine, any casualties?" Rogers yelled.

"Negative, everyone is still alive. Angie is with Adrian and Oliver, while Jennifer is with Rosann. Shall I…"

"Stay your ass here, and watch Erica," Rogers commanded. "I'm going out to get them."

A shaken Erica grabbed his arm before he left.

"Come back with them," she ordered.

He nodded as he ran through the doors, diving into the black smoke and fire filling the base.

~ ~

Rosann stumbled around in the middle of hell. Coughing and hacking from the suffocating smoke, she followed Jennifer, leading her to the central command while avoiding four-alarm blazes. The fire control system kicked in, working overtime as it sprayed foam to kill the fires that had erupted about the base.

"How much further?" Rosann coughed.

"We're almost there," Jennifer confirmed.

Erica and Rogers's dread before the blast passed onto Rosann as booming footsteps forced her to back up.

Out of the smoke that could have killed an elephant emerged the sadistic Draugr looking to kill something. And now the monster stood before her.

With full knowledge of what the monster was capable of, a terrified Rosann stood her ground despite her fear. Summoning up courage, she ran her hand across her fossil bone bracer and transformed into a human hybrid version of a Kodiak bear matching the Draugr size for size.

She bellowed a roar, brandishing her claws, challenging him.

Jennifer, also prepared to fight by Rosann's side, converted into combat mode. Her back opened up, allowing her to reach and pull out two hi-tech hilts made for samurai swords. Another section of her back opened up, producing the blades; she attached the hilts, drawing out two razor-sharp swords. They both squared off, flanking the monster, ready to attack.

In an instant, Jennifer's eyes widened like Maxine's before she defended an attack against a dual metal pipe-wielding Ghoul using them like escrima sticks, leaving Rosann to fight the Draugr alone.

With a savage grin, the Draugr roared back and attacked. Knowing that he was far more powerful than her despite her current form and could tear her apart once he got a hold of her, Rosann stuck to moving in and out of his swings, swiping and clawing at him with her thick dagger-like nails.

Her plans were thwarted as her razor-sharp nails cracked and chipped against his super-thick skin.

The android and EVO duo held their own against the Viking powerhouse and the speedster until Rosann was clipped by a powerful backhand, sending her into a tailspin. She hit the floor hard, saved from any additional injury by her dense bear physiology. She slowly reverted back to her human form in her unconscious state.

Seeing Rosann down, Jennifer ran to her side, but a faster-moving Ghoul blocked her path, laying into her with powerful strikes from the dark metal forged pipes he wielded, forcing her to defend herself.

Jennifer ran defensive battle scenarios in nanoseconds, calculating how to get past the murderous speedster to protect Rosann from the beast now standing over her. None of them had a survival rate of over five percent for Rosann. Rosann's survival rate decreased as Nachzehrer attempted to blindside Jennifer with her own pipe swinging for her skull.

Jennifer's 360-degree vision and sensors helped her barely duck the head-removing swing only to take a chest full of pipe from a faster-moving Ghoul. She tumble-rolled backward with the hit to avoid further damage and get some distance between her and her attackers. Unfortunately, it also put additional space between her and Rosann, dropping her survival rate to zero.

The Draugr prepared to stomp down on Rosann's skull like a grape in his own world. A powerful bluish-white electrical blast from Oliver's electrical plasma form staggered him. Bellowing a battle cry, he struck the Draugr with a powerful plasma ion blast, burning a hole into his chest while propelling him several yards through a destroyed structure.

He did the same to Nachzehrer, knocking her into the wreckage of the Tornado, while an armored Adrian ran to his sister's side with Angie to check on her.

"She has a severe concussion and a cracked collar bone." Angie determined after quickly scanning her. "We have to get her out of here now."

Oliver wrapped up his one-man mop-up by showing Ghoul that lightning speed was always faster than sound. He charged and strafed at a rattled Ghoul, witnessing his team's fall, clobbering him with an energy-charged right cross. He did not have time to scream from the electricity, leaving fourth-degree burns on his face as the jolting hit fired him across the base into the obliterated mess hall.

"Get to the central command," Oliver yelled at Adrian. "I'll buy you some time!"

Another sliver of blessing came their way as the power returned within the base. Relief came over Oliver as the Sergeant finally appeared with a rifle in tow, finding them. It was quickly dashed away as he witnessed his oncoming death.

Oliver saw her before Rogers did. Charging out of the smoke, she prepared to tear Abe apart in seconds. His plasma form turned from a bluish-white to a blinding deep blue for a split second.

With will and adrenaline pushing Oliver, his new form allowed him to get to her before she got to Rogers, blindsiding her with a flying shoulder charge that even she could not see or block.

The energy-charged strike detonated like a micro supernova tearing through the base, knocking everyone off their feet while sending the mystery woman tearing through the other side of the headquarters.

Adrian, Angie, and Jennifer huddled on the ground to cover a badly injured

Rosann from the explosion.

A groaning yet still alive, Rogers, caught in the middle of the blast, fought to his feet. Smoke wafted from his body from first-degree burns that quickly healed via his regenerative abilities. Through his blurry vision that slowly cleared up, Oliver stood defensively, still crackling in his blue and white electrical plasma form, facing where he believed he had knocked their powerful intruder.

"She's not dead."

"Then let's get the hell out…" Abe commanded.

"It's too late. I can feel her, she's coming," Oliver shot back, "you guys got to run now! I'll buy us some time!"

Rogers was about to admonish Oliver, ordering him to screw the heroics and get his ass in gear with the rest of them until he heard the rumbling starting to get closer.

"Go, Sergeant! Go!" Oliver frantically screamed. "I'll be right behind you! Go!"

Rogers reluctantly nodded as he motioned to Adrian, cradling his sister in his arms, to start running. Both men reluctantly turned back, giving Oliver one final hard look before running to the central command with the android sisters following.

Oliver stood trembling, not just because he felt the pain from his possibly fractured arm, which was caused while knocking the female powerhouse across the base, but because fear was swimming around in his gut. Oliver's chances of walking away from this were significantly against him, but he had to hold the line for his team to escape and survive to fight another day.

As Oliver predicted, she returned in a matter of seconds. He wasted no words as he focused on drawing power from the base again to reach his deep blue hue form. Her obnoxious smile unsettled him as he unleashed a barrage of streaming bolts at her.

Before bolting, the woman covered up, weathering through heat ten times hotter than the sun. Oliver's hat trick was unsuccessful the second time around. Not only were his most potent shots ineffective against her, but she was also terrifyingly faster than him.

Oliver found himself again in another woman's grip, and the motherly aura he felt from Sophia was nowhere in the female's eerie yellow glowing eyes. She gave him the creeps as she appeared to be checking him out.

"My… you're cute," she declared with a savage grin.

"And you're an ugly ass…"

The pressure she applied to his throat silenced Oliver, sending him into a gagging fit.

"Please, baby, that's the anger and adrenaline talking," the woman scoffed. "I know I look hot."

"If you're…going to kill me," Oliver gagged, "then… do it."

"Kill the tough talk, handsome. No one is anxious to die… especially you."

The power within her seeped from her pores, crackling and snapping, forming a ball of energy in her hand. She aimed it in the direction the rest of the Regulators fled to.

"No," Oliver groaned, struggling. "What are you doing? No!"

"Proving a point."

~~~~~~~~~~~~~~~~~~~~~~~~~~~~~~~~~~

Erica spun around to the opening of the central command doors. Rogers stormed in with Adrian holding his sister and the android twins.

"Where's Oliver?!" Erica frantically asked, looking around.

"Buying us time," Rogers said.

"What?!" she yelled back. "You left him?!"

"He stayed so we could live!" Rogers shot back. "Did you reach Dennison?!"

"We had to do some rerouting after that last blast," Erica reported, "we're attempting to connect now!"

~~~~~~~~~~~~~~~~~~~~~~~~~~~~~~~~~~

Thousands of miles away, Sophia was in cruise mode, two miles off from her island. Her little joy flight had expelled the anger and frustration after her encounter with her younger sister, Gemma.

She thought of Kimberly and spending the rest of the day with her. She'd break the news over dinner about how happy and excited her grandmother was to find out about her and that she would see her grandparents for the first time tomorrow and spend the weekend with them.

Sophia began planning to take her back to the States to do some shopping early tomorrow so she would have some presentable clothing that she could pick out herself.

"Excuse me, Ms. Dennison." Vincent came in through her earpiece, breaking her train of thought. "Ms. Champion is hailing you. It appears to be urgent."

"Put her on, please."

"Sophia!" Erica screamed.

Her distressed voice rattled her, forcing her out of mid-flight. She regained her bearings and came to an instant hover in the middle of the Pacific Ocean.

"What is it? What's going on?" Sophia frantically asked.

"Tell me you have some long lost sister with your exact powers!"

Her words brought a gruesome shiver to her entire body.

"No… I do not," Sophia nervously answered.

"Then, you need to get here fast!" Lady Tech shrieked, "because there is a white clone of you tearing the Ranch apart! She also broke out…"

"Another massive power buildup," Maxine announced, "trajectory is aimed in our direction!"

"Drop us, Maxine! Drop us now!" Erica screamed.

Rogers did not have the chance to ask what she meant by drop as the entire central command went into a freefall descent. Seconds after it dropped, Oliver screamed as he watched the woman once again unleash a powerful Earthshaking blast that ripped through the base, atomizing everything in its path, including the main door to the central command. Had it still been there, everything and everyone within it would have been vaporized to less than ash.

A thunderous booming sound shot through the earpiece, causing Sophia to jolt. The line became silent.

"Erica? Erica!"

Sophia exploded across the sky, flying at supersonic speeds toward the Ranch. The fear of nausea pushed her to soar even faster as she raced to California. Sophia prayed Lady Tech was wrong. She prayed that the dead had not risen.

~~~~~~~~~~~~~~~~~~~~~~~~~~~~~~~~~

The elevator converted central command continued to plummet down the cylindrical shaft as everyone, human and non-human, clung onto something to prevent it from hitting the roof. Still, Adrian held onto his sister in a transformed metal state while Angie stooped down, magnetically locked her feet into the floor, holding onto him.

"Nearing two-mile mark in twenty seconds. Preparing to slow down," Maxine reported. "I am also detecting falling rock debris within the shaft."

"Electromagnetic stabilizer one is no longer functioning," Maxine relayed. "Stabilizer three functioning at twenty percent. Please brace for possible impact."

The central command slammed violently into the ground, jolting everyone. The Regulators' troubles were not over as they hit the floor, covering their heads. Parts of the shaft and boulders, rock, and dirt rained down in the tons, burying the central command. Everything went black for a second before the red emergency lights booted up.

~~~~~~~~~~~~~~~~~~~~~~~~~~~~~~~~~

Back up top, Oliver continued to groan and struggle in the grip of the blonde dreadlocked woman as the three formally captured members of the Zombie Nation surrounded him.

"I'll kill you!" Oliver whimpered, clawing the air to get to her. "You bitch! I'll kill you!"

She increased her grip on his throat, making his body stiffen as he struggled to breathe. With a slight flex of her arm, her hand began to glow, siphoning energy from him through the pores of her skin. Her eyes glowed brighter as she nourished enough power to drain him to his blue and white form.

"No need to get uppity, baby. You will be joining your team very soon."

She pulled him closer to whisper in his ear.

"Do you know why energy wielders like you die when you drain them of all their power?" she softly asked.

He groaned to break free of her iron grip, knowing what was coming next.

"It's because the power within you is the same energy that allows you to function and live. The electricity running through your nervous system and brain is all the same. So when that is drained… all brain functions and vital organs slowly shut down. I understand it's a very terrifying way for your type to die."

She flexed her arm tighter, causing her hand to glow brighter. Oliver frantically yelled, struggling to break free as the power within him was painfully being ripped away from him and into her.

She was correct; he did not want to die. He did not want to leave this world, his family, and his new family. Most importantly, he did not want to leave her. He had so much to say, to tell her, and this woman smiled as she took it all away.

His plasma form went from bluish-white to his greenish-white state before disappearing. As his breathing became difficult due to his lungs failing, his eyes began flicking as he weakly struggled to break free. Even his falling tears did not sway her from taking his life as she looked him dead in the eyes.

His eyes went cold, his body limp, as she squeezed every spark of power out of him until there was just a shell to release.

No one even winced as his body hit the floor.

Her eye shined brighter from the power she absorbed from a lifeless Oliver. She looked intoxicated as she glanced at her glowing hand crackling with a red electrical discharge before powering it down.

"She'll be here any minute, so I will go up first to distract her," she instructed them. "Asses back to the base, and wait there till I return. Understood?"

They all nodded as she took off, flying back up through the massive tunnel she made to the top. The Draugr and Nachzehrer used their powerful legs to leap to the surface, while the Ghoul used his speed to run past them all the way back to the top. They all waited inside what was left of the hangar as the mysterious blonde powerhouse was the first to exit as planned.

~ ~

Sophia's heart quickened as she flew to see the black smoke wafting from the obliterated hanger. She touched down, throwing off the backpack her mother gave her as someone emerged from it.

The blood in her veins began to burn as the woman got closer and closer. Her eyes and hair were indeed different, but there was no mistaking that obnoxious, sadistic smile as she confidently swaggered over to her.

#3 grinned, throwing her hands up.

"I know! I know! For a woman who was supposed to die screaming, I look damn good, right?"

Sophia's whole world became white as she detonated the air around her, taking flight. An inaudible sound of blind rage emitted from her lips sent animals within earshot running for cover as she propelled herself toward the woman she knew as #3. Surprisingly, #3 stood her ground as she prepared to take a hit equivalent to ten thousand exajoules of force.

The impact unleashed a sonic boom sound similar to a mini-nuke as Sophia struck #3 with a flying shoulder tackle, taking both airborne. The speed she was moving at was beyond Mach 20. Blinded by rage, she lost track of direction; Sophia took #3 halfway around the world, putting her through the Matterhorn.

The most renowned mountain bordering Switzerland and Italy shattered in one stroke. Massive chunks of mountain rained down, causing an avalanche obliterating everything in its path.

The ride did not stop as a reckless Sophia sent them crashing into the heart of the Forest Fun Park, bringing down trees with zip lines and other structures. Visitors and tourists ran and screamed, searching for safety. At the same time, those within the aerial tramways bawled and cried, clinging onto whatever they could grab, including one another, as it swayed back and forth.

Sophia dragged herself off of a downed tree. Realizing what her unchecked emotions had done, Sophia quickly pulled herself together. First, she had to save a male tourist from falling from a snapped zip line and then stabilize the shaking structure attached to trees.

Her hair stood on the back of her neck as Sophia leaped through the sky, catching the screaming zip liner in midfall setting him down. She could not stop to check if he was okay as she bolted to secure the massive metal tower. She pushed it down into the ground to secure it.

It was all for knot as an orange and red energy blast blew the tower's top apart, snapping the cables and sending two suspended carts falling and crashing to the ground.

"Noooooo!" Sophia screamed.

#3 stood sneering in the center of the chaos. With a hand gesture, she beckoned Sophia to come at her. Drenched with fury, she obliged, propelling herself toward her. It sounded like a bomb detonated as she slammed into her again, driving her through the dense forest.

As Sophia drove her backward through thick foliage to beat her to death in an isolated area. Ice chills ran throughout her body as she realized she was slowing down.

#3 bared down, straightening her body into a slanting position, trenching the ground with her feet.

Sophia stopped her forward thrust, landing on her feet. She planned to grab #3 by her legs, lift her up, and then go airborne again, straight up. Before she could put her plan into motion, #3 revealed that she was disturbingly stronger and faster than Sophia.

She leaped up before she could react and delivered a crushing elbow to the upper part of Sophia's spine. She felt every bit of it.

In the almost seven years since her reawakening, she had not felt pain—the type that #3 delivered to her. Not even the Draugr's lucky shot to the nose hurt as much. The elbow to the back felt as if her spine was shattered.

#3 followed up with a knee to the gut that felt like she cracked several of Sophia's ribs. So much so that Sophia could not prepare for the earthshaking uppercut knocking her into the planet's upper stratosphere. Blood poured and froze as it left

Sophia's mouth while her eyes witnessed literal stars and planets.

The cobwebs and pain rattling her body and mind were dispersing too slowly for her to defend herself.

#3, now airborne, had caught up with her in seconds. This time, it was #3's turn to deliver a swooping shoulder tackle to the gut, which hurled both women back down to Earth. Their atmospheric reentry lit up the heavens.

The material used to create Sophia's new outfit gifted to her by Lady Tech held against their downward angled plunge's scorching heat.

#3's leather ensemble also held, though it took more damage and abuse from the god-like roughhousing. She did not care as she cackled insanely while strafing across the skies of England, looking to pay Sophia back for the Matterhorn.

The target of her aggression was innocent Big Ben.

Realizing where she was heading, Sophia fought to break from her grip, but it was too late.

The famed clock tower exploded, similar to an egg in a microwave; those watching the scene in horror ran for their lives as debris from the Elizabeth Tower rained down, crushing everything and everyone unfortunate to not have gotten out of the way. The rest of the tower's weakened structure gave way and came crashing down while #3 and Sophia plowed into the Palace of Westminster.

It went up like a lit M-80 stuffed inside of a birdhouse. Smoke billowed everywhere while pieces of the historical structure collapsed into itself; some fell outward, falling into the River Thames. The seismic hit also claimed the Westminster Bridge, tearing it apart and sending it into the river. The destruction and loss of life were immeasurable.

Sophia groaned as several tons of the Palace laid on her while a high-pitched ringing went off in her ear. She employed her eyebeams to slice a path through the rubble. With a couple of swipes and kicks, she unburied herself.

As quickly as it came, the ringing disappeared as Sophia slowly staggered to her feet. Now filled with fire, structures crumbling, and the screams of the trapped and dying, she clutched her chest, looking around at the destruction and mayhem. Black smoke blotted out the little sun that shined, making it nearly impossible to see. It was hell on Earth that she was partially responsible for creating.

"No... no... no," Sophia coughed out, close to tears.

Her ears also picked up another sound through the madness. It was the insane laughter of joy.

"Whoooooo! That shit was **hot**!" #3 howled. "Nothing like a bit of mass destruction to make you feel more alive!"

Her bright yellow glowing eyes and ear-to-ear grin made her look more monstrous as she stood basking amongst the ruin.

"What did you do?" a male voice screamed. "What did you fucking cunts do?"

Both women turned to see five mortified superhumans dressed in colorful British flag attire and body armor; the UK's superhuman military unit known as the Lions of Elizabeth.

Their leader, Knight Light, was a powerful Apollo class EVO and one of the few to channel and manipulate photon energy on a dangerous level. He was the only one hovering above his team, adorned in a bodysuit with a star on his chest and forearms and the Union Jack flag over the entire bodysuit. Like Sophia and other energy wielders of the solar and electrical spectrum, his eyes glowed a yellowish-white. He was also the one who crudely addressed them.

"Look around, "bright boy. What do you think happened?" #3 callously asked while gesturing. "My girl and I happened to be roughhousing and did a little remodeling of this piece of shit country of yours. Fuck you very much. Now piss off before you piss **me** off."

"Take them!" Knight Light howled his orders to his team. "Dead or alive, take them both!"

"No, wait... I'm not with...!" Sophia yelled while throwing her hands up.

Her attempt to reason with them was cut short by a furious gust of water capable of punching a hole through a brick wall. She could have powered through it if she was not caught off guard. Instead, she was blasted a good thirty feet by the team's water wielder, codenamed the Lady of the Lake.

Sophia quickly recovered, rolling to her feet, only to be set upon by the water wielder and the Mercurian speedster, Sir William Swift.

His Union Jack bodysuit was styled with a flashy wind pattern design. He also wore a ballistic mask with the same pattern to hide his identity. Furiously, he circled Sophia, moving six times the speed of sound. He moved in and out of his circular running pattern to get close enough to strike her with a right cross that could remove a human head at his running velocity.

The act was nothing but annoying to Sophia. She would have grabbed him had it not been for the Lady of the Lake slamming her repeatedly with typhoon salvos of water. An impressive technique they both mastered.

Through the blur and the water pelting, Sophia could see that Knight Light and the rest of his team consisting of Jack the Giant, a Titan class EVO, and Foundation, a female Elemental EVO with abilities similar to Adrian, attempted a triple team on #3.

It was going worse than she feared.

Knight Light's powerful photon blast, capable of cutting an aircraft carrier in half, did not even sear her skin. Sophia had a gut feeling it was also strengthening her. The woman, known as Foundation, placed her hand on a broken column of the Palace, transforming her body into its properties. She then grasped the fifteen-ton column, breaking it off to use it as a blunt object.

Jack the Giant attempted a Mixed Martial Arts shoot to tackle her to the ground, but a far more powerful and skilled #3 stuffed his attempt and upended him with a knee that lifted him off his feet.

Unlike Sophia, who only expelled a couple trickles of blood, Jack the Giant found himself on his knees, clutching his gut. His body violently trembled from the devastating hit as he threw up blood and bile.

Sophia had to remove her before she caused more senseless deaths. In one swift move, she extended her arm, clotheslining Sir William Swift out of his running pattern and into a painful tailspin. She ensured to strike him in the rock-solid upper part of his chest instead of his neck to avoid beheading him. He hit the floor brutally hard but would recover in minutes.

Sophia then powered through the Lady of the Lake's powerful hydrostream blasts, grabbing both of her arms. She applied enough pressure to stop her from channeling any more water molecules.

"Ow! Ow! Ow!" Lady of the Lake screamed.

Sophia could see the anger and tears in her eyes mixed with fear.

"I'm not the enemy, so stop hitting me with water," Sophia said sternly, "You and your fast friend over there need to focus on putting out these fires and helping the wounded. I'll deal with that madwoman before she hurts or kills anyone else. Understood?"

The Lady of the Lake frantically nodded that she would comply. Sophia released her long enough to see #3 standing punt kick Jack the Giant through an already broken wall structure and smash the column Foundation attempted to use as a club into rubble with a swat of her forearm. With blinding speed, she grabbed her by her throat, lifting her off her feet, forcing Knight Light to end his futile photon barrages in fear of hitting his teammate.

#3 grinned as she prepared to crush her marble stone neck, popping her head off.

Sophia blindsided her with another shoulder tackle and whisked her into the air, saving Foundation from the gruesome death. She hit the floor hard. Clutching her throat, she was visibly shaken, even in her transformed state. Knight Light landed, running to her side to check on her. He briefly turned, looking up at the sky with rage and sadness.

Several thousand miles up, the two women cursed, screamed, clawed, punched, kneed, and kicked at each other at unimaginable speeds. Neither one paid attention to their flight pattern as they flew over the Sahara.

In midair, #3 executed a Judo Tomeo-nage or Circle-throw, hurling her off. Before Sophia hit the sand, she grabbed a handful of #3's blonde dreads.

#3 screamed as Sophia pulled, slinging her down by her hair.

#3 tore through a sand dune and kept tumbling while Sophia impacted the sand, sliding across it at high speeds, spraying sand everywhere before stopping. She spat up a mouthful of sand that she ate as she slowly rose to her feet.

As the blazing sun beat down on her, no innocent soul was in sight. Her ears popped up to the sound of foul language. Slowly, Sophia turned to see the person she had been trying to kill for the second time in the past forty-five minutes, dusting herself off.

"Asshole!" #3 screamed with a snarl on her face. "If you wanted to get me alone to talk, all you had to do was ask! I swear if you pulled out one dread."

As #3 checked her hair to ensure none was ripped out, a blindly enraged Sophia attempted to rush her again. Two feet away from closing the gap, #3 extended her right hand, charging an orange and red soccer ball size of energy, stopping her in her tracks.

"Careful!" #3 warned. "You know how one of these works once I let it fly. How many towns do you think I can destroy in a single blast before you get to me? Now, are we going to talk like adults or make more bodies to bury?"

"How are you still alive?!" Sophia screamed.

"Search your thoughts, Luke," #3 sneered. "After the trouncing, you gave me before you kamikazed me into that nuke, which let me go on record to say was **way** over the fucking line to anything I've ever done to you. I should have been dead. Blown to bits, atomized ashes, so what did you do to ensure my survival?"

Sophia began searching her memory, fast-forwarding, freezing, and analyzing their one-sided battle before their supposed nuclear end almost seven years ago.

"I'll give you a hint," #3 said. "It was before you said... "That's... for Charlie."

Sophia staggered backward, shaking her head as her memory fell on that moment before her remark.

"No." Sophia gasped, shaking her head.

"Oh yeah," #3 confirmed with a grin, "your knack for being a petty little bitch is what saved my ass. My already enhanced cells, combined with your blood, allowed me to heal and adapt faster than you. Mind you, it wasn't enough juice to even the odds against you in our first scuffle, but it was enough to open my cells up and absorb the energies from the nuke that engulfed us both. Kind of makes you wish you had blown me to ashes like you did #1."

Her words took some of the fight out of Sophia, allowing her to ease up and power down the pulsating, crackling ball of death she held.

"By the way, I go by the name 'Peace' now, #3 is my slave name."

Sophia fought to regain her focus.

"Where...?"

"You mean, where I've been hiding?" Peace chuckled, "off-planet!"

Sophia swayed where she stood, a bit stunned.

"Off planet? You mean space?"

"Shit! I mean, I traveled to Mars, Saturn, and then I backtracked to Venus, which is like a twenty-four-seven acid trip! After that, I spent like a month and a half on Mercury! Let me tell you, girl! Clothing is not optional! The upside is no tan lines!"

Peace snickered, pulling the straps to her outfit, revealing she had none. She began to stroll around.

"Now, the backstory, if you must know, is that I apparently woke up after you. Not sure how long, but it was definitely after you."

"You woke up in a sack, too," Sophia deduced.

"Oh yeah, I don't know about you, but there ain't nothing more fucked up than waking up at the bottom of the ocean with no memory, in jellyfish afterbirth, and glow in the dark fish floating all around you."

Sophia furrowed her brow while folding her arms.

"I never lost my memory."

"Typical." Peace snorted while rolling her eyes. "Anyway, I broke out returning topside a basket case; I didn't even remember that I had powers. I don't know how I figured it out, but I ended up swimming all the way to South America. Murdered like two Great Whites and a Mako on the way there… pesky little shits."

Sophia was unsure if she should continue to listen or begin slugging her again.

"On the way there, which took about three days," Peace sighed, "my memory started to come back. Not gingerly, mind you; it came like tsunami waves that I had to ride out. Believe it or not, our little fight seven years ago actually traumatized me to the point I had a terrifying fear of you."

"That's comforting to know," Sophia scoffed.

Peace glared at her, then decided to ignore her comment.

"Anyway, with the gut feeling that you were out there somewhere, I went into deep hiding. I mean, I went native, like Amazon rainforest bush bitch native. It was pretty easy considering that I didn't really need to eat, didn't need a lot of clothes, or even shelter, for that matter. During the day, I kept a low profile; at night, I worked on mastering my abilities."

Peace opened the palm of her right hand, facing up. A red electrical charge snapped and crackled from it before producing a red and orange sphere of pure energy. With a thought, she dispersed it.

"I can make bigger ones and even full streams; I can also do this."

Peace's eyes became ablaze as she unleashed a reddish-orange eyebeam blast straight at Sophia. On instinct, Sophia threw up her forearms to block the shot; her bracers constructed of dark metal deflected the heat beams hitting the sand of the Sahara, crystallizing it. The bands held, although the blast left a searing mark on them.

Sophia's eyes blazed as she got ready to fight again. Peace cackled, backing up with her hands held high.

"Okay! Hold up, I'm just messing with you! No need to start brawling again. Very nice what you did with your 'wonder bands,' though. Throw a cowl with some ears on you, and you're the Trinity rolled up into one."

"What do you want?!" Sophia's voice boomed.

"The first thing I want is to finish my story." Peace said, getting serious again. "So there I was, building my confidence. I gained some sense of peace. The indigenous thought I was some witch or goddess; they'd bring me food offerings from time to time, but they pretty much left me alone. I would have probably stayed there to my own devices had you not shown up one day in my backyard."

Sophia searched her memories, remembering the day she visited the Amazon rainforest, a record of six times.

"You were there?" Sophia asked, stunned that she did not detect her.

"Oh yeah, I saw you coming a mile away. I buried myself in the mud like Dutch while you were strolling around uprooting trees for your fancy-schmancy garden. The fear I had for you paralyzed me. It was friggin humiliating. After you left, I concluded that it wouldn't be too long before you found me that the world was just too small for the both of us. If I was truly going to be safe, I should look to the stars."

Peace pointed up with a glint in her eye. Sophia briefly glanced up herself before returning her eyes to her mortal enemy.

"So after a couple of midnight test runs when I knew you weren't buzzing around," Peace continued, "I stole the proper attire and provisions that I believed I needed for space travel and said farewell to this beautiful dirtball planet. Let me tell you that breaking through that stratosphere into that big black nothing is one hell of a rush! But you already know what it's like to be unbound. Anyway, it took me a day and a half to get to Mars, which was a disappointing red rock of nothing."

Peace rolled her eyes before looking down at the ground, doodling a pattern with her boot.

"So I left; it took me three days to get to Saturn. Don't ask how I knew how to get there. And as I stood on one of Saturn's many moons preparing to set off again on my journey to the unknown. I realized I had no friggin idea where I was going! And then it happened at that moment. The fear I had for you faded away, and the rage and hatred set in. Unfortunately for Saturn, it is now short a couple of moons."

Peace looked up at her with the same eyes as when they had their first one-on-one conversation at Mount McLoughlin.

"You see, the only other person to put fear into this little black heart of mine other than you," Peace said, "was my dear old dad, may he rot, burn, and suffer in hell. I had to tag-team two of his closest friends and promised them to split his meth and a profit of two hundred thousand dollars if they slit his throat and emptied several rounds in him. They ended up tag teaming me again against my will. Left me five hundred dollars for my troubles, but it was worth it to remove that fear forever."

Peace smirked as she advanced one step closer with her arms folded behind her.

"But I forgot who I'm talking to. You don't give a damn about my 'hard life.'"

Peace brandished a sarcastic smile, looking Sophia up and down as she glared back at her, giving her ten seconds to get out of her face. Peace, not wanting another confrontation, just took the subtle facial hint to retreat one step.

"So anyway, I about-faced heading back here to take the moon and cram it down your throat. Then something else happened on my journey back. Little by little, that rage and hatred started to fade as well, and I had a moment of clarity that allowed me to think and see straight in… god knows how long. You weren't my problem, and I had no reason to hate you."

Peace lowered her head in frustration, rubbing her eyebrow. As she raised her eyes to her, Sophia realized in disbelief that she was mustering up the courage to apologize.

"If I was you, and you did to me what I did to you, I would have probably done the same and worse. And although I was given orders to carry out, I think I took such pleasure in f-ing up your life because my own up until then was so shitty. My issue was not with you but with people who were supposed to care for me, who failed me, and a world that didn't give a shit about me. So I turned into an animal to survive, and you became just another prey. For what it's worth… you didn't deserve that, and I'm sorry."

She almost fell out just by Peace's words. Sophia, now with narrowed eyes, stepped forward, trying to wrap her brain around what she had just said.

"You attacked the Regulators' base an hour ago, reducing it to rubble." Sophia replayed the events, leading them to where they stood. "You released three of the most dangerous superhumans on this planet."

Peace shrugged, agreeing with a nod.

"Yeah, I did that; I also killed one of their team members; actually, I think I killed all of them. But if you're going to bitch about us roughhousing in the UK, remember you started it by slamming me into the Matterhorn. I just want to point that out."

"You do see how what went down is going to make it difficult for things to be good between us, basically making your apology worthless, right?" Sophia asked with a sarcastic smile of disgust.

"I don't really see how; I mean, you destroyed a base, like, seven years ago and killed a whole lot of people. You don't see me throwing a fit about it."

Sophia wore a look, realizing that she was genuinely crazy and she was taking part in an insane conversation with her.

"And it's the UK," Peace emphasized, "who really gives a shit about the UK? It rains there all the time, and the people are certified assholes. I mean, despite all of that, considering how well shit turned out, I don't see a reason for us to have any ill-will toward each other. Do you?"

"You're a psychopathic murderer!" Sophia screamed at the top of her lungs. "You murdered my husband and framed me for it! That's going to make it pretty hard for you and me to be girlfriends! **Like never!"**

Peace snarled while lowering her head for a minute, taking in some air, and then raised it, displaying a scowl. She stepped toward Sophia, who crossed her arms and stood her ground.

"All right, let's gain some perspective here; **I** was an **ex-con** turned **assassin** by the United States Government, who had no choice but to follow orders due to the nanites implanted within me promising a slow and painful death should I refuse them. **Your husband** was a lying sack of shit with **daddy issues**! No one put a gun to his head to join our unit, so you need to put the blame where it belongs!"

Peace turned storming away as if she was actually arguing with a girlfriend. In frustration, she kicked up a cloud of sand while throwing her hands in the air.

"I mean, Jesus! How are we supposed to work together to change this dirtball of a planet if we're fighting over a man?! And a dead one at that!"

Sophia raised an eyebrow, zeroing in on the vital part of her statement.

"What do you mean 'work together'?"

"You think I was bullshitting you seven years ago about us making the world the way we want it to be?" Peace asked while turning to her. "I was as serious as a stroke the day you decided to play chicken with a nuke and our lives."

"You mean us being "gods" again?" Sophia scoffed with an eye roll.

"Oh, no, no, no, my dear deluded 'sister.'" Peace cackled, waving her off. "I told you I evened out. I have no desire to become a god. Gods are nothing more than egotistical contradictory sons of bitches, and I also have no desire to be some queen or ruler. Subjects are like rugrats, always needing a tit to suck on or someone to wipe their ass, and I hate kids. I love my independence."

"Then what?" Sophia inquired, becoming impatient.

"Like I said," Peace said, looking at her as if she was deaf, "make the world as we want it to be. Look around you. How long do you think this planet has left at the state our inferior counterparts are running it into the ground? Another decade, maybe two? They're like a bad television sitcom that keeps getting worse year after year after year. It's time to cancel their season and try something new, don't you think?"

Sophia narrowed her eyes.

"If you're talking genocide…"

"I don't like using that word... such a nasty term. Plus, I know we still need the little knuckle draggers if we're going to increase our stock. I propose a quick, systematic fade out, like when a new model phone or car comes out. You don't keep making the old one."

"You just keep pushing the envelope on how crazy you are," Sophia grumbled while shaking her head.

"You know what's crazy?" Peace spat while taking a step forward. "Half of our wildlife gone in less than forty years! That is crazy! Deforestation, global warming, idiots butchering rhinos over their horns because they believe it will cure them of limp dick disease! Our world is dying because we are a species created weak in both body and mind! We consume and don't give back; we prey, especially on one another, because he who has the power makes the rules! Just look at our history!

You won't give us your oil? We'll pretend you were behind the fall of some towers and are hiding weapons of mass destruction, and then we'll drop bombs on you from afar and then take it! You don't want to give up your land? We'll kill you for it with our guns, and while we're at it, we'll murder your women and children, driving your race to near extinction!

Do you want to fight for your freedom? We'll crucify you, your family, and your friends from one town to the next as a warning not to oppose us! You don't want to obey and worship me? I'll drown you all and start anew!"

Peace looked up into the sky as if to spit at God and give Him the finger.

"For centuries, we've been in that afternoon program where the father confronts his kid about smoking weed. But what if this was a world where **everyone** had power, where **everyone** was like us, or close enough?"

She started to walk around Sophia in a circle, continuing her lecture. Sophia stood listening for now because there was no destruction while talking, giving her the time to figure out a way to put her down for good.

"You ever been to a bar where everyone was packing?" Peace asked. "Of course, you haven't; you're a 'Miss Goody Two Shoes.' I'll have you know it's one of the most peaceful and safest places to be, except for those who are not armed. Because everyone knows that the guy next to him is holding, and the last thing you want is a bar packed full of guns blazing."

"You want to bring back the Wild West?" Sophia inquired while following her movement.

"I want to make us all truly equal," Peace answered. "I want us to be independent of trivial things that we really don't need! I want to get rid of our old parasitic shells that continue to drag us down and become the race that we were meant to be! One solely focused on reaching our true potential! You tell me how much more noble can one get than wanting that for her people?"

"Why the rush?" Sophia asked. "Another ten years the next generation will have matured, and if the birth rate of superhumans continues steadily as it has, we'll be what five maybe ten percent of the population?"

Peace turned to her with a gaze of disbelief.

"You really have blinders on, don't you? You really think those cockroaches are going to allow that to happen? Just because they haven't gone and 'William Strykered' us yet does not mean the so-called 'powers that be' aren't working on a way to either thin out our herd or eliminate us all together should we 'dare' step out of line or overtake them. They're quiet now because they know they can't match us. And now they have some of us taking up sides with them against each other for worthless things such as 'loyalty' or 'money.'"

Peace turned, spitting in disgust into the sand. Her act brought back more demons from their past.

"This so-called new 'Cold War' is against **us**! Maybe if you pulled your head out of the sand of that island of yours, you'd see it! If we're against each other, we're not against them! And as long as they keep us plugged into their madness, we are destined to repeat the insanity of their failed miserable race! To grow and thrive, see each other as one race, and not separated by our skin color, stupid flags, fucking religion, or money, we must become unplugged permanently! The human race must die along with their poison!"

Peace stood waiting for her to buy her pitch. She could already tell from Sophia's facial expression that it was not a sell.

"You're about to tell me to go F--- myself, aren't you?"

"And I intended to use the full four-letter word while doing it," Sophia answered with a snide smile. "What gave it away?"

"You've been collecting the heads of warlords." Peace pointed out, lecturing her. "And breaking the bones of white slavers among other devious things. Yet you continue to remain on the fence because you still see what? Redeeming qualities about them?"

Peace leaned in as Sophia wore a stunned glare over the fact that she knew so much about her activities.

"Oh, yes, Dr. Dennison, I have been keeping very close tabs on you. I have a theory about our little intimate time in the heart of the nuclear explosion. You see, I think a little of you got into me, while a little of me... got... into... you."

"I'm **nothing** like you," Sophia growled.

"Save that movie line for someone who will buy it," Peace snorted. "The eyes tell all. You've got some rage in you long before you knew I was still alive. Come on, deep down, you know what I am saying is the truth. You want hands off your family? That little island you got there? I'm a woman of compromise. One island and a couple of normals from your bloodline aren't going to hurt the cause. What else do I have to do to get you on my side?"

Sophia exhaled, mustering up the strength to reason with her.

"Why, everyone? Why not just eradicate those that do evil?"

"Because they're all the problem! The weak are just as guilty because **they are weak**! This twisted circle of life bullshit that we are trapped in is the reason for our society's downfall. We must shatter it and wipe the slate clean, and the only way to do that is for every last one of us to be strong! There can be no chink in our armor for us to succeed!"

"You brought up the 'flood' a couple of minutes ago," Sophia scoffed. "What makes this plan any different than that one?"

"Rolling out a better product line."

"And that's the end game?" Sophia asked. "A world of just superhumans. I guess you didn't take the possibility of overpopulation into consideration."

"Which would be like what a hundred or so years from now?" Peace calculated. "Yeah, I did, but by that time, our planet would have been healed, and we would be ready to write the next chapter in our soon to be epic history."

Sophia looked up, figuring out her long-term plan.

"You're planning on going back out… there?"

"Very good, I told you I have no intention of being a leader, but a conqueror of worlds I can do. And with the discovery of several super-Earths around the known universe, we'd be crazy not to claim them as our own, thus also solving our population problem."

"That's not just it," Sophia said, shaking her head. "You doing this because you want an army… for what? What do you know?"

"Come on." Peace replied with a dull glare. "I don't need a college diploma to know that the virus that made us what we are now wasn't created in some Petri dish in a lab."

"What do you know of Project EVOlution?" Sophia asked, forgetting that they were talking about worldwide genocide for the moment.

"I love this one-sided ass relationship we have where you think you can just ask me anything without giving anything back." Peace snarled while sarcastically rolling her eyes. "When you torched #1 on that day at Mount McLoughlin, you also obliterated the tablet that held all of the data concerning Project EVOlution. But the times I got to snoop around Rosen's files after I put him to bed with my good stuff, I learned that our universe is not only as vast as we may think, we are definitely not the only ones in it."

Sophia's eyes widened with interest.

"What are you talking about? What did you see?"

"I didn't see jack," Peace sneered. "It's what I read. When the US Forces invaded Nazi Germany and liberated the Ohrdruf concentration camp, they found an entrance to a secret research lab that ran underneath the camp. There they found what they codenamed 'The Holy Grail.' They took it and everything else that was there, detonated the lab, and smuggled it out of Europe and back to the US."

"You didn't see any pictures of this Holy Grail?" Sophia asked.

"Nope. Whatever they had, they didn't want anyone to know what it looked like. It was all extremely cryptic. I do know whatever it was, based on what I read and could figure out, they were taking samples from it. Samples that they used to create the first strain of the virus."

At that moment, Sophia wrestled with whether it was a curse or blessing that she was still alive, as she willingly gave vital information about the origin of their new life.

"So now that we've had this very groundbreaking sentimental conversation between us," Peace got back to business, "I got to know right now if you're in or out."

"No," Sophia flatly answered. "I cannot and will not allow you to do this. It's not that I don't agree with some of the things you said, which is hard for me to even admit, but the way you intend to implement change is not how to go about it. Getting to the ends will not wash off the ocean's worth of blood the means will bring."

Peace wore not a face of anger or disgust. It was one of disappointment as she turned her back to her, stepping away.

"For whatever reason, we survived that nuclear explosion," Sophia said, reaching out a hand to reason with her, "we're alive. I have plenty of reasons to hate you. But maybe if I had your life, I would have turned out the same as you or even worse. Time has opened my eyes, where I can see the bigger picture. I can forgive in time. If a better world is what you want, I'm in, just not this way. Surrender, pay for your crimes, and maybe we can work toward achieving that goal together."

Her words were earnest and tactical; #3, or Peace as she called herself, was not the same woman she pulverized seven years ago. She was powerful, maybe even stronger than her. To fight with her again would mean possible destruction on a global scale. She had to use all means of diplomacy to prevent that from happening.

"A tempting offer," Peace sighed before turning back to her with a dull look. "But one, I am afraid I will have to decline. And since we both can't reach an accord on the fate of this world. I regrettably have to ask you to leave. And by leave… I mean the planet."

Sophia looked stuck for a minute as she held up a hand, unsure if her perfect hearing had just heard what Peace ordered her to do.

"Did you just tell me to leave the planet?" Sophia requested confirmation.

"Yeah, I did," Peace answered while vigorously nodding. "You see, we're currently at a discord. I had hoped that you would come to your senses and join me, but I also made preparations to do this without you. And as much as I would love to throw hands with you again, I kind of need the planet and the people here intact to implement my plans. Really sorry, wish there was another way, but you really need to raise up out of here."

"Oh, really," Sophia snorted. "And how do you intend to do that, aside from going another couple of rounds with me?"

"It's already done the second I hit the Regulators' base. Revenant is currently having afternoon tea with your dear old parents at their house, while Wendigo is right now hovering over your little island."

Sophia's eyes expanded again with shock and fear. Slowly, the rage grew on her face.

"And if you attempt to fly off," Peace warned, "or put your hands on me again, my young resident telepath who has been monitoring this conversation has been instructed to tell Revenant to turn your parents to bone and dust while Wendigo kills everyone on your island and then sinks it back to the bottom of the ocean that you raised it from to the tune of 'Kill Everybody' by Skrillex. I'm personally more of a Halestorm type of gal, but you can't tell kids shit about their music these days. Oh, and if you think I'm bluffing."

Peace quickly reached into a small pocket on the inside of her tight red leather pants, pulling out a little carbon fiber-looking case. She opened it up, revealing an earpiece. She checked to ensure it was still intact, tapped the button on the side to turn it on, and then tossed it to Sophia. She snatched it out of the air and quickly put it on.

"Hello?" her voice quivered.

"Hello, Ms. Dennison," a gloating Revenant came over the other line, "you have a lovely set of parents. Your mother, in particular, is a very colorful and charming woman; I can see where you get your fire from."

"Sophee!" her mother came loud and cleared over her headset.

She fought back panic and tears.

"Mummy!"

"Nuh worry bout we baby!" Mrs. Dennison yelled. "We nuh fraid ah no godless jangcrow dog! Look pon you! Yah fava ah ole whore!"

"Like I said," Revenant sighed, "colorful woman."

As he hung up on his end, Sophia removed the headset, crushing it in the palm of her hand. Her eyes blazed as tears streamed down her face, burning a hole through Peace, who tanked her glare.

"Whatever chance you had of me not hating you anymore, you just lost it."

"Yeah, I know, but for the greater good, I'm willing to take that hit. You're not going to believe me because you're all pissed off, but this is not personal between you and me."

Sophia narrowed her eyes as she fought to control the building rage.

"You made it personal… again."

Peace walked up, standing toe to toe with her to look her in the eyes.

"Baby girl," she whispered, "if I wanted to make it personal, I wouldn't need stooges to wipe out your entire bloodline and everyone you ever loved and cared about. A month baking on Mercury, where I adjusted to and then harnessed, the full power of the sun is all I need to do that. Hell… I could have wiped out the entire planet with one blast, leaving just you and me to fight to the end of the universe or till I kill you, and there is a way to kill you."

She made a popping sound, motioning to her head; her yellow eyes blazed, showing the unfathomable power coursing through her as the two women again sized each other up.

"But it's like I said, it's not about you," Peace snarled. "So when I came back, I stayed under the radar and made preparations to exploit your most obvious weakness. Do I really need to say what it is?"

She slowly began to stroll around her as Sophia lowered her head, grinding her teeth.

"To do that, I needed to find a team both heartless and lacking a conscience like I was," Peace explained her master plan. "That I thought was going to take a while until I tracked down the Zombie Nation. They really are a bunch of Satan worshippers who believe their powers came from the 'Dark One,' a bunch of friggin idiots."

Peace laughed at herself, shaking her head.

"Wasn't that hard to bring them to my side of the force, especially when I tore their leader's heart out and reduced him to ashes right before them. I think his name was Dybbuk. Anyway, I had my team; I just needed to do some intelligence work to ensure that you and I were the only current heavy hitters on the planet. As impressive as they looked, all the other superhuman units around the world proved no threat to me.

Nor did any of the so-called independent 'heroes.' I thought I had all the intel until I learned that the US commissioned its own superhero squad. Yay! Attacking Times Square, which was my idea. I wanted to see what this new team was capable of. The bonus was watching that A-Hole Captain Omega die, although I would have preferred to have been the one to pull the trigger myself. You have to stop underestimating the Draugr; he does some fine work. And the double bonus was watching you swoop down to save the day. I really thought you shied away from grandstanding, but you had me fooled there. I also didn't factor in the Egyptian. He really took me by surprise. A real mystery that one. You wouldn't happen to know his name?"

Sophia looked up with a sneer, telling her where to go and do with herself.

"Bah!" Peace snorted, waving her off. "Doesn't matter; he may seem formidable, but with you out the picture, easily dealt with. Now I must tell you, although Anchimayen can't read your mind for some reason, his 'astral signature' range of detection is extremely friggin impressive. That means once he gets within proximity of you, like in Times Square, he can track the energy your soul gives off almost anywhere. That's how he explained it anyway. That's how we were able to find the Regulators' base. I mean, this kid can tap, detect, and pinpoint me from space!"

Peace sighed with some motherly pride.

"Under that robe is the most beautiful little boy I've ever seen, with an, unfortunately, nasty disposition. Did you know when he acquired his powers, he removed both his parents' tongues by the root and then made his mother watch as he broke every bone in his father's body? He then tore each of her limbs off one by one, leaving her head for last. All because they denied him dessert for not finishing his vegetables."

Peace acted as if she had the jitters telling the story, while Sophia wore a face of disgust.

"I believe we've now come to an understanding, right?" Peace asked. "That the life of your parents and everyone on that little fantasy island… including your daughter depends on you not returning to Earth. In return, I will ensure that not a hair is harmed on any of their little heads. The rest of the planet is another story; I make no promises on that. And after fifty, maybe a hundred years after you've roamed the universe and found yourself, you can come back and see all the wonderful work that I have done. By then, everyone you pretty much loved would have croaked. I won't be able to use that trump card forever."

She finished her carousel walk around Sophia, standing face to face with her again.

"Except for your little girl, she'll be a grown woman by then, but she'll be here waiting for you. Now I know I said I'm not paternal material, but for you… I'll do the best that I can. I can't wait to have that girl talk about boys."

Sophia sighed, letting out a nervous laugh as she lowered her head. When she raised it again, a smile was plastered over her face as her body trembled uncontrollably.

"Somehow, someway, I will be back," Sophia promised, "and as God is my witness, I'm going to make you wish that nuke had killed us that day."

"Yeah," Peace coughed. "Your track record for keeping promises hasn't been so good. Shall we?"

The two women slowly ascended into the air; neither one bothered to increase speed as they stared at one another throughout the entire trip into space. Through no words, they understood that in their subsequent encounter, even if it was a thousand years from now, one of them would die at the other's hand.

Sophia followed her past the moon, where Peace slowed, coming to a stop. She signaled that where they floated was as far as Sophia was allowed to go near the planet. She turned with a wave, parting ways with her blasting off back to Earth, signaling the beginning of Sophia's exile.

Sound in space only exists in electromagnetic vibrations inaudible by the human ear, but Sophia screamed anyway. Her eyes blazed brighter than any star. If the sound did carry, the entire universe would eventually hear her and tremble as her mind swam with sadistic thoughts of murdering Peace—every method, extremely slow and painful.

In her mind, she would not be returning in fifty or a hundred years. Before the end of the week, Sophia would see her daughter again and feel her hands around Peace's throat, choking the life from her. She roared that promise to whatever god or beings were listening.

CHAPTER 21

Sophia hovered in the darkness of space. Her rage subsided; she now had to focus, think, and put a plan into action.

If Peace's warning was definite, Anchimayen's ability to sense her even in space meant she had few options. Sophia remembered her bracers and personal AI. She touched her ear, realizing her earpiece was gone. It was either lost or destroyed during the battle. She slid open the compartment, revealing a touch LCD screen.

Bracing herself, Sophia began to type, "Vincent, are you there?"

"Yes, Ms. Dennison," Vincent projected words via the screen. "How may I help you?"

"Can you call Earl's number?" Sophia typed.

She prayed the answer was 'yes,' desperately needing to know the situation at Sanctuary.

"Negative. Even if I connected to local satellites, distance from the planet and Mr. Earl's phone's limited capability would not allow for a direct phone call. However, you can send him an email or text message. It will take ten minutes for the message to reach his phone."

"Let's do it!" Sophia frantically typed.

"Whenever you are ready," Vincent announced.

Sophia quickly typed a message, getting directly to the point.

"Message sent," Vincent confirmed.

She prayed it reached them in time.

"Can you connect me with Lady Tech?" Sophia typed.

"Attempting to connect with local satellites to increase the range to connect to her," Vincent responded.

She patiently waited for a response.

"No response," Vincent relayed, "shall I keep trying?"

"Yes," Sophia typed.

"Emitting encrypted beacon signal, it will conserve power while sending a signal. Once Lady Tech responds, I shall connect you."

Sophia sighed and prayed that everyone was still alive at the Ranch. Her finding a way to return home and stop Peace depended on it.

Until then, she floated in the cold black void with no home to return to.

~~~~~~~~~~~~~~~~~~~~~~~~~~~~~~

Back in the buried central command, everyone, save for Adrian holding his sister and Angie kneeling beside him, stood as the chaos outside settled.

"Maxine rotate us to the entrance," Erica commanded.

"I already attempted to do so, Miss," Maxine informed her. "A massive amount of debris has jammed the servos. We are unable to rotate."

"Why do we need to rotate?" a panicked Adrian asked. "Rotate to where?"

"A mini base, and a way out," Erica answered, "if we can't rotate, we're good as buried down here. Rogers let Rosann touch you so that she can heal."

Abe marched over to her as Lady Tech glided her hand over the digital touch screen, pulling up multiple holographic screens. Rogers took Rosann's hand into his own, but nothing happened.

"Not responding," Rogers answered.

"A rush of adrenaline will activate the barbs in her hand," Erica responded. "Angie, help her."

"What are you going to do?" Adrian nervously asked.
~~~~~~~~~~~~~~~~~~~~~~~~~~~~~~

"A slight push on her broken collarbone will activate her pain receptors," Angie explained. "I can then ensure that it is properly aligned to rebind properly. She will feel some discomfort."

Angie's eyes lit up as she scanned the broken collar bone, then went to work, positioning it together. It was painful enough to force a groan out of an unconscious Rosann. Her body stiffened as she clutched Abe's hand. The microscopic barbs in her hand protruded, piercing his hand, sucking in his blood. Her skin color changed to match his own, while her frame became denser, duplicating his Titan abilities. Abe's regenerative healing mended her collarbone and other injuries.

She awoke with a gasp, attempting to sit up. Her brother and Abe subtly restrained and steadied her.

"Easy, don't try to get up yet," Rogers ordered.

"Where am I? What happened?"

"We're in the central command," Rogers explained, "a couple miles down from the base, we were attacked."

"The Draugr," Rosann muttered, attempting to move. "I was fighting…"

"Relax," Rogers calmly ordered, "don't move and don't try to get up. Just stay here with your brother until we figure this out."

Rogers rose to his feet, returning to Erica's side to help assess the situation.

"How far down are we?"

"Approximately three miles," Rosann indicated while feverishly working, "and no, we can't bust through the other side of the wall. It's a ten-inch thick wall of dark metal and behind that is a sixty-inch thick wall of mantle shielding us from a river of lava. That's why I built this damn thing to rotate; I didn't calculate on dealing with another version of the Source bringing parts of the shaft down on top of us while we were trying to escape her turning us to ash."

"Oliver," Rosann asked, "where's Oliver?"

Silence fell over everyone as Adrian turned to Erica and Rogers for an answer for his sister.

"Adrian, where is he?" Rosann inquired, searching for him.

"Sis," Adrian swallowed, "he chose to stay behind to buy us some time."

Rosann struggled to get up.

"Then we have to go back and get him."

Rosann's eyes became glassy as he stopped her.

"We can't go back, sis."

"Yes, we can!" Rosann snapped at him. "Get off me. Adrian! We can't leave him up there!"

Even with her Titan strength being less than Rogers, Rosann was a handful as she fought to break free from her brother's grip. Angie aided him in trying to restrain her.

"Get off me!" Rosann screamed. "Get the fuck off me! How could you leave him up there?! You know what they'll do to him! You know what they'll do to him!"

Rosann screamed and bawled as if she was dying. It made Adrian wail as he held onto his sister. The fight finally taken out of her, she clung to her brother, sobbing to the near point of hysteria.

A powerless Abe stood watching as his team fell apart. He turned to see a frantic Lady Tech punching away at her digital keyboard. She pulled up screens and swiped them out with little rhyme or reason.

"Miss?" Maxine asked concernedly, "Miss, can I…?"

"I got this, Maxine! I got this!"

Rogers stepped in, pulling her away from the screen. Erica fought to get away from him, throwing a fit as he held her close.

"Let me go, Rogers! I got this! I got this!"

"You have my permission to cry," Rogers ordered.

Erica began banging her head against his chest.

"I don't have time for this! I told you I got this! I got this!"

Rogers continued to hold her, weathering through her useless barrages.

"You have my permission to cry," Rogers said again.

Erica went into a sobbing fit, collapsing into his arms. He held her like his little girl and allowed her to breakdown.

Angie looked worried as she gently touched Adrian's back to comfort him. She turned to her sisters and found the same confusion and concern in their eyes.

Rogers remained the foundation of his team. He could not and would not afford himself the luxury of tears for their sake. Rogers would allow them to fall apart. He needed it out of their system to build them up again. For vengeance to be theirs, he would need them fiercer than ever.

~~~~~~~~~~~~~~~~~~~~~~~~~~~~~~~~~~~~

An unhappy Nachzehrer arrived at the Dennison residence in Mount Vernon, drawing attention. Her scantily clad outfit was the same as her original except that the chained bikini she wore was silver color instead of pink, and a black pleated schoolgirl skirt with rings adorned the waist with safety pins that held together with a high slit as opposed to leather hotpants.

Parked in front of the Dennison's residence were two vacated police vehicles. One with its doors still opened, while the other sat charred and flattened like a pancake.

Decorating the Dennisons' driveway gate was a female police officer scorched with fourth-degree burns nearing death. The officer's wrists were fused to parts of the gate, placed there as an omen for those that would dare enter. Inside the yard, the steps and grounds were littered with the clothing, gear, and small bone fragments of the other officers who accompanied her.

Nachzehrer stopped to admire Revenant's work before casually strolling to the front gate entrance. She ripped it from where it was secured with one arm, tossing it aside. Walking up the steps, she shot terrified onlookers peering out of their windows and doors with a dirty, murderous look, daring them to say something to her. She knocked on the door, purposely delivering extra force, cracking the wood.

A minute later, Revenant opened it, looking her up and down.
~~~~~~~~~~~~~~~~~~~~~~~~~~~~~~~~~~~~

"Reporting for coon watching duty," Nachzehrer sneered, snapping a salute.

"Thank the devil himself," Revenant sighed. "The father isn't too bad; he's been trying to talk me into turning my life around and converting. The mother can be a handful; she has a knack for hurling insults and scripture verses attempting to 'cast me out.' If you want to have fun with her, recite some satanic verses. I've never seen a woman's eyes open so wide."

"I could just shove my hand up her…"

Revenant held a finger up, stopping her from finishing.

"Do remember not to lay a finger on any of them. The last thing you need to do is incur any further wrath from you know who."

"Remind me again how the fuck I drew porch monkey babysitting?" Nachzehrer inquired with a scowl.

"You got caught, my dear, when you weren't supposed to," Revenant reminded her.

"This is bullshit, you know," Nachzehrer yelled, pointing a trembling finger at him. "You promised to get us out of this servitude shit! You promised!"

Revenant grabbed her by the back of her head, pulled her close, and kissed her deeply to calm her. Nachzehrer groped his crotch area and licked his lips with sinful, unsavory thoughts in her eyes. He nuzzled his nose against hers, whispering in her ear.

"I am working on it. Till then, I need for you to do as you are told and behave yourself like your life depends on it. Do not cut, injure, maim, rape, sodomize, cripple, or kill anyone inside this house. Outside, as you can see, is fair game. Are we clear?"

"If I promise to be good," Nachzehrer asked with a mousey voice, "and you find a way to kill that bitch… do you promise to ravage me on their mutilated corpses?"

He grinned while pulling the back of her chained one-piece bikini upwards, wrenching it in between her legs to force a moan out of her.

"For a whole week," Revenant murmured in her ear.

She grinned and then nipped at his ear. During the sordid display of affection,

Mrs. Dennison stepped into view, making her presence known.

"Listen here, yuh ole whore," Mrs. Dennison barked while pointing at Revenant, "me can barely stand your ugly ungodly mug, but you nah bring ya ugly ass dawg inna me house! Look pon har! Har face wash out like Vybz Kartel! Uno fee come out!"

Mr. Dennison walked up, grabbing her.

"Nopel!"

He attempted to guide her back into the living room, but she refused to move.

"Wha yuh do?" Mr. Dennison scolded her. "Stop ramp! Yuh want dem kill yuh inna here?"

"Dem nah do nuttin to us babes, if dem know what good fe dem!" Mrs. Dennison yelled back. "Ah, hostage situation dis! Me say gweh botty bwoy wit yuh dutty gyal! Yuh face bumpy-bumpy like jackfruit!"

Nachzehrer glared at her, and then Revenant raised a finger warning her to keep her promise.

"Step back, and shut the fuck up, you shit slinging old ape," Nachzehrer warned her, "or I'll gut you slowly."

"Ah, who yuh ah talk to?" Mrs. Dennison shot back. "Yuh want me take sometin and open ya head up? Listen, you dry-head, picky-picky, jeyes-ears, horse-mouth, buck-teeth, bandy-leg, bat-ears, snaggle-tooth dutty gyal! Ya betta kill me now cus one ah us gone dead inna here today!"

Revenant slowly closed the door behind him as a full-on verbal war ensued within the Dennisons' house. He prayed for it to remain just vocal, knowing Nachzehrer's hair-trigger temper.

Stepping out into the open, he politely waved to the terrified neighbors looking in his direction before channeling dark matter to propel him into the air to his next destination.

~~~~~~~~~~~~~~~~~~~~~~~~~~~~~~~~
~~~~~~~~~~~~~~~~~~~~~~~~~~~~~~~~

Back at the island, Kimberly, now in a yellow and blue two-piece sports bathing suit, was on the beach playing with Kyle, Akram, and the rest of the children. From boogie boarding to volleyball to tag, she enjoyed the perks of being the daughter of a woman who owned her own island. By playing, she learned to control her strength and speed. It did not make her weak to run slower or hit the ball softer. It was okay not to be the first at everything. The other children made her feel normal, a regular yet taller, ordinary girl.

Although she still missed her friends, she was unsure if they would react to the newly improved her as her new friends did.

Kimberly stopped amid her frolicking to look up at the sky, wondering when her mother would be home. It had been almost five hours since she had left. She presumed she would see her flying back home by now.

Mixtures of emotions overtook her when she realized she had an actual flesh and blood mother who willingly laid claim to her. During her euphoric realization, Kimberly noticed that a child was not participating in the beachside fun.

Three-year-old Melanie, one of the few children born on the island, stood on the beach's shore in her pink and white polka dot one-piece bikini. While everyone played, she stood looking up at the sky. Kimberly, noticing her, walked over.

"Hey Mel," Kimberly said, smiling as she knelt beside her, "what's wrong? Don't you want to play with us?"

"There's a lady," Melanie softly said while pointing, "floating up there in the sky."

Kimberly looked up where she pointed and saw only clouds. She smiled, thinking she was using her imagination to see the clouds as a woman.

"Yeah, I think I see her too."

Melanie shook her head.

"No, you don't. She's hiding in the clouds. I can help you see her."

Melanie touched the side of her face as she continued to look up in the sky. Instantly, Kimberly saw what she saw. A pale-skinned young woman with a clean-shaven head wearing black hovering in the clouds by some unknown vibrating force. The evil smile she displayed told her she was not a nice person.

A shaken Kimberly pulled away, also realizing that Melanie, like her, was not ordinary.

Kyle and Akram ran up with the rest of the children to see why Kimberly stopped playing with them.

"Hey, what's up?" Kyle asked. "You found something?"

"Melanie telling you about the imaginary people she sees?" one of the other boys jokingly asked.

Kimberly picked her up and fretfully turned to them.

"We need to get back to the village, like right now."

"What's the matter?" Akram asked nervously.

"More people are coming," Melanie informed her.

"Show me, honey," Kimberly asked.

The child again touched the side of her face, showing her what she saw. Five miles off and getting closer were three more superhumans. Two were flying: one with long black hair, with what appeared to be the face of a demon, flew via a column of flames, while the other with long blonde dreads and glowing yellow eyes flew by some form of propulsion that appeared to be similar to her mother's. She carried a massive man by a harness, which looked like a Viking wielding a colossal sword and ax. The bad feeling swirling around in her stomach turned into a horrible feeling.

"We need to get back to the village now!" Kimberly fearfully yelled, "Come on!"

She tried to run as quickly as possible, but holding a precious bundle and ensuring the other kids kept up with her greatly hindered her superhuman speed. By the time they reached the village, it was too late. The skies overhead were covered in flames, igniting a chorus of screams from everyone below.

Kimberly was lucky enough to find Earl standing dumbfounded and other villagers looking up at the red flaming sky.

"Mr. Earl! Mr. Earl!" Kimberly yelled, getting his attention.

"Kimberly!" A shuddering Earl inquired. "What the hell is going on?!"

"Where's my mom?!" Kimberly frantically asked. "Is there a way to get in touch with her?! Mr. Earl?!"

Earl shook himself out of his transfixed state to reach into his pocket for his Samsung Smartphone. He quickly punched in his passcode, hit her number on speed dial, and tapped the speaker option.

He shook his head as the phone went straight to Sophia's voicemail.

"Something's not right. Wait… there's a text message!"

Earl clicked on the message from Sophia, which read, "No time to explain! Evil people are coming! Run! Hide! Get everyone to the boats!"

Earl and Kimberly looked up from the text message, seeing they both wore the same fearful look.

The next thing they heard was what sounded like a bomb dropping. The gigantic Viking she saw flown in by the blonde-headed dread had crash-landed into one of the huts, leveling it in one shot. Luckily, no one was home during the impact.

Kimberly handed Melanie to Earl.

"Take her! And get the kids and the villagers to safety!"

"Kimberly, no!" Earl forcibly yelled, "I'm supposed to look out for you!"

"My mother's not here," Kimberly tensely returned. "I'm... I'm the only one who can do something!"

She bolted before he could say anything more to try to stop her.

The fire witch Jiang Shi cackled hysterically as she used her flames to corral the villagers like a herd moving in one direction. Wendigo's mere presence and vibrating sonic sphere, which shook the huts almost to collapse, forced them to move in another direction.

Peace's eyes blazed as she strolled up to villagers attempting to escape in her direction, stopping them in their tracks into a backpedal.

"Wrong way, kids! Back that way! Move! Move!"

The Draugr was less subtle. With a swipe of his ax, he sliced through one of the huts. He roared like an uncaged lion shaking the Earth with just his steps. As everyone else ran back to the center of the village, a terrified Mr. Norton sat in the monster's path. Finding a sliver of courage, a frightened Zeek ran back to his side, grabbing him.

"Mr. Norton!" Zeek screamed. "You got to get up! Get up!"

"But this is Sanctuary," Mr. Norton mumbled. "We're safe here in Sanctuary... we're safe."

Unable to get the old man up, Zeek held him tight, covering him with his frail body, praying that the beast would pass them by. A savage grinning Draugr, with not a pint of mercy in his cells, would not as he raised his sword high.

"If you don't run," Draugr frothed, "you die!"

He brought his sword down to cleave them in two until a powerful shot to the chest sent him flying. He roared, tumbling and crashing through two huts.

Zeek looked up to see Kimberly sitting on her rear. She sprung to her feet, turning to them both.

"Run... run now."

Zeek nodded, pulling Mr. Norton to his feet ushering him to safety.

Kimberly trembled like a leaf, slowly moving in the direction she sent the Draugr flying. She had never been in a fight before. Her ability to duplicate martial arts moves to show off during recess, and gym class was an excellent deterrent for anyone with the thought of challenging her. Though she was young, she knew the monster she had just knocked down would not run away from a simple showcase of her skills.

As the Earth trembled, her reluctant paces became slower and slower. As the enraged Draugr with murderous intent written on his face came into view, a terrified Kimberly searched the skies for her mother.

"Mom, where are you?"

Realizing he was embarrassed by a mere child, the Draugr bellowed with rage and charged. Kimberly screamed, scrambling backward as he went berserk, swinging both sword and ax in an attempt to cut her down.

The terrified child dived out of the way, barely missing his sword swipe, cutting through one of the nearby huts like paper.

"Leave me alone!" Kimberly cried.

Showing the last ounce of bravery she could muster, Kimberly uprooted a large nearby palm tree like she did her first day on the island. She swung with all her might, hoping to knock the Draugr back like she did before when she surprised him.

This time, ready for her, the monster stood his ground, taking the full brunt of the hit, snapping a part of the tree like a twig. She attempted to swing again. He responded by hacking another piece off with his battle ax. The Draugr toyed with her; he advanced, slicing the tree bit by bit until the vibration of the hacking forced her to drop what was left.

The Draugr buried his sword in the sand, clutching his trusty ax to finish the job. Kimberly attempted to fake him out, pretending to run. She exploded into the air for a super leap. However, the monster revealed uncanny speed, grabbing Kimberly by one of her legs, snatching her out of the air, and violently slamming her to the ground.

His shadow was now cast over her.

"Mommy…" a shaken Kimberly sobbed.

"You shall see your mother again, child," Draugr salivated, "as you both become whores of hell!"

He raised his ax, bringing it down on top of her.

Kimberly covered up, screaming her lungs out.

The blow, however, would not be delivered. Now hyperventilating, Kimberly looked up to see the woman in the leather outfit and long, dirty blonde dreadlocks stopping the Draugr's ax blow with one hand.

"What the hell are you doing?" Peace snarled. "Did I give you permission to go 'Games of Thrones' on anyone up in this bitch? Did I?"

The monster groaned and whined in frustration, glancing at Kimberly and then the woman. Effortlessly, she shoved him backward.

"Go take a walk before I backhand you. Now!"

The Draugr looked at Kimberly again, yelping like a wounded pup. He then turned away, howling. He unleashed his frustrations on a nearby hut, turning it to rubble.

"Grow up!" Peace yelled at him, "and don't bring down no more huts after that one! Spoiled brat."

She reached down, grabbing a near-catatonic Kimberly, pulling her to her feet.

"Up you go," Peace sighed. "Come on, walk it off. He didn't hurt you that bad. I saw the whole thing."

"Who… are… you?" Kimberly said between short breaths. "Where's my… mom?"

Peace leaned down a bit to look Kimberly in the eyes.

"Okay, the first thing, I can't have a serious conversation with you crying and wheezing like that. This is not a good look with you being the very first superhuman and all."

Her words made Kimberly give her a better look over.

"I know you. You're that lady my mom fought with at the mountain. The one she flew away with…"

"Almost seven years ago," Peace said with a smile and a nod. "Yeah, that's me. I go by the name Peace now, or you can call me Auntie Peace."

"Where's my mom?" Kimberly asked again.

"One tracked minded, you are," Peace pouted. "Where's my mom? Where's my mom?" No, "How come you look different?" "What's up with your eyes?" "What'd you do with your hair?"

Kimberly put on her 'refusal to talk anymore unless her question was answered' face. Peace rolled her eyes, wrapping her hand around the back of her neck, leading her back to the center of the village.

"Okay, kid," Peace coughed, "I'm not going to sugar coat anything. I sent your mom away."

Panic filled Kimberly's belly and swirled.

"What?"

"Now, now."

Peace rubbed the back of Kimberly's neck while gripping her.

"Let me explain. You see, I put your mom in a situation where you, these villagers, and the life of your grandparents hung in the balance. See, as powerful as she is, I got people, as you can see, each with a body count. So she took the only option I gave to her… exile."

"Where?"

"Where?" Peace scoffed, shaking her head. "Come on, kid, use your head; with people possessing our abilities, exile to someplace like Bermuda would be just retarded. So what's the only other option left?"

Kimberly shuddered as she looked straight up. She attempted to pull away, but a much stronger Peace pulled her closer, wrapping her arm around her neck.

"See, you can't do that," Peace scolded her. "Where you going to run? Where you going to go?"

Peace paused for a minute with a perplexed look on her face.

"Think I heard that line in a movie. Anyway, as I was saying. There's nowhere to run to, especially after tomorrow."

"What's happening tomorrow?" Kimberly blurted out her question.

"What's going down tomorrow is grown folk business," Peace replied, wagging a finger at her, "which is none of your business. Now I also promised your mom that I would look after you. She's a little pissed at me right now, but give her a century or two, she'll get over it. Till then, you're my responsibility, and for the sake of the lives of all these norms here on this island, you got to do as I say. You get what I'm saying? Are we on the same page?"

Kimberly stopped in her tracks, forcing Peace to stop. She turned to her, knocking her arm away from her neck, and mustered up the bravest defiant scowl she could pull off.

"It's not going to take a century or two for my mom to come back. She'll be back, and she's going to kick your ass again."

Peace gave her a blank stare at first, which turned into a sarcastic smirk as she sighed.

"I'm going to let you have that cheesy cliché remark because you're all emotional now with me sending your mom away and all that. Not to mention if it wasn't for you, this little trailer park trash girl from the Midwest wouldn't be the most powerful being on this planet about to usher in a new age. So I owe you, that's why I let your mom live, and I'm going to let you slide… this… one… time."

Peace moved forward, towering over Kimberly and backing her up against a palm tree. Kimberly, clearly intimidated, did her best to maintain her tough front.

"But make no mistake, little girl," Peace warned, "we're not kin, which makes your situation a billion times worse because I can't even stand my own. You step out of line or grow a sac to try to challenge me, I will mop the planet with you, and then give what's left of you to the guy I stopped from hacking you to bits. Please note he does not like being embarrassed, so you are forever marked on his shitlist."

Kimberly clutched the tree, fighting to stand firm. Peace's terrifying threat weakened her legs to where they shook violently.

"Now that we've had our little girl talk," Peace said with a beaming smile, "let's break the news to the rest of the family!"

With a hand gesture to start moving, Kimberly willed herself to walk, with Peace following close behind. She quickly glanced up at the sky, praying that if her mother was up there, she was thinking of some way to get back home.

~ ~

Back at the town square, the villagers huddled close to one another as Wendigo and Jiang Shi hovered high, watching them from below like hawks. Kimberly finally showed up, and both relieved and terrified eyes were focused on her.

As she fast-walked over to stand by Earl and everyone else, she got a quick side glance of the Draugr brandishing his massive ax and sword, zeroing in on her like a lion hunting a gazelle.

Peace finally walked up and paused to clear her throat before announcing.

"Ladies and Gentlemen, if I may have your attention! I have an announcement! This here island is under new management!"

Peace pointed to herself with a smug smile as she made eye contact with everyone.

"Now under my supervision," Peace explained, "means as long as everyone follows the rules, the status quo will remain the same... for now. If you don't follow the rules, you get punished. It's that simple. I normally demonstrate this by randomly pulling five or six of you out and killing you in front of everyone else."

Everyone screamed and cried while the Draugr savagely grinned along with Jiang Shi, who wore a sinister smirk, praying for her to do it.

Peace held her hands up in a calming gesture.

"However, because I made a promise, I'm going to go with the honor system here. You all seem somewhat intelligent, not requiring a tutorial to get my point across. Unfortunately, I won't be able to hang around to get to know all of you better, due to some business I have to attend to. So right now, we're going to take a formal headcount, and everyone is going back to their homes for a mandatory..."

Peace paused, realizing she did not know what time it was. She pointed to Earl.

"You. Yeah, you with the watch. What time is it?"

Earl took a jittery double look at his watch before answering.

"Four PM."

"Pacific time?" Peace asked.

"Yeah," Earl swallowed with a nod.

"Dammit, I'm running late, anyway, people, for today, there will be a quick 4:15 p.m. curfew after we do this headcount in the next five minutes. Now, for those whose homes got wrecked or damaged during this invasion, my bad, but you'll have to sleep over at your neighbor's house until we get you sorted out. Tomorrow at 9 a.m., you will all come out and do another headcount! At 10 a.m., you will then go back to your home.

Then another one at 12 p.m., and at 1 p.m. you will return to your homes, and finally at 4 p.m. where you will return to your homes at 5 p.m. I am generous to allow you to stretch your legs outside for an hour, so don't abuse it. This will go on until I get back. So please remember the times. Your lives will depend on it. Until then, my associates here will be watching over you. Allow me to introduce them to you."

She first walked over with a smile to the Draugr, gesturing to him.

"This big handsome man over here is the Draugr. He has a hard-on for killing and eating people and not necessarily in that order."

Her introduction made various villagers squeal, cry, and cling to one another for comfort.

"And the lady in the colorful ensemble and face tattoo is Jiang Shi; she loves to burn things and people."

Her second introduction made everyone feel worse than her first.

"They have been instructed to not lay a finger on any one of your heads as long as you obey the rules," Peace informed them. "They also have been known for their extreme short fuse and nasty disposition. You all heard about what went down in Times Square, New York, right? That was them. I think they're willing to sign autographs if you ask them nicely."

No one got her joke.

"Again, following the rules is for your safety because any prolonged contact with my associates will get one of you killed. These are not stable people; they are only here to watch you. So do as you are told and avoid all eye contact as much as possible. Now, this may seem really bad right now," Peace continued, "but trust me, this is actually the safest place on the planet, especially after what's about to go down tomorrow. So do me a solid, follow the rules, don't piss my friends off, and I will see you when I see you. Now let's get this headcount done people, I got an interview I have to get to. Come! Come! Time is money!"

~~~~~~~~~~~~~~~~~~~~~~~~~~~~~~~~~

Back at the destroyed Ranch, three miles down within the descended central command now at fallout level covered underneath the rubble, the crying and mourning had ended for now. Rosann sat in one of the swivel chairs with an emergency Mylar thermal blanket wrapped around her. It was more for comfort than warming her up. Erica wanted to administer a sedative to her, but she asked her not to. Expressionless, she sat there, every now and then, removing tears that formed before they ran.

Adrian sat with her for a while, but she kindly asked him to give her some space. He now stood beside Rogers, watching Lady Tech work magic to get communication back up and running while also figuring out how to get them topside to the base's main level.

"How's it going?" Rogers calmly asked.

Lady Tech sighed as she glided her fingers over the touchscreen keyboard.

"We are buried; there are several tons of rock equivalent to a small mountain preventing us from rising back to the top. At least ten small Doozers are still functioning, all the others have been destroyed, and they don't have enough firepower to cut through the rubble and get us out. The main generator was shut down due to damage, but the backup is up and running. They're working on getting some form of communication channel open. Hopefully, we can contact someone and figure out what's going on topside."

"What about the SAM armor?" Rogers asked. "It's got an independent AI; couldn't you command it to blast us out of here?"

"Would love to if it wasn't unfortunately buried, and I didn't remove its entire brain for an upgrade which is sitting in my lab. Now it's just a shell, and judging from the rubble covering it, it'll take at least a day, maybe two for those pint-size Doozers to uncover it, barring that nothing else comes down on top of them while they're at it."

A satellite dish symbol appeared on her holographic screen's top right-hand side, blinking before holding strong.

"And we have a connection," Lady Tech said with a faint smile of relief.

"Incoming encrypted message from Ms. Dennison's AI named Vincent," Maxine announced, "patching her in now."
~~~~~~~~~~~~~~~~~~~~~~~~~~~~~~~~~

Everyone's attention, including Rosann's, turned toward the screen as Sophia appeared with a black starry background behind her. It was clear that she was in a weightless environment. She began to frantically type as Vincent became her mouthpiece.

"I'm alive and exiled into space," Vincent verbally translated her typing. "Peace, the woman who attacked your base currently has Revenant holding my parents hostage in their home, and the one called Wendigo hovering over my island ready to destroy it. I had no choice but to leave. Is everyone all right?"

"Most of the base has been destroyed," Rogers stepped in, talking to her. "We were forced to descend to a lower level and are currently buried under several tons of rock. We also lost Oliver."

Sophia bowed and shook her head. She started typing again.

"I am so sorry," Vincent translated for her.

"I think you need to tell us who we're dealing with," Rogers sternly requested, "since it appears you know her so well."

She nodded and began to type again.

"I will tell you everything," Vincent translated for her.

CHAPTER 22

Back at a locked-down Sanctuary, Kimberly stood in Kyle's home with his parents, older brother, Earl, Akram, his mother, and a couple of other adults. As they nervously talked amongst themselves, the Draugr purposely made his presence known using heavy footsteps that shook the village.

She mustered the courage to peer outside the window, where the monster gave her a vile animalistic glare undeserving of any child her age, much less a full-grown adult.

"Kimberly, honey," Earl called back, gesturing, "get away from the window. Don't look at the evil man out there."

"Where's Sophia?" Mrs. McArthur stammered. "Why isn't she back yet?"

Kimberly nervously stepped up to explain.

"The woman named Peace said she exiled my mom."

"How," Kyle's father asked, "to where?"

"She's in outer space," Kimberly answered. "The woman said she has my grandparents captive and threatened my mom that if she didn't leave the planet, she would kill them and everyone on the island at the same time."

"Sophia sent me a text message," Earl said, backing her up, "trying to warn us that they were coming and to run and hide. Unfortunately, we got it too late."

"So what do we do now?" one of the men asked.

"Mr. Earl, can I borrow your phone, please?" Kimberly asked.

He quickly pulled it out, punched in his passcode, and handed it to her.

"You're going to try and text your mom?"

"Yes," Kimberly said with a nod. "I have a feeling she sent that last message from space. If that's the case, hopefully, we can send another message and let her know what is happening here."

Kimberly began to speed-type a detailed message while everyone around her silently prayed for it to reach her.

~ ~

Three miles underneath the destroyed Ranch, the surviving members of the Regulators attentively listened to a space-exiled Sophia as she speed-typed, debriefing them with the aid of Vincent verbally translating what she wrote.

Sophia told them who Peace was and how she was related to her. She also told them her intentions toward the human race. Sophia even told them about her daughter Kimberly. However, she did not know her ultimate plan to bring the world to its knees.

"I knew there was something off about this witch," Lady Tech sneered.

She quickly threw up a video feed of Peace shrugging off energy plasma barrages from the first initial Doozer attack.

Rogers stepped in, examining the footage with her.

"What did you find?"

Lady Tech slowed down the footage as three plasma blasts from the Doozer assault struck Peace's red tank top shirt, leather corset, and her biker outfit's upper thigh leg pants before dissipating, leaving only burn mark patterns.

"Those three hits should have left three large holes in that Coyote Ugly outfit of hers," Erica explained, "instead, it just grazed it, leaving burn marks, which means that's not leather she's rocking."

"She has gear like us?" Rogers gruffed.

"Not like us," Lady Tech sighed. "Probably first-generation bodysuit armor fabricated into that gawky getup."

"How?"

"If she is who Dennison told us she is," Erica replied while grinding her teeth, "she could have commandeered any of the other project EVO facilities and got ahold of both gear and tech."

"What other facilities?" Vincent translated Sophia's typed question, mirroring the anger now on her face.

"Mount McLoughlin was one of many research facilities that were a part of Project EVOlution," Erica answered. "You didn't think a project this big would be housed underneath one roof. There were R&D installations built, in any number of cities and states."

"Like Area 51?" Adrian asked.

"Area 51 is a decoy facility," Erica scoffed, "created to focus the attention of simple-minded conspiracy theorists like dogs to a bone."

"Wait, so there's nothing there?"

Wearing a disgusted sneer, Lady Tech turned to answer a perplexed Adrian.

"The only thing there is a heavily armed guard detail rotated every two months to look like their guarding something important and three partially dismantled Lockheed SR-71 Blackbirds painted a metallic silver to look like crash-landed space crafts."

"Can we find these facilities?" Rogers demanded to know.

"Nope," Erica huffed.

"Why not?" Rogers snapped.

"Because they're completely off the grid." Erica leered back at him, not appreciating his tone, "They've been so for over seventy years."

"But you know of them," Adrian followed up.

"Because of some intelligent research and educated theories," Erica impatiently barked at them, "come on, people! Think! In the age of Snowden and other whistleblowers, how is a project like EVOlution safeguarded from becoming a WikiLeaks page?"

"By keeping it literally off the grid-like the Umbrella Corporation did in Raccoon City," Adrian answered, snapping his fingers.

"Raccoon, what?" Abe asked, turning to him.

"Resident Evil, sir, a video game turned blockbuster movie. To keep something like EVOlution off the grid, it would have to be either a distant location or plain sight like a gated residential community. Everyone would be monitored 24/7.

The main facility would have to be underground. There would have to be no Internet or satellite connection to the servers or supercomputers so hackers or spies could not attempt to access it. Only certain people would have the authorization to pull the data. No paper trail, so no one could steal files."

Rogers did not know whether to be stunned or impressed at Adrian's breakdown, while Erica clapped with approval.

"I would have left out the whole gated community bit, but very well done, Mr. Esposito. Couldn't have explained it better myself."

"But I thought Project EVOlution was shut down after the Big Bang Two Incident?" Rogers asked her.

"Yeah, and Oliver North acted alone," Lady Tech snorted. "The D.E.A.D project was shut down. You really think they're going to let go over seventy years of research because one of their viruses got loose?"

"Something I don't understand; how come you were able to track Dr. Dennison but not this chick?" Adrian inquired.

Erica kneaded the bridge of her nose before she answered him.

"Good question; the answer is based on what we've been told about where she's been; she's operating on a whole different energy frequency. If she's actually been baking on Mercury, her power levels are monstrous, which means her output frequency is similar to white noise. It's there, just undetectable to my sensors."

"So, how powerful is she?" Rogers inquired.

"Let's just be glad she wants this planet for whatever she needs," Erica swallowed before she told him. "or there would be no planet."

"So we're screwed?" Adrian huffed.

"Not necessarily," Erica replied while folding her arms. "Because she cheated to increase her strength, she's done some damage that her RDH had to compensate for. If she's emitting a high frequency of bioenergy that I cannot detect, it means her body is constantly bleeding off power, not storing it like Dr. Dennison. It's like filling a balloon with constant gushing water; for it not to pop, you have to make a small hole for some of the water to leak out. So even though she's operating a peak capacity, which is on a global killing scale, there's still a limit to her strength."

"Unlike me, whose body gradually stored energy over the years," Vincent translated Sophia's message.

"Correct, you have the potential to surpass her if you can tap into that additional power within you."

Out of nowhere, Vincent displayed the text message from Kimberly that finally reached her. Her eyes widened while her body trembled. Sophia fought to control herself to remain stable in her current drift.

"What is it?" a concerned Rogers asked.

"Dr. Dennison's daughter sent her a text message," Vincent answered. "It said they were unable to escape. The woman known as Peace has taken over the island. No one is hurt, but everyone has been locked inside their homes on a form of curfew, and two superhumans known as the Draugr and Jiang Shi have been left to guard them."

Everyone wore mirrored looks of concern at the sound of the Draugr.

"Well, how much does this suck?" Adrian muttered.

"It's tactical," Abe answered, "between those two, they could wipe that whole village out in a matter of minutes."

"If she switched up Jiang Shi for Wendigo, that means either the Ghoul or Nachzehrer is at the Dennison's house," Erica said. "I doubt she'd leave a heavy hitter like Revenant to babysit two elderly people."

"Miss," Maxine interrupted, "you will want to see this. The Second Source is on Channel Eleven's six o'clock news."

"Put it on," Erica commanded.

The screen lit up, revealing the inside of the PIX 11 newsroom. Peace sat with her hands clasped between a visibly unnerved Scott Stanford and a clearly frightened Tamsen Fadal. She brandished a massive Cheshire grin after successfully storming and interrupting the six o'clock edition of the news.

"Good evening, world," Peace began with a chirpy, upbeat introduction, "allow me to introduce myself. I go by the name Peace!"

She quickly threw up a Valley Girl peace sign.

"The official alpha dog queen bitch of this entire fucking world," Peace said dryly, leaning forward. "And, yeah, I cursed on national fucking television, I care not for offending your delicate ears, or that of your little hell spawns, especially when they hear and say far worse behind your backs in one session of 'Call of Duty.' In fact, my second order of business as the new shepherd of planet Earth is to wipe the FCC off the face of the planet. So if you happen to work there, you might want to put in your resignation starting tonight. I'm talking scorched Earth, bitches. But before I jump ahead of myself, I must first attend to my first order of business."

Peace took a minute, reaching over to grab Stanford's cup of water, taking a sip, pretending to quench her throat. She nodded to him, putting the cup back down and returning to the cameras.

"Ready for it?"

Peace's grin became more profound as she rubbed her hands together.

"Tomorrow morning at nine o'clock Eastern Standard time, I will be heading to the nation's capital of Washington, DC, to kill the President of the United States of America."

A sickening silence fell over the country for all those watching. With a grim look, Rogers turned to Erica, who wore one of disbelief.

"To all those watching or streaming, there's nothing wrong with your television speakers or whatever device you are watching this on. You heard me correct. Tomorrow at nine o'clock in the morning, I will kill POTUS, followed by the Vice President, whose shotgun I intend to ram up his ass till it comes out the other end. But it doesn't end there; next, I will move onto the United Kingdom, where I will kill the Prime Minister, and just for the hell of it, even though she's just a figurehead, the Queen of England. You hear me, you, old bitch! I'm going to deep throat you to death with your own scepter!"

Peace cackled as she pounded the anchor desk, cracking it; Tamsen Fadal, now in tears, appeared as if she was about to lose it on national television.

"Then I move onto Russia, where I will rip Putin's heart out of his 'manly' bare chest and feed it to his Prime Minister before I snap his neck. Does everyone see where I am going with this? Iran, Poland, North and South Korea, China, South Africa, Australia. Basically, if you are a 'world leader,' and I happen to know the names and locations of all one hundred and ninety-two of you, you're pretty much dead come tomorrow."

Peace snapped her fingers as if she remembered something.

"Oh, and for my grand finale, I plan to kill both Pope Francis and Benedict… the pussy, Syedna Mufaddal Saifuddin, and Louis Farrakhan at the same time, just because they're the only religious figures that really matter in this day and age."

Peace adjusted herself in her seat as a stern visage appeared on her face.

"Now, you may be asking, what is the purpose of this massive and monumental bloodletting. The primary reason for this mass extermination of all world leaders is clear psychological warfare intended to last till the end of time. You see, tomorrow, I expect to meet with some opposition. Hell, I expect to meet with some opposition the second I walk out of this building. The reason I can sit here with absolute confidence and tell you everything I plan to do tomorrow in great detail is because I'm that friggin powerful."

"Let me paint you a clearer picture," Peace sighed while leaning back in her seat, "if you created ten exact clones of the 'late, great' Captain Omega, you'd still need at least a billion more to make me break a sweat. You begin to understand the lesson for tomorrow, kids? Resistance is fucking futile."

Rosann walked over to stand by her brother. She glanced at him as they both wore mirrored faces of unnerved. Rogers stared at the screen with a granite-breaking scowl while Lady Tech shook her head. Vincent translated what he picked up from Peace's exclusive via Sophia's screen.

"Now, I could do something more humane like."

Peace tossed her hands up in the air as if to grasp for an idea.

"Demanding a show of submission and obedience by bowing on one knee to me like in the movies. But history has shown us nothing grabs a person's attention, like, say, if I murdered Tamsen right here on national television."

Tamsen squealed, grasping the desk in maddening fright, fearing for the end, while her colleague on the opposite side of Peace watched powerlessly and incredibly concerned for her well-being.

"Calm down, Tam, no need to wet yourself," Peace jokingly reassured her. "I'm not going to kill you; my plan was always to kill Scott."

"What...?" Stanford stammered.

Peace leaped out of her seat in one swift motion, grabbing Scott Stanford by the back of his head. She slammed him face-first into the anchor desk, shattering his skull and breaking his neck simultaneously. Tamsen stood, letting out a blood-curdling scream as Stanford's lifeless body crumpled into a heap on the floor. Additional yells and shrieks erupted from the terrified broadcast crew who witnessed the brutal murder of their fellow colleague right in front of them.

"Bitch," Peace erupted, "if you don't stop screaming in my ear, I'm going to rip this dead bastard's right arm from his body and fist you to death with it on national television. Sit down!"

Tamsen Fadal whimpered as she sat back down in her seat. Her initial trembling appeared to be a full-blown seizure, as she was clearly in total shock. Everyone else followed suit to avoid becoming a victim of her sadistic wrath. Peace rolled her eyes while flicking her blonde dreads back, retaking a seat as she recollected her thoughts.

"Now, as you can see, that's the effect I'm going for tomorrow, just on a much larger scale. Let me also reassure you that my intentions for doing this aren't driven by politics, religion, money, power, world conquest, or any of that other worthless shit. My actions are much purer than that. This is about the preservation of my race and this planet, and by race, I mean the 'superhuman' race."

"Let's face it, people," Peace proceeded to lecture, "the current version of humanity, which is you ordinary people out there, sucks balls. Most of you are obese; if you're not a porky pig, you're malnourished and dying. Then, let's add a society of drug and technological dependence, greed, over-indulgence, and outright hatred for your own species because of differences in trivial things such as class, race, religion, sexual preferences, and so on.

And don't get me started on how you brutally and savagely raped and abused this precious planet of ours; global warming is real, you dumb fucks; anyone says differently… I'll kill em! In a nutshell, the failed experiment, which is mankind, is destined to eventually die out, and sadly may take this planet with them in the process."

"But that was until something wonderful happened near the end of 2008," Peace said with a cheerful grin, "in an explosive flash for the entire world to see; a process began where the genetically weakest of our race died off due to the Judgment Day virus, while the same virus allowed the strongest to evolve into more powerful beings. Surpassing the pathetic status quo, which is you, and we are multiplying like rabbits, people!"

"Now I know what many of you are thinking, "Is this the eve of our Auschwitz?" Hell no," Peace reassured while holding up a hand, "because even though the rest of you have not evolved to become as glorious as me, you still serve an essential purpose. You see, what your soon-to-be defunct government does not want you to know is that although you, the majority population worldwide, may not have symptoms of illness or evolve into superhumans, everyone on the planet is infected with the virus.

It is a part of our ecosystem; there is no cure, and shit is not going anywhere. The totally awesome news, which many of you have probably noticed, is normal humans like you who do the horizontal nasty have the potential of siring more superhumans!"

Peace jumped up and down in her seat excitedly like a little girl on her birthday.

"Isn't that wonderful?" Peace gleefully asked. "What better incentive for getting knocked up than the advancement in the evolution of the human race? Now allow me to reassure all of you out there who step up and do their new civil duties that you will be generously compensated and cared for! We're talking two cows and a Lambo in every driveway or something like that."

"This bitch is crazy," Adrian sneered.

"Rabid dog crazy," Rosann chimed in.

"As for those incapable of producing superior stock," Peace sighed while leaning forward with clasped hands, "I'm not going to blow smoke up your ass like a politician. You see, for this to work, the regular human gene pool must wither and die while we superhumans flourish, which means those that can't produce… got to go.

"Now, I don't know if we're going to implement some form of euthanasia or exile you to a remote location of the planet where you can live out the rest of your short and miserable lives. I'll have to mull over it after the massacre tomorrow. But you do have my word…"

Peace savagely grinned while pointing at the camera.

"You all will be the first to know after a decision has been made. Now, to all of my fellow brothers and sisters who've taken up the mantle of being a 'superhero.'"

Peace coughed, attempting not to laugh.

"I would heavily advise you not to attempt to be one tomorrow. You're not going to come and save the day because none of you are on my level. I know this because I am the reason you evolved in the first place. Well, me, and a now exiled Sophia Dennison."

"Aw, shit," Adrian muttered with a headshake. "Cats out of the bag now."

"You heard right, kids, me, and the first female superhuman you saw in 2008! You owe your rebirth to your two mothers who made hot lesbian love with a nuclear warhead! And although it would really break my heart to do so, I will not hesitate to kill any of you who attempt to stand in my way. Not to mention, look around you. Why would you want to protect any of them?

Do you think they love and respect any of you? Wake up! They fear, hate, and loathe all of you, especially those in 'power,' because they know they cannot kill, control, or become like us. And don't think for a second they're not trying to do all three behind our backs. And while they're doing that, they have enticed some of our kind with worthless trivial things like money and fortune to join their puny little armies to fight and protect them from each other, starting a whole new cold war with us as the weapons!"

Pure, unadulterated rage was written all over Peace's face as she stood up, knocking her seat over, making Tamsen Fadal cower further in her chair, whimpering as quietly as possible. Her yellow eyes blazed brighter, causing the feed to distort slightly as she reared her fangs.

"Well, let me tell you something, my fellow superhumans… my children, we are not weapons, heroes, or any other ridiculous label these lesser primitive shells of our former selves think they can call us. We are the closest things to gods these backwater apes will ever see, and my children… it is time we start fucking acting like it. It is we who shall inherit this Earth, not the meek! That's right, us, the strong!"

Peace violently slapped her left breast.

"We, who do not need cars, planes, or boats that poison our atmosphere and the very planet itself when we can fly, leap, or run to our destination at the snap of a finger. We, the strong, capable of surviving the harsh, ever-changing environments of this planet, most of us do not get sick or even need food to survive. And we do not need to be divided by retarded ideologies such as race, religion, creed, or color because aside from power levels and abilities, we are all equal in terms of being superior beings."

Peace placed her hands firmly on the table, leaning forward. She looked at the table, allowing strands of her dreads to fall across her face. She raised her head again to glare at the cameras.

"For far too long, words like peace and change get thrown around, speeches like 'Yes we can!' are only good for erecting nipples and soaking panties. The truth is this is a world of 'No, you can't' if you're not a part of the one percent. If your ideas and views fuck with our bottom line, then 'No, you can't.' An ideology that has saturated itself, infesting all aspects of life on this planet. And as we all know, the only way to treat an infestation is through thorough cleansing and eradication."

Peace took a minute to look at the nails on her right hand as she cracked a smile.

"It's never clean or fun to do. Well, it's going to be a lot of fun for me. However, this must be done for the human race to thrive and go on. It will be traumatic; many people will want to drink, shoot up, or seek heavy therapy after tomorrow, not in that order.

But after tomorrow has come and gone, and centuries have passed, future generations will look back at tomorrow as the day when the real cancer of this planet was finally cut out, giving this world a real chance to heal and us as a race the opportunity to thrive and reach our maximum potential, as we should. Maybe in a decade or two, we might just make tomorrow a worldwide holiday, like Burning Man and shit."

Peace cackled, shaking her head.

"In closing," she sighed, "to POTUS and the rest of our soon to be dearly departed world leaders. My advice to you in these last fifteen hours you have of life. Go fucking nuts. Drink what you want, smoke, inject or snort what you want; go bang anyone or anything you want anywhere you want. Go to town! Because come nine o'clock in the morning tomorrow, this pretty little face shall be making the rounds to visit each and every one of you… and shake you from mortal coil."

Peace allowed her ominous message to linger for a minute before clapping her hands, dawning a bright smile, making a near-catatonic Tamsen Fadal almost jump out of her skin.

"Thank you all for tuning in to this very special edition of the Pix 11 six o'clock news. Be sure to tune in tomorrow for Tamsen and whoever her new anchor might be. "Two and a Half Men" is up next!"

Peace cued the station's theme music to play as she turned and appeared to be thanking a distraught and spaced-out Tamsen for co-anchoring with her before stepping over Stanford's body and walking off the set.

With a wave of her hand, Erica closed out the feed. Everyone looked around the room at one another with similar expressions and thoughts. How were they going to overcome such a menace?

"Miss, I patched into the video surveillance cameras on 42nd Street between 2nd and 3rd," Maxine reported. "The Defenders of Justice are outside the building, preparing to ambush her."

"Oh no," Erica gasped.

"Aren't they based out of Chicago?" Adrian asked.

Erica looked up at Rogers with fear in her eyes.

"It's going to be a slaughter."

"Maxine, pull it up," Rogers ordered.

The holographic video screen came to life again; this time, it was an outside view of the building.

Peace walked out whistling and humming as if she had just gotten off work and was heading home. Unlike Sophia's news announcement seven years ago, which brought down almost the entire local, federal, and military forces of Washington D.C., down on her, the streets of 42nd Street were a ghost town with no single soul in sight.

Peace stood around, slightly disappointed that she did not receive the same reception Sophia did until she was side-blinded by a New York City Transit bus. Some unknown force hurling it drove her into the side of a nearby building. The mysterious power did not stop as it compacted the massive vehicle into an accordion to flatten her like a pancake.

A woman in a black domino mask wearing a blue, black, and yellow costumed rubber bodysuit with black boots and a long flowing blue cape descended, hovering twenty feet off the street. On the right breast of her suit, she bore the brain's symbol with some form of energy bursting out.

"She's down!" the woman called out.

Either leaping, running, or flying from their respective hiding places, her teammates each appeared.

Next to her descended the team's flame wielder, dispersing flames like thrusters from her palms and feet to keep her elevated. She donned a skin-tight red and yellow bodysuit with matching booties designed in a flame pattern. The emblem of a fiery bird sat on her right breast. Her outfit appeared to be created from a material that could withstand the heat and flames she produced. With red streaks in her raven hair, she wore no mask to cover up her identity.

The female speedster of the group, Mrs. Quick, wore a black full-body compression suit with blue lighting graphics designed into it and Nike running shoes with similar colors to her outfit. She wore a lightning-styled domino mask to cover up her identity.

The rest of their team's outfits were reminiscent of the rubber costumes used in the 1989 Burton and the 1995 Schumacher movies, with color schemes and symbols to match their heroic identities.

Standing next to the Mercurian was a male Titan wearing a sleeveless rubber suit with a black and yellow color scheme. He also wore a simple yellow domino mask. On the mask and in his chest center, he bore the letters "VJ," which stood for Victory Jones.

Closer to the totaled bus stood a woman with Titan abilities and flowing red hair in a full pink rubber suit with white boots and a flowing white cape bearing the letters BB on her chest for Bruiser Betty. Her identity was, too, covered by a type of white domino mask.

Finally, standing beside her was her husband, also a Titan class. He was also their leader recognized throughout Chicago and most of the world as Power Hour. His outfit was all red with yellow and black accents. Unlike his teammates and wife, he wore a full red cowl to hide his entire face. His symbol that he proudly wore on his chest was an exploding hourglass.

"Nice work, Mindblast," congratulated the flame wielder.

"Thank you, Flaming Jay," Mindblast cheerfully replied.

"Let's not get cocky people!" Power Hour yelled, "not till we confirm if the target is really down and out!"

Before they could assess if Peace was defeated with one blow, the bus effortlessly moved as she pushed it back and tossed it with one arm. It landed crashing on its side as the Defenders of Justice took defensive stances, ready for a fight.

Peace took her time stretching and cracking her back before giving them all a disappointed look.

"You all are shitting me, right? I purposely laid pinned up between that nasty ass New York City bus for three minutes waiting to hear some iconic superhero shit, and that's the best you all could do?"

"We're not here for your amusement, lady!" Power Hour roared.

"No, you're all here to die."

Peace folded her arms, rubbing her chin as she evaluated them. The only one in the group unnerved by her glowing yellow eyes and deadly confidence was Flaming Jay.

"Let me tell you how tonight's lesson is going to go down."

Peace pointed at Power Hour with a loathing sigh.

"I'm going to remove the Jean Grey knock-off's head from her body in under five seconds for throwing a bus at me. Then I'm going to put you and each of your little friends in critical traction and then force **you** to watch as I kill them all in one fail swoop before I kill you."

"Not if I strike first!" Power Hour roared.

He exploded, tearing up concrete before leaping to tackle her to the floor.

"I said you're **last**!" Peace yelled with irritation.

With a simple backhand moving a thousand times faster than him, she swatted him away, knocking him out of his trajectory. His body painfully crashed through the glass lobby windows of the building on her left side. He kept going as he tumbled into the front lobby security desk, obliterating it.

The rest of the Defenders of Justice, now shaken after witnessing their leader so quickly dispatched, slowly turned to a grinning Peace, looking at them as if they were dinner.

"First lesson."

Mindblast, not waiting to be her first victim, employed her telekinesis to lift two blocks of various vehicles and launch them at Peace like missiles. Peace swatted two of them out of the way and then went supersonic airborne, tearing through the rest of her barrages like snow going straight for her.

It was over in a matter of seconds as vehicles fell from the sky along with Mindblast's headless body smacking into the streets of Manhattan.

The rest of the Defenders of Justice stood beside themselves as she slowly hovered back to the ground, clutching their fallen team member's lifeless head by her long, dark mane.

Finally, realizing what had happened, they all began howling and screaming as she casually tossed her head onto the ground like a ball.

Before they could mount an avenging offense, Peace was on them using hypersonic speed on foot. With a Muay Thai side leg kick, she destroyed Ms. Quick's leg at the kneecap, breaking it in half and upending her. Victory Jones became her next victim as she crushed the left side of his ribcage with a savage knee and then severed his spine with a jackhammer elbow. Bruiser Betty was next to fall as she shattered and dislocated her jaw with an explosive haymaker.

Flaming Jay watched in horror from above as her teammates were decimated on the ground.

"Screw this," Flaming Jay quivered. "I didn't sign up for this."

She soared away, deserting her team, using her flames to rocket her out as far and as fast as they could take her.

As Bruiser Betty collapsed to her knees, dazed and bloodied with her broken jaw hanging by just skin from her face, her husband, Power Hour, finally staggering out of the building, ran to her aid. He would never get to her as Peace latched onto his throat, taking the male Titan high into the air. She slammed him violently into the concrete, creating a crater with his body. She kept a vice-like grip on his throat as she reared her fangs, pulling him to his feet and holding him high.

"Second lesson."

She extended a handout, pointing toward the badly injured members of the Defenders of Justice. Red and orange energy burst from her pores, flowing into her hand, forming into a golf ball's size.

Power Hour weakly got out, struggling to break free of her grip.

"No, nooooooo!"

"Bang," Peace sensually whispered.

In an instant, the ball expanded into a stream of pure raw energy the height and width of the Empire State Building if it was laid on its side in the middle of 42nd Street. Anything in its path turned to either ashes or atoms starting from the center of Second and Third Avenues, past the FDR Drive, over the river into Long Island City, and beyond. Buildings toppled, as well as parts of the highway on the FDR.

A couple of teeth, tiny melted rubber bits from their costumes, and scorch marks were all left of the Defenders of Justice members.

"Well, now, has the lesson been learned?" Peace asked Power Hour.

He defiantly mustered the strength to spit in her face. She slowly wiped it off in disgust.

"So, that's what it feels like," Peace noted.

She increased her grip on his throat, teetering on the borderline of crushing it.

Power Hour groaned and gagged, struggling to breathe.

"You stupid fuck! Normally someone buys me dinner before they do that," Peace howled. "And now you're going to die in that ridiculous costume for nothing! So the question I got to ask before I end you is, was this all worth it? To die knowing that you changed nothing, you saved no one, and in about another five seconds, you will be no one! The question "Raymond" is how does it feel to know that comic books are bullshit because, in real life, the "good guy" does not win in the end?"

Through his gurgling and near lack of oxygen, Power Hour forced a grin on his tear-stained face.

"I know… comic books are not real, heroes are… and I am thankful I lived my dream to become one. I die here today knowing I stood against you… and that… my act… will hopefully champion others… to do… the same."

"Wow," Peace scoffed. "Very inspirational there. My little bean just pulsated from that. Now allow me the honor of giving you a hero's death. God speed… oh wow… I don't even remember your name."

Peace's eyes went ablaze as she unleashed a powerful eyebeam blast into his face. His red cowl melted as he screamed in agonizing pain from his eyeballs roasting while his skin popped and blistered. Eventually, his body went limp as his skull exploded, leaving just a searing jawbone.

She released the rest of his remains to hit the ground with a sickening thud, forcing a wince out of Lady Tech, watching along with the rest of the Regulators.

"What a waste." Peace shook her head.

She exploded into the sky, darting away, once again leaving her calling card of death and destruction.

Lady Tech turned away, shaking her head, while Adrian dropped his head, burying it in his chest. Rosann stood there with an emotionless expression, grinding her bottom teeth into her top.

"We can't let this go down," Abe grumbled.

Erica turned to Rogers, pointing at the screen.

"We just saw her slaughter five EVOs by herself; three of them were Class 9!"

"There's got to be a way to beat her," Adrian said, stepping in.

"With Dennison, yes, we stand a chance," Lady Tech answered. "Without her, we're good as dead. Peace holds both her island and parents hostage on opposite sides of the world with the help of her goon squad and powerful Promethean monitoring not only our every move but hers if she gets anywhere near Earth's orbit. I don't see what other options we have that don't involve the disgusting words collateral damage."

"So that's it?" Adrian asked, tossing up his hands in disbelief. "We've lost?"

A frustrated Erica turned to him.

"We need to be in three different places attacking at the same time. The only way to do that is for me to invent teleportation in the next fifteen hours. From down here, where we are buried, I don't see that happening. I'm good, but I'm not that good."

Everyone, including Sophia, now bore faces of frustration. No one wanted to admit it, but Peace had covered all her bases, checkmating them. Erica turned her back to her team, placing her hands on the central command console with her head lowered. She silently racked her brain, searching for some scenario to put them back in the game. To her dismay, she could find none.

Amid their backs against the wall, the three android sisters' eyes widened, causing everyone alarm.

"Maxine, what is it?" Erica asked nervously.

"Energy anomaly building within this vicinity." Maxine indicated.

Out of thin air, electricity crackled and expanded, licking and searing the floors and walls around it as the light appeared to spill from whence it came. It grew larger, opening into the size of a large oval doorway. On the opposite side of the portal, everyone had a bird's eye view of what appeared to be a reflective veil of various worlds and dimensions colliding.

Rosann and Adrian morphed while Abe grabbed his rifle. The android sisters also went into combat mode, anticipating an attack. Lady Tech was the only one who did not feel threatened as she walked toward the portal like a moth to a flame.

Out of the portal stepped the Egyptian demigod from the battle in New York. That girlish heart-fluttering feeling returned to Erica as she gazed into his golden-brown eyes.

"Everyone power down, or lower your weapons," Erica advised with a wave of her hand. "I think the cavalry has arrived."

They all did as told while Erica gazed at the gentle smile directed toward her.

"Hi."

"Hi," he answered with a deep rumbling voice.

"All right," Rogers stepped in with a protective fatherly tone. "I take it you're here to help us fight the forces of evil."

"I am the Eye of Ra," he formally introduced himself. "And I am here to help."

"Great, glad to have you." Abe got down to business. "Think you can get us topside to our main base with whatever you just stepped out of?"

"Yes, I can."

"Can you make more of those portals," Erica inquired, jumping in, "or just one?"

"I can open as many as you need," Eye of Ra confirmed.

"From anywhere?" Erica asked.

"Yes."

Abe turned to the rest of the team.

"Then, we have a plan to put together."

"Whatever plan you have," Vincent translated for Sophia, "I'd like to add to it."

Rogers nodded in agreement.

"Let's get to work, people," Abe brought his rallying voice, "we have less than fifteen hours to save the world."

~~~~~~~~~~~~~~~~~~~~~~~~~~~~~~~~~~

Far off near the North Pole's remote area, Peace soared high as she streaked across the sky, immune to that region's harsh cold environment. She touched down hard, spraying snow a few feet while startling a family of polar bears that ran away to safety.

She walked a couple of feet to a massive iceberg. As she neared it, the view of a colossal barge ship encased in part of it appeared. She walked up the frozen boarding deck steps covered in icicles, stepping onto the ship's main deck.

Heading to one of the main doors, she strolled along the frozen deck, where some of the ice had a deep reddish color.

The red icicles that hung from the guardrail pointed down to the deep, dark, frozen waters where the former occupants' remains lay.

Nonchalantly, she keyed into the security panel, opening the door. She stepped inside to an actual lift that brought her down to the bottom level of the ship. She exited into the fluorescent lights of an experimental R&D lab and a waiting Revenant, Wendigo, Ghoul, and Anchimayen.

"Did they catch my good side?" Peace asked. "I didn't look bloated, did I?"

"Ya looked like a million bucks," Ghoul shrugged, assuring her.

"An imposing display of power," Revenant congratulated with a smirk. "Think you overdid it?"

"It had to be done, though; I took no pleasure in it. 'Overdoing it' ensures that others will think twice about trying to oppose me. If preventable, we don't need any further bloodshed or loss of our own species. Anchimayen, have you located the Egyptian yet?"

A hovering Anchimayen sitting cross-legged floated over to her.

"No sign of him either on the normal or astral plane; it is as if he does not exist
~~~~~~~~~~~~~~~~~~~~~~~~~~~~~~~~~~

or has a soul."

This new information made Peace rub her chin. Concern appeared on her face for a split second, which Revenant caught.

"New plan. Ghoul, you're no longer benched. You'll be accompanying me Revenant and Wendigo to DC in case the 'Scorpion King' makes another appearance. Anchimayen, you will stay here as eyes and ears. The Regulators I'm not too concerned about, but this new mystery player, and especially Dennison, are top surveillance priority."

Revenant sighed as he examined his fingernails.

"Maybe if you killed her, you'd only have one…"

He could not finish his sentence as Peace wrapped her hand around his throat at lightning speed, taking him off his feet. He put up his protective shielding on instinct as she slammed him violently into a nearby metal wall, making an impression of his back into it.

Peace moved closer to him as if she was about to kiss him. Her hand glowed as her increasing grip drew some of his power from him, forcing him to groan and gag, saying otherwise. Wendigo slowly went to reach for her iPod and turn up the volume, but Ghoul turned to her, raising a subtle finger to stay out of it.

"Let's get an understanding, shall we, you piece of oozing diarrhea out of the crack of Lestat's ass. This ain't no Starscream slash Megatron type of shit. You're not going to test my patience episode after episode till I kill you in some blockbuster movie. I keep you alive because you serve a purpose.

The second my new world is created, and I feel you no longer serve a purpose. I will end you as quickly as a horse flicks a flea. Now the next time you attempt to reprimand me, I will reach up your stink hole and use your spinal column as an anal bead. Are we clear?"

"Perfectly," Revenant choked.

"Good boy."

Peace hammered him violently into the wall, embedding him further into it for good measure before releasing him. Her hand and eyes, momentarily glowing purple and black from draining a fraction of his power, reverted to her yellow glow as her hand-powered down. He leaned against the wall nursing his throat, slowly sucking new air into his lungs, as Peace turned to the rest of them.

"I'm going to my room to sit in my underwear and play some Xbox Live; unless it's something urgent, do not bother me until tomorrow."

Peace walked off to be alone as the unscathed trio watched her depart. They then turned to their secondary leader.

"Well, that was bloody stupid," Ghoul admonished him.

"But necessary to determine that miserable cow's plan for us once we no longer serve a purpose," Revenant shot back at him.

"All I heard was as long as we're useful to her, we can keep breathing in her new world," Ghoul answered, "which is fine with me. Personally, I find being a fanatic Satanic worshipper to be no different than any other religion. Overrated and with a very short lifespan. At least I know what I'm dealing with when it comes to her."

"She may be powerful," Revenant sneered, "but she is no god; she has fears and weaknesses. She fears the Egyptian."

"I'm afraid of the Egyptian," Ghoul snapped back. "I don't think you understand our dire situation. We've gone from serial killings with a side of cannibalism to full-on terrorism on a global scale. If we're to survive without a bounty on our heads, we need her New World Order!"

He walked away with Anchimayen following behind him. Wendigo approached Revenant, touching his chest to see if he was all right. He looked down at her with a simple smile, stroking her left cheek; she nuzzled against his hand like a kitten.

"No worries, my dear, we will let her have her new world. And then we shall find a way to kill her and take it from her. The Egyptian is the key. She did my work for me when she dispatched Dybbuk. When I take the Egyptian's power and merge it with my own, it will help me in usurping her and claiming this world for myself. And then the real fun will begin."

CHAPTER 23

0500 AM Pacific Time, the Regulators worked through the night, preparing for vengeance and battle. With the Eye of Ra's assistance, they used one of his dimensional portals to return to base level without detection from Anchimayen. It was an experience none of them could put into words.

The first thing they did was search for Oliver. A part of them prayed he was waiting for them. Maybe a bit banged up, possibly injured, but alive and waiting for them. It made it all the more real when they found him, bringing back tears and heartache they tried to exercise while confined in the central command.

Even though his face remained stone, Abe's eyes could not stay dry at the sight of Oliver lying there.

Rosann stopped them before he and Adrian stepped in to take him to the medical bay as tears rained from her eyes.

"I want to take him. I want to take him."

Rogers nodded, extending his hand. Rosann grasped it, duplicating his Titan strength again, allowing her to lift him. She closed his eyes and cradled him close, slowly carrying him to the medical bay as if he were sleeping. He still felt warm to her.

Rosann laid him down, covering him with one of the medical blankets. She found a rag to wipe the dirt and dry blood from his face and mouth. Standing there fighting to smile, she stroked his cheek, making her way down to place a hand on his chest. None of her caressings woke him up.

"I love you," Rosann's heart broke as she said, "from the first time I saw you. Every day, I wondered what your kiss tasted like, what kind of beautiful babies we'd make… silly, right?"

A smile popped up on her face for a brief second; her joke did not wake him.

"I know my dad would have liked you, no one is ever good enough for his little girl, but he would have liked you a lot. My mom would have loved you."

Rosann leaned in, laying her head on his chest. He still did not wake up. She blubbered like a child as she patted a hand on his forehead. She fought to smile again.

"Thank you… for sharing your life with me. I'm going to see you again soon… okay… I promise. Just wait for me… okay?"

As Rosann kissed him goodbye, her body shook, waiting for him to wake up, but he did not.

Forcing herself off him, Rosann hollered till her legs almost gave out. Unfairly robbed, her body could not sustain the weight of the grief she carried.

Still aided by Abe's strength, Rosann bent and crushed a part of the metal table Oliver rested on until her sorrow turned into a blinding rage.

She began to tear the medical bay apart, searching for something.

Happening upon one of the medical kits, Rosann tore it open, pulling out a syringe.

Ripping it out of its packet, she trudged to where Oliver lay.

"Let's fight together one more time. You and I... we're going to kill them all… so you can look down at them as they burn in hell."

~ ~

Rosann returned from her time with Oliver with all of her emotions ripped from her. She uttered nothing as they assessed and salvaged what weapons and equipment remained intact.

The Tornado was gone, but the Warthog was surprisingly still intact and functional despite being buried. Erica's SAM armor, which descended to its own fallout bunker, returned undamaged and ready for battle.

The ten miniature Doozers that survived the base's attack and destruction repaired the minor damages the Warthog may have sustained after Adrian, Rogers, and the Eye of Ra removed the rubble from it.

After ensuring that her armor was intact and functional, Erica supervised preparing and loading the weapons and equipment they needed for their mission.

As they worked tirelessly through the night to prepare for war, Abe, Erica, and Adrian found a couple of minutes to individually slip away and say their goodbyes to Oliver.

Now suited up carrying every clip he could lug, Rogers, brandishing the M1 Ballistics rifle, walked up to Rosann, adjusting the straps to her tactical gloves.

"You ready, Esposito?"

Rosann locked eyes with him before she answered.

"If you don't mind, sir, my call sign is Merge. And I am ready."

Her eyes were devoid of emotion. Her demeanor was a mixture of coarse salt and raw iron. Although Rogers needed the end product he would have preferred, she was hardened another way.

Rogers moved onto Adrian; his aura was not as grim as his sister's, but the light had also left him. He was in a dark place, thinking dark thoughts. He wanted his friend back and had to settle for vengeance. Rogers instantly noticed the changes to the color scheme and wording on the thigh of his bodysuit.

"Heavy Element," Rogers read out loud.

"Sir, yes, sir."

Rogers gazed into Esposito's eyes and saw his sister's mirrored gaze, only slightly less intense.

"Good name."

Finally, Rogers glanced over at Erica, who changed out of her regular colorful bodysuit for a dark gray one. She sat on the Warthog's steps, adjusting body armor fittings on her forearms, biceps, knees, and shins. She kept her goggles over her eyes so he could not read what was behind them.

"All right, children," Rogers grunted.

He got their attention but did not expect them to fall in.

Rogers looked into Lady Tech, Heavy Element, and Merge's faces while the Eye of Ra observed them all. They were hardened faster in one day than a platoon of Marines who had done several tours. The tears were gone as their eyes filled with rage and the desire for payback. They could also tell he wanted it, too, and was going to lead them to it.

"Speeches are for politicians, coaches, and actors; it's simple, those sons of bitches took Oliver from us. So we're going to take everything away from them… and I do mean everything. Any questions?"

"Sir, no, sir!" the trio roared.

"Then let's get it done."

They piled into the Warthog. Rosann sat alone with her head down in her thoughts. Occasionally, she ran her hand against a small ammo compartment on her left thigh.

Adrian glanced at his sister with concern but gave her the respected space she needed. He knew she did not want his help or to save her from what she was going through. She needed him on his A-Game, fighting at peak condition with everything in his gut and arsenal like she would be. She desired nothing more from him or anyone else.

"Lady Tech, play something motivational and turn it up." Rogers requested.

"Got it."

Adrian got up from his seat, leaning in, whispering into Lady Tech's ear. She turned to him, raising an eyebrow.

"I heard him playing it a lot in his room."

Lady Tech smiled with a nod.

"I got the song."

As Adrian returned to his seat, Erica selected the song he requested. Skillet's "Rise" rumbled throughout the audio system of the powered-up Warthog. Rubbing her hands together, she grasped the two hand controls, ready to go.

~~~~~~~~~~~~~~~~~~~~~~~~~~~~~~~~~~~

0850 AM, Washington, DC:

The streets throughout the capital were cemetery dead. Peace's news broadcast and savage obliteration of the Defenders of Justice left people cowering in their homes, refusing to come out while taking the fight out of all superhumans around the globe. The District of Columbia residents huddled together close to their loved ones under structures that gave them very little protection. They clung closer to one another as the sky began to tremble.

Flying overhead, Peace was in cruise mode on her way to the White House. Adding to the sky's rumbling was Wendigo thumping "Narcissistic Cannibal," performed by Korn, Featuring Skrillex and Kill the Noise to give her propulsion, while Revenant flew as her right wingman.

Below, the Ghoul ran ahead of them, tearing through abandoned DC streets to reach 1600 Pennsylvania Avenue.

Peace's emotions were half and half that morning. Half pleased that she had no opposition and half disappointed that there was none. She at least expected a squadron of F-22As or several fleets of M1 Abrams in strategic parts of the streets with some M167 VADS on the rooftops of buildings looking to shoot her down. They would all fail miserably to stop her, but she was a bit disappointed there was not one piece of military equipment ready to defend the President of the United States.

As Peace approached the White House, her face turned from slight disappointment to one of trouble. She hovered a block from her destination, bringing both wingmen to a halt. They all wore the concerned look of flying into a trap.

Peace expected the entire block in front of the main gate and the lawn to be flooded with every heavily armored weapon and personnel they could deploy in less than twelve hours. Instead, the street and grounds were as vacant as the rest of the city, save for one lone soul standing on the lawn.

The President of the United States himself.
~~~~~~~~~~~~~~~~~~~~~~~~~~~~~~~~~~~

"Anchimayen," Peace projected her thoughts, *"is that the real President of the United States down there?"*

"Yes, it is," the child returned from the safety of their North Pole hideout. *"He has not left the White House all night. That is him standing before you."*

Peace looked up toward the skies.

"Where's Dennison?"

"Still in space in the outer orbit where you left her," Anchimayen answered. *"She has not moved since you exiled her there."*

She nodded before looking down at the free world leader standing alone, facing his imminent death.

"You're just hell-bent on showing the world what a big pussy Bush was, aren't you?"

Peace shook her head in disbelief.

"Big bad Bin Ladin Al-Qaeda ninja drone killer now standing on the lawn of the White House with his gangsta lean facing down a world killer like me."

Peace grinned, biting her lip.

"Kind of sexy! Makes a girl wanna come down there and do the ole Monica on you."

"I stand out here, so that good Americans do not die needlessly," the President nobly responded, "so that…"

"And then he talked." Peace groaned, rolling her eyes in disgust. "And turned something that I found really hot a second ago into something that just pisses me off to no end. Ghoul…"

Ghoul strolled up to the front gates brandishing his new blades, slicing a section down with a couple of well-placed swipes, all that stood between him and the President.

"You see, this martyr shit does not sit well with me," Peace dryly informed him. "Sends a bad message of hope where there should be none. Now had you cowered under your desk like you were supposed to, I would have given you a quick, somewhat painless, death. But since you want to come out here like Harrison Ford, I'm going to have Ghoul here butcher you on the front lawn while your wife and kids watch screaming from the windows. And then right before the last breath leaves your body, I'm going to make you watch as I obliterate the White House with them inside of it."

A sweat-drenched President slowly turned to a rabid, grinning Ghoul, pointing one of his machetes at him getting ready.

"This is for da homeland, you cunt, whether dey appreciates it or not."

A smile returned to Peace's face as she realized her plan would come to fruition in two seconds. She would finally win, all due to her perfect plan.

With the vital player taken off the board, there was little resistance. The Defenders of Justice's demise meant no annoying heroes. Not even the Regulators, who she suspected were not dead, came out of their hiding place to make a final stand against her. She would decide later whether to hunt them down or leave them to rot in the hole they cowered in.

Peace basked in the euphoria of her perfect plan until she realized it was more than two seconds, and Ghoul had not moved an inch to dip his blades in Presidential blood.

It was because he was transfixed on the portal that opened up behind the President.

In two seconds, Peace watched her perfect plan go up in smoke as a female speedster in a high-tech gray and white bodysuit wearing a Kabuki mask to cover her identity popped halfway out of the portal.

"Sike!" the mystery superhuman yelled while flipping her off.

She wrapped her arm around his waist and snatched up the United States President, pulling him into the portal with her.

"No!" Peace roared.

She unleashed a powerful stream of raw power that sheared the air itself. However, the portal closed as quickly as it opened, causing the blast to only leave a massive crater on the White House lawn.

"The goddamn Egyptian who I told you to find!" Peace howled, turning to Revenant with murderous intent. "Find them! Find out…!"

Before Peace could finish her rant, two more portals opened midair several feet from them. In the first one, the Egyptian demigod flew out and floated with a grin that quickly turned into a sneer as he locked eyes with Revenant, who brandished a devilish grin.

Peace did not need to guess who was coming out of the second portal. She could feel her coming. Somehow, she always found a way. Something Peace both respected and loathed.

The Earth trembled as EVO Zero barreled through the portal with all the rage of hell on her visage. Revenant and Wendigo wisely scattered while Peace covered up, bracing herself for the first impact.

Even though Peace had her guard up protecting her face, Dennison's building-leveling haymaker knocked her clear across the skies of DC. She felt the blow in her bones. She hit the brakes to stop her reverse momentum and get her bearings, but Sophia was already on her with murder in her eyes.

The next thunderous punch connected, smacking Peace out of the sky hurling her through the Jefferson Memorial. The seventy-one-year-old monument did not stand a chance against her wrecking ball body crashing through it. Parts of it exploded like an eggshell, while another part collapsed in on itself. Peace bounced violently off the grass lawn behind the monument, producing several large craters before sliding to a stop.

Peace rolled to her feet, shaking out the cobwebs and dusting herself off. She realized in their second fight, Sophia was holding back. Her strikes were more brutal and actually caused pain. That was all the time she had to think as Dennison landed, putting a massive crater into the lawn. She did not hesitate or utter a word, charging straight for Peace, sending dirt and well-cut grass spraying everywhere. Sophia let her fists talk for her as she roared, throwing left and right bombs at breakneck speed, tagging Peace across her jaw, both sides of her ribs, and the left side of her face.

The word of the day was attack… and to keep attacking.

~ ~

At the same time, Sophia returned to Earth, the bay window to the Dennison's home, and a good portion of the front of their house detonated. Its cause was a body hurled at incredible speed, sailing over the gate and crashing into a black Ford Fusion across the street.

A dazed and furious Nachzehrer pulled herself from the wreckage of the car while Sister Shareef appeared from out of the new hole made in the Dennison's home. She traded her prison attire for a black and purple version of Heavy Element's bodysuit, matching boots, and black bracers similar to Sophia's bracers.

"Heffa, you done picked the wrong house to threaten!" Sister Shareef yelled out.

Shareef leaped from the house, clearing the fence and landing in the middle of Seventh Avenue. A rabid Nachzehrer, with her knife still in hand, wasted no time pouncing on her. They both slammed into a Hyundai RAV 4, crushing the vehicle between themselves and the curb. Nachzehrer roared, fighting to overpower her so that she could drive her blade into either her neck or chest, while Shareef, with a vice grip lock on both her forearms, muscled back to keep her at bay.

The commotion drew everyone in the neighborhood onto their porches while Sophia's parents looked through the new hole in their home. A livid Mrs. Dennison appeared to want to get in the middle of the fight while her husband held her back.

Feeling the knife edging closer, Shareef broke the stalemate with a neck-snapping headbutt to the face, stunning her; she repeated the process twice for good measure.

With a three-second window, Shareef tucked her head under Nachzehrer's right arm while reaching across her chest and around her neck with her near arm, allowing her to control both her knife arm and upper body. Using her pistons for legs, Shareef propelled herself into the air, slamming Nachzehrer violently back-first into the already totaled Ford Fusion. A chorus of "Oooooooh!" rang through the neighborhood of witnesses as Shareef, now in control, wrenched the knife from Nachzehrer's grip, tossing it away.

"Rock Bottom! Rock Bottom!" an onlooker screamed out.

Shareef straddled Nachzehrer and proceeded to rifle her with a sledgehammer right haymakers to the face.

"Dat's right!" Mrs. Dennison screamed, throwing her own left and rights shadowboxing. "Lick out her what's it not!"

"Nopel!" Mr. Dennison yelled, holding her back. "Mind your blood pressure!

Mind your blood pressure!"

~~~~~~~~~~~~~~~~~~~~~~~~~~~~~~~~~~~

At the same time, Shareef's portal opened up in Mount Vernon, and another opened on Sophia's island at 6 a.m. Pacific Time. This one was ten times larger than all the other gateways. The Draugr and Jiang Shi turned mystified while Sanctuary residents, still awake, exited their homes to witness something straight out of a science fiction movie. Many were terrified; some, like Kyle and Akram, were fascinated, while Kimberly saw hope.

A fearless Draugr walked toward the portal to cleave whoever or whatever came through in half. Instead, he got a chest full of a 41.6-ton assault vehicle plowing into him like a wild boar. The impact knocked the monster off his vertical base, sending his battle ax flying. As he rolled back onto his feet, still brandishing his sword, Lady Tech inside the Warthog locked her main cannon onto his chest.

"Choke on this, you son of a bitch."

With two simultaneous button pushes from her hand controls, the Warthog's long-barreled main cannon lit up, displaying a white light. A build-up of kinetic energy unleashed a plasma shell round, striking the Draugr dead center, lifting him off his feet, tearing through the village, causing destruction and a chain reaction of explosions.

Still gripping his sword, the monster crashed and landed yards from where the village ended and the beach began.

Jiang Shi, coming to her senses after the Regulators' startling entrance, shot up into the air via a column of flames while channeling flames through her hands, preparing to turn them and the village to ash.

"You shall all…!"

"Jiang Shi!" Merge screamed, getting her attention.

Standing in the Warthog's open-top hatch, Merge injected herself with a syringe filled with Oliver's blood. Her skin color instantly changed to match Oliver's, while her hair turned into a frizzy white afro. Her eyes blazed white as she focused on channeling an electrical charge, propelling herself from the top of the vehicle toward the fire witch.

Jiang Shi rocketed higher into the sky to get some distance between her and an
~~~~~~~~~~~~~~~~~~~~~~~~~~~~~~~~~~~

enraged Rosann, now locked on her with a bloodhound mentality.

The skies blazed with fire and lightning over the island as a vengeance-seeking Merge picked up where Blitz left off.

"All right, girls," Erica ordered, "Time to get to work."

Additional parts of the Warthog opened, jettisoning the android sisters. Angie and Jennifer landed on the Warthog, while Maxine brandishing two automatic plasma rifles, touched down before the frightened villagers.

"Ladies and Gentlemen, if you will please follow me," Maxine instructed them, "we are going to the far side of the island until the fighting is done."

Everyone was still too frightened to move until Kimberly found the courage to speak up.

"Come on, people! We have to follow the lady robot!"

"The correct term is android," Maxine rectified, "but, yes, please follow me."

"What is everyone waiting for?!" Earl howled, also helping to lead. "Let's move people! Move it! Grab smaller children and help the older people! Let's go!"

Merge strafed across the skies, evading Jiang Shi's flame attacks. The flame witch became erratic, unleashing volleys and streams of intense plasma heat, trying to turn her into a cinder. Even with half Blitz's power levels, her speed outmatched the fire witch's accuracy. Rosann was purposely frustrating her, patiently waiting for her to make a mistake.

Spotting an opening, Merge darted by striking her across the face, spinning her around in midair. It was like pulling a pin out of a grenade as she screamed in rage, turning the sky red and creating a firestorm. All the villagers running to safety with Maxine leading them looked up into the sky, fearing hell blazing above them.

"Think we should give Merge some help?" Lady Tech asked as she drove the Warthog.

"My sister's got this," Heavy Element answered. "Let's just worry about mowing down that big ugly son of a bitch."

Jiang Shi halted her flaming rampage to see if Rosann's charred body had fallen from the sky. Instead, she received a roaring Merge bursting through her flames, slamming right into her. The strike was so fast and hard that it sent them flying half a mile from the island. Unable to recover from the blow, the fire witch plummeted into the Pacific Ocean back first. Rosann released Oliver's power while straightening her body into a diving position. Before hitting the water, she rubbed two fingers across the bottom bone slab on her wristband.

A gagging Jiang Shi swam back to the top and frantically looked around. She was in an element that rendered her abilities useless. She prepared to swim back when Merge rose from the water, pouncing on her.

Jiang Shi screeched as Merge, taking the form of a human hybrid sea otter, sank her razor-sharp claws into her arms, forcing her back first into the deep, dark depths of the ocean. The fire witch struggled to break free, but Merge's sea otter DNA granted her superhuman strength and greater lung capacity. Merge watched the life fade out of her as her lungs filled up with water. Her vengeance was almost fulfilled until Oliver's words from when they spoke in the hallway echoed in her mind.

Rosann reluctantly shot back up to the top, breaking through the ocean surface where the early morning sun beamed down on them. Jiang Shi weakly hacked up the water she took in and groaned as Merge strapped her into an arm under-chin headlock. She used her powerful legs to swim back to shore with her.

Back at the island, her teammates continued their assault on the Draugr.

"Full throttle," Rogers ordered. "We have to keep that bastard on the beach."

"Yes, sir," Lady Tech acknowledged.

She gunned the high-tech assault tank, tearing through the village while tracking the Draugr's trajectory trail to pinpoint where he landed. It was not hard to find him; the man-beast charged straight at them with thoughts of slaughter in his eyes.

"Dennison's gonna kill me for tearing up her island," Erica muttered with gritted teeth. "Time to let it fly, Angie!"

"Yes, ma'am!"

The bubbly android locked her tripod feet into sections of the tank to stabilize herself as a compartment in the Warthog opened in front of her, pushing up two gargantuan rifles half the size of her body. Her sister armed up, and her back opened up once again, allowing her to connect and pull out her swords.

Angie grinned, raising one of her hand cannons as her targeting system locked onto the Draugr. She pulled the trigger, causing the gun to hum before discharging an energy projectile round, striking him on the right side of his helmet.

The heat and impact forced his head to turn and buckle while causing superficial damage to his helmet. It did not stop him from charging but motivated him to increase his speed.

Angie adjusted her stance, raising her guns and opening fire, unleashing one round after another from both barrels. Most of them found their mark, knocking the big man around, but it did not stop him from coming.

Lady Tech answered his challenge, pushing the accelerator gunning the Warthog straight for him.

"What the hell are you doing?!" Rogers yelled.

"Este hijo de puta quiere jugar pollo conmigo?!" Lady Tech snarled. "Then let's go!"

As Rogers and Adrian glanced at each other, Heavy Element transformed into metal form while Abe braced himself.

"Get ready, girls!" Lady Tech screamed.

Jennifer and Angie simultaneously coiled their legs, waiting for the point of impact. The Draugr launched his massive half-ton frame into the air. His intention was clearly to cut the Warthog wide open.

Angie and Jennifer leaped at the same time he went airborne, but in opposite directions, away from him and the vehicle.

"Time to get FUBARed!" Lady Tech howled.

Upon her command, various compartments of the Warthog opened up, revealing various anti-air missiles. She unleashed them all at the Draugr, who had no time to cover up. The explosions consumed him, the vehicle, and anything within range of the blast. Still gripping his sword, a roaring Draugr was hurled again like a meteorite back onto the beach. The Warthog, battered and smoking with cosmetic damage, survived the explosion.

"You guys, alright?" Erica asked.

"Oh, yeah," Heavy Element groaned. "I feel like I just came out of a Michael Bay movie, but I'm good."

"Go get him, girls," Lady Tech commanded.

Angie and Jennifer bolted, going into full combat mode, hunting the Draugr. The nearly unstoppable goliath rose to his feet again, wafting with smoke. His superficial wounds healed instantaneously as his armor told the tale of the hell he endured. White smoke blew from the vents in his helmet as he turned to begin mortal combat anew.

The Draugr would not have to wait for it as Angie tore down the beach, kicking up sand, firing salvos of plasma rounds, and hitting vital parts of his body that should have proven fatal. He weathered the storm of barrages and broke into a run for another game of chicken between himself and the cannon-toting android.

Draugr could not see Jennifer hidden during his berserker charge as she ran behind her sister. With their battle plan synced, Angie hit the brakes, sliding across the sand while firing two rounds, kneecapping the behemoth in his left leg. As he crashed and burned face-first into the sand, Jennifer, using her sister's back as a springboard, propelled herself into the air and came down, sinking her dark metal-forged swords into his back.

Draugr roared furiously, fighting to stand on his uninjured knee while his bad one healed. Still on his back, Jennifer set up to attempt a decapitation, but the big man tumble rolled forward, forcing her to leap off his back so she would not be crushed.

The rear hatch to the Warthog opened, allowing Heavy Element and a rifle-toting Rogers to exit the vehicle.

"I'll be with you guys in a minute once I suit up," Erica radioed.

"Roger that," Abe answered before turning to Adrian. "Let's go have some fun."

The two broke into a sprint, heading toward the Draugr and battle.

"Sir," Heavy Element asked, running side by side with him, "ever play ball in school?"

"Call me Sarge," Rogers replied. "Centerfield in high school and QB in college and Marine Corps. I assume this has to do with a plan."

"Yeah, it's called a fastball special."

Rogers shook his head.

"Never heard of it."

Adrian halted several yards from the battle.

"Stop, and I'll show you."

The Sarge halted, wondering what his metal teammate was up to.

"Hold your hand out palm up," Heavy Element instructed. "Bring your arm down lower."

Adrian, holding onto Rogers's shoulder, hopped with both feet into the palm of his hand.

"I take it that I just aim and throw," Rogers confirmed.

Adrian stooped down, readying himself.

"That's the plan."

"You sure about this?" Rogers asked.

Heavy Element shook his head.

"No, but let's do this anyway."

The Sarge took a Colin Kaepernick stance and hurled him with a patriot missile force at the Draugr. The mad Viking finally got the upper hand on the android sisters, destroying one of Angie's guns with a slice of his sword. The internal power source detonated in her hand, badly damaging it while knocking her to the sand. The Draugr pounced on her before she could recover, driving a boot into her chest. The softness of the sand and her extra dense form was the only thing that kept him from breaking her like an egg.

Draugr raised his sword to drive it through her skull just as Jennifer rushed to attempt to save her sister.

Heavy Element got there first with a roaring thunderous right caving in the side of his helmet. It also turned slightly, inhibiting his vision. He landed, tumbling and rolling on the sand.

Jennifer dashed behind him, letting both her swords fly as she sliced the back of his left leg and calf open. The Draugr roared again in pain and frustration as he stumbled forward, giving Angie the opening to roll out of the way.

Everyone scattered from the vicinity of the Draugr as a now-airborne Lady Tech in the SAM armor powered up and fired an ion blast from her main chest cannon. It tore through the air, hitting him dead center in the face and upper chest; the Draugr fell backward, sending sand spraying everywhere. On his feet, Adrian waved away the stench of burning flesh emitting from him.

"Well, that was easy!" Heavy Element yelled to his teammates.

Lady Tech touched down next to Rogers, getting into a combat stance.

"It's not over," she reported.

Insane cackling confirmed what her readings revealed. The Draugr sat up and rose to his feet as if the team did not lay a scratch on him. He grabbed his sword and ripped off his helmet-tossing it away, revealing the inhuman demonic insanity in his eyes.

Heavy Element rolled his eyes in disgust.

"I am the Draugr, you cunts!" he howled, raising his sword. "Satan's champion and eternal enemy of God! You can not kill me!"

Draugr's sinister rant was answered with a high-powered plasma round to the face, sending him reeling and roaring with pain. His mouth frothed with saliva as his hand hovered over the now tender side of his face, blistered from the scorching heat.

"Give us a minute!" Sarge yelled back, brandishing the smoking rifle. "We'll think of something!"

~~~~~~~~~~~~~~~~~~~~~~~~~~~~~~~~~~~

Back in Washington, Sophia's initial plan of attack was not faring too well. A recovered Peace had found her rhythm fighting back just as viciously as she was. She realized that this battle would not be as easy as their first one seven years ago.

Back then, Sophia overwhelmed her with sheer brute strength and speed. The skill she also displayed was just the icing on the cake.

Though Sophia was fighting on par with her, Peace's strength and speed were slightly higher than hers were, and she was a trained combatant forged from the pits of the D.E.A.D project.

Fighting and killing came as naturally to her as breathing and eating.

Although Sophia possessed many fighting techniques, Peace had actual combat experience, which made her realize she was a champion that had never been tested until now.

Sophia found an opening through the barrages of punches and kicks, delivering a legsweep, dropping her flat on her back. Peace responded by rolling and scissoring Sophia's legs, slamming her face-first into the Jefferson Memorial lawn. Peace rolled again, driving a backhand fist to the back of Sophia's skull, sinking her further into the dirt. Sophia rolled out of the way, evading another hit that cratered the soil with her fist.

As Sophia sprung back to her feet, Peace performed a Kip Up back to her vertical base. The two began to circle one another like lionesses preparing to fight over territory or a kill.

"However way you and Mr. Stargate pulled off your little Houdini act," Peace seethed, "it doesn't matter. After I kill you, he and everyone you ever loved and cared about are dead by my hands!"

"Not going to happen, you monster!" Sophia fired back.

"Tell me why you misbegotten bitch!" Peace screamed. "Why do you continue to defend these blood-sucking parasites who ass rape everything they touch, including your life?!"

"I swear by God the Father in Heaven, Jesus Christ, His only begotten Son, and the Holy Spirit to keep according to my ability and judgment. The following Oath and agreement," Sophia recited, "to consider dear to me, as my parents, him who taught me
~~~~~~~~~~~~~~~~~~~~~~~~~~~~~~~~~~~

this art; to live in common with him and, if necessary, to share my goods with him. To look upon his children as my own brothers, to teach them this art; and that by my teaching, I will impart knowledge of this art to my own sons, and to my teacher's sons, and to disciples bound by an indenture and oath according to the medical laws, and no others. I will prescribe regimens for my patients' good according to my ability and judgment and never harm anyone.

I will give no deadly medicine to anyone if asked, nor suggest any such counsel, and similarly, I will not give a woman a pessary to cause an abortion. But I will preserve the purity of my life and my art. I will not cut for stone, even for patients in whom the disease manifests; I will leave this operation to be performed by practitioners and specialists in this art. In every house where I come, I will enter only for the good of my patients, keeping myself far from all intentional ill-doing and all seduction and especially from the pleasures of love with women or men, be they free or slaves.

All that may come to my knowledge in my profession or daily commerce with men, who ought not to be spread abroad, I will keep secret and never reveal. If I keep this oath faithfully, may I enjoy my life and practice my art, respected by all humanity and in all times; but if I swerve from it or violate it, may the reverse be my life."

Peace glared at Sophia as if she was the one who was insane.

"What the fuck did all that mean?!"

"For your simple mind to comprehend, I took an oath as a doctor to save and preserve all life using all of my abilities. So there's no way I plan on standing back and watch you enact mass genocide on the world. You're going to have to go through me to do it!"

A frustrated Peace emitted an inhuman animalistic roar similar to when Sophia was resurrected from Mountain View seven years ago. She detonated from where she stood, taking flight and crashing into Sophia, going airborne. Through mid-flight, Sophia performed her own Judo Tomeo-nage or Circle-throw in midair, tossing her off her.

Sophia came in at full speed, throwing a powerful right; Peace sidestepped the punch, grabbing her and performing a Judo Uchi-mata Inner-thigh throw, hurling her through a fifty-story building. Halfway through, as Sophia slammed on the breaks to stop, Peace barreling through plowed into her, bursting through the other side of the building, putting her through two more. Exploding through the third building, they both broke free of one another, crash landing on opposite sides of Pennsylvania Avenue in Downtown Washington DC, taking out cars, storefronts, and anything else unlucky enough to be in their path. Abandoned building number three collapsed into itself, sending smoke and debris in opposite directions within a twelve-block radius.

Sophia fought to her feet, shaking off the cobwebs in the middle of a closed Radio Shack that she demolished with her crash landing. Most of Washington had apparently taken the hint after Peace's televised speech and did not come to work, which was lucky for them. She walked through the hole she created where those who did not take the hint ran screaming, biking, or driving to safety.

Sophia turned, spying Peace through the massive dust four blocks away, already standing and glaring in her direction. She turned, taking a deep breath, knowing that she was not only in for the fight of her life but that the end could only have one outcome. Two of the most powerful EVOs on the planet launched toward each other to begin battle anew with no more words to be spoken.

~~~~~~~~~~~~~~~~~~~~~~~~~~~~~~~~~~

On the other side of Washington DC, the Ghoul stood alone as the skies and streets lit up with battle again after seven years between his teammates, Peace, Sophia, and the Egyptian.

"Well, this went all tits up!"

Before Ghoul could contemplate whether to join his teammates in fighting the Egyptian Warrior or save his own skin, his reflexes kicked in as the female speedster that rescued the President appeared again out of nowhere, now brandishing twin swords of her own.

With a swing, she attempted to sever his head from his torso with one blow. He barely put his blades up, which took the impact of the sword swipe. The force of her swing took him off his feet and slammed him into a parked Lincoln town car, caving in the passenger door.

Ghoul shrugged it off, returning to his feet while sizing up his new opponent.

She stood an impressive six feet in height. Her gray and silver second-skin bodysuit was designed to look like the body without skin revealing the muscle tissue underneath. Her matching high-tech split-toe shoes seemed as if they were attached to her outfit. Her identity was covered by a blue, red, black, and silver Kabuki mask.

Her dark raven hair was neatly cornrowed into thin braids. The last thing he spied on as they circled each other were her futuristic gunmetal gray ninjato-style swords with Japanese caricatures etched into the blades. They looked hefty and could cut through
~~~~~~~~~~~~~~~~~~~~~~~~~~~~~~~~~~

almost anything with a single swing.

Ghoul pointed his blade at her.

"And who might you be love?"

"Your executioner," she responded with a distorted voice, "but you can call me Shintobe."

"Never seen a bomb watcher as tall as you," Ghoul spat back.

"Oh, that's my Irish side," Shintobe answered with a cutesy voice. "Guess what my other side is."

She twirled the sword in her right hand with insane speed, producing a wind he could feel as she prepared to end the small talk.

"Before I dice you into sushi," Ghoul snarled, "do tell to what do I owe this apparently personal invitation of combat?"

"Lady Electrify was a good friend of mine." Shintobe emitted bass in her voice. "You butchered her like a dog in the street. The only reason I didn't get back in enough time to watch your entrails spill before you is because I was on the other side of the world, killing scumbags like you. By the time I heard the news and got back, the Regulators already hauled you off to the deep dark hole you should have stayed in."

Ghoul sarcastically stumbled around in shock.

"So this is payback then? I'll have you know your little friend bawled and squealed like a stuffed pig as I did her in those dirty streets, and I enjoyed watching the light go out of her!"

"Thank you," Shintobe shot back.

"Thank you for what, you cunt?!" Ghoul roared.

"Now, I'm really going to enjoy killing you," Shintobe calmly answered.

~ ~

In Mount Vernon, Sister Shareef held a bloodied and pummeled Nachzehrer by the throat, letting up to see if she surrendered before delivering her forty-first punch.

"You give up," Shareef barked, "or do you want some more?!"

Nachzehrer answered her the same way she responded to Heavy Element in Manhattan by hacking blood-laced spittle into her face.

"Oh no, that nasty bitch didn't!" someone yelled from their front porch.

Before a disgusted Shareef could respond with another thunderous haymaker, Nachzehrer took the split-second opportunity to wrench a fist full of dirt from the sidewalk grass, hurling it into her face, blinding her.

Nachzehrer followed up by backhanding her, knocking her off. A stunned Shareef tumbled and rolled off the wreckage of the Focus. As she stumbled to her feet, Nachzehrer already up charged, nailing her with a shoulder tackle to the gut.

She lifted her off her feet in one motion, plowing her back into a parked red Yukon, which slammed nose-first into the back of a parked BMW. It continued to cause a chain reaction of crashes while Nachzehrer, with a handful of Sister Shareef's locks, slammed her skull repeatedly against the back of the caved-in vehicle.

Shareef went for a head-removing elbow to back her up and get some breathing room; a faster Nachzehrer ducked it, locking her up. She lifted her into the air, delivering a textbook wrestling back suplex, drilling her head and shoulder first into the back of the SUV. Unlike the staged sport, she was unprepared for the savage bump, taking the full force of the blow.

An enraged Nachzehrer, refusing to give her breathing room, latched onto her right leg. Using a one-armed swing, she hurled her into the skies of Mount Vernon.

Shareef's point of impact was the basketball court attached to the Seventh and Eighth Avenue projects. Players and locals hanging out scattered, screaming as Shareef took out one of the steel basketball hoops, bringing it down. She rolled to her hands and knees, groaning.

"Dear Lord, I'm too old for this shit."

The hairs on her neck stood to attention as something screamed for her to move.

Out of the corner of her eye, Shareef saw the totaled Yukon toward her, guided by a cackling airborne Nachzehrer.

She rolled out of the way, thwarting Nachzehrer's attempt to crush her with it. The vehicle folded like an accordion as it smashed into the concrete of the ball court.

The older woman on her feet covered up as a younger, faster Nachzehrer began to batter her with what was left of the SUV. With her guard up, Shareef tanked some shots, looking for an opening. She miscalculated, dropping her defense for a second, taking a face full of a wrecked SUV, knocking her into a violent and awkward tailspin.

Shareef's skull was the first to hit the pavement. On instinct, she rolled to her hands and knees despite her vision going blurry. She was unprepared for her, bringing the wrecked SUV down on top of her. A wide-eyed, drooling Nachzehrer delivered a secondary blow for good measure.

Nachzehrer pulled the wreckage off Shareef as onlookers cursed and screamed at her from afar. Once again on her hands and knees, Shareef continued to fight to rise. Blood from healing open wounds dripped from her skull, nose, and mouth. Her body trembled in pain despite her regenerative healing working to help her recover.

Nachzehrer snapped off a steel beam from the undercarriage of the SUV. It was not a clean break producing a sharply jagged edge. She ran the edge across the ball court's concrete several times to make it even sharper. She then sashayed around with it in her grip, taunting Shareef.

"You know… I could give two shits what Peace says."

Nachzehrer raised her left hand into a fist.

"The only true master race is the one with **this color**!"

Nachzehrer bolted, delivering a savage punt kick to Shareef's ribcage, lifting her several feet off the ground. She hit the court back first, emitting an agonizing groan as she clutched her ribs. Nachzehrer could have field goal kicked her out of the court. She held back, wanting everyone to see what she would do next.

Nachzehrer dropped onto Shareef's chest, pinning her upper arms by the biceps. She then grabbed Shareef by her dreads, lifting her head up a bit, running the sharp edge of her makeshift shiv across her face.

"And I'm going to make it my business to finally exterminate you knuckle-dragging…!"

Nachzehrer's speech of hatred screeched to a halt as her eyes widened while her entire body quivered.

Shareef removed her hand from Nachzehrer's left thigh to reveal an ion body damper attached to it, sending thousands of volts of electricity directly into her nervous system, overloading it. She had pulled one out from one of the compartments in her forearm bands during her beating. Lady Tech instructed her that it had to be attached to the back of her opponent's neck to be one hundred percent effective in delivering the charged pulse to the spinal cord, cerebellum, and brain.

However, in Sister Shareef's current situation, she figured nerves were still in any part of the body.

"What's that?" Shareef coly asked. "I can't quite hear the shit coming out your mouth."

Sister Shareef delivered her backhand to Nachzehrer, knocking her off her, which sent the shiv in her hand flying. Shareef sprung back to her vertical base, grabbing her by her Mohawk and pulling her to her feet.

Shareef made the end quick and fast as she hammered both sides of her jaws with thunderous lefts and rights, followed by a spine-blowing gut check, doubling her over. Measuring Nachzehrer up, Sister Shareef exploded with a neck-breaking uppercut, lifting her ten feet into the air. Another chorus of "Ooooooh!" rang out from the onlookers witnessing the knockout punch.

Nachzehrer came back down on the back of her neck, folding like a lawn chair for about a second; she flipped over onto her face, never to rise.

"She got knocked the you know what out," an elderly woman stated from afar.

"That's the problem with you kids today," Shareef huffed, "you talk too darn much."

Nachzehrer groaned in agony as Shareef pulled out another ion body damper from her bracer, slapping it down on the back of her neck, completely incapacitating her.

"One more to grow on, ya nasty heffa."

Sister Shareef stood tall, cracking her neck and back while collecting herself as onlookers howled and cheered her on. She looked toward the skies, praying that Sophia and everyone else were as successful as she was in her mission.

CHAPTER 24

The violent rhythmic clanging of blades echoed throughout the streets of DC as the Ghoul and Shintobe fought to see who would slice the other into ribbons.

Their swords moved at such blinding speeds; sparks spurted amid the exchange. It was hard to tell who was on the offensive and defensive. Both combatants stood their ground, unleashing a hailstorm of slashing moves from various angles to score a deep cut. Neither one attempted a thrust nor parry; for Ghoul, he probably believed any over-the-top attempts would leave him open to Shintobe taking his head for a trophy.

It also did not sit too well with Ghoul that her mask shrouded her face, making it impossible for him to read her. Shintobe's poker face body movements frustrated him. Even though this was clearly vengeance for her, she did not attack like someone looking for blood. She moved as if she was performing a dance or playing an instrument. She was not rushing to deliver death to him; she slowly led him to it with a waltz.

Ghoul snarled as he thought he had found an opening. He went for a diagonally downward slash, slicing her half from her left collarbone to her right hip.

Had she stood in the way of his blade.

Shintobe moved into the Ghoul's personal space, getting out of the range of his machetes. She kissed him with a vicious mask-enforced headbutt to the nose, staggering him. Shintobe executed a barrel jump, sailing into a back kick to his chest with a shotgun force.

It took Ghoul off his feet, plowing him back into a brick wall, caving it in. He fell to one knee, still clutching his machetes. Pieces of broken brick fell from his imprint behind him, breaking into smaller pieces as they hit the concrete. His left hand nursed his chest as he spat blood on the ground. Slowly, he looked up at a waiting Shintobe bearing his fangs.

"Why am I not surprised," Ghoul hissed. "Ya probably wank off with those things."

"Yeah, and if you were going to live to see tomorrow," Shintobe returned. "Guy Ritchie would be suing you for stealing his shit. Lucky for you… you won't. So how about we get this over with? I got a bath waiting for me to scrub off your funk."

An enraged Ghoul rose to his feet.

"The only one taking a bath is me, bitch! In your blood!"

Shintobe erupted with laughter from underneath her mask.

"You're gonna bathe in my blood! Dude, seriously, how long have you been waiting to use that cliché line?"

Ghoul howled, going rabid as he launched himself toward her. Shintobe stood her ground, meeting him head-on as he entered a berserker rage attack. Their second clash was more savage than the first, with Ghoul increasing his offensive.

Shintobe's speed also increased to match his ferocity but not his demeanor. She was as cold as ice. Something else she was doing disturbed Ghoul and pushed his rage to a fever pitch; through all of the clangings of steel, he was sure she was singing the hook to Lady Gaga's "Bad Romance" under her mask.

Five seconds more, the fencing contest that would make the most skilled masters faint ended as Shintobe did a simple duck, spin, and tumble roll back onto her feet and out of the range of the Ghoul's blades again. This time, she turned her back to him.

"It's over," Shintobe sighed, "say 'hi' to the devil for me while he's cornholing you."

"What do you mean it's over you…?!" a bewildered and enraged Ghoul spat.

He would not finish his sentence as both his forearms detached from the rest of his limbs, still clutching his machetes.

"Impossible…" Ghoul stammered. "Your swords don't have…"

A gust of wind blew off his entire hood while his head fell from his shoulders. His torso was the last to fall, separating in half from his left collarbone to his right hip, leaving him nothing more than body parts in a blood pool.

"In the words of the most legendary speedster to grace this planet," a victorious Shintobe recited, "Beep, Beep."

With a sonic boom, she rocketed toward the battle between the heroic Egyptian, Revenant, and Wendigo, tearing apart portions of DC. She knew vengeance would not bring her friend back, but she prayed it would help her rest better in peace.

~~~~~~~~~~~~~~~~~~~~~~~~~~~~~~~~~~

The skies of Washington, DC, roared with a sound greater than thunder. People cowered as they watched their atmosphere abused with unearthly energies wielded by beings battling against one another.

Revenant channeling dark matter energies unleashed it with sinister intent at the Eye of Ra, who deflected volley after volley with his staff. He returned fire with a powerful cosmic blast of his own. Revenant strafed away to avoid the hit, unconfident that he could tank the stream with his protective shielding as it scorched the air.

Ra powered up to let off another volley until Wendigo's sonic attack forced him to go on the defensive. His energy shielding weathered the storm of Disturbed's "Into the Fire," beating down on him while tearing apart the tops and sides of buildings below, raining debris and glass into the streets.

Revenant found the opening he needed to create a massive animated dark matter construct of a tank-size hellhound. It lunged at him, moving with twice the speed and force of a bullet train, plowing him into the top floor of a small building, taking out the first full three floors.

On command from his creator, the dark matter beast clawed and snapped at its prey, trying to rip him to shreds. Wendigo hovered next to Revenant to take in the view of the slaughter.

They levitated there like proud parents watching their child at play until an Earth-quaking surge of bright white and gold energy tore through Revenant's pet, turning it into the atoms it was created from.
~~~~~~~~~~~~~~~~~~~~~~~~~~~~~~~~~~

The couple's morbid grin disappeared as the Eye of Ra looked up at them. They could not tell if he had a displeased look because a golden face mask one would find on an ancient Egyptian statue now covered his visage. He gripped his staff, charging it with the raw energy he used to obliterate the hellhound construct.

Revenant narrowed his eyes.

"Interesting."

The Eye of Ra took to the air once again, torpedoing right toward them, forcing them to separate.

The sadistic couple attacked him again on both his flanks. Eye of Ra disappeared with a portal, evading both of their attacks, sending their volleys at one another, causing them to scatter.

During this time, Shintobe, now on the scene, gunned it at full speed, running up a skyscraper's side. Getting high enough, she leaped off with sword cocked and ready to remove Revenant's head from his body when a protective Wendigo unleashed a sonic blast knocking her away from her target.

Shintobe twisted and turned to recover in midair, going into a dive. Seconds before she impacted the ground, she performed a high-speed tumble roll, relying on her enhanced durability and regenerative healing to save her.

Springing back to her feet, Shintobe tore through the streets of Washington as a furious Wendigo gave chase.

As Revenant watched the scene unfold, he was unaware of the Eye of Ra appearing out of a portal to his right side. With a mighty swing from his staff, he swatted him out of the sky, sending him through several buildings and impacting an unmanned city bus in the streets below. Thanks to his dark shielding protecting him from the fatal blow, he slowly staggered to his feet, swaying.

There would be no rest for the wicked as the Eye of Ra came crashing down on top of him with high-powered staff reared back, looking to crush him with a single strike. Revenant quickly launched himself into the sky, barely evading the blow that obliterated what was left of the bus and the street it sat on.

"You're… you're mad…" Revenant gasped and shuddered while looking down at him. "You're bloody mad!"

Now desperate with fear, he unleashed a rapid-fire volley at the Egyptian demigod, who tanked the shots by twirling his staff in a cross pattern reminiscent of Shaolin monks from old Kung-fu movies. Tired of being on the defensive, he launched himself into the sky, barreling towards Revenant, spooking the fight out of him and forcing him to take flight.

~~~~~~~~~~~~~~~~~~~~~~~~~~~~~~~~~~~

Maxine successfully guided the villagers to the island's far side, away from the battle back at the beach. As she stood guard, maintaining a protective perimeter, Earl and the other council members began taking a headcount to ensure no one was lost or left behind during the journey.

During the headcount, Kimberly looked around, realizing some people were missing.

"Kyle?!"

Mrs. McArthur looked around, confirming her suspicions.

"Kyle! Where are you?! Kyle!"

"What happened?" Mr. McArthur asked. "Where is he?"

"I saw him keeping up with us!" Mrs. McArthur frantically screamed. "Joseph, where is your brother?!"

Kyle's nervous and bewildered older brother shrugged at both his parents.

"He was with me a second ago!"

"Akram!" his mother also cried in her native tongue, "Akram! Are you here?! Where are you?! Akram!"

"Idiots!" Kimberly muttered under her breath, rolling her eyes.

She knew where they were; despite all the chaos, the comic book buffs would not pass up a chance to see a real live superhuman battle as she turned to Earl.

"I think I know where the Dynamic Doofuses are. I'm going after them."
~~~~~~~~~~~~~~~~~~~~~~~~~~~~~~~~~~~

"Negative," Maxine replied, overhearing her. "It is far too dangerous. I will..."

"Too late!" Kimberly yelled.

She was gone with a superhuman leap, landing a mile into the jungle. Kimberly proceeded to run on foot in search of her friends.

"Miss, I have located Ms. Dennison's daughter," Maxine reported to Lady Tech. "She's heading back into the jungle to search for two boys unaccounted for during the evacuation."

"Why'd you let her go?!"

"Ms. Dennison failed to mention that her daughter currently possesses Titan level abilities," Maxine indicated, "possibly beyond."

"Then, stay there!" Erica said, "We're doing everything possible to keep the Draugr on the beach and bring him down! She should be okay searching for them until then!"

~ ~

It took Kimberly a minute to get within three yards of the village again. She put on the brakes as her heart twisted while her stomach turned to the jolting sound of intense battle on the beach.

"Kyle! Akram! Where are you guys?! Kyle! Akram!"

Kimberly wore a face of fret, fearing that they were somewhere hurt and alone. In a short time, they got to know each other, the two managed to grow on her. She stood, deciding to either check the village or move toward the fighting, when she heard the familiar screeching of Sir George.

Running toward the sound, she hid her misting eyes with a hand swipe.

Strolling up to her as if it was just another regular day was the duo walking side by side with Sir George sitting on Kyle's shoulder.

Her relief quickly turned to anger as she stomped over to them.

"You blockheads!" Kimberly screamed at them. "Your parents are worried sick about you, and you're out here lollygagging while there's a superhuman fight going down on the beach?! This is not a stupid comic book! You could get killed!"

"First of all, we're nowhere near that madness!" Kyle yelled back, "and secondly, we came back to get Sir George!"

"He's a monkey! He knows how to run and climb a tree when there's trouble!"

"Dude, she does have a point," Akram said, agreeing with Kimberly.

"Whose side are you on?!" Kyle yelled at his best friend.

"The side keeping me from the crazy lady who likes to burn people, and that ax-wielding Skaar wannabe!" Akram fired back.

"Technically, he's pretending to be a dead Viking." Kyle corrected his friend.

"We don't care!" Akram and Kimberly both yelled at him.

Sitting on his shoulder, Sir George shared their sentiment by popping him with his tiny fist on the top of his head.

A thunderous boom broke up their argument. Kimberly looked around, realizing they were very close to the beach.

"Follow me," she ordered, "and stay close!"

"You're not the boss…" Kyle said with a sneer.

Kimberly shut him up by grabbing him by the back of his neck and dragging him with her. Sir George jumped on her shoulder, taking a seat as Kyle yelled in protest. Akram, shaking his head, obediently followed.

Three minutes later, they came upon the battle. Kimberly, Kyle, and Akram watched in fear and disbelief as Heavy Element, Abe Rogers, and Lady Tech in her SAM armor, backed by Jennifer and Angie, fought the Draugr feverishly in an attempt to keep him quarantined to the beach and bring him down. It was not going well for them; the Regulators' combined and coordinated attacks barely kept the sheer brute strength of the sadistic monster at bay.

"This is bad," Kyle uttered.

"Doomsday bad," Akram chimed in.

A frustrated Kimberly ran her hands through her braids. Even if she joined the fight, which terrified her, she would not be strong enough to make much of a difference.

"I've got to get stronger," Kimberly muttered to herself.

Then she remembered her mother's talk about their abilities and how she got stronger. She turned to look toward the village's electrical power generator. During the tour, her mother told her that although it was small, it could generate enough power to light up half of Manhattan.

"Sir George, hide," Kimberly ordered.

It obeyed, leaping from her shoulder onto a palm tree and running up it.

Kimberly grabbed her friends around their waists without hesitation, lifting them into her arms.

"Hold on tight," she warned.

Kyle and Akram grabbed each other's arms to hug Kimberly close as she coiled up. She exploded into the air with them. They both screamed in unison as an airborne Kimberly soared over the island, clearing the town with her precious cargo.

"Brace yourselves!"

The duo screamed again, holding on as tight as they could. Kimberly made the landing as comfortable as possible without jolting them badly, stopping several yards before the massive electrical turbine generator. She set Kyle and Akram down before trotting over to it.

"What are you going to do?" Kyle frantically asked.

"I have to get strong like my mom to beat that guy!"

Kimberly walked up to one of the enormous cables connecting the generator to the town, lifting it up.

"What doesn't kill me," Kimberly whispered to herself. "On three. One …"

Kimberly did not hesitate as she dug her fingers through the protective outer layer of the cable, touching the wires surging massive amounts of heart-stopping electrical power. She could not even scream as her body seized up. Giant sparks and explosions erupted as Kimberly stood on the tips of her toes with her back arched while massive amounts of electrical current surged through her body.

Kyle, filled with tears, rushed to save his friend. Akram tackled him to the ground, preventing his own electrocution.

"Let me go! She's dying! Let me go!" Kyle screamed, fighting to get free.

"You will die too stupid!" Akram yelled back, struggling to keep him down.

Amid their struggle, the generator flatlined. Kyle and Akram looked up from the ground to see Kimberly still standing. White smoke wafted around her. She released the thick, ruptured cable, which hit the ground, kicking up dirt with a thud. Not even a spark spat from it as it lay there dead.

"Kim?" Kyle quivered.

Fear of her falling flat on her back overtook them. It lifted as she slowly turned to face them.

Kimberly's eyes said it all as they glowed a blazing bright white like her mother. She survived the deadly ordeal, absorbing the generator's electrical output now stored within her cells.

"Holy shit…" was all both boys could utter in amazement.

"You guys stay here," Kimberly commanded, "I'll be back in a split second."

"But the battle is that way," Kyle stated while pointing.

"I need to generate speed if I'm going to deliver an IMP to Mister oogly."

Before they could ask her to explain, Kimberly took off with a leap, going airborne. She closed her eyes as she soared higher and higher, her mind focusing not on thoughts of fictional characters she watched on YouTube but on her mother.

Kimberly filled her head with images of her soaring through the sky, racing to save her from her first attempt at flight. No longer did she have to dream or wonder who her mother was. If she was a good person, if she ever loved or wanted her. Her picture was clear, and her mother was who she wanted to grow up and be.

"Now fly," Kimberly whispered to herself.

Unlike her mother, the electrical power within her surged and crackled about her form before concentrating around her legs. It caused an ion thrust, igniting an earth-shaking sonic boom, propelling her at unimaginable speeds through the air. There was no time to be fascinated with her achievement. Kimberly had to go faster to circle the Earth and save her friends.

Akram and Kyle stood flooded with emotion, being the first to see their friend take flight.

"Dude, did… she say… she was going to do an IMP?" Akram asked.

Kyle's eyes widened as he, too, realized what his friend just said.

"Infinite Mass Punch!" They both screamed, jumping up and down with joy.

"Dude! Let's get back to the beach!" Kyle shouted, "we definitely don't want to miss this!"

They both scurried as fast as their young legs could take them, returning them to the battle.

~ ~

Back at the beach, the fighting was at a very bad stalemate. The Regulators did their best to switch off attacks to keep the Draugr at bay, but their best assault tactics only staggered him. It did not help that he was enjoying the battle immensely.

"More! Give me more! More!" he roared.

The Draugr swung his massive broadsword, missing Heavy Element, who ducked just in time. Although he knew his dark metal form could withstand the hit, he feared the strike would knock him to the other side of the island. He would not allow a stupid move to take him out of the fight alongside his teammates.

"Oh shit!" Heavy Element yelled, using his forearms to block.

The Draugr again revealed his inhuman speed as he followed up with a savage front kick from his size thirty boot. Even in his metallic form, it radiated down his arms through his spine, knocking him off his feet, back first into the sand, several yards away. He had no time to recover as the Draugr leaped into the air to bring his gargantuan sword down on top of him.

Heavy Element covered up the best he could for the blow he would never feel as an orange-haired Angie leaped on top of him to take the full impact of the strike to her back. She smiled at a stunned Adrian as the Draugr's blade sunk deep into her back.

"I got you, sweetie," Angie whispered to him.

She gently stroked Adrian's cheek with the back of her hand before the Draugr ripped her away, tearing her in two before him. He simultaneously flung her upper and lower halves yards away from each other.

"You son of a bitch!" Heavy Element howled.

Draugr raised his massive blade high to deliver another murderous blow.

"You shall join your tin bitch…!"

He never finished his obscene sentence, nor did he get to go for the kill.

An ear-deafening sonic boom sandstorm overtook Heavy Element and the rest of the team. When it settled, the Draugr was no longer on the island.

"What the…?! Where the hell did he go?" Adrian demanded, looking around.

Rogers pointed to a blip in the sky that he believed to be the Draugr whisked away by something or someone.

~ ~

With a waist full of Draugr, Kimberly soared higher and higher into the heavens.

The terror and fear that crippled her during her first flight attempt were gone. Anger and determination filled her as she focused on removing the invading behemoth from her mother's island.

A disoriented Draugr, hammered by the elements, realized too late what Kimberly, traveling five times the speed of a space shuttle, had in store for him.

Kimberly's speed increased the second she exited Earth's atmosphere, ripping out of Earth's orbit. She counted ten more seconds in her head before putting the brakes on releasing the Draugr into the vacuum of space, where he howled with insanity, still clutching his sword.

Disorientation also overtook her as Kimberly spun out of control in the freezing, weightless black. She calmed herself, using short bursts of energy from her hands and feet to upright herself.

Kimberly finally stabilized and took in her surroundings. She was a ten-year-old floating in the vast universe, and it was beyond beautiful to her. Kimberly cupped her mouth, trembling with emotion; the Earth looked like a pretty sea-blue marble to hold in her hand. She snapped out of her euphoria, remembering she had to return to the island and find her mother. She powered up again, rocketing back to Earth.

~~~~~~~~~~~~~~~~~~~~~~~~~~~~~~~~

The Regulators regrouped back on the beach while attempting to figure out who quickly dispatched the Draugr before their very eyes. Merge violently threw a soaked and restrained Jiang Shi onto the beach's sand while her brother recovered the two halves of Angie. Despite the psychopathic juggernaut tearing her in two, she still functioned as she chirpily wrapped her arms around his neck while nuzzling against his chest.

Adrian gave in to her this time, chalking it up to her weird AI programming, saving him from a possible deadly blow. Angie's sister, Jennifer, stood off to the side, sneering at the bizarre scene of affection.

"Why don't you two get a room, or better yet take that crap to the other side of the island."

"Don't hate because you ain't got a man," Angie said.

"I'm not your man." Heavy Element groaned while rolling his eyes.

Rogers walked over to Erica, sitting in the open cockpit of the SAM armor, looking up at the sky.

"What the hell happened?"
~~~~~~~~~~~~~~~~~~~~~~~~~~~~~~~~

"Someone with a huge ion reading just swooped in and took him," Lady Tech answered flatly.

Rogers nodded as if he was accepting her answer.

"Took him where?"

"From the traces of energy signature left behind. I'd say straight up," Lady Tech said, pointing, "and whoever did it… is coming back… like right now."

The battle-weary team did not bother to go on the defensive as Kimberly touched down on the sand before them with her clothes partially tattered and scorched.

"Let me guess," Rogers said, walking up to her. "You're Dennison's kid."

"Yeah, where's my mom?"

Before Rogers could answer, Akram and Kyle ran down the beach to meet up with their friend.

"What the hell was that?!" Kyle yelled. "I thought you were going to do an IMP!"

"I did too do an IMP!" Kimberly yelled back at him.

"That was no IMP!" he shot back.

"It was too!" She got louder. "I was moving too fast for you to see it!"

"What the hell is an IMP?" an irritated Abe asked.

"Infinite Mass Punch," Lady Tech and Heavy Element recited in unison.

"Dude, you did an RFB, and you know it!" Akram jumped in.

"An RF what?" Rogers inquired with a cocked eyebrow.

"Remove from battlefield," Lady Tech and Heavy Element recited in unison again.

"All right!" Rogers raised his voice, throwing his hands up. "You two knock off the acronyms! Young lady, what did you do with the Draugr?"

"He's either headed to the moon or Mars," Kimberly answered with a shrug.

Erica cracked up, laughing in her cockpit.

"Good riddance," Heavy Element chimed in.

"Now, where's my…?" Kimberly started to ask again.

The sound of thunderous shockwaves shaking the heavens answered her unfinished question. Kimberly's new keen eyes and Erica's headset were the only ones to view Sophia trading godlike blows with Peace as they streaked across the skies, jockeying each other for position.

Kimberly advanced to take off again, but Rogers quickly grabbed her arm.

"Whoa! Where do you think you're going, young lady?"

Kimberly turned to him with a glare.

"I'm going to help my mother."

"I think you need to sit this one out," Rogers advised her.

"I think you need to let go of me, mister."

Kimberly's eyes surged brightly, revealing her emotions; Erica decided to step in before everyone witnessed Sarge embarrassed by a little girl.

"You can't go dressed like that," Erica interjected. "Jennifer, take her to the Warthog to get the spare gear. It should fit her just fine."

"Yes, ma'am, come on, super mini-me, let's get you suited up."

Rogers reluctantly released Kimberly. She did not glance at him as she ran, following the android back to the Warthog. Abe turned disapprovingly to Erica for usurping his command.

"Don't give me that look," Lady Tech bluntly fired from her cockpit. "You weren't going to stop her on your best day. We also need the extra muscle to end this quickly. Peace and Dennison are too evenly matched, and judging from my readings, if we don't end their fight immediately, a lot of people are going to die, and we might not have a planet left when all is said and done."

CHAPTER 25

Goddesses warred on high, shaking the blue sky as they continuously clashed, searching for an opening and a blow to fall the other. This was Sophia's first aerial hand-to-hand combat fight, especially with her equal, who was possibly stronger than her.

Sophia had six years to become a natural flyer, pulling from countless resources depicting feats of flight and fighting. Peace was also a skilled aerial combatant.

As she charged to deliver a blow, Peace strafed to avoid it, coming back with a punch of her own to take Sophia's head off. She would not be there as she used her version of an aerial flash move to evade her attacks, a trick Sophia picked up from watching anime cartoons. With a thought, she executed powerful bursts of speed.

The times they were lucky enough to land a shot weren't enough to knock the other out of the sky, as they would quickly recover and return to attack again.

During their fight, Sophia realized that Peace possessed all her physical attributes on a greater level but none of her mental abilities. A relief that gave her some edge. With that knowledge, she decided to get creative.

Sophia brought violent thunderclaps to the skies over North and South America as she executed a series of flash bursts around Peace. As she expected, it was enough to overwhelm and frustrate her. Sophia found a big opening. Enough to deliver a seismic right cross.

Peace would not recover this time as she spiraled out of the sky, crashing into the heart of Rio de Janeiro. Sophia cursed herself, wanting to avoid further destruction, but there was no way to contain this fight like before. She dived to where Peace fell. Her mind raced with still no clue on how to stop her.

Before Sophia could even land, a recovered and enraged Peace knocked her out of the sky and through the top floors of a JW Marriot hotel. Her recovery time was truly far superior to Sophia's.

Peace's other edge was her disregard for life or property as she tore a giant hole through the hotel to get to her.

Residents and tourists ran through the streets, screaming for safety as they crash-landed through the second floor of an office building. They went through the floor, exploding out the front window of a restaurant located on the bottom floor on the opposite side of the building.

Sophia shook the cobwebs out on her hands and knees before springing to her feet. She had no time to process the insanity of the fight she was in. Sophia shut out the cries and screams around her to focus. Peace had figured out how to employ her version of Sophia's flash step, hitting her with a powerful forearm that she barely blocked. The force of her blow pushed her two feet backward.

Sophia retaliated with an arsenal of strikes she pulled from all three Ong Bak movies and "The Raid: Redemption."

The ground shook and trembled as Sophia unloaded a barrage of elbows, forearms, knees, and shin kicks with bone-breaking intentions. The shots she got in could total a tank. However, Peace was her physical equal and not without a fighting style, which also consisted of forearms, elbows, knees, and, when all else failed, picking up something heavy and hitting her with it.

First, Peace picked up an old dirt bike, clobbering her with it. She went to hit her again, but Sophia swatted the cycle away, opening herself up to a kick to her chest, drilling her back first into a car. Peace charged going on the offensive. Sophia managed to sidestep her barreling through, using her momentum to slam her face-first into the vehicle's roof. She did it thrice, caving in the driver's side of the car with her face.

Peace stopped the skull-bashing by using her forearms to block the next hit. She spun around, delivering an elbow to knock her off. Sophia rolled with the blow, gripping the driver's side hood. Lifting the entire vehicle up, she swung it with ferocity. The split second before it connected, Peace fired an eyebeam blast cutting through the car, which ignited the gas tank, blowing it up in both their faces.

Flames, smoke, and shrapnel were all Sophia saw for a couple of seconds, forcing her to spin around. It left her wide open for a chokehold, crushing her breathing. Feeling Peace's legs attempting to wrap around her, she widened her stance to keep from being pulled down, knowing that if she succeeded, it would be over.

Sophia's first thought was to take to the sky and shake her off, but she would have to bring her legs together to achieve flight. Right now, between fighting to keep her chin tucked in, holding her stance, using one arm to prevent a scissors leglock, and the other attempting to pry one of her arms from around her neck in hopes of slipping out, Sophia was in horrible shape.

As Sophia struggled to break free of her planetary crushing grip, she felt intense heat-generating near her face. The inside of Peace's semi-clutched right fist began to glow as she focused on channeling raw energy in the palm of her hand.

"Science question for you, Doc." Peace seethed. "How much nuclear energy do you think is needed to blow up this dirtball of a planet? Let me give you a hint, an estimated fifty thousand kilotons times sixteen thousand. Now the next question is how long you think it'll take me to generate that amount of power."

"No!" Sophia groaned.

Sophia began to violently thrash around, fighting to break free, but each move allowed Peace to cinch in her rear neck, body scissors choke even tighter. She could feel the energy she was channeling increase with intensity as her arm moved from the side of her face near the back of her head. Sophia gurgled and fought to stay on her feet as she struggled to grab her hand, harnessing raw Earth-killing energy while attempting to keep Peace's arm from sinking into her neck.

"Now… now," Peace growled, "you can't have both. You can't stop me from finding an opening to tear your head off and save the planet at the same time. You have to **choose**. Personally, I'd choose the one I know I'd probably survive in the next sixty seconds."

Sophia's eyes became blurry. Her body trembled as her neck was losing the battle to stay tight. Her heart quickened as she realized that if she did not stop struggling, everyone she loved and cared about would be dead in a flash. It was the opening Peace needed to finally slither her arm around her neck like a python and clamp down around her with her body scissors lock. She dispersed the energy in her fist to focus on pulling. Sophia's mind went semi-blank on the first tug as she gasped at the immeasurable force she was using to rip her head from her torso.

Sophia's body went into a violent seizure as she fought to remain on her feet through the ordeal. The only thought echoing through her mind was that she regretted wishing to die back in 2008. She wanted to live. Three days was not enough time; she needed more time.

"You know why I chose to exile you instead of killing you on the sand of the Sahara?" Peace snarled. "Because as crazy as this may sound, you were the only semblance of family I had. Whether you want to believe it …that nuke bonded us. All you had to do was stay gone. Now, this only ends one way."

Sophia squealed as Peace continued to pull. Her eye began to flicker as she felt her neck about to snap in two.

"And just so you know, this little sacrifice of yours saved no one." Peace whispered to her. "I intend to pull real slow… so I can hear you die screaming. And then I and your pretty little head will be making family visits… and my first stop will be…"

Peace's words were silenced by the shaking of the Earth and the sound of exploding glass. It was as if a fighter jet was flying at street level. She turned to see the source of the mayhem coming right at her—the topic of her unfinished sentence.

Peace became so transfixed on what she saw her grip loosened, not bothering to evade what was coming at her. A screaming Kimberly delivered her version of the Infinite Mass Punch, connecting with the side of Peace's face. The entire area detonated with a seismic blast that shattered windows and brought down already weakened structures.

Peace sent flying lost her grip on Sophia. She crashed through several small buildings, racking up mileage before slamming into the side of Sugarloaf Mountain. A landslide of rubble buried her.

Sophia lay on her side, curled into a ball, trembling and groaning as she clutched and cracked her neck while severely stretched vertebrae and torn muscle fibers began to heal. Kimberly landed and then ran, sliding to her mother's side to check on her.

"Mom! Mom! Are you okay?!" Kimberly frantically asked.

Sophia, realizing it was her daughter, forced herself to sit up. She grabbed her, looking her up and down and then into her eyes with rage and fright.

"Oh my god!" Sophia screamed. "What did you do?! What did you do to yourself?! You promised!"

"I came to help you!" Kimberly responded with a hurt look.

"I don't need your help! This is not a stupid game or comic book!"

"I know that!" a frustrated Kimberly yelled back.

"Then you need to get out of here!" Sophia sternly ordered her daughter.

"Mom, no! Let me help you!"

"I said to go!" Sophia roared at her daughter, "Get out of here now!"

"Mother, no! Listen to me, dammit!" Kimberly shrieked back at the top of her lungs.

Sophia fell quiet as Kimberly's white glowing eyes blazed, mirroring her emotions. At that moment, she saw anger and determination. She saw herself.

"Mom," Kimberly said with a calmer tone, "when this is over, you can treat me like a little girl all you want, but right now, I have to be your equal. If we don't work together to stop Peace, many people will die, and the planet might not survive. Your fighting could eventually destabilize the planet-destroying it. Lady Tech told me this."

Kimberly's words brought Sophia to her senses. She turned to where a buried Peace lay. She figured they had less than a minute before she busted out. Realizing Kimberly had similar bracer gear to hers, Sophia quickly grabbed her arm, sliding open the compartment, revealing another personal computer.

"Did Lady Tech show you how to set this up?" Sophia feverishly asked.

"No, she..."

Sophia cut her off with a hand wave, opening the compartment to her computer.

"Vincent, are you still with me?" Sophia asked her personal AI.

"I am still functional, Ms. Dennison," he responded through her bracer's speaker system.

"Can you patch into my daughter's bracer and then guide her to the location of the Eye of Ra?"

"Yes, I can," Vincent confirmed.

"Who?" a bewildered Kimberly asked.

"Do it now," Sophia commanded him before turning to her daughter. "His name is the Eye of Ra. He won't be too hard to spot. When you find him, tell him this."

Sophia quickly grabbed her daughter, whispering in her ear. Kimberly's eyes widened as she absorbed her mother's instructions.

"Do you understand?"

"Yes," Kimberly answered with a quick nod.

Sophia pulled the earpiece from Kimberly's bracer, attaching it to her right ear.

"Put this in your ear. Vincent will tell you where to go. Once you find him, text me immediately. Now go. Go now!"

An explosion of rock and rubble announced that it was too late as a savagely enraged Peace torpedoed herself toward Kimberly. Seconds before contact, Sophia intercepted her furiously, sending them both crashing and rolling to the ground. Sophia managed to get a mounting position, straddling her while holding her arms down.

"Go!" Sophia turned, screaming at her daughter.

Kimberly shook herself from her frightened trance, turning on her heels and, taking to the sky again, flying as fast as her power could propel her.

Sophia turned her attention back to Peace only to get hit with a head-removing eyebeam blast to the face. She screamed as it felt like she was being scalded by a blow torch. She grabbed her right hand, gripping it around Peace's eyes to block the beams. Peace retaliated by rifling Sophia's ribcages with machinegun body blows and then backhanding her off.

Sophia rolled off, springing to her feet, while Peace performed another Kip Up, landing on her feet.

Sophia performed her version of a flash step, darting over to Peace, executing a whirlwind legsweep, taking her feet from under her, and dropping her on her back again. Sophia then leaped into the air, roaring as she delivered a trademark Bruce Lee double foot stomp.

Peace employed her flash step to roll out of the way within milliseconds of being stomped as she cratered the ground, descending a good fifteen feet.

Sophia exploded out of her hole, taking to the air as an oncoming semi-truck was javelined at her. She eradicated it with a low-level energy blast from her hand, unaware that it was just a diversion tactic used by Peace to slam into her, propelling them both into the sky at crushing speeds.

~ ~

Back in Washington, Shintobe's body was brutally cannoned through a skyscraper. She would have stopped if the building she tore through was not sheared in half by Wendigo's sonic blast, sending her slamming violently into another building.

Dropping a good twenty feet, Shintobe was able to get her feet underneath her, landing on them. The impact blew out her right knee in the process. She used her right-handed sword to keep herself propped up. Her left-handed sword was lost during the building's first impact as she clutched her ribcage on the right side. Her breathing was shallow and difficult, signaling that her ribs were cracked. If she stayed put a couple more minutes, they would heal along with her knee.

The trembling of the ground and the vibrating of the windows to darkcore music meant she did not have a couple more minutes. Shintobe quickly pulled up her mask, revealing her lips and spitting blood on the concrete before pulling it back down again.

Wendigo hovered ten feet from her with a sadistic Cheshire grin. She had been toying with her mouse, and now it was time to feast. With no striking distance and a bad wheel to run on, she prepared for the worst.

"Your music sucks ass!" Shintobe yelled, gripping her sword.

Wendigo raised her left hand-delivering the killing blow.

It was delayed by Kimberly plowing into her. Her sonic shielding was the only thing saving her from being broken in half as they cratered the streets of downtown DC. Now, in the heart of Wendigo's sonic output, Kimberly's body shook as her vision became blurry, and her brain felt as if it was about to explode from her skull while she held onto the front of Wendigo's trench coat.

Wendigo screamed and howled, fighting to get away as part of her headset slid from her skull, significantly reducing her sonic powers' effect. A dazed Kimberly realized that she was trying to protect her iPod Touch.

Fighting through the soundwaves that could pulverize an average human's bones to dust while turning their brain to goo and detonating their heart, Kimberly tore the Apple device from her grip. The sadistic Wendigo reverted to a sobbing, bawling child reaching for her iPod.

Kimberly crushed it in her hand, stopping the music and her power. Wendigo collapsed onto the ground, wailing hysterically. She curled into a fetal ball, clutching and clawing at her skull, unable to be consoled.

Kimberly stumbled around, getting her vision back as her body and insides stopped rattling. Shintobe, almost healed, limped over to her, placing a hand on her back.

"Thanks for saving my ass. You alright?"

Kimberly held a finger up as she turned and hurled up the remaining food in her system and bile.

"Yeah, you're alright."

"Have… to… find… Eye… of Ra," Kimberly groaned.

"Don't think he'll be too hard to find," Shintobe said.

Kimberly turned to where she pointed to see a purple and black fireball crashing two blocks up from them, tearing up the street.

A rattled Revenant struggled to his feet as the Eye of Ra descended, landing in the streets with a concrete cracking thud.

The second in command of the Zombie Nation wasted no time retaliating as he unleashed dark matter energy at the Egyptian demigod. Ra raised his staff, absorbing it.

"We should help him!" Kimberly yelled, preparing to take flight.

Shintobe placed a hand on her shoulder.

"Hold on. I think the big man wants to handle this little scuffle 'hombre a niño.'"

"But we don't have time!" A frustrated Kimberly shouted, turning to her.

"Trust me."

Shintobe gave her a pat.

"I don't think this will take long."

The Eye of Ra waded through Revenant's energy attacks, advancing toward him with purpose. Realizing that his streams and volleys were ineffective against him, the dark matter wielder switched to channeling dark, solid constructs. By focusing, he created two ginormous fists that mimicked the physical movements of his own hands.

This show of power did not halt the Eye of Ra's forward motion. Revenant roared as he threw a right haymaker that tore through the street, heading straight for him. Ra responded, meeting the blow head-on with a cosmic-charged right fist, shattering the construct. It sent a shockwave that shattered windows and drove parked cars into storefronts. He continued to advance.

"Stay back!" Revenant frantically yelled.

This time, he dropped his right constructed fist for a hammer blow. Using his staff, the Eye of Ra created a gold construct of an ancient Egyptian shield to block and destroy his second attack on impact. His continued advancement broke Revenant's nerve.

Revenant's first thought was to flee as he took to the skies, but a faster and stronger demigod also took flight, facing him twenty feet up. With a backhand fist, he swatted Revenant out of the sky, dropping him awkwardly onto the hood and windshield of a Toyota RAV 4.

"Ooooh! He brought out the Egyptian pimp hand!"

Kimberly quickly turned to a cringing, energetic, and highly vocal Shintobe, wondering who was the woman under the mask as they watched the one-sided beating taking place.

Revenant slowly rolled off the damaged mini SUV as the Eye of Ra returned to Earth-shaking the ground now towering over him.

Revenant held a hand up, displaying a twitching smile, attempting to reason with him.

"Now… now. No need for any further violence. You've proven your point exponentially, dear sir. I surrender."

"You must be punished for your crimes," Ra's voice calmly boomed from underneath his mask.

"Yes… I imagine I should be punished for my crimes, but not today!"

Revenant lashed out with one final act of defiance, touching the Eye of Ra's armor breastplate with his hand to absorb and destroy its properties. Instead, the armor temporarily changed to the black and purple color scheme of the dark matter energy he wielded before reverting back to gold.

"I… don't… understand." Revenant gasped while falling back against the vehicle. "I have the power to absorb matter itself… I wield the darkest of powers…"

"But I wield the oldest," Ra answered, "one that gave birth to the universe itself."

Before Revenant could honestly plead for his life, the long metallic scorpion tail attached to the back of the Eye of Ra's helmet coiled up and struck him deep in his right side, taking him three inches off the ground before releasing him.

Revenant dropped to his knees and hand while clutching his right side, going into convulsions with drool pouring from his mouth. His eyes' black and purple glowing hue slowly disappeared, turning to his normal light blue eyes.

"What… did… you… do… to me?" Revenant asked while scraping the ground.

"I manipulated your DNA," the Eye of Ra retorted, "sealing your power to absorb matter. And now for your crimes against humanity. I banish you to quadrant 674910."

"Where… is that?"

"You pride yourself as an agent of hell," the Eye of Ra replied. "Allow me to reassure you that what awaits you in quadrant 674910 will make your romances of hell seem like a heavenly paradise. The beings there have ways of keeping you alive for centuries as they fulfill their curiosity, slowly figuring out what you are. My advice to you the second you hit the ground… is to run, hide, and pray not to be found."

The Eye of Ra's staff lit up, creating a portal underneath a screaming Revenant falling into the unknown. Kimberly covered up her ears to shut it out. The portal was sealed with the dimming of the staff.

"Now that's gangsta," Shintobe said with an approving nod.

Kimberly cautiously walked over to him as the faceplate to his helmet slowly retracted, revealing his warm, dark face and piercing golden-brown eyes. He turned to face her, startling her enough to jump back one step.

"My mom… needs your help; she said you'd know what to do."

The Eye of Ra nodded, ready to give assistance.

~~~~~~~~~~~~~~~~~~~~~~~~~~~~~~~~

Sophia stood up in the middle of downtown Mexico City. Around her once again was destruction, screaming, and people running. It was the apparent theme of the entire day.

"Run! Get far away from here!" Sophia yelled in Spanish.

She remembered Peace taking her high into the sky after throwing the truck and using it as a decoy. Before they got too high, Sophia rang her bell with three stiff elbows to the back and side of her skull. She slipped out of her grip and turned the tables on her, taking her downward at tremendous speeds. Nothing in their way stood standing or was unscathed when they hit.

"All I wanted was a husband, two-point three kids, a house, and a Pug named Puddles."

Sophia sadly shook her head.

"Now, this is my life."

She had to stop this mass destruction world tour as quickly as possible. She prayed that Kimberly found the Eye of Ra to help her put an end to this. First, she had to find Peace, whom she lost in the impact.
~~~~~~~~~~~~~~~~~~~~~~~~~~~~~~~~

"Where are you, you bitch?!" Sophia screamed at the top of her lungs.

Her answer came from a war cry and a bomb-dropping kind of sound. Instead of dashing out of the way, Sophia threw her forearms up to take a double forearm axhandle strike meant to split her head open. The ground cratered on impact. Sophia roared back, wrapping her arms around Peace's waist like a python, and detonated an overhead belly-to-belly suplex, hurling her through the front window of a small local bar.

Sophia charged into the bar after her, only to get the literal bar thrown at her. With a backhand, she swatted it out of the way, giving Peace the opening she needed to deliver a charging shoulder tackle, sending them both into an old car, turning it into a boomerang while putting it halfway through the front window of a restaurant on the other side.

Sophia battered her back with a series of elbows, refusing to let up herself. Tired of getting her back pulverized, Peace shot up, knocking her arm away, smacked her with a right cross, staggering her. Peace then threw a left, which she blocked with the right forearm. Sophia's bell still rang as she fought back, cracking her nose with a vicious headbutt and then caving in her chest with a dropkick, putting her through the wall of a building across the street.

Sophia pulled herself to her feet, leaning up against the wrecked Cutlass. The ringing disappeared as her brain stopped swimming, allowing her vision to focus again. Enough for her to see Peace also staggering through the wall; she got knocked through. She stopped to blow blood snot from her nose. It was clear they were both inflicting severe damage to one another. Their regenerative healing worked overtime to keep up with the fatal injuries they sustained.

"You selfish bitch!" Peace howled. "You couldn't do a hundred fucking years!"

Sophia felt her arm vibrating. She knew it was a message from Kimberly telling her she found the Eye of Ra.

"If you're going to start monologuing, you can choke on it," Sophia shot back, "because you're done."

"Now who's monologuing, bitch?!" Peace returned fire. "Either that or you have somehow officially gotten brain damage from me bouncing your skull from country to country! Popping shit like you got a final form to pull out of your ass!"

Sophia answered her remark with a smug look.

"Bullshit," Peace scoffed.

Sophia's face did not change. Peace's face turned into a scowl, building to infinite rage.

"Bullshit! I'm calling bullshit!" she screamed at her. "You're a lying ass bitch!"

Peace stomped around, throwing a fit while pacing back and forth.

"There's no way! There's no goddamn way you're that powerful!" Peace pointed at her, roaring. "You would have shown it already! Bullshit!"

Sophia gazed down at the ground before answering her.

"You know I'm not a real fan of that anime. The fight scenes and power increases are drawn out and ridiculous. I prefer the type of anime where power is defined by mere action."

The Earth violently shook as Sophia sank into the solid concrete that could no longer hold her weight. She had to hover to keep from falling further, which made things worse as her thrust's sheer force created a massive sinkhole underneath her. The circumference of the hole was so immense Peace had to hover over the ground, and surrounding buildings disappeared from around her. The bottom of Sophia's boots began to tear apart, unable to contain the thrust she was discharging. Slowly, her eyes began to blaze and pulsate, along with the veins and major arteries within her body glowing through her skin.

God-like power brought silence between the two for the first time since their battle began in Washington.

Peace's disgusted glare said it all.

"You always find a way to make me feel small, and I hate you for it."

Sophia's glare said, *"I don't care."*

~ ~

Back at Sanctuary, the Regulators mended their wounds, surrounded by the liberated villagers. Lady Tech, leaning up against her SAM armor, stood up, startled by the instruments on her bracer lighting up and screaming at her.

"Oh shit."

Erica broke into a sweat as she deciphered the readings.

Rogers walked over to find out her reason for using profanity.

"What is it?

Erica nervously turned to him.

"Remember that additional power I recorded from Dennison? That I said, she can only tap involuntarily?"

"She can tap it at will."

"Uh, huh."

"How bad is it?" Rogers asked.

"Judging by this, she's slowly building her own gravitational field."

"Like a planet?"

"Like... the sun." Lady Tech answered, shaking her head in disbelief. "And if she doesn't stop or get away from the Earth in the next five minutes, she'll rip this planet out of its orbit and tear it apart."

~~~~~~~~~~~~~~~~~~~~~~~~~~~~~~~~

Regret filled Sophia's heart with what she was doing, the destruction she was causing. All of this was on her; somehow, she would have to make amends. This was a last resort she pulled out of her deck to put her plan into motion.

A fearless Peace was not intimidated seven years ago, and she would not be scared now as she closed the gap between them with a flash step.

Peace's attempt to close the gap led her into a right cross, juddering half of the planet. It sent Peace from the middle of Mexico City across the Atlantic Ocean, heading to Africa's Northern tip. The world came to a standstill as the entire planet quaked from
~~~~~~~~~~~~~~~~~~~~~~~~~~~~~~~~

Sophia's movement, darting across the sky to catch up with her. Just as she expected, Peace had not recovered from the first hit, leaving her open for the second one before she hit Western Sahara.

An uppercut shook the planet again, sending her upwards into the upper atmosphere. Sophia, like a bloodhound, hunted after her. The farther she moved from the Earth, the less it vibrated. Once again, she caught up in seconds, slamming into Peace, taking her into space.

Sophia's current speed took them past the moon in seconds. Anything in their path was obliterated upon impact, including a near-Earth asteroid almost half the moon's size. She kept going, closing in on their destination, one of the Eye of Ra's portals. This one was made massive, so she could not miss it.

Sophia knew within the vacuum of space and the short distance to the portal, Peace would not have the time to fight back and escape. However, for it to be successful, Sophia had to go through the gateway with her. She closed her eyes as tears froze on her face and broke off. Her heart was shattered because she would have to break her daughter's heart again.

Sophia's eyes opened as she felt something powerful slam into her right side, breaking her grip on Peace and taking her out of the range of the portal. Shocked and dismayed, she realized it was Kimberly with her arms wrapped around her waist. She released her mother while reversing her thrust. Sophia, stabilizing herself, finally realized that her daughter had changed her plan.

The Eye of Ra, also floating in the dead of space, powered up his staff, shining brighter than any star in the known vicinity. He unleashed a powerful stream of cosmic energy, striking Peace. The force of the blast sent Kimberly into a nearly uncontrollable tailspin. Sophia also had difficulty stabilizing herself. It felt like the entire universe shook from the raw, unbridled power.

Evading the blast was unavoidable for a disoriented Peace. It was unclear how much physical damage his attack had caused. It was, however, strong enough to knock her through the portal. It closed and dispersed within seconds.

~~~~~~~~~~~~~~~~~~~~~~~~~~~~~~~~

Exiting the portal, a slow-recovering Peace realized too late that she was in the middle of a part of the ending universe. With all of her strength and power, she would not be able to escape.
~~~~~~~~~~~~~~~~~~~~~~~~~~~~~~~~

Consumed by the crushing ancient force of a black hole wiping out a small patch of the universe light-years away, Peace screamed and roared to her doom.

~~~~~~~~~~~~~~~~~~~~~~~~~~~~~~~~

Back in Earth's solar system, Kimberly finally regained control, ended her spiraling, and flew back over to her mother. She slowed herself down, using small bursts to float over to her. Kimberly noticed the veins and arteries underneath Sophia's visible skin glowed blue like her eyes, which blazed like a newborn star. They slowly died down, turning her skin back to normal. Sophia swayed a bit, fighting to stabilize herself; the taxing pressure of focusing so much power took an unknown toll on her body.

"Are you all right?" Kimberly asked, using sign language to communicate with her.

It was then Sophia realized a new change within her daughter. Kimberly's eyes had gone from a glowing white to a bright golden hue similar to the energy the Eye of Ra wielded.

"Oh my god," Sophia frantically signed back, "what did you do?"

"First, I hitched a ride with him," Kimberly smiled while signing. "Traveling through his portal is crazy! But before that, when I told him of my plan to save you. He told me I wouldn't be able to catch you at my current level. So he let me borrow a fraction of his power. It was the only way to pull this off."

"No." Sophia shook her head. "This is not what I wanted. I did not want this."

"I wanted this," Kimberly sternly signed back, "nothing is taking you away from me again. So I did whatever it took so I could save my mother because I knew you'd do whatever it took to save the world. That's the type of mom Mark told me I have."

Ice formed again around Sophia's eyes, which she knocked away as she pulled her daughter close. They held each other close as the universe melted away, leaving just them.

~~~~~~~~~~~~~~~~~~~~~~~~~~~~~~~~

They flew back to the Earth accompanied by the Eye of Ra, who did not pull another disappearing act. Thanks to Sister Shareef, they first headed to Mount Vernon to find her parents safe and alive.

Although unplanned, it was also an excellent introduction to the granddaughter they never knew they had. Her parents encouraged them to go to Sanctuary while Sister Shareef hung around to look after them. They decided to use one of the Eye of Ra's portals to take a captured Nachzehrer.

~ ~

Arriving at the island in a matter of seconds, they found the Regulators and their other extended family on the beach where the battle took place. They found that the village was much worse for wear after locking Nachzehrer in a stasis pod on the Warthog next to Jiang Shi.

Aside from some scrapes, bruises, and one still functioning android torn in two, no lives were lost, making it an all-around perfect victory. The Regulators' hearts became heavy, primarily for Sophia and the villagers, remembering it was not a clean victory for them. None felt it more than Rosann, who sat on the beach alone, staring into the endless ocean.

Erica started to walk toward her, but her brother touched her shoulder, halting her. With a headshake from him, she understood that Rosann needed some space and that no amount of words would console how she felt.

Brave children and some older adults crowded around the Eye of Ra, enthralled by his appearance. He bowed, greeting each of them with a humble smile, and picked up a couple of toddlers that wished to be held by him.

Sophia found a minute to personally thank him for his pivotal help in defeating the Zombie Nation, especially Peace. He respectfully bowed to her with a child in one hand and his staff in another.

"It was an honor assisting you… Ms. Dennison."

With a smile, Kimberly came up behind her to thank him.

"Thank you for helping me save my mom, but if you don't mind, I'd like to give your power back to you, if it's possible. I don't need it anymore."

A look of astonishment was plastered all over Sophia's face as she turned to her daughter.

"What?" Kimberly said with a shrug. "I'm a child. I'm not ready for this kind of responsibility."

"The energies of the Wakening will always be bonded to you," the Eye of Ra revealed, "but I can bleed off some of the energy so it will grow with you. In time, you will be ready for it."

As she agreed with a nod, he extended his staff for her to grasp. It appeared to be burning her hand as it glowed. However, Kimberly felt no pain as the golden pulsating energies revealed through her eyes slowly dimmed to a faint, warm white glow. As the staff powered down, she swayed slightly as a concerned Sophia grabbed her.

"Whoa!"

"I'm okay," Kimberly replied, steadying herself. "I'm okay."

"Very few beings in this universe would willingly surrender such power," the Eye of Ra stated with a smirk. "I had faith it would be in good hands before I gave it to you. I was correct."

Erica walked over to the trio with a broad smile on her face.

She pointed to the Eye of Ra before turning to Sophia.

"You and I really need to talk. And you, Ms. Dennison, are just full of surprises. The type that makes one want to wet their shorts, but surprises, nonetheless. So a black hole."

"Yep," Sophia answered with a sigh. "It was the only force in the universe that I knew that was more powerful than the energies she absorbed and that her RDH ability could not defend against. Hopefully, she'll be forever trapped within its crushing gravitational pull, and with no energy to draw from, she'll eventually burn out in a century… maybe two."

"What about that energy projectile you hit her with?" Erica asked, turning to the Eye of Ra. "It registered off the chart with my readings."

"Solid light photons, she absorbed no energy from me."

Erica thoughtfully pointed to him again.

"We definitely have to talk. So how long have you been able to tap your reserve energies?"

"Since 2011," Sophia said while looking down at the sand, embarrassed. "During one of my trips to deep space, I tried to duplicate a certain technique that will remain nameless. Next thing I knew, my veins began to light up like Christmas trees, and nearby asteroids began to form an orbit around me."

Erica and Kimberly looked at each other and then burst into laughter as the Eye of Ra brandished a smirk on his face, comprehending the joke.

"Don't laugh!" Sophia pouted with a stomp. "I was out there for like two days figuring out how to power down, which was almost impossible because I kept absorbing vacuum and electromagnetic energy! It also takes a massive toll on my body!"

Her plea and explanation did not end the laughter.

"I'm sorry!" Erica choked. "I'm just picturing you out there screaming and waiting for your hair to turn yellow!"

Amid the laughter and celebration, Rogers's communicator went off. He checked the caller's I.D. on his bracer and patched in via his headset.

"So, how long am I suppose to babysit David Draiman's illegitimate offspring?" Shintobe's voice came through. "She's just laying here drooling all over the pavement of DC. It's like mad depressing."

"I can ask the big man in gold to open up one of those portals so you can bring her to us," Abe said with a smirk. "I'd like to thank you personally for a job well done."

"Now, you damn well know I retired from the spotlight," Shintobe scoffed. "You want to thank me. Buy me dinner sometime."

"You got a deal. We'll be there in a couple of minutes to collect her. Thanks for everything… champ."

"You too… champ," Shintobe returned.

Abe cut off his communicator, turning to see Lady Tech looking at him from afar with a sly smirk.

He made a gesture, wondering what her problem was.

"Oh, nothing," Erica grinned, whispering in his mind, *"just wondering when*

you were going to tell me that you had the Queen of Queens on speed dial."

"Don't know what you're talking about," Rogers shot back, *"and get out of my head."*

"Sure, you don't."

After checking to see that every last one was alive, not severely injured, and counted for, Sophia went to the Rogers to extend her gratitude for saving her island and people.

"I'm in your debt, Sergeant," Sophia said while holding a hand.

"This isn't all our doing," Rogers answered as he shook it, "that little girl of yours takes after her mother. She's the one who took down the Draugr."

A wide-eyed Sophia, in disbelief, slowly turned to point to Kimberly a few feet off, talking to Kyle, Akram, and the rest of the kids about how she had helped her mother save the world.

"She did?"

"She sent that son a bitch to an ice-cold hell where he belongs," Rogers explained while pointing upward. "That's one hell of a kid you got there."

Sophia smiled, looking at her.

"I'm finding that out every day."

"Miss, I am detecting an EVO inbound," Maxine announced out of nowhere. "Energy signature is similar to..."

Before she could confirm, the intruder landed, sending sand spraying everywhere. Villagers scurried away, screaming behind Sophia and the battle-ready team, curious to know who would attempt to attack them when they were at their strongest. As the mini sand storm rested, the beach became silent in disbelief.

"What did I miss?" an exhausted Oliver asked with his left arm in a sling.

The uneasy silence remained as Erica covered her mouth while her eyes poured like a fountain. Her body trembled as if she was about to collapse.

Adrian also stood there, running his hand through his hair and shaking his head. His eyes could not keep dry either as he shook his head in disbelief.

Rogers was the first to move as he holstered his sidearm and walked up to Oliver. He stood toe to toe with him, giving him a slow look over.

"Sir, I…" Oliver began to formally report in.

He was stopped as Abe grabbed him by the back of his neck, pulling him in for a hug that took everyone aback, especially Oliver. He held him tight as if he were his son, making it impossible for Oliver to contain his emotions.

Rogers finally released him, still holding the back of his head as he looked him in the eye in disbelief that it was him.

"Thought we lost you, son," Rogers's voice cracked.

"I thought I lost you all," Oliver said with a smile.

A wide-eyed Erica stepped forward, searching for an explanation.

"How? You were gone… for almost two hours… you weren't breathing, there was no heartbeat, no brainwaves… how?"

Oliver pulled out Adrian's platinum crucifix from his sling, holding it up. Erica, close to falling out, turned to him.

"You? You did this?"

Adrian answered with a shrug, wiping his eyes.

"I couldn't let my best gaming buddy go without a fight."

"But how?" Lady Tech pressed.

"It's from your lessons, you stressed how the virus genetically transformed our bodies, making us different from regular humans. When I went to go see him off, I touched his hand; it was still warm even after all that time. It was a gamble, but I figured brain functions took longer to die for people like us. Something you probably missed because you were distraught like the rest of us, so before I left, I took a chance and hooked up the defibrillator to him. I set it to its highest level, hitting him with a jolt every two minutes for thirty minutes. Everything else I left at the Big Man's feet upstairs. Hoping He understood that we needed him more than He did."

Erica smiled, realizing how amazing Adrian was when he was not acting like an adolescent and how she was still one in some ways.

The awkward silence returned as a doe-eyed Rosann slowly approached. Everyone on the beach and the world disappeared at that moment, leaving just her and Oliver. Inches from him, she seemed as if she was about to back away and run as he smiled at her. Slowly, she reached out, touching his chest. Her eyes widened as if it was the first time she felt it. The more she touched it, the less she could contain her tears.

Rosann traced her hands on both sides of his chest; she gave it a hard tap before running her right hand up to his neck to his face, touching his cheek. He grabbed and held her with his good arm as her legs went out from underneath her. Her uncontrollable sobs of joy delivered tears to everyone watching.

"You heard me," Rosann cried in his arms. "You heard me and came back to me."

"No, I didn't," Oliver whispered with a smile, "but you can tell me again."

Rosann told him again with a deep kiss. He answered her back, kissing her deeper.

It triggered cheers and applause from everyone, even those not privy to the whole story. To them, it was as memorable as "The Kiss" photo. The battle was over; Sanctuary and the world were safe once again.

Amidst the celebration, Lady Tech saw Rogers with a sour look returning to his face. She indiscreetly sauntered to him to see what troubled him amid their monumental victory.

"There's still more work for us to do. Isn't there?"

"Yeah, we have a lot of work to do."

~~~~~~~~~~~~~~~~~~~~~~~~~~~~~~~~~
~~~~~~~~~~~~~~~~~~~~~~~~~~~~~~~~~

1000 Defense Pentagon, Washington, DC:

Rogers marched through the Pentagon's halls with Erica in tow, making a beeline for Secretary Graves's office. Anyone who attempted to stand in his way he violently threw out of it. Those who witnessed his act of violence wisely moved out of his way. He pushed through Graves's double Oakwood doors to find him sitting behind his desk as if waiting for them.

"By all means, do come in and have a seat," Graves greeted them with sarcasm.

Rogers, walking up, pulled out one of the visitor seats. He removed his sidearm, placed it on the desk facing Graves, and then sat.

"Now, what may that be for?" Graves inquired, motioning to the gun.

"It's to shoot you in the face with, if I find out you've been lying to me," Abe flatly answered.

He turned to Lady Tech, doing a scan via her visor.

"Found it," she confirmed.

She extended her hand, employing telekinesis to rip the metallic disk from Grave's forehead and the fake skin patch.

Rogers finally turned to Graves, giving him a dull look.

"My team and I just got back from the North Pole," Abe began, "where we tracked down and captured the last member of the Zombie Nation held up in a barge partially stuck in an iceberg. We confirmed that all of the original occupants except one were dead. They kept this poor bastard alive to fabricate the weapons and gear they used against us. The rest were killed and tossed overboard to be chow for fish or polar bears.

Interestingly, this barge was top to bottom R&D we found from body armor, weapons, and a butt load of other tech that only my friend here could decipher their application. All this shit fell into the hands of a murderous psychopathic bitch, and her equally psychopathic goon squad. And what gets my goat is that this barge and everything on it is related to a project that was supposed to be completely shut down seven years ago. This is where you determine whether I ask Ms. Champion to wait outside while I shoot you in the face."

Graves inhaled and exhaled as he leaned forward in his chair to look Abe in the eyes.

"The genetic side of Project EVOlution was shut down," Graves dryly answered, "however, that was only a small fraction of the project. As you are both well aware, not all of us are blessed with your "attributes." We still employ several hundred thousand non-superhuman troops who defend this country. The latest tech and weaponry are under development, and our other facilities are meant to equip them in the near future.

As you probably already figured out, we shuffled D.E.A.D members to the facilities when they needed to familiarize themselves with weapons or equipment for their missions. Not the other way around. This is why she knew the location of that facility and possibly others."

"How many others are out there?" Rogers demanded to know.

"That information is classified," Graves huffed, "and you will have to shoot me before I divulge that to you. However, I will say ninety percent were closed near the ending and beginning of 2008 and 09. And before you chew my head off about irresponsibility, Sergeant, the report after the destruction at Mount McLoughlin was that all four members of the D.E.A.D were D.E.A.D."

"You knew she had possession of that barge," Erica snarled, "didn't you? How long?"

"Does it really matter?" Graves answered with a simple smile, "it's over. The members of the Zombie Nation are either dead or captured, #3 finally eliminated, the world and its leaders all safe because of your efforts."

"You're not making an argumentative case for me putting a slug in your brainpan." Abe declared while leaning forward.

"For what, Sergeant?" Graves scoffed, "a couple hundred casualties? You're a soldier; you know battles are never clean. And the majority of that blood is on the hands of #3 and your new best friend. You want to kill me because of our government's methodology of warfare? I hope you brought enough bullets because you'll have to shoot everyone in this building, the Senate, the House, and then make your way to the White House."

Abe and Erica glared at Graves, hoping to burn a hole through him. His Teflon demeanor made him impervious to their death stares.

"You superhumans think you know real power because you can lift heavy objects, fly, or move things with your mind. Real power is about progression and building a network of like-minded individuals to ensure that progress continues to move forward.

That network would happen to be the United States Government, and our progression is superior to any known force in the universe. The world believes that Asia is now the leader in technological advancement, which we want them to feel. Because the final key to real power is a better poker player than everyone else, they never ever see your hand… until it is too late."

Graves's words unsettled Erica.

"No need for the disturbed looks." Graves exhaled while rolling his eyes. "This is how we've done business since the founding of this nation. And in my opinion, it's far more honorable than using religion to brainwash simpletons into suicide bombings."

If there was humor in Graves's last statement, neither Abe nor Lady Tech found it, and Graves did not care as he picked up his own tablet and started to scroll through his email.

"Now that we've established that we're still on the same team, you will excuse me as I have more pressing business to attend to. Consider your saving the world a free pass on intending to assassinate me in my own office."

Rogers sat there for a minute more as Erica looked at him, wondering what else he had planned. He slowly rose from his chair, holstering his pistol from the table. He then about-faced without a word, leaving Graves's office. Erica cut the Secretary of Defense one final dirty look before following him out.

"Why did we just walk out?"

"Was he lying about anything?" Rogers flatly asked.

"Don't answer a question with a question," Lady Tech shot back, "and no, shockingly, he was telling the truth."

"He was telling the truth about some things. He's still a lying son of a bitch and hiding something."

"Language," Lady Tech reminded him.

"Sorry," Rogers said flatly. "We still don't have any grounds to blow his brains out."

"So, what's the plan?"

"The plan is to keep doing what we're doing," Rogers answered, "while working to find the answers while on the inside."

"Which means remaining dogs of the military," Erica sighed.

"Say what?"

"An anime thing," Lady Tech dismissively said, "explain to me why we didn't bring up the Holy Grail?"

"Because he would both deny it and know that we know about this Holy Grail," Abe responded, "as long as he doesn't know, we're free to search and find out what the hell it is."

"I like that plan," Erica nodded.

"Me too," Rogers grunted.

~ ~

Graves continued nonchalantly sitting and reading his tablet as Mendes walked into the Secretary of Defense's office.

"Are we clear?" Graves asked.

"Yes, sir, we've also swept the office; there are no traces of a bug of any kind."

"Well, that was interesting." Graves said, clearing his throat.

"I don't understand how you were able to hide the truth from her, sir," a baffled Mendes said.

"Ms. Champion should have taken the time to focus on her natural abilities, then maybe she would have been able to pick up what her devices could not detect."

Mendes still wore a face that said he did not know what Graves was talking about until a woman with light brown hair and gray eyes in a black two-piece power suit walked into the Secretary's office, standing at attention before him.

"This is agent Lockwood." Graves introduced her. "One of our top C.I.A field agents and also a Promethean Class Ten EVO. She's been monitoring the Regulator team and informed me that the good Sergeant was en route to this office, which is why I ordered you to tell security to stand down when he arrived. She was a couple of offices down monitoring the conversation. She's capable of cloaking herself from Ms. Champion's scanners while feeding me 'mental whispers.'"

"Subliminal suggestions that helped him believe whatever he spoke at the time was the truth," Lockwood clarified. "I was also able to hide confidential information about Project EVOlution within his mind from Ms. Champion. She was doing quite a bit of browsing."

"While she was snooping in my skull, did you find anything in Rogers?" Graves asked.

"Unable to, sir," Lockwood answered. "She had a mental tether on him, sort of like a security system. If I attempted to enter the Sergeant's mind, she would have known I was there. Even at her level. She also employed some form of psionic field to shield their conversation as they left the building."

"The little minx does cover her bases," Graves nodded.

"By the way, sir," Agent Lockwood relayed, "Dr. Alexander wanted me to relay to you that the crops have been fertilized and that we shall have a perfect harvest."

Graves smiled while flipping through another screen.

"Thank you, Agent Lockwood."

With a nod, Lockwood exited the office, leaving Mendes and Graves.

"Sir, what should we really do about Sergeant Rogers?" Mendes asked.

"He and his team saved the world, which includes our current Commander in Chief. There's not much we can really 'do' about him for now."

"With what we now know of Dennison?" Mendes hesitantly inquired, "is it wise for us to continue?"

"Now more so than ever," Graves said with a sigh, "if this incident has taught us anything, we must bolster our efforts to create a response to ensure that nothing like this ever happens again. I have just been informed that after my term of office is over, I will be directly appointed the official new head of Project EVOlution, and I will need a second in command."

Mendes swallowed deeply as he positioned himself as straight as an arrow.

"I would be honored if you consider me for your possible second, sir."

Graves gave a dry smile without answering him, still reading his tablet.

"Oh, look, it appears we may have a possible chocolate shortage… and I love chocolate."

~~~~~~~~~~~~~~~~~~~~~~~~~~~~~~~~~~

The Grand Canyon National Park, 2,245 miles away from the nation's capital, at an undisclosed location at the bottom of the ancient riverbed, housed a government research facility one mile down underneath the canyon. Doctor Alexander strolled around the facility with a tablet, viewing readings from four huge metallic vats.

On a table, his assistants handled DNA samples labeled Doctor Senji Kumamoto, FBI Houston Forensics office, on September 3, 2008. The name S. Dennison was printed at the very bottom. Positioned next to them were refrigerated samples labeled male reproductive cells. One batch of samples was labeled "R. Matheson – April 2002," and the other was labeled "B. Matheson – October 2012."
~~~~~~~~~~~~~~~~~~~~~~~~~~~~~~~~~~

CHAPTER 26

Three months after the epic battle around the world, a sense of normalcy had returned to the planet. Despite the carnage and destruction, the human race moved forward as always.

Because the Ranch sustained severe damage, mainly in the prison area known as Purgatory, the only option left to deal with the remaining members of the Zombie Nation, Jiang-Shi and Nachzehrer, was giving them the same fate delivered to Revenant. Exile. With the Eye of Ra's assistance, he banished the remaining adult members to two hundred and fifty uninhabited planets with Earth-like atmospheres, not under the territory of the Dominion Council's races. No one bothered to inquire what the Dominion Council was.

The unspoken truth was Erica could have easily repaired Purgatory and placed them back in confinement. Given the opportunity, no one felt they deserved to be anywhere on Earth, and the Regulators weren't executioners.

The Eye of Ra departed through one of his portals without clearly explaining who he was or where he came from. He promised he would not be far or hard to reach if the Regulators or Sophia needed him.

As for those not exiled, it was agreed that Wendigo was dubbed mentally incompetent despite her horrendous crimes to understand the atrocities she caused. Her current catatonic state also made her a threat to no one. Erica mercifully found a low-level frequency to ease her suffering while preventing her from using her abilities.

She also contacted her parents, informing them that their daughter was alive. However, they declined to see her when she explained who she was and what she had done. She did not need to read their minds to know it was out of fear and embarrassment.

Everyone also reluctantly agreed to show some leniency to Anchimayen due to him still being a minor. Identified as six-year-old Michael Westgate, they confirmed that Peace's grizzly tale was accurate from Caron City, Nevada. With Sophia's help, Erica created neural dampeners to prevent him from using his mental abilities even at his heightened level.

Both Wendigo and Anchimayen were placed by Erica in an undisclosed facility until the repair of Purgatory, where they would receive special psychiatric treatment in hopes of reversing the perverted psychological damage done by the Zombie Nation.

Justice was not the only thing dispensed. The world had to bury their dead and mourn, especially those who paid the ultimate price to keep it free from Peace's clutches. A special memorial for superheroes dubbed "The Garden of Heroes" was created in Washington, DC, remembering the bravery of the fallen Defenders of Justice, Heat Seeker, Lady Electrify, and Captain Omega.

Captain Omega's statue depicting him in his costume stood in the front of the Memorial next to Power Hour's monument, also shown in his costume.

Upon his direct and ironclad orders, Abe sent Oliver and the twins home to be with family. Before Oliver could go home, he had to visit Rosann's family. As she told him, her mother immediately took to him while her father wore the wall of no one being good enough for his daughter. It lasted fifteen minutes as Oliver endured and survived a brutal grilling of his intentions toward Mr. Esposito's youngest daughter. Adrian playfully chiming in from the sidelines did not help matters. Three days later, she would journey with him to Milwaukee's hometown to endure the same treatment from his mother and three older sisters. She, too, would barely survive due to the antics of her twin.

Erica followed suit, taking some much-needed advice, and went home. Just as Sophia predicted, a family was waiting for her.

~~~~~~~~~~~~~~~~~~~~~~~~~~~~~~~~

Sophia took her own advice, traveling with her daughter to a residential part of Queens, New York. As expected, their landing drew attention, especially in a white and brown painted row house with a green chain link fence. Her three nieces and nephews were spilling out of the front door with joyously shocked looks on their faces.

"Auntie Sophee! It's auntie Sophee!" they all screamed, ecstatic to see her.

They all became quiet, standing at the gate as they noticed Kimberly standing
~~~~~~~~~~~~~~~~~~~~~~~~~~~~~~~~

beside her. Sophia looked up to see her nervous little sister, close to tears, standing in the doorway of her house. The children all backed up as they entered the gate.

"Children, this is your cousin Kimberly." Sophia introduced her with a smile. "My daughter. She's ten years old."

Kimberly shyly waved at everyone. They all waved back with the same shyness. Being around her age, Gemma's eldest was the first to walk up and greet her with a bright smile.

"Hey, I'm Natasha,"

"Hi," Kimberly answered, returning the smile.

"You like Dance Revolution?"

Kimberly nodded, then turned to her mother for approval.

"Go introduce yourself to your aunt first," Sophia instructed, "and remember… light steps."

"Yes, Mom."

Kimberly walked up the steps, standing before her aunt. Gemma did not hesitate to hold her hands and give her a look over.

"Nice to meet you, Auntie Gemma," Kimberly addressed her with a nervous smile.

"It's so great to meet you, Kimberly." Gemma greeted her with a trembling smile of joy as her eyes ran with tears. "You are so beautiful."

"Thank you," A blushing Kimberly replied.

"Please go on inside; I hope you like cookies and bun and cheese."

"Yes, thank you."

As all five children entered the house, Gemma cautiously walked down the steps to meet her sister in the middle of her yard. Sophia's demeanor became similar to their last encounter as she neared her, stopping Gemma in her tracks.

"You hurt me, you really hurt me, Gemma, and I don't know if I can forget about what you said and did to me."

Gemma bowed, preparing for the ax her sister had grinding for her.

"But I have to find some way to forgive you," Sophia's face softened as she said, "Almost losing Mom and Dad put a lot of things into perspective, that and watching Frozen a couple of times."

Gemma was unsure if she should lift her head until she felt the warm touch of her sister's hand on her face, igniting her to burst into tears again.

"You're a spoiled, miserable little brat… but you're my baby sister," Sophia reaffirmed, "and I still love you."

Gemma rushed into her sister's arms, bawling as she buried her face in Sophia's chest. She clung to her for dear life as if she feared falling.

"Sophee, I'm sorry! I'm so sorry!"

Sophia fought back her own tears as she held her sister.

"You tell me, 'I'm sorry' one more time; I'm going to crack your neck like a chicken. I'm tired of sorry. Let's just be good to each other, like we're supposed to be."

Gemma slowly raised her head, nodding in agreement.

"I'd like that."

With her arm around her little sister, Sophia walked into a home she had not acknowledged in over seven years. Each step she took extinguished the anger and hatred that had been burning throughout her. Dropping the most massive weight she ever had to carry, she could breathe easier again; Sophia learned that she could still mend and heal even the deepest of wounds.

~~~~~~~~~~~~~~~~~~~~~~~~~~~~~~~~

Back when the Ranch was still under construction, big and small Doozers performed repairs and rebuilds to return the Regulators' base to the operational status it once was before Peace's attack. Rogers stood alone in the central command with a smile on his face. The cause was his infant grandson on the large screen flailing his arms,
~~~~~~~~~~~~~~~~~~~~~~~~~~~~~~~~

making baby sounds, and blowing spit bubbles at him. Holding him in his arms was his second eldest son, with his wife beside him.

"He's definitely a Rogers," Abe acknowledged with a grin. "You two did a wonderful job."

"Well, she did all of the work," his son laughed. "I just started screaming when the head came out."

His wife playfully nudged him.

"Thank you, Dad," Rogers's daughter-in-law replied.

"Your mom would be proud of you both."

"So… Thanksgiving?" His son asked, changing the subject.

The wounds were still raw; she was always missed.

"And Christmas," Rogers confirmed. "I'll be there. I can't wait to hold him and see all of you."

"Sergeant Rogers, sorry to interrupt," Maxine spoke from the audio system, "The Miss is on the other line; shall I have her call back."

"No, I'll take it, just give me another minute."

Rogers turned his attention back to his family.

"I got to run."

"It's okay." His son said with a nod. "Dad… Mom would be proud too."

"You know I love you guys, right, Mike?" Rogers asked, lowering his head. "You, Oscar, and Sarah… I love all three of you."

"We love you too, Dad," Mike answered with a grin. "Talk to you soon."

The screen switched to a beaming Erica sitting in her bedroom with an anime t-shirt. She snapped a playful salute.

"Sergeant."

Rogers returned with a causal two-finger salute.

"Lady Tech, how's the family?"

Erica rolled her eyes and shrugged before she answered him.

"The first day was your typical crying and glad you're home stuff. The next two days were kind of awkward, but I'm learning to keep my mouth shut and listen. It's not perfect, but it's getting better."

"Good to hear."

"Maxine informed me our recruitment headcount has reached one hundred and fifty," Erica said with a smile.

"Something we can deal with when you get back," Rogers sternly reminded her.

"On an off-topic, I spoke to Oliver and the twins."

"Me too, I spoke to Oliver last night, and Adrian reported in today," Rogers replied. "They all wanted to come back this coming Friday, but I ordered them to take the additional week; I think it's too soon for anyone to be here."

"Then why are you there?" Erica asked with a motherly tone. "Maxine and the girls are there; the base is self-automated and practically runs itself. You don't need to be there to oversee the repairs."

Rogers bowed his head and grunted before he gave her his answer.

"I'm a… superhero now, someone has to be here."

A deep smile from Erica formed from his words.

"See you soon, Sarge."

Rogers tilted his beanie to her.

"See you soon, Lady Tech."

He signed out on the screen, alone once again.

"Maxine, let's start from the last candidate we left off from," Rogers requested.

"That would be candidate fifty-eight," Maxine answered, "shall I read off the file to you like before?"

"Sure, why not."

The screen lit up again, revealing a file of an EVO candidate for the Regulator program. Maxine began with her name and age.

~~~~~~~~~~~~~~~~~~~~~~~~~~~~~~~~

Sophia stood on the sands of her island with Sister Shareef, looking out into the ocean's blue waters. With her and Kimberly's help, Sanctuary residents completed all repairs to the island in under a month. Thankfully, no soul was lost during the battle with the Draugr and Jiang-Shi.

Sister Shareef stood in her white tank top and jeans shorts, gripping the soft white sand with her toes while drinking in the island's beauty and the beach. It had been almost two decades since she had seen the sunshine over anything other than prison walls. Sophia glanced at her friend in her black and yellow bikini top and blue jeans shorts, who was now free and felt complete.

"Damn, beautiful place you got here, girl." Sister Shareef acknowledged. "Damn, beautiful."

"You know there's a home ready for you if you want to stay," Sophia said, extending an invitation.

"Island life ain't for me; I'm a Texas girl. I was born there, and I will die there. Not to mention I got family I got to get back to and fences to mend."

"Well, you know, if you need anything," Sophia said while nudging her. "You got family here."

"Well, I got to come back," Sister Shareef smirked. "Seeing as Mr. Earl has been talking me up, something fierce these past few weeks. He got a thing for big girls like me."
~~~~~~~~~~~~~~~~~~~~~~~~~~~~~~~~

"Shareef, you've been locked away a long time. Please, do not kill that man."

"The man's a former soldier," Sister Shareef scoffed. "He's been in dangerous places before."

"Shareef," Sophia emphasized her name with a bit of bass, fighting to be serious.

"I ain't gonna hurt him!" Shareef's voice went up a couple of octaves to reassure her friend, "too bad."

The two women, no longer able to fight it anymore, broke down laughing. Sophia was close to tears as she touched her friend's shoulder.

"So now that you've saved the world **again**, what are you going to do? All eyes are on you now." Shareef inquired.

Sophia took in some air and then exhaled as she gazed out into the ocean.

"I can't turn my back this time, even if I wanted to. The funny thing is, I feel ready, kind of welcoming it."

An impressed Shareef stepped back a bit.

"Okay, now. What brought this on?"

"You remember the last white slavery brothel I shut down in Ukraine?" Sophia asked.

Sister Shareef nodded, remembering the uncomfortable story.

"Well, I went back to shut down my counter operation. My handler, Olia, wasn't too pleased, but she understood after I explained to her the new direction I had to take. I released the criminals I brought down, taking off their collars, which were for the best. Their reputations made it impossible for them to carry out the tasks I set them to do.

I then warned them to find a more legitimate profession because I would be back to shut them down for good if they started up again. One of them said I need not worry because between myself and someone named "Brother Paul," the skin trading business was no longer worth it. Curious about who this Brother Paul was, I asked around and went looking for him."

A deep smile grew on Sophia's face as she continued her tale.

"I arrived at this once abandoned monastery. It looked like it had some major renovation work done to it. You can hear the children's laughter before walking through the gate. They were of all ages, along with a lot of women, both young and old. Some of the older women tended to the children; you could faintly see that they all came from someplace not so pleasant, but their smiles told otherwise.

As I walked around and talked to some of the women, they began to tell me their stories of slavery and the day this "Brother Paul" liberated them, brought them here, took care of them, and began helping them build back their lives. A lot of the women actually stayed on to help him take care of the younger children. After a couple more minutes, I finally saw him and almost fainted."

"You knew him?" Shareef asked.

"I sure did," Sophia said with a nod. "It was the superhuman from the last brothel I took down. His name is Kostyantyn Yurchenko. He walked up to me a bit nervous at first, and the first thing he asked is if he could give me a hug."

Sister Shareef instantly swatted away mist as she listened to the beautiful tale of redemption.

"We walked for a while, and he began to tell me about his life before we met. How he grew up poor with his mother and no father, and how he watched the men his mother brought home walk all over her and abuse him. It taught him to be hard to survive.

He said he never personally abused women and children, but he also had no respect for them. When he got his powers, it was an added bonus to make more money, especially as a hired bodyguard, until the day he ran into me. He said the scolding I gave him stuck more than anything else. No one had ever talked to him like a mother to a son."

Sophia shook her head with a smile and some disbelief that this was her life.

"At first, he didn't know what to do. He wandered around, picking up odd jobs here and there. Then he came upon the monastery. He didn't know what overtook him, but something told him to fix it. Before he knew it, he took orphaned children and runaways off the streets and gave them a place to eat and sleep.

He kept doing odd jobs to pay for food and clothing and encouraged them to attend school. Next, women who were either homeless or in abusive situations started to come seeking protection, and he just took them in as well. One day, he overheard some men talking about going to have some fun at a brothel similar to those I brought down. He followed them there, busted the place up, took the women with him, and cared for them. All of them."

"Wow." Sister Shareef gasped. "How's he financing that operation?"

"He flat-out jacks the pimps," Sophia laughed, "all of it goes toward the victims and the monastery's upkeep. He calls it their 'donation' in repentance against their wrongs. Apparently, it's set off a chain reaction of some kind. Through him, a lot of the women have found the strength to take back their lives.

He's become their big brother and father to the children. I gave him a sizeable donation, which he tried to refuse, and I introduced him to Olia. With her information network, they can work together to track and end these horrific operations."

"So you were the blinding light that struck him down on his road to Damascus," Shareef chuckled. "And put him on the right path, hence the name "Brother Paul."

"I guess so, but he wasn't the only one who learned something on that day. I learned I don't need to break bad men to make a better world. I just need to inspire good ones."

"Amen," Sister Shareef rejoiced, "Amen."

"I remember telling Charlie, when I decided to pull that stunt in Washington in 08, that I was tired of running," Sophia confessed. "Since I came back after surviving that nuke, all I've been doing is running. Fighting Peace again was a revelation, the world has changed, is changing, and I played a huge part in it. I can't turn away from my responsibilities anymore. Ten, maybe fifteen, years from now, a whole new generation of EVOs will reach maturity; if we don't want a repeat of what happened three months ago, I have to lead by example. Try to make a better world for everyone to live in."

"Well, girl, you know I got your back."

"You really gonna suit up?" Sophia asked with a cracked smile.

"Child, I'm a pardoned ex-con, fifteen years shy of retirement age, and now a grandma." Sister Shareef answered, cutting her eyes. "What else am I going to do?"

"I'm glad you're my friend," Sophia came out of the left field, telling her, "It's the only good thing that came out of what I went through at Mountain View."

Sister Shareef nodded as the mist began to form again around her eyes; she quickly wiped them, flicking them away.

"You're not my friend," Shareef corrected her; "you are **my sister**."

As the two women gazed upon one another, reaffirming their friendship, a gust of wind picked up, drawing their attention to Kimberly in her wetsuit hovering several yards up. She returned from swimming with Kyle, Akram, and the other children.

Kimberly tilted her head with a perplexed look.

"Were you two going to kiss?"

"No!" both women yelled back at her while putting some extra distance between each other.

"Oh, okay, Auntie Shareef, can I speak to my mom for a minute?"

"Sure, sugah, I'm about to go find me some Mr. Earl anyway."

Shareef spun on her heel, walking back to the village.

"See yawl later."

"Shareef!" Sophia yelled, getting semi-serious. "Do not kill that man!"

"Not listening to you!" she responded, adding a little more sashay to her walk.

Sophia shook her head, watching her leave as Kimberly slowly descended back down to Earth.

"Why is Auntie Shareef going to kill Mr. Earl?" Kimberly raised an eyebrow, asking.

"No, honey," Sophia blushed. "She's not really going to kill him, she's..."

Not prepared to have that talk with a daughter she has only had for a couple of months, she decided to change the subject with a smile.

"What would you like to talk about?"

Kimberly looked down while using her big toe to doodle in the sand.

"School is around the corner, and I miss my friends in DC."

Sophia nodded with a smile that fell a bit.

"You want to go home."

She wanted to avoid this talk for a bit longer. The past few months, even throughout the island rebuild, saw their relationship grow exponentially. It took her several days to get over Kimberly calling her mom without breaking into tears.

However, a small part of her knew that homesickness would kick in; her child built a life for a second time without her, and as much as she wanted to keep her, it was not fair for her to keep her from it.

Kimberly met her mother's gaze with a sad, confused look.

"I thought this was my home?"

This made Sophia bewildered.

"Okay, I'm confused," she vocalized. "You want to go back to Washington to live with Michelle, right?"

Kimberly quickly shook her head.

"No. I just want to go back to my old school. Flight time is like thirty to forty-five minutes both ways, depending on how fast I go. Maybe you could take me till I'm old enough to fly on my own."

"Yes!" Sophia blurted out. "Yes, I will take you."

She smiled as she cupped her daughter's face.

"And this is your home," Sophia reassured her.

"Uh, Mom." Kimberly fumbled around her next question.

"Yes?" Sophia coaxingly asked.

"When I was born, and if we never got separated, what would you have named me?"

Sophia's eyes filled with tears as her heart felt like it would pop into her chest. It was a question mixed with both joy and sorrow.

"I wanted to name you after my Aunt Vannie on my mother's side, short for Vanessa."

"Well, I'm kind of use to Kimberly being my first name, but Vanessa could be my middle name… Kimberly Vanessa… Dennison."

Her words opened up the floodgates within Sophia, who moved closer to her.

"I'd like that," Sophia whimpered. "I really would…"

Sophia kissed her daughter's forehead and grabbed her, whisking and twirling her around as if she was still an infant.

"Mom!" Kimberly screamed. "I'm ten years old!"

Sophia pulled her in for a hug.

"And you're still my baby. You're still my baby…"

Sophia broke down, crying with joy as she held her daughter. It would not be the last time she would weep; she was sure of it. Nevertheless, that heaviness in her heart and the emptiness in her stomach were forever gone. Kimberly also gave in, breaking down; that feeling of loneliness and abandonment would never return. She was home; she was truly finally home.

"Mommy…" Kimberly groaned between her sobs.

"Yes, baby?" Sophia asked.

"You're… still... stronger… than me."

Sophia erupted, laughing with joy in between her cries. She loosened up her grip, but she never let go. She would never ever let go again.

CHAPTER 27

Two weeks later, Sophia sat in her powder room in a robe surrounded by her daughter, Sister Shareef, Michelle, her little sister Gemma, and her mother with a no-too-pleased look.

In front of her sat a silver case delivered yesterday by Abe Rogers himself. It was her new outfit constructed by Lady Tech.

"Honestly, I don't know why we're making a fuss over this?" Sophia asked, rolling her eyes.

"Mom, it's your coming out party," Kimberly lectured. "People worked really hard for this."

"For what?! I'm wearing some stupid costume, not coming out of the closet! And even if I was, I wouldn't make this much of a fuss! And what was wrong with the original outfit I had?"

"Gal, you a supahero!" Mrs. Dennison scolded her, "You fi look like a supahero, not like ya ah come from dance hall!"

Her grandmother's comment made Kimberly cackle. She quickly stopped as her mother said, "No, you are not laughing at me glare."

"Okay," Sophia huffed, "let's get this over with."

She stood up, flying open the latches to the case opening it up. Sophia reached in, pulling out another full bodysuit-with a hood attached in a different red and black color scheme minus her old suit's silver pattern. It appeared as if the red and black seamlessly flowed together. The new material had a dull shine to it. Inside were also new boots and bracers to match the outfit.

What caught Sophia's attention were the emblems on both shoulders of the outfit. The Fawohodie, a West African symbol of freedom, was designed in gold. She slowly ran her hand across it.

"Everyone in the village helped me pick it out," Kimberly said with a smile, stepping in. "I contacted Lady Tech and asked her to work it into the design."

Sophia swallowed, understanding the responsibility of such a symbol.

"I… I'm not…"

"Yes, you are," Kimberly stopped her. "Everyone who I spoke to about this said the same thing. Whether it was from oppression, poverty, abuse, drugs… you gave them back their freedom, and that's what your name should be."

"Amen," Mrs. Dennison's rejoiced with a crackling voice and glossy eyes. "What a powerful name! Betta den some of dem foo-foo names out dere!"

Sophia saw a chain reaction of waterworks about to begin and decided to break it up with a clap of her hands before it got contagious.

"All right! Out! Everyone out, so I can put this thing on and come out! Everyone but Michelle, I need her to help me with something."

Michelle closed the door behind her as the rest of the women exited the hut. She turned perplexed to see a near-teary Sophia motion for her to come closer.

Sophia was hesitant as she held both Michelle's hands, looking down at the ground before looking up at her with a trembling bottom lip.

"I never got the chance to properly thank you for taking care of my baby."

Michelle broke Sophia's grip, cupping her face to wipe her eyes as her tears fell.

"Thank you for sharing her with us and for giving **me** back my husband."

They hugged each other, confirming a bond never to be broken, one to last for an eternity.

~~~~~~~~~~~~~~~~~~~~~~~~~~~~~~~~~~~

A half-hour later, the door to the hut opened. Sophia slowly walked out onto her porch, adorned in her new suit. Her heart swelled and overflowed, gazing out at the reception, waiting for her.

Before Sophia stood a sea of people who were now her family. She knew each of their names and all of their stories. It did not dawn on her till she stood there, seeing them all together in one place what she had done.

A tidal wave of emotions overtook her as she covered her mouth, failing to fight back running tears.

Her reaction brought tears to other people's eyes. A misty-eyed Earl clapped and cheered, encouraging others to do the same to break up the waterworks.

It gave her the courage to walk down her steps and stand before them.

"Honestly, I don't know what type of hero I'm gonna be crying on day one."

"An awesome one!" Mrs. Dennison yelled from the crowd.

Creating a sea of laughter as her father held her mother's hand. Sophia began her speech by looking directly at her mother.

"I told one person the reason why I really created this island. What I did not tell her was I did not save one person standing before me today. You all... **saved me**."

Sophia turned, looking at all the faces before her.

"You took away my anger and brought back my humanity. When I look into each of your eyes, you remind me that there is still goodness in this world. That no matter how dark things get, we can rise through it into the light. If evil tries to break us, we can mend, becoming stronger than we were before, and no matter how lost we may feel, we can find a way back. This is what I learned from all of you, my family."

"Amen! Amen!" a choked-up Mr. Norton yelled.
~~~~~~~~~~~~~~~~~~~~~~~~~~~~~~~~~~~

Standing by him, Zeek threw a brotherly arm over his shoulder while wiping his eyes. Mr. Norton did the same, pulling the young man close to him.

"And now, onto why I am wearing this colorful outfit."

Sophia quickly posed before getting serious again.

"I can't ignore anymore that we live in an age of wonderment. In an age where people now have powers and abilities to make a difference for good or evil, which I am responsible for, many good people gave their lives to open my eyes to that fact. With Earl and the council's help, things will continue to run when I am away. Which hopefully won't be for too long."

"We'll hold things down for you, Soph, don't you worry!" Earl yelled.

She touched the emblem on her right shoulder.

"I know why you all chose this symbol for me. Honestly, I don't think I am worthy to carry it or the name, but I give you all my word… I will become worthy, and I will make you all proud."

As Sophia finished her speech, Akram, Kyle, and the village children stepped forward.

Akram began to sing.

"When I get older, I will be stronger

They'll call me freedom just like a wavin' flag."

The children sang their rendition of K'naan's "Wavin' Flag."

Amid the song, Sophia slowly ascended. She looked down at her blood family and extended family cheering her on. Nadiya Romanenko and the twenty-seven, now spread apart within the crowd, standing on their own with their heads held high again. Alison Jefferies, the light she once lost, returned to her eyes, no longer alone.

Most importantly, her little girl with tear-filled eyes looked up at her with pride because she was her mother.

"Go, Mom, Go!" Kimberly screamed.

On her command, Sophia Dennison, now Freedom, streaked off into the blue skies.

~~~~~~~~~~~~~~~~~~~~~~~~~~~~~~~~~~~

Twenty minutes later, Freedom stood on the White House lawn for about an hour and a half. Fifteen minutes after her arrival, a White House correspondent backed by a twelve-man Secret Service team asked what she wanted. Her response was an audience with the President, and she would not leave until she got it.

She looked around, impressed that remnants of the battle from months before were gone.

Eventually, Mohammad came to the mountain. With the detail of six Secret Service men, the President walked onto the lawn to meet her with an extended hand.

"Dr. Dennison, or is it… Freedom now?"

Freedom smiled at his perception and shook his hand.

"Something, my family from my island, came up with."

"So what do I owe this visit from the woman who saved the world… again?" he asked.

"The UN General Assembly is in two weeks." Freedom said, getting down to business. "I am asking you to please play this on my behalf."

Opening up the compartment in her bracer, she pulled out a memory stick, extending it to him. Surprisingly, he took it from her without hesitation.

"May I ask what this is regarding?" The President inquired, raising an eyebrow.

"Peace was a psychopath," Freedom answered, "and her plans for this world would have been horrific. However, through madness, some truths cannot be ignored anymore. Our world has changed; in the next fifteen years, not only will the superhuman race have increased, many will have reached maturity. Some will have powers and abilities to rival my own. That is a fact that cannot be ignored. If we don't want a repeat of several months ago, Mr. President. It's pretty simple… we either evolve… or we die."

He reluctantly nodded in agreement.
~~~~~~~~~~~~~~~~~~~~~~~~~~~~~~~~~~~

"What are you proposing?"

"It's more of an ultimatum." Freedom bluntly corrected him.

The President's face switched from curiosity to concern as Freedom looked up at the sky.

"It's said that God created the world in six days and rested on the seventh. I think seven years is enough time for you and the rest of the world's leaders to get their acts together."

"You want us to remake the world?" The President asked, attempting to understand her weird statement.

"No, I want you to fix it. Let's face it, Mr. President. You all have not been doing a very good job. When representatives selected by the people getting benefits and paid exceptionally well from taxpayers' dollars can shut down the government to fulfill their own agenda… then a good job is not being done.

When the one percent's bottom line is more important than the realistic threat of global warming, something I have personally seen, a good job is not being done. When we are afraid of those who should be protecting us… then a good job is not being done.

When we permit murderous warlords, despots, and cartels to run rampant when we hold white slavery and the exploitation of women and children on a lesser scale to a person walking around with a nickel bag… then a good job… is not being done. And that's just the sprinkle of the problems this world currently has. This world is long overdue for an uprising."

The Commander in Chief lowered his head, contemplating the best Presidential response to her statement.

"Dr. Dennison…"

"I don't want your jobs, Mr. President," Freedom said. "I wouldn't want it in a billion years. I prefer to be a mother… a good one. However, I cannot close my eyes and ignore the millions of people screaming for change that is continuously denied to them because of bureaucratic red tape.

You're going to create real change in this world… all of you. You will all find a way to work together, to do so without compromise. Your timeline is seven years, starting the first day of the General Assembly, whether you choose to play that video or not."

"What happens if…?" he asked slowly, afraid to hear the answer.

"I step in and affect change," Freedom answered, knowing his question. "And so you know I mean business, I'll be doing little projects here and there, so that all of you will know that this matter is not up for debate."

"What if you meet with opposition?" the President inquired.

"They're welcome to try, although I think you've seen how pointless that would be." Freedom laughed. "Like I said, this is not some new tyrannical rule. It would help if you considered it motivation to get your ducks in a row and begin to do the right thing. In time, you won't see this as something you are forced to do; you'll see it as something that should have been done long ago, which was well overdue.

Your actions and mine will inspire humans and superhumans alike that this can be a better world and that we must all work together as a family to achieve that goal. We cannot expect the world and future generations to change and be better if we do not lead by example, and we must start leading by example, not tomorrow, not two years from now, but today."

The President smiled and nodded. Sophia hoped the look in his eyes read that it was hard to argue with her logic. It would not change her decision, but she still prayed he understood.

"You have my word that the UN Council will see your message," the President promised.

"Thank you, Mr. President. Now, if you'll excuse me. I have to do this superhero thing."

"What's that?" He asked with a chuckle.

"Go look for trouble."

The President backed up as Freedom smirked, coiling her legs and launching herself into the air with a mighty leap.

He watched with amazement as she rocketed off, taking flight into the clear blue skies.

He nodded with approval.

"Go get 'em, Dr. Dennison. Go get 'em."

~~~~~~~~~~~~~~~~~~~~~~~~~~~~~~~~~~~

Freedom flew through Washington DC, cutting her speed to a slow cruise, allowing people to see her. Next, she rocketed to New York, doing the same in Times Square, Los Angeles, Houston, and San Francisco before heading to other major cities worldwide.

Freedom wanted everyone to know that, despite losing many fallen champions, one had risen to take up the mantle as their protector. Regular people raised their heads and felt safer that day, while other heroes looked up and saw something to aspire to.

Freedom picked up speed, soaring higher and faster into the skies, remembering those who sacrificed their lives, those who stood beside her and continued to stand beside her. She lost a lot but gained a billionfold in the process. Her only regret was that it took so long for her to realize it. She added another promise to pay it forward.

Freedom tore through the Earth's atmosphere long enough to plummet to the other side of the world.

She did it one time for Charlie.

Freedom imagined him laughing and cheering her on from on high as she finally embraced her destiny willingly.

The world needed a hero… and a hero from that day forward… is what she would be.
~~~~~~~~~~~~~~~~~~~~~~~~~~~~~~~~~~~

CHAPTER 28

Today would be the worst day of Fazilah Abusalih's life. Today, Fazilah turned five years old. Fazilah was born in a small village in Eastern Sudan between the Red Sea and Kassala. She was the youngest child of two sisters and a brother. The night before her birthday, her mother gave her the most considerable portion of Asseeda (porridge), and sheep cooked and slaughtered the night before. That night, her older sister stained her hands and feet with henna.

At dawn, her mother woke her up, gave her breakfast, and took her for a walk. The walk took about a half-hour. As they neared the hut at the end of the village, her little heart began to beat faster. She remembered playing with her sisters in this area less than a year ago and hearing a little girl's screams and cries. When she tried to see where they came from, she was shooed away by some of the village's habobat (grandmothers). The wails became so loud that she had to cover her ears as she ran away. Haunted by the experience, she never returned to play on that side of the village.

Fazilah looked up at her mother, who held her hand tighter as they entered the fenced-in yard. As they walked around the large hut to the back of the yard, all the village's habobat was waiting for them. Her tiny body began to tremble. She was the only little girl in the yard.

Fazilah looked up again at her mother, hoping she would look down at her. She prayed she would look down and see in her big brown eyes that she was terrified and wanted to go home.

As hard as she searched, Fazilah could not find her mother's eyes.

Instead, she would feel her mother's grip loosen as one of the habobat came to take possession of little Fazilah's hand, leading her into the circle of female elders now formed.

In this circle of elders, little Fazilah would be mutilated.

They would force her to lie on the mat in the center of the yard. Several kinswomen would weigh down her torso. Two others would pull and hold her legs apart. The Miriam or the midwife would then take a sharp knife and quickly slice away her clitoris and labia minora; the rejected tissue caught in a bowl they would later toss away.

No words could describe the excruciating pain and suffering of little Fazilah, nor how shattered her heart would be as she screamed out for a mother who would not save her.

Miriam would remove a surgical needle from her midwife's kit to add to her suffering. Threading it with suture, she would sew together the child's outer labia, leaving a small opening at the vulva.

If Fazilah was lucky to survive the procedure or the infection that could occur, on the day she consummated her marriage, her would-be husband would slice her open one more time with the help of a "little knife." This would allow him to penetrate her to impregnate her if she could have children after the damage was done. Even if she was lucky, there was a great chance she would still die during childbirth.

Fazilah's eyes remained on her mother as the habobat laid her down on the mat.

Her little heart began to beat out of her chest. Fazilah squirmed and whimpered as four of the habobat held her down by her tiny torso. She felt almost suffocated.

The tears began to fall as they pried and held her legs open; the screams and cries followed as the knife came into view.

"Mommy! Mommy! Mommy!" Fazilah screamed her lungs out in fright.

Fazilah desperately searched through the cloud of elders, pinning her down, bawling for a mother who would not save her. Despite her petite size, she fought to get free; the Miriam stepped in, forcing her down while scolding her.

"Be still, child! And let us do what needs to be done," the Miriam ordered.

Fazilah gurgled and cried as the habobat used additional force to keep her down. They stretched her little legs further apart as if to rip them off.

As the Miriam prepared to administer her first cut, a mighty wind blew, sending dust flying while the ground shook.

The force of the wind increased as a shadow cast over the group of women in the yard.

Fazilah would not feel one cut as the knife dropped from the Miriam's hand while the many hands of the habobat removed themselves from her tiny body.

Fazilah quickly sat up, seeing her mother again, now on her knees, clutching her mouth in fear. She quickly glanced little Fazilah's way, then back up at the sky.

Screaming began, this time from all of the habobat looking in the same direction as Fazilah's mother and the Miriam.

Fazilah wiped her eyes of tears and stood up, looking to the skies at a memory forever etched into her mind of her fifth birthday.

On her birthday, Fazilah witnessed a hooded, wingless angel in red and black clothing with skin as dark as hers and radiant blue eyes that pierced the day itself. On her shoulders, she wore the symbol of freedom known throughout her homeland.

"Cry for freedom… and I will come."

EPILOGUE

Billions of light-years away from the Earth's solar system, something floated amongst the stars, answering the question as to whether humans were alone in the universe. It bared the shape of a killer whale with two aircraft carriers' length and width lined up behind each other. Its dark metallic form blended with the harsh black environments of space. Red glowing hieroglyphic-like etchings around its nose and hull, along with the blue glow of the dormant thrusters that powered it, were the only things that made it viewable amongst the blackness and stars.

It was dark and cold within what appeared to be the main bridge. The same lights that glowed on its outside also illuminated its insides. Sitting at designated stations controlling it was a crew of eight. For the most part, their features were similar to humans, possessing two eyes, two arms and two legs, a mouth, a nose, a pair of ears, and five fingers and toes on each hand and foot.

The difference between their race and that of Earth became all too obvious after that. Their skins were smooth with a scale-like pattern similar to a snake, while their large elfin ears made them appear as if they came out of a fantasy novel. Physically, their bodies were muscular, toned, and powerful.

All the females on the bridge with womanly features similar to Earth possessed different skin shades that matched their lips. Their finger and toenails were also shiny black mirrors, while their eyes were void of irises, and shiny black fangs popped, matching their nails.

Like their male counterparts, their hair came in different colors: black, red, bright orange, white, blue, and purple. They wore their hair in a braided Mohawk style of four to six braids.

The males were similar to the females except for nails, eyes, and teeth gleaming bright white. Some wore their hair similar to the women, while others wore it in a regular Mohawk or just straight and long.

Both males and females sat dressed in versions of what could be described as ancient single-shoulder Roman or Greek togas. The women's legs and arms were adorned with greaves and bracers similar to gold, silver, or crystal, while the men wore heavy metallic gold or gray bracers with ancient etchings of their race.

Sitting lazily in a throne-like captain's chair with his right leg over the armrest, the commander of the massive vessel, wearing just a long red loincloth, sat with his chin resting on his fist as if he was about to fall asleep. His skin was pearl white with yellow undertones on different body parts, and he wore his long blue mane in a Mohawk with three thick braids. Though he does not appear larger or more muscular than most of the males on their bridge, it is clear how he earned his station.

Aside from his golden bracers with etchings that glowed red, similar to the ship he commanded, a powerful deep blue glow illuminated his eyes, signifying the immense power that coursed through his veins.

Not to be outdone was the female who stood to the right of his chair. Her skin was pitch black like the universe outside their vessel, with red undertones on different parts of her skin, while her blood-red Mohawk-styled hair was done with six braids. She adorned a near-sheer pink toga with metallic gold accents. She wore bracers and greaves with similar etchings to the commander's bracers on her arms and legs, also possessing a dim red glow. A sharp red light shined from her eyes as she wore a face that could slaughter a million legions by itself.

To the left of his chair was a shiny black orb the size of a basketball floating via a propulsion system.

The two spoke small talk in a language older than the first words a human man ever uttered.

Their conversation topic was the holographic image projected by the orb of a blue, green, and white third planet from a lone star.

~ ~

In the lower levels of the massive vessel, insane cackling could be heard. Behind a transparent energy barrier, the dead hung naked against a cold metallic wall within the cell's confines. Each of her appendages was confined to a humongous metallic cocoon-like restraint, which hummed while its parts emitted a green glow. Her blonde dreads masked her face with her head bowed as she laughed and laughed.

FREEDOM AND THE REGULATORS WILL RETURN…

AND SO WILL THE EYE OF RA…

ABOUT THE AUTHOR

Kipjo K. Ewers was born on July 1, 1975. At an early age, he had an active imagination. By the time he started kindergarten, he would make up fictitious stories; one of his favorites was about a character named "Old Man Norris," who hated everyone except for him.

When he attended our Lady of Victory Elementary School in Mount Vernon, he continued writing and reading stories to his classmates. Sometimes, the children would laugh. His teacher, Mrs. Green, would remind them that some great stories they read came about that way.

After elementary school, he went to Salesian High School in New Rochelle, NY, and then to Iona College.

He would work for several major firms and companies in New York, but his passion was becoming a journalist/writer. Therefore, it is not surprising he decided to write his first book/novel.

Kipjo began working and creating a new superhuman universe, finding inspiration and solace in losing his first daughter due to an unfortunate miscarriage that devastated both his loving wife and him; he began writing a hero origin story now titled "The First."

After publishing "The First" in 2013, Kipjo wrote two more follow-up novels to the series, a spin-off novel titled The Eye of Ra and a romantic supernatural story titled "Fred & Mary."

Now known as the EVO Universe, Kipjo continues to write to expand the series and create new projects for the foreseeable future.

Thank you for reading and for your support.

Made in the USA
Columbia, SC
14 August 2024

0b88a71f-21ca-4363-b5d3-d2d771d7ecfbR01